## Shamrock Green

'Let me change your dressing.' Her voice was soft, even softer than Sylvie's. 'Come on, Private McCulloch, big brave chap like you. What would your wife think of you, scared of having your bandages changed?'

He did not deny that he had a wife, but he did not confirm it either.

To appease her, he said, 'All right.'

The dressing came away from his face in one piece. Cold morning air pressed against his lids. His eyes were a mess. He knew they were a mess. He kept them shut. He could see threads of colour, though, and the darkness was no longer white but black. He felt the icy solution dribble down his cheeks.

'Open your eyes.'

He opened his eyes and saw natural light and in the light the nurse's face, solemn and sallow and drawn with concern.

'Can you see me?' she asked.

Beautiful, he thought, she's quite beautiful. But all he said was, 'Yes.'

*Also by Jessica Stirling in Coronet Paperbacks*

The Spoiled Earth
The Hiring Fair
The Dark Pasture
The Deep Well at Noon
The Blue Evening Gone
The Gates of Midnight
Treasures on Earth
Creature Comforts
Hearts of Gold
The Good Provider
The Asking Price
The Penny Wedding
The Marrying Kind
The Island Wife
The Wind from the Hills
The Strawberry Season
The Workhouse Girl
Prized Possessions
Sisters Three
The Piper's Tune

The Haldanes (*as Caroline Crosby*)

*About the author*

Born in Glasgow, Jessica Stirling is the author of
twenty-two heartwarming novels, many with
Scottish backgrounds.

# Shamrock Green

Jessica Stirling

CORONET BOOKS

Hodder & Stoughton

A CIP catalogue record for this title is available from the
British Library

ISBN 0 340 81848 4

Typeset in Bembo by Palimpsest Book Production Limited,
Polmont, Stirlingshire

Printed and bound in Great Britain by
Mackays of Chatham plc, Chatham, Kent

Hodder and Stoughton
A division of Hodder Headline
338 Euston Road
London NW1 3BH

*M&B™ and M&B™ with the Rose Device
are trademarks of the publisher.
Harlequin Mills & Boon Limited, Eton House,
18-24 Paradise Road, Richmond, Surrey TW9 1SR*

SUMMER FEVER © by Harlequin Books S.A. 2008

*Rex on the Beach* © Stephanie Bond 2007
*Getting into Trouble* © Leslie A Kelly 2007
*Shaken and Stirred* © Heidi Betts 2007
*Summertime Blues* © Kate Austin 2007
*Kokomo* © Alison Hart 2007

*ISBN: 978 0 263 86671 1*

24-0708

*Printed in Great Britain by
Clays Ltd, St Ives plc*

**Stephanie Bond** believes it's a privilege to write romance for the greatest, most loyal readers in the world. She lives with her architect/artist husband in her own happily-ever-after in Atlanta, Georgia, where chances are good that at this moment she is either reading a romance novel or writing one. Visit Stephanie and find out more about her books at www.stephaniebond.com

Stephanie also writes for Mills & Boon® Blaze® – *She Did a Bad, Bad Thing* is out now!

**Leslie Kelly** has become known for her sassy, sexy novels with strong heroines and to-die-for heroes ever since releasing her first book with Mills & Boon! For excerpts, contests and more, visit Leslie at www.lesliekelly.com or pop into www.plotmonkeys.com to check out her latest blog.

Don't miss Leslie's brand-new Mills & Boon® Blaze®, *Overexposed*, available in November 2008!

**Heidi Betts** likes to create stories that sizzle, charm and delight from the first page to the last. She loves to read, write, watch movies (and just a little too much television) and surround herself with furry, four-legged friends in her home in the beautiful hills of Central Pennsylvania.

Heidi's next book, *Christmas in His Royal Bed*, will be available from Mills & Boon® Desire™ in December 2008.

**Kate Austin** has worked as a legal assistant, a commercial fisher, a brewery manager, a teacher, and a technical writer, while managing to read an average of a book a day. Go ahead – ask her anything. If she doesn't know the answer she'll make it up, because she's been reading and writing fiction for as long as she can remember! She'd be delighted to hear from readers through her website, www.kateaustin.ca.

**Jennifer Greene** lives near Lake Michigan with her husband and two children. Before writing full-time, she worked as a teacher and a personnel manager. Michigan State University honoured her as an "outstanding woman graduate" for her work with women on campus. She has written more than fifty romances for which she has won numerous awards!

# Rex on the Beach

## Stephanie Bond

This story is dedicated to every woman who's
ever had an unforgettable summer romance!

# *CHAPTER ONE*

"NO, I'M NOT there yet." Lucinda Belvedere winced into her cell phone, wryly noting how much her phone conversation with her client, Eugenia Sampson, resembled her pillow talk with her last bed partner.

"Where in Florida are you?" Eugenia asked.

"I'm just leaving Fort Myers, so I'll be on Captiva Island within the hour. The weather's nice." Lucinda glanced up at the postcard-perfect sky, wishing she could have afforded to rent a convertible for this surveillance job. But a private investigator had to be prepared to live in her vehicle. Her five-year-old mini SUV, with a nondescript beigy gold paint job, allowed her to blend in with traffic, while offering plenty of space for storing clothes, wigs and other props—and for sleeping on the air mattress she kept in the floorboard for emergencies. Besides, a car rental would eat a big hole in her profit… and she didn't plan to be here long enough to enjoy the weather.

"It's raining here in Orlando," Eugenia said morosely.

Granted, the woman had a right to be morose—her bridegroom had left her at the altar three weeks ago and had since disappeared into thin air. Lucinda had tracked

missing girlfriends, wives, boyfriends and husbands countless times, but runaway groom Michael Gaines had proved to be elusive. When she'd discovered that his best man, Rex McCormick, owned a second home on Captiva Island, she'd decided to see if Gaines was hiding out there.

"Cheer up," Lucinda said. "Maybe I'll have news for you soon."

Eugenia made a disparaging noise. "If you see Michael, will you shoot him?"

Lucinda laughed. "Only with a camera."

"Oh, come on, I know you have a pistol."

"Only for protection and emergencies."

"This *is* an emergency, Lucinda. I can't get on with my life until I know why Michael did what he did. And Rex McCormick told me he doesn't know where Michael is. If he's lying, you can shoot him, too."

"I will," Lucinda promised in mock solemnity. "And if Michael isn't visiting his friend, then I'll figure out a way to get Mr. McCormick to tell me what he knows."

"Good luck. You'll have to hypnotize Rex to get him to tell you where his lousy best friend has slunk off to."

"You leave that to me," Lucinda said in her most assuring voice.

Eugenia made a disparaging noise. "To be honest, Lucinda, I'm not just mad…I'm worried, too. Michael has a tendency to party too much. What if he was in an accident and is lying somewhere in a coma?"

"Eugenia," Lucinda said gently, "the first check I ran was on John Does in area hospitals and morgues."

"I know," Eugenia moaned. "But I can hope, can't I?"

Lucinda pursed her mouth—in her experience, there were no limits to how far a lovesick person would go to justify another person's disappearance. "Just keep thinking good thoughts, Eugenia, okay? By the way, do you know what kind of women McCormick likes?"

"Michael said once that Rex has a thing for redheads, if that's what you mean."

"Thanks. I'll check in as soon as I have anything to report."

She disconnected the call and shook her head. Why Eugenia wanted to spend so much money to track down a man who didn't want to marry her, Lucinda didn't know. In hindsight, she wished that she or her ex-husband had had the courage to flee their wedding—it would've saved them two years of grief and a heap of legal fees. The only thing that Lucinda had gotten out of the short, ill-fated marriage was discovering that she had a flair for investigating. The pictures that she'd taken of her ex cheating were still legendary in the county court system where she'd filed for divorce.

As she entered Captiva Island and located the high-rise in which she'd booked a one-bedroom condo, Lucinda focused her thoughts on one Rex McCormick, mentally reviewing the details in his file. The man was a land developer in Atlanta and had appeared on Most Eligible Bachelors Under 40 lists in a couple of magazines. His pet cause was the J. N. "Ding" Darling National Wildlife Refuge on nearby Sanibel Island. And he spent most weekends at his beachfront home here in Captiva.

Was he also harboring a wedding fugitive?

Before checking into the rental unit, Lucinda asked to tour it alone, barely registering the brightly hued decor as she walked through the small living area and out onto the covered balcony that offered a northwesterly view. She removed binoculars from her purse and scanned until she located a modern three-story blue-gray house that was mostly glass and clearly afforded its occupant a spectacular view. *Thank heavens for Internet aerial maps.*

Lucinda whistled low under her breath. Rex McCormick was pulling down some serious jack to afford that kind of a spread on one of the most expensive stretches of land in the continental United States.

As she watched, a man dressed in dark swim trunks and holding a longneck beer walked out onto the uppermost balcony to the edge of the railing and turned his attention to the expanse of the Gulf of Mexico that was the house's front yard. Her pulse skipped higher. Rex McCormick was taller and bulkier than his picture had led her to believe, and he carried his athletic body in a way that told her he spent less time behind a desk than she imagined a land developer would.

The tip of her tongue slid out to whisk away the salty perspiration on her upper lip. The intense heat of south Florida in July was getting to her, but better the heat than the man who was her target—she couldn't afford any mental distractions. It was a good thing that she was immune to the charms of charmers.

"Been there, done that," she murmured, although her indifference didn't keep her from noting that this man had more assets—physical and otherwise—than her ex.

She watched a few minutes longer to see if Michael Gaines would join McCormick on the balcony, but he remained alone, nursing his beer and seemingly engrossed in his own thoughts as he stared out over the water. She scanned the area around the house for any sign of Michael Gaines's car, but she saw only a black Porsche that she knew from the file belonged to McCormick.

Not exactly the kind of car to blend in with traffic.

She trained the binoculars on each of the house windows, but detected no movement inside. And darn it, the house was gated front and back—there would be no sneaking up to take a quick peek inside. She wasn't above trespassing, but made it a practice not to breach gates and fences. Dogs and outdoor security systems were the bane of private investigators, and she didn't need a breaking-and-entering charge on this lucrative job.

She'd have to get inside the house the old-fashioned way—by invitation.

And even if McCormick was alone, it still didn't mean she'd have clear sailing where he was concerned; Rex McCormick was, his dossier said, notoriously aloof and a bona fide bachelor. She didn't care about his personal life except as a means to get close enough for him to divulge the whereabouts of his best friend. If Michael Gaines had revealed to anyone where he was going, chances are it would've been to the best man in his aborted wedding.

As she eyed the unwitting target of her investigation, Lucinda almost felt sorry for him. She'd never had an

unsolved case in her career as a P.I., and she wasn't about to start now. And while she'd never slept with anyone to get information, she had no qualms about turning on the sex appeal if the situation warranted it. She'd had the forethought to bring a few two-piece bathing suits and lots of tanning oil. A smile curved her mouth. The man wouldn't know what hit him.

She lowered the binoculars and returned them to her purse. When she walked out into the hallway, the rental agent gave her an anxious smile.

"We have a few units left with balconies that face the ocean. The views are much better there."

"I'll take this one," Lucinda said, snapping her sunglasses back into place. "The view is absolutely perfect. And can you give me directions to the nearest drugstore?"

REX MCCORMICK stared out over the peaceful, gentle waves of the Gulf of Mexico and took a long draw on the icy cold bottle of Corona. The ocean was like a woman, he decided wryly. On the surface, it was welcoming, alluring…irresistible. But a few feet under the surface, an earthquake could be churning, giving rise to an emotional tsunami that could upend a man's life in the blink of an eye.

He'd thought things were going well with Ginger. They had dated for almost a year now. She was amenable to his busy schedule. They didn't argue. The sex was still pretty good. He'd thought they were happy—which was why her demand that they get married had blindsided him. His philosophy had always

been not to mess with a good thing. He'd never planned to marry. He was pretty sure he still felt that way.

He expelled a noisy sigh.

On the other hand, when it came to wife material, he could do worse than Ginger. And if he waited too long, she might not be available. Ginger's biological clock was ticking and she'd made it clear that if he didn't buy a ring and set a date soon, she was taking her ovaries elsewhere.

Rex leaned against the warm wood of the railing, willing the right answer to come to him as he swallowed another mouthful of beer. True, he didn't grow giddy when he thought about the possibility of getting married, but in all fairness, he wondered how much of his hesitation came from his friend Michael's recent near miss with matrimony.

At the time, he could've throttled the man for leaving him standing at the altar in a too-tight tux to explain to the guests that there wouldn't be a ceremony after all. But afterward, he was glad his friend had backed out of the wedding if he truly felt that Eugenia wasn't the woman for him, or that marriage in general wasn't for him.

Except Michael hadn't handled the situation well, simply fleeing the scene and dropping out of sight. And considering the explosive fallout from the bride, Michael had better be prepared to remain in hiding for a while. At least Eugenia had stopped calling *him*, asking if he knew where Michael was.

Because right or wrong, he couldn't give up a buddy.

Which still didn't bring him any closer to an answer to his own dilemma. He only hoped that a week on the beach

would bring him enough solitude—and beer—to reach a decision about Ginger that he could feel good about.

Rex glanced down at the nearly deserted beach and felt the pull of the water, the need for a quick swim in the cool chop and a long nap in the shade of a dune. That's what he needed—a little R&R to clear his head, here on the quiet, conservative beaches of Captiva where people came to pick up shells instead of dates. And far away from women trying to get an answer out of him.

## CHAPTER TWO

LUCINDA SIGHED in frustration and wiped another blob of sunscreen on her nose. McCormick had been lying on a low chaise lounge shaded by a dune for so long that she was starting to think that he'd died.

If so, he was one good-looking corpse, she conceded. Even at rest, his long-limbed, bronzed body was contoured with enough muscle to garner glances from every passing female over the age of twelve. A knot of elderly women stopped to take pictures of the sleeping man whose swim trunks had dried molded to his, um, *trunk*. They giggled like school girls before moving on.

Lucinda had read three magazines while frying in the sun on her rented beach towel, waiting for the man to move one of those bulging muscles. She had taken pains with her new flame-colored hair—a temporary color covering her mousy blond—pulling it back into a poufy, flirty ponytail instead of twisting it up in its usual two-second banana-clip do.

Then she'd donned her bikini, sheer coverup, and nonsensical rhinestone sandals. And for the last hour and a half she'd been sitting here sweating, waiting for Rex McCormick to wake the hell up and notice her.

The only person who'd noticed her so far was a crusty old man in a floral print shirt trying to wow her with lame jokes. Thankfully his wife had appeared to drag him away.

But during her surveillance, she realized that she needed a reason for being a good distance from her condo on this stretch of sparsely populated beach that ran in front of the megamillion-dollar homes—something that would make crossing paths with Rex McCormick seem less contrived.

At the sound of a voice carrying on the wind, Lucinda turned her head to see a woman standing on the edge of the shoreline giving some kind of lecture to a group of children and adults who had gathered with pails and long sticks. With nothing else to do, Lucinda wandered over in time to hear the woman launch into a spiel about Captiva being a prime spot for shelling, attracting collectors from all over the world.

The woman went on to explain that it was illegal to remove "live" shells—ones that were still inhabited—and held up examples of native shells that were plentiful along the beach, although perfect specimens were hard to come by.

"And the most coveted prize," the woman said, holding up a small brown spotted shell, "is the junonia. Shellers who are lucky enough to find a junonia shell get their picture in the local newspaper."

Everyone oohed and aahed as the rare shell was passed around.

"I've got dozens of all the other shells," Lucinda overheard a boy about twelve years old tell another boy as

he showed him a clear shadow box of mounted shells with a glaring blank spot. "But I haven't found a junonia yet."

As Lucinda listened, an idea came to her. "Hey, kid, are you willing to sell your collection?"

He looked up at her. "Sure, I guess so. I got plenty more at home."

"How much?"

"It doesn't have the junonia."

"That's okay."

He shrugged. "Twenty bucks?"

"Here's twenty-five," she said, fishing the money out of her wallet to trade.

"Thanks!" the kid said, taking the money.

"Thank *you*," Lucinda murmured as the boy scampered off.

Now she had a reason to be walking the beach. She would be in pursuit of the rare junonia shell…while she was in pursuit of the whereabouts of the also rare Michael Gaines.

She frowned toward the sleeping form of Rex McCormick. Time to get this show on the road.

REX WAS jarred awake by something landing on his, er, privates. He glanced down to find a floppy pink hat covering his pride and glanced up in time to see a redhead—correction, a *gorgeous* redhead—jogging up to him with an apologetic smile.

"Sorry," she said, "my hat got away from me in this breeze."

"No problem," he said, sitting up for a better view.

With the sun at her back, her hourglass figure was outlined perfectly. His body reacted immediately— thank goodness the hat hid it.

"Are you here on vacation?" she asked, flashing the most engaging smile.

"Sort of," he answered evasively, waiting for his I-have-a-girlfriend filter to drop into place. Every decent guy in a monogamous situation with a woman had one. It prevented him from flirting, teasing, speaking in double entendres and otherwise coming on to other women. Although at the moment, his seemed to be snoozing.

"Sort of? What does that mean?" she asked with a laugh so appealing that he immediately wanted to hear it again.

Rex stood, hoping the vertical movement would activate the filter, to no avail. If he were going to honor his relationship with…what was her name?…he was going to have to do it through sheer willpower.

"I have a place here," he heard himself say. "So I come down when I can get away."

"Get away from what?"

It was the perfect opportunity to tell her that he had a girlfriend, one whom he was considering marrying. But that would sound as if he came down here to get away from his girlfriend. "From my job," he said.

"Sounds demanding," she said, reaching for her hat. "I'll let you get back to your nap."

But he held on to her hat for no reason other than that he didn't want to see her go. He'd seen his fair share of good bodies, but this woman was so…refreshing. "Are *you* here on vacation?"

She nodded. "I came to Captiva for the shelling."

His eyebrows rose. "The shelling?"

From her beach bag she withdrew a small acrylic box holding a mounted sea shell collection. "I have all of them but the junonia, and I'm determined to find one before I leave."

Okay, not what he expected out of the statuesque stunner, but kind of...sweet. "A junonia—that's a brown-spotted shell, isn't it?"

Her eyes lit up. "You've seen one?"

"Not today," he said with a laugh. "And your best chance to find one is first thing in the morning, when the tide is out."

"It sounds like you know something about shelling."

"I know a little about the wildlife around here," he admitted. "And pardon me for saying so, but you don't seem like the type who collects seashells."

She dimpled adorably. "Call me old-fashioned. My father used to take me to the beach when I was young, and seashells bring back good memories."

He couldn't fault a woman for being old-fashioned, although there was nothing old-fashioned about her beachwear. The woman was toned but curvy, and the tiny blue string bikini had his brain short-circuiting his tongue.

"Are you here alone?" she asked.

His malfunctioning tongue froze in his mouth. He nodded.

She smiled widely. "Thanks for the tip on low tide. Do you have any suggestions on where to go for dinner?"

Rex hesitated, feeling the pull of her smile on his body. And those green eyes...wow. The woman was like

a tall, voluptuous stick of candy—if he had her, he'd be satisfied for the moment, but later he would feel guilty and a little juvenile. Still, he involuntarily wet his lips.

Then the image of Ginger crowded his mind. She was a nice person who deserved an answer about their future. It would be easy for him to let this beauty distract him from the decision he'd come here to make, but if he had an affair, there would *be* no decision. He'd dated a lot of women in his thirty-six years, but he'd always remained faithful within a relationship.

"The Blue Marlin has good food and a nice atmosphere." He would make it a point to eat at Sharkey's instead.

"Thank you. I'll give it a try. It was nice to meet you."

"Nice to meet you, too," he mumbled, realizing that he didn't know her name, although that was probably for the best. But she stood there, as if she expected something more from him.

"Uh…my hat?" she said, her eyes dancing.

"Oh." A flush crawled up his neck as he handed the floppy pink hat to her. He watched her walk away, conceding that it wasn't often that a woman knocked him off balance. He noted with consternation that the back of her looked every bit as good as the front of her. Rex turned away from the mouthwatering view and pulled his hand down his face. He was an adult—he could resist temptation.

Then he craned his neck and watched until the mystery seashell-collecting redhead disappeared. But he would *not* go to the Blue Marlin tonight hoping to run into her, no sirree.

# CHAPTER THREE

"NO SIGN OF Michael yet?" Eugenia asked.

"No," Lucinda said into her cell phone. She sat at the bar of the Blue Marlin where she could see patrons walk in, nursing her second margarita and worrying that Rex McCormick hadn't taken her bait. "I watched the house for most of the day, and it looks as if McCormick is the only person there." She'd set up her high-powered zoom lens camera on a tripod and had snapped a few photos for good measure.

"When do you plan to talk to Rex?"

Lucinda shifted on her seat, reliving the impact of the man's intense pale blue eyes raking her body. "Actually, I struck up a conversation with him on the beach already."

"Gorgeous, isn't he?" Eugenia asked wryly.

"He's…handsome, yes." The picture in Rex McCormick's file had not done justice to his strong, sharp features, his square jaw, his thick, dark hair that was tousled endearingly in the wind like a little boy's—

"Be warned—Rex and Michael are two of a kind. The men are masters at making women fall in love with them."

"Trust me, Eugenia, Rex McCormick is just a means to an end."

"Yeah, well be careful that you don't 'end' up in his bed."

The door opened and the topic of their conversation walked into the dimly lit restaurant, looking just as good in jeans and a white short-sleeved shirt as he had in his swim trunks, if that was possible. "I have to go, Eugenia."

She disconnected the call and turned away from McCormick, but her stomach fluttered with excitement, the way it always did when a case started to fall into place. She took another sip from her glass, then turned toward McCormick in time to make eye contact.

She smiled with feigned surprise as he made his way over to her, but when he stopped to level those ice-blue eyes on her, she realized with dismay that the disturbance in her midsection had little to do with the way the case was progressing.

"Hi," she said, with what she hoped was the smile of a confident redhead. "Imagine running into you here."

"Yeah," he said. "Well, everyone on the island ends up here sooner or later."

"Are you meeting someone?"

He hesitated, then shook his head.

"You weren't planning to eat alone, were you?"

He grinned. "I guess I hadn't thought that far ahead." Gesturing vaguely around the bar, he asked, "What about you? Eating alone?"

She laughed. "More like drinking alone."

"That's no fun. Mind if I join you?"

This time Lucinda hesitated, which was crazy. Wasn't

this exactly what she'd hoped would happen? But something about this man had all of her warning systems on alert—what was it that Eugenia had said? That he was a master at making women fall in love with him. Lucinda averted her gaze to regain her composure, then nodded to the empty stool next to her. "Please."

McCormick settled himself on the stool and ordered a beer. His nearness elicited a response that she blamed on the low lights and the alcohol she'd already ingested. She couldn't remember the last time a man had affected her this way. Maybe she should become a full-time redhead.

"I'm Rex, by the way," he said.

"I'm Lucy." Close enough for undercover.

"What do you do when you're not looking for sea shells, Lucy?"

"I'm a real estate agent."

"Really? I'm into buying and selling property myself. Mostly commercial."

"Around here?"

"No, in Atlanta."

"Ah. Atlanta's a great city."

He nodded, although his eyes clouded for a split second. "Yeah. Where are you from?"

"Orlando. Have you ever been?"

"Sure. In fact, I have a friend who lives there."

"Oh?" She smiled at him over the top of her glass. "Man or woman?"

"Man. A friend from college."

"What's his name? I might know him."

His mouth twitched downward at the corners before he

answered. "Michael Gaines. He's into liquor distribution."

She laughed gaily to cover the spike in her pulse. "That's a great friend to have. But I don't think I know him. Is he single?"

To her consternation, his beer arrived, interrupting their conversation as he handed over his credit card and instructed the bartender to put her drinks on his tab as well.

"So your friend in Orlando," she said to try to steer the conversation back to where they'd left off, "is he single?"

Rex pursed his lips. "As a matter of fact, Michael *is* single. Maybe I should introduce you two since you live in the same town."

"Is he as handsome as you?" Lucinda asked, leaning close enough to get a whiff of his earthy cologne.

His laugh rolled out low and sexy, then he drew on his beer. "Do you want to get a table, order some dinner?"

The band that had been playing returned for a second set and while the music had been good, Lucinda realized it would be difficult to talk over the noise. She reached forward to touch Rex's arm, and the shock of his warm skin beneath her fingers almost made her forget what she was going to say. "Actually, it's such a clear night I was thinking of getting a bucket of shrimp and heading back to the beach. Want to come?"

He hesitated too long, drawing on his beer again. Something was wrong. Had she asked too many questions? Did he suspect she wasn't who she said she was?

Finally he set down the beer and his mouth dragged upward into a smile, as if reluctantly. "Sounds like fun. Let's do it."

# *CHAPTER FOUR*

IT WAS ONLY a bucket of shrimp, Rex reasoned as they picked their way along a moonlit path to the beach. He was just being friendly to a friendly tourist.

Who happened to be the hottest redhead he'd ever seen.

Wearing the shortest skirt he'd ever seen.

And emitting the most decadent fragrance of musk, tequila and woman.

He closed his eyes and groaned.

"Are you okay?" Lucy asked.

"I'm fine," he said. "I, uh, stepped on something."

"Here, take my hand."

He relented and knew he was in big trouble as soon as her soft, slender hand slid into his, thumbs interlocking. If anything, holding hands made the passage more awkward since their other hands were occupied with food and drink. But crazily, Rex didn't want to let go. They leveraged each other's weight, feeling their way down the path as Lucy's laughter carried on the night air.

Fear nudged him along his spine. How could he be so instantly and intensely attracted to this woman? Had Ginger's ultimatum pushed some kind of retaliation

button inside him? He had promised himself he wouldn't go to the restaurant where he'd sent Lucy, and now they were a shrimp bucket away from doing something that might change the trajectory of his life.

"What a beautiful night," Lucy said, squeezing his hand as the path ended, opening onto a deserted stretch of the beach a good quarter mile from his house. He was purposely avoiding taking her there—that would be suicide for his relationship with Ginger. As of now, he hadn't done anything he couldn't recover from.

The sand gave way beneath his feet, spilling into his new shoes, but he didn't care. The pale-colored beach glowed in the moonlight, providing plenty of reflected light for him to take in Lucy's profile—the tilt of her nose, her full mouth.

A few yards ahead of them, frothy waves broke and then receded into the blackness of the ocean. The horizon was a shimmering ribbon of light where the moon met the water. All in all, everything was way too romantic for a platonic meal.

"How about here?" she asked, pointing to a log, a chunk of palm tree, felled in a long-ago storm, that had washed ashore.

"Fine," he said, assuaging his guilt by telling himself that this was a test. This was only a test. If he could get through the evening with the gorgeous, intriguing redhead with his fidelity and integrity intact, then he would be all the more in the right frame of mind to make a decision about Ginger…and him.

He set down the bucket of beers, and Lucy set down the bucket of shrimp. He lowered himself to sit in front

of the log, but Lucy kicked off her shoes and remained standing, lifting her face and arms to the starless sky. "Isn't it the most beautiful thing you've ever seen?"

Rex stared at her, mesmerized. The wind lifted her hair, tousling it around her shoulders. The white halter top she wore hugged her breasts. The full, flirty skirt rose as she stretched to reveal rock-hard thighs. Her slender, tanned legs ended in toes that were dug into the sand.

"Yeah," he said hoarsely, trying his best to think himself out of an erection. He cracked open a can of beer, hoping the alcohol would cool his libido. "Ready to eat and drink?" he asked, opening a beer for her, too.

She smiled and took the beer, then settled a few inches away from him in the sand. Oblivious to soiling her clothes, she spread her legs and plopped the bucket of shrimp between her shapely limbs like an eight-year-old. "I'll peel."

"No argument here," he said, leaning back against the log, forcing himself to focus on the natural beauty before him to keep his mind off the natural beauty *beside* him.

It was, indeed, another exquisite night in paradise, the sight and sound of the water so soothing that it could lull a person into thinking that the rest of the world didn't matter, didn't even exist. If he looked to the far left, the lights of the distant Fort Myers skyline would remind him that the world *was* waiting for him. But he didn't look left.

Instead, he accepted a peeled shrimp from a sexy woman who expected nothing from him, dredged the

bite-size morsel in spicy cocktail sauce and popped it into his mouth. "Umm."

Lucy popped a shrimp into her own mouth, murmuring in agreement. Her nimble fingers moved quickly, peeling the shrimp and shucking the coral-colored husks in the bucket as fast as he could help her eat them.

"What kind of real estate do you deal in?" he asked.

"Mostly residential, investment properties." She shrugged. "Nothing too exciting. How about you?"

"Commercial development. Atlanta is booming."

She nodded. "What do you do for fun?"

"I come down here."

"This seems like a sleepy place for a single man. I would've pegged a guy like you for Miami or maybe the Keys."

"My family was coming to Sanibel and Captiva before the causeway was built," he said. "It brings back good memories, and I prefer the quiet."

"You don't entertain friends and family while you're here?"

"Occasionally," he admitted.

"But you're alone at the moment?"

"Yes," he said, telling himself that he was being truthful.

Not honest, but truthful.

"Here's to being alone," she said, raising her beer.

He drank to that and felt himself warming to her even more. He couldn't remember having such an instant connection with a woman. Their chemistry was undeniable. And there was something so sexy about them sharing a simple meal, eating with their hands.

And then she offered him a shrimp dangling from her long fingers, her eyes teasing. He hesitated as desire pulsed through his body; then he opened his mouth to take what she offered. Her soft, wet fingers brushed his lips, lingering longer than necessary. He flicked his tongue to remove the juice from her fingers, and his erection surged.

She withdrew her hand and bit into her lip as the color rose on her cheeks. Rex chewed slowly, overcome with the urge to touch her. He was both relieved and frustrated that she also seemed to be holding back. The pounding surf filled in the silence with a rhythm that echoed the lust flooding his body.

"So how often do you come to Orlando to see your friend?" she asked before taking a drink of her beer.

"I was there not too long ago," he admitted. "I was best man at his wedding."

Her eyebrows went up. "I thought you said he was single."

"He is. The wedding didn't happen."

She winced. "Who changed their mind?"

"My friend."

"Oh. Bet that was awkward."

He gave a short laugh. "You can say that again. I had to cover for him."

"Oh?"

"Yeah. I had to tell the bride and all the guests that Michael had, um, changed his mind."

She gasped. "He didn't even tell his fiancée?"

"No."

"So he just left?"

He nodded wryly. "Yeah."

"Where did he go?"

Rex tipped up his can for another drink, then said, "No one's seen him since."

She gave a little laugh and licked a drop of cocktail sauce from her finger. "But you were his best man—surely you know what happened to him."

He stared as she continued to lick her fingers, then before he could stop himself, he had clasped her wrist and pulled her to him for a kiss. It wouldn't be that special, he told himself, and then the spell would be broken.

But the feel of her lips on his was like an electric charge. Her tongue darted out to meet his and he thrust back, delving into her sweet, warm mouth. She was reluctant, he could sense it, and her shyness fueled the fire within him. His body hardened with an intensity that surprised him. There was something about this woman that had all his warning flags flying—she was refreshing, irreverent and irresistible...

But he had to resist.

Drawing on a flicker of clarity, Rex ended the kiss abruptly. "Uh...I have to go."

LUCINDA BLINKED and touched her lips that were still vibrating from the pressure of his. They couldn't stop now, not when he was finally, er, *talking*. "Go? But it's still early."

"Sorry," he said, pushing to stand and pulling her to her feet with strong hands. "Let me walk you back to your place—where are you staying?"

He was talking too fast. Something was wrong. Maybe she'd spooked him with the questions again. Her mind was still spinning from his unexpected kiss, but she forced herself to relax. "I'm parked at the restaurant," she said breezily, brushing sand from her skirt. "I'll just go back the way we came."

"I'll take you," he offered, retrieving their buckets of leftovers.

But she knew when it was time to cut bait—she could cast her line again tomorrow. "That's okay, I'll be fine by myself. I can see the restaurant from here." She smiled broadly and picked up her shoes, trying to hide her own haste to put distance between them. "Guess I'll go turn in so I can get up early to look for a junonia shell."

He nodded and wet his lips. She could feel the lingering voltage of their kiss crackling in the air. She wanted the information on Gaines, but not this way. McCormick was too intense. "Good night."

"Good night," he said. "And good luck finding what you're looking for."

"Thanks," she murmured, her chest tightening unexpectedly. She couldn't start feeling guilty about doing her job—she had a one hundred percent success rate to protect.

Lucinda turned to retrace her steps down the path to the restaurant, trying to figure out what had just happened. When she reached the crowded outdoor patio, she turned back to see that McCormick was still watching her with those amazing eyes. He lifted his hand in an offhand wave, then turned to disappear in the direction of his home.

Lucinda sprinted to her SUV and was back at her condo, binoculars and camera in place, by the time McCormick reached his house. Thank goodness for modern architecture and minimalist decorating taste—lots of panoramic windows and no curtains to hide behind. She watched the lights go on room by room as he walked through them, seeming restless, with a beer in hand and a cell phone pressed to his ear.

She bit her lip. Was he talking to Michael Gaines? Was he suspicious of her?

As she watched, he set down the phone and ran his hand through his hair. Whoever he'd been talking to, or whatever he'd been talking about, had left him feeling agitated. He walked to his bedroom, found a baseball game on the wide-screen television and began to undress.

Her heart, still hammering from the exertion of running back to her room, sped up again. Lucinda swallowed hard but kept watching, even though it was evident that McCormick was alone and wasn't expecting company.

There was no information for her to gain here, just personal pleasure.

With agonizing slowness he unbuttoned the white shirt and tossed it to the floor, revealing the wide, muscular chest she'd seen on the beach earlier today. Then he unzipped his jeans and stepped out of them.

Lucinda's pulse bumped higher with anticipation. His white briefs revealed more skin and muscle than his swim trunks had. The man had great abs, a superb behind, and well-developed thighs—a cyclist, she guessed. He walked across the bedroom, moving with

a wide-legged stance, then lowered himself to the floor and launched into sets of rapid push-ups.

He was, she realized as he challenged his body, working off some sort of frustration. The ripple of muscle and the sheen on his dark skin sent desire pooling in her midsection. From the intensity of their short kiss, she had the feeling that Rex McCormick had physical passion to spare and wouldn't leave a woman wanting in bed. She wondered if the evening had progressed past the kiss if he would be doing push-ups over her body right now.

While the unwitting vision of having sex with Rex McCormick formed in her head, he stood and shucked his white briefs, tossing them onto a pile of clothing, and stretched tall.

The moisture left her mouth. She'd seen her fair share of naked men, but Rex McCormick topped them all. Her thighs tingled, and moisture surged to intimate places. She wanted him, she conceded with a shock. Wanted that long, lean body next to hers, making her dig her heels into the mattress and dig her nails into his shoulders.

Dismayed by her visceral reaction to McCormick, she cursed and tossed the binoculars onto the bed. She never let a man rattle her, and she wasn't going to let this one. She had a job to do and that was to get something out of McCormick.

Something other than what would probably be the perfect orgasm.

REX STEPPED UNDER the trio of showerheads and expelled a pent-up sigh, one that he'd been holding since he left Lucy.

With a start, he realized that he didn't know her last name.

But her smile, her red hair and her blazing body were seared into his brain. Worse, he couldn't figure out why this stranger affected him so, although he suspected it had something to do with his impending decision about Ginger.

He'd felt relieved, then guilty, that Ginger had been unavailable when he'd called her earlier. As a result, he'd left a message that sounded falsely cheerful even to his own ears.

He gritted his teeth as the image of the woman he was supposed to love was replaced with the image of another woman sprawled in the sand with a bucket of shrimp between her legs.

His body reacted and he reached down to clasp his thick erection, tempted to placate his physical urge if only out of defiance. Instead he grunted, turned the water to cold and let the icy temperature cool his desire.

He could resist her…he could. He'd been able to walk away after that scorching kiss, hadn't he?

Rex turned off the water, dried his face, then wrapped the towel around his waist and walked out onto the balcony. The wind had picked up and so had the surf, creating a peaceful cadence of ebb and flow, of waves breaking and receding. He could taste the tang of salt in the air, and he never tired of the faint fishy scent that eventually permeated everything here.

This place had always given him answers to questions—when to enter into a business relationship, when to pass and when to reconsider. He was hoping it would

be equally helpful in reaching a decision about a personal relationship. Instead, it had delivered up a complication that he hadn't counted on.

And just like that, the redhead was back in his head.

Rex gripped the railing, determined to avoid the woman for the duration of his stay. He would eat in or go to Sanibel Island for dinners, play a round of golf, get caught up on movies he'd missed, take long solitary runs to the wildlife refuge.

But he would *not* be walking the beach in the morning at low tide, hoping to run into Lucy, no sirree.

## CHAPTER FIVE

LUCINDA FOUGHT a yawn as she pretended to poke her digging tool into the wet sand. It was Rex McCormick's fault, damn him, that she hadn't gotten any sleep. Walking around naked or with just a towel around his waist. The man showed absolutely no mercy to Peeping Toms.

The sun had barely risen in a pink sky, sending golden light across the water. At low tide, the beach stretched at least fifty yards past where it normally merged with the sea, revealing shells and other sea creatures that were normally hidden.

Gulls dipped and soared, searching for food. Other shell seekers dotted the beach, moving alone or in clumps, dressed for the early morning breeze that was a bit chilly coming off the water. Stabbing blindly at the sand while shells crunched under her feet, Lucinda desperately hoped she wasn't mauling something that someone else was looking for.

She kept one eye on the sand to avoid stepping on jellyfish that had been beached and one eye on the shore. She'd passed McCormick's house several minutes ago, and all had been quiet. She could still see the house, barely, and had dawdled as much as she

dared. With a sigh, she decided that her shell-collecting story had fallen flat with McCormick and that she might have to invent yet another reason to walk up and down the beach hoping to run into him.

"Any luck?"

Lucinda jumped, then turned around to see the very man she'd been pondering dressed in running gear, his perspiration-drenched T-shirt clinging to his broad torso. Her senses went haywire.

"Oh. Hi." She gestured vaguely to the sand. "There are lots of shells, but no junonia...yet. Out for a run?"

"Just finished."

"I think I'm giving up, too," she said, rubbing the back of her neck. "At least for today." Then she nodded toward other shellers, now everywhere. "Tomorrow I'll have to get a better jump on the competition."

"I'll walk back with you as far as my place," he offered.

She remembered to play dumb. "You live near here?"

He pointed. "The blue house that's just visible."

"Okay," she said, falling into step next to him. She had vowed that when she saw him again, she would remind herself that he was a subject under surveillance—a job. But she'd forgotten about this *magnetism* that he exuded.

And the fact that she'd seen him naked.

"White with brown spots?"

"Hm?" she asked, eyes wide.

"The junonia shell—it's white with brown spots, isn't it?"

"Oh. Yes, that's right."

He scanned the ground in front of them and she pretended to do the same as they walked along silently. Her mind raced for a way to bring up Michael Gaines, but at the moment, her mind was fully occupied with Rex McCormick.

"I had fun last night," he said, surprising her.

She gave a little laugh. "The way you left, I thought I'd done something wrong."

"No," he said. "It was me, something…something I'd already committed to."

"And forgot about?" she asked lightly.

"Something like that," he admitted.

"So did you take care of it?"

His step faltered. "I, um, postponed it for now."

They were nearing the stretch of beach in front of his house, so she knew her time was running out. "Uh, Rex—"

"Would you like to go biking today?" he asked. "We can ride to a section of beach that most tourists don't know about. You might get lucky and find your shell."

"Well, that's an offer I can't refuse. What time?"

He glanced at his watch. "How about noon?"

A smile curved her mouth involuntarily. "I'll bring lunch. Where shall we meet?"

"The bike rental place on the corner? My road bike isn't appropriate for touring."

"Okay."

"Okay." He backed toward his house, gave a little wave, then jogged toward the boardwalk that led to his home.

Lucinda smiled all the way back to her condo, and

her entire body thrummed with anticipation at spending the afternoon with him. It wasn't until she was riding up in the elevator that she remembered going biking with Rex McCormick wasn't a date.

He had simply taken the bait she'd offered, and now she had to set the hook.

## CHAPTER SIX

REX STOOD in front of the bike rental place, staring at the display on his ringing cell phone.

Incoming call from Ginger.

He pinched the bridge of his nose, trying to relieve the pressure there. He must be insane to have invited Lucy bike riding when he was supposed to be on a personal retreat to think about his future with another woman. He checked his watch—two minutes after noon—and was buoyed by the prospect that Lucy might have changed her mind. If she didn't show, he'd be off the hook.

"Rex!"

He turned to see Lucy striding toward him, her wide smile hitting him like a sucker punch to the gut. He knew almost nothing about this woman except that he felt compelled to spend time with her. And a bike ride was safer and less intimate than a late-night picnic on the beach as a way to get to know her better…to discover that they probably had nothing in common.

Hopefully.

Suddenly he realized that his phone was still ringing. He hit the Silence button and slid it into his pocket, then turned a smile toward Lucy.

She was dressed in red shorts, a white bikini top and tennis shoes, with her marvelous red hair pulled back into a thick ponytail. She arrived on a fresh breeze, her green eyes sparkling, her nose and cheekbones sun-kissed. "Hi!"

"Hi, yourself."

She patted a small insulated bag. "I brought sandwiches. Are we ready?"

He swept his gaze over her, once again plagued with guilt that he was heading down a dangerous path. If he were smart, he'd tell her that something had come up—namely, his conscience—and that he wouldn't be able to join her after all.

"Is something wrong?" she asked, sinking white teeth into her lower lip.

Here was his chance to save himself from himself and to let her go so she could meet someone else to have fun with, someone who might be able to offer her more than a couple of distracted days on the beach.

"Yes, something is wrong," he admitted.

A concerned light came into her eyes. "What?"

"I...I...don't know your last name," he said, exhaling.

She grinned. "Oh. That's easy enough to resolve. It's Bell. Lucy Bell."

As in ringing his, he noted wryly.

"And yours?" she prompted.

"McCormick."

"Well, Rex McCormick, I'm counting on you to help me find what I'm looking for today."

It was his turn to smile. "I'll do my best."

They went around the corner to the storage lot to select bicycles. Most of them were for gentle, sitting-upright riding, with baskets in front or back for parcels. They were a far cry from his own sleek bike, but built for leisurely fun.

An older woman emerged from the office and glanced back and forth between them. "I have the perfect bike for you."

Rex traded a puzzled glance with Lucy, then smothered a laugh when the woman produced a bicycle built for two. "The person riding in the back can't steer," the woman said merrily, "but the person riding in front can't go very far without their help pedaling."

Rex started to protest until he saw the expression on Lucy's face.

"It sounds fun," she said. "What do you think?"

He sighed. "I think I'm going to regret this." A more far-reaching statement than even he knew, he realized. He paid the woman, then he and Lucy practiced riding the awkward bike in the lot—with many laughs and near tumbles—until they got the hang of it. Then, with her bag tucked in the basket, they set off for the stretch of beach that Rex had in mind. He was hyperaware of the woman behind him, of how quickly they had gotten into synch on the bike, and how perfectly she moved to counterbalance him to keep them steady. Plus, she was just so easygoing and eager to spend time with him—it was a heady combination that had his thoughts and body in a bind.

It was another beautiful, hot day on Captiva Island. Lightweight helmets and sunglasses protected them

from the harsh rays of the sun, and the air rushing past them kept them cool. Along the way, he pointed out landmarks—the tiny wooden church that was an island original, the public library—and was pleased beyond reason when she touched his back or shoulder to shout a question. He wondered if Lucy had any idea how irresistible she was…the kind of woman who could persuade a man to do something against his better judgment.

The island was small and soon they had reached the section of beach that he'd described, a fifty-yard section cut off from shoreline foot traffic by mounds of foliage debris from past storms. As promised, the sand was thick with shells. "Think you'll find what you're looking for here?" he asked over his shoulder.

Behind him, Lucinda took in the deserted, secluded beach, the gentle surf and the swaying palm trees, but her gaze strayed back to the expanse of Rex's broad shoulders, the way his damp hair curled around the bottom of his helmet, the way the muscles moved in his forearms. A tickle of foreboding lodged in her stomach, but she forced a light tone into her voice. "Let's go see, shall we?"

They parked the bike, but Lucinda struggled with the twisted strap of her helmet.

"Let me," Rex said, and reached up to gently unfasten the clasp.

Lucinda found herself unable to look away from his piercing blue eyes. The kiss they had shared the night before came back to her full force, and she moistened her lips. When he lifted the helmet from her head, she

reached up to run her fingers through her flattened ponytail. "I must look a fright."

"Not at all." He fingered a lock of hair that had come loose from her ponytail. "Did I mention that I love red hair?"

She swallowed hard. "Oh? How...*fortuitous.*"

He put his hand at the nape of her neck and drew her closer, claiming her lips with his. She put her arms around his neck and the kiss quickly escalated to a full-body encounter. His hands slid down her back to cup her rear. When she felt the ridge of his erection against her navel, she sighed into his mouth and pressed herself closer.

He lowered his mouth to her neck, then to her shoulder, swirling his tongue against sensitive skin, then grabbing the end of her bathing suit tie with his teeth.

She had time to stop him, heard the slide of the string as it was being undone, felt the bathing suit top loosen from her breasts, but she didn't want him to stop. When air hit her naked skin, her nipples sprang to attention, full and distended. With a groan, he cupped her breasts in his hands and claimed her mouth in a deep, burning kiss.

Desire flooded her body, and her hand went to his fly to stroke him through his clothing. He moaned in response, fueling her own fire. His hands were working magic on her breasts, kneading, gently squeezing her nipples until she cried out for more.

His breath rasped in her ear, letting her know that his arousal rivaled hers. Then suddenly he stilled, and his mouth moved to her ear. "We have company,"

he murmured. "Don't worry, they can't see you." Keeping their bodies pressed together, he lifted her bikini top and quickly retied the strings behind her neck. "There," he said, stepping back, regret and something else—relief?—in his eyes. "No harm done."

While he turned and offered a friendly wave to the three people walking toward them who were talking and oblivious to what they'd interrupted, Lucinda looked at Rex with a mixture of wonder and fright.

*No harm done?* Speak for yourself, she wanted to say. This *attraction* was getting out of control. She was supposed to be using their chemistry to extract information from Rex, but instead he and his incredible blue eyes—and undeniable sex appeal—were making her forget the reason she was here in the first place.

Hardening her resolve, she suggested that they look for the junonia shell. She stood a better chance at getting him to talk if they weren't touching.

Rex seemed relieved and didn't mention what had transpired between them. Even though her body still smoldered with the fire that he'd ignited, she pretended to look for the rare shell as they picked their way across the beach using sticks to dislodge large piles of shells. She didn't come across any junonias, but she couldn't resist picking up some particularly gorgeous specimens of other types of shells, perfect in their formation and stunning in their coloration.

"Pretty incredible, isn't it?" he asked. "To think that each of these shells once housed living organisms."

"Yes," she agreed. "It makes a person feel...small."

He nodded. "We think that our problems are so monumental, but when we look at nature, it reminds us that we're really a very tiny part of the universal equation."

"Preservationist and land developer seem to be at opposite ends of the spectrum," she observed lightly.

When he didn't respond, she glanced over to see a blanched look on his face.

"I'm sorry," she said. "I didn't mean to judge you."

"No, it's okay. You're right. It's easy to talk the talk."

Irritated with herself for delving too deeply into personal beliefs, she cast about for a way to guide the conversation back to Michael Gaines. "I saw something on TV last night that made me think of your friend, the runaway groom. It really is a fascinating story."

He didn't respond.

"Do you think they'll get back together?"

"Not unless Michael decides to come out of hiding and face his problems."

She punched him playfully. "You know where he is, don't you?"

He shrugged. "Maybe."

"Tell the truth—did he run off with another woman?"

"Nope."

"Run back home to Mama?"

"Nope."

"Go on a Vegas gambling junket?"

He laughed. "Nope." Then he angled his head. "You sure are asking a lot of questions."

She recovered in half a heartbeat. "I just think it's

interesting what people will do when faced with the prospect of marriage—some people really get freaked out by it."

His mouth tightened as he punched the ground with his stick. "That's true. Have you ever been married?"

"Once," she said, thinking it was okay to tell the truth in this instance.

"And?"

"And it wasn't for me. And considering the divorce rate in this country, it's not for about two-thirds of the population."

"So because the odds of success are low, people shouldn't bother?"

She lifted her hand in denial. "All I'm saying is that your friend must have had a good reason for running out on his wedding and for hiding."

He didn't respond, just kept walking, scanning, poking shells. "I think it's time for a lunch break," he said. "Then I have to be getting back."

"To that commitment of yours?" she asked.

He nodded, but remained silent. And his mood was pensive while they ate, despite her effort to keep the conversation light. She did coax him into feeding their sandwich leftovers to the gulls, but had the feeling that Rex had erected some kind of wall around himself. He was quiet on the return trip, leaving her to memorize the way his back muscles moved underneath his shirt, to remember her bikini tie clasped in his teeth, to relive his hands on her breasts.

"I'm sorry we didn't find the junonia," he said when they returned the bike.

She gave a dismissive wave. "Maybe I'll get lucky tomorrow morning."

"How long are you staying?" he asked, and she thought she detected a bit of reluctance in his voice.

Lucinda shrugged. "I still have a few days of vacation. I'd like to stay until I find what I came for."

He nodded absently. "It's supposed to rain in the morning."

"Then I'll look in the afternoon." She had to give him a chance to cross paths with her again, to get close enough that he might confide in her.

"Would you like to go sailing tomorrow afternoon?" he asked. "I know a little island not too far away that hasn't been shelled like the beaches. We can look for the junonia there."

"Sounds good," she said, immensely relieved. "Where and when should I meet you?"

"One o'clock, at the marina across the street?"

She smiled. "I'll be there. Thank you, Rex, for being so helpful."

But the earnest look he gave her stirred guilt in her stomach. "No problem," he said. "See you tomorrow."

Trying not to read anything into his reaction, she focused on being happy that she'd have another chance tomorrow to endear herself to him. She decided that a trip to the public library for a crash course in sailing might be useful.

For hours she pored over books and watched a DVD on sailing techniques, although she found it hard to focus because her mind kept wandering back to their erotic encounter on the bike ride. Their intense physical

chemistry was a factor she hadn't counted on. She idly wondered how far she would have allowed things to progress today before her emotional brake would have engaged. In hindsight, she hadn't even been close to stopping him when they'd been interrupted.

On that disturbing note, she left the library and stopped to get takeout for dinner. When she got back to her condo, she phoned Eugenia to give her an update.

"Nothing from McCormick yet on Michael's whereabouts, but I think I'm getting close. Hopefully I'll have news for you tomorrow."

"Good," Eugenia said. "I'm ready."

Lucinda frowned. *Ready for what?* "Eugenia, you promised me that if I could track down Michael, that you wouldn't…harm him."

"I know," Eugenia said quickly. "I meant that I'm ready for this to be over."

"And it will be soon," Lucinda said, picking up her binoculars and finding Rex in them. He was in the hot tub on the balcony outside his bedroom, *thankyouverymuch.*

"Do you promise?" Eugenia asked.

"One hundred percent success rate," Lucinda reminded her absently. "I'll call you tomorrow."

She disconnected the call and, her food forgotten, she increased the magnification on the binoculars and focused on Rex. He was sitting in the water up to his chest, his head leaning back. She didn't see the shadow of clothing beneath the water and imagined that he was probably nude. While she watched, he stood and climbed out of the tub, confirming her suspicions. He wrapped a

towel around his waist, but shed it when he walked into his bedroom and closed the sliding glass door.

Mesmerized, she watched as he reclined in the large bed on top of the covers. He was drinking a beer, but the television wasn't on. She imagined that he was listening to music, some kind of sultry jazz, and was lost in his own thoughts. And while she watched, his cock suddenly hardened. He grimaced and reached down to grasp its length, then with his eyes closed, began a slow massage.

Lucinda ripped the binoculars away from her eyes, her heart pounding, her breasts heavy. This was going way beyond the bounds of her job, this was getting personal. She put her hand to her forehead and turned her back to the window. She'd never had a problem keeping her mind on the task at hand before.

Why now?

Because she'd never run into the likes of Rex McCormick before—a man who seemed to bypass her brain and talk directly to her body.

She couldn't deny that the man could do things to her with a glance that other men hadn't been able to do with both hands and feet…and various props. She closed her eyes and groaned, too tempted by the knowledge of what was going on in his bedroom, all for the viewing.

No one would be the wiser.

She turned and lifted the binoculars, her lips parting in a sigh to find him in her sights, to find him clasping the part of him that she wanted inside her.

Lucinda slid her hand into her waistband, then under

her panties, pressing her fingers into her wet folds...wet for Rex. She imagined it was his hands on her, readying her for his entry.

Breathless, she matched his movements stroke for stroke, taking cues from his expression to know when he was close to climaxing. The beginnings of an orgasm coiled low in her belly, making her strain against her hand as the tremendous pressure climbed higher and higher. She moaned his name as the orgasm began to claim her, slow and intense, sweeping her along on a wave of intense pleasure. She nearly dropped the binoculars, but managed to keep them trained on Rex to see his body jerk, then his seed spill on his bare stomach that contracted with the effort of his release.

Their bodies pulsed together in quiet spasms of recovery. She watched until he rose and disappeared from sight—to the shower, no doubt.

Shocked and a little appalled at her own behavior, Lucinda dropped onto the bed and conceded in a swell of satisfaction that his act was probably a culmination of what they'd started on the secluded beach, and that he'd been thinking about her while he climaxed.

Then she bit her lip. Or had he been thinking of someone else?

## CHAPTER SEVEN

THE NEXT DAY, Rex stood on the dock staring down at his sailboat, wondering if he were developing Tourette's syndrome because being in proximity to Lucy made him blurt out the exact opposite of what he'd told himself he'd do—inviting her to go sailing with him when he should be sailing alone to become one with nature, to clear his head, to help him sort out whether or not he had a future with Ginger.

Instead, all he could think about was becoming one with Lucy.

But he held out hope that his self-gratification episode last night had cured him of these obsessive fantasies. And that the more time he spent with her, the sooner he would uncover something about her that proved they could never be a couple, that he was better off settling down with Ginger.

At the sound of footsteps on the dock, he turned to watch Lucy approach, his chest expanding in sheer admiration, along with dismay that, if anything, he wanted her more.

Blue shorts hugged her thighs, and a white T-shirt molded the glorious breasts that had overflowed his hands. Her long legs were tanned and ended in a pair

of sensible flat tennis shoes. Her sassy red hair was pulled back in a ponytail, and she wore sporty wrap-around sunglasses.

"Hi," she said, then pushed up her sunglasses.

*Wow, those eyes.* "Hi, yourself."

"What did you do last night?" she asked playfully.

Heat climbed his neck. "I took care of something that I couldn't ignore any longer. You?"

"Same," she said with a little smile.

Somehow he doubted that, although the image of Lucy getting herself off sent a sensation through him that did not bode well for his concentration this afternoon. But he kept telling himself that the sooner they found a junonia shell, the sooner Lucy could return to Orlando, and chances were they'd never see each other again.

Unless he happened to run into her when he was visiting Michael.

Assuming that Michael returned to Orlando from his little side trip.

"Nice marina," she said. "Which boat is yours?"

"That one," he said, pointing to the white-hulled, teak-inlaid, open-bowed boat just a few feet away. "It's called a—"

"Thistle," she finished for him. "It's beautiful."

He blinked in surprise. "Do you sail?"

"My father had a sailboat, an old woody. I used to go out with him. He taught me how to run the jib sail and the spinnaker, but I'm a little rusty."

He nodded, pleased. "Don't worry, you'll be back up to speed in no time."

He stepped down into the boat, then extended his hand to help her down. She took his hand and awareness shot up his arm. She must have felt it, too, because she locked gazes with him, her sparkling green eyes suddenly unsure.

"Static electricity," he murmured.

"It's in the air," she agreed, then stepped in next to him, her body brushing his. "Where do you want me?"

Several unsuitable answers flitted through his mind before he said, "Up front. Put on this life jacket. When you're settled, I'll untie the lines and push off."

The winds were with them and after the mainsail was raised, he was able to navigate them into open water fairly quickly and easily.

Lucy had her face turned into the wind, a smile on her lips. "This is wonderful!" she shouted, and he had to agree. Sailing was one thing that Ginger did not enjoy.

He frowned. Come to think of it, there were a lot of things that Ginger didn't enjoy. The two of them didn't really have fun together.

And just like that, the answer seemed crystal clear. He couldn't marry Ginger, for both their sakes.

"Rex, can I take over the jib?" Lucy asked, pointing to the front sail.

He looked into Lucy's sunlit face and felt a jolt to his system—he barely knew this woman, but he loved spending time with her. A happy grin lifted his mouth as he untied the line that had been holding the jib steady. She seemed tentative at first, but soon they were working together to keep the sails tight and the boat

moving forward at a nice clip…a further extension of their rare chemistry.

He spotted the tiny unnamed, uninhabited island that was their destination and pointed it out to her. The rocks and the shallow approach kept most boaters away, but the Thistle handled the obstacle course well and soon they were beached on the patch of sandy land boasting only a handful of trees.

"It's beautiful," Lucy said, stepping out into knee-deep water to wade ashore.

"And lots of shells," he added, bending down to pick up a particularly nice whelk.

"Yes," she agreed, almost as an afterthought.

"And to improve our odds," he said, pulling a piece of paper from his pocket, "I brought a picture so I could keep it in my mind's eye." Although the picture in his head changed instantly when Lucy lifted her T-shirt over her head to reveal a tiny bright yellow bikini top covering her generous breasts.

Rex cleared his throat. "Why don't we start over there?"

"Looks good to me," Lucy said.

*I'll say.* Rex puffed out his cheeks in a slow exhale, and began scanning the shell-scattered sand for the brown-spotted junonia.

"How long have you been looking for it?" he asked.

Lucinda caught herself before she said, "What?" He meant the junonia, of course. "Uh…I can't really recall."

"Is this shell on your life list?"

"Something like that."

"Along with what else?"

She pursed her mouth to think—it had been eons since she'd thought about what she wanted to do with her life. After her divorce, financial security had been the most pressing item of business. To get her private investigator's license had required hours of study, a lengthy exam and a certain number of hours apprenticing under another P.I. before she could get her own license. After that, her life had been about building her business and her reputation.

"Success, I suppose, in my job."

"That's good, but what about your personal life?"

"I work a lot," she said, suddenly feeling defensive. "I don't have a lot of time for relationships."

"I know what you mean. Do you have family around Orlando?"

"My three brothers are scattered across the country, but my parents are there, both retired."

"Does your father still sail?"

She felt a pang of guilt over what now seemed like such an unnecessary lie. "Uh, no. But he loves to fish." And it struck her suddenly that Rex would very much like her father, and vice versa. "How about your family?"

"My parents are both gone."

She didn't remember reading that in his dossier. "Oh, I'm sorry."

He gave her a reassuring smile. "I lost them when I was in college. It was rough at the time, but I learned to cope."

"Do you have any brothers or sisters?"

"No."

She felt another pang of sympathy and saw an opening to bring up his friendship with Michael Gaines, but something made her stop. Instead, she asked, "What's on *your* life list, Rex McCormick? Or have you already achieved everything that you set out to?"

He laughed. "Not quite. I guess I don't think about it much. I'd like to travel more, I suppose. Maybe do good things where I can."

"A family of your own?" she asked for no good reason.

His expression turned serious. "I've thought about it. I don't know. I don't think you can plan those things. I think they come when they're supposed to."

She averted her glance, and turned her attention back to the shells at their feet. She didn't like the direction of the conversation, the things that being with Rex McCormick made her think about, made her feel.

They walked in silence for a long while, and when a stiff gust of wind kicked up, Lucinda realized that more than an hour had passed. And instead of trying to think of ways to bring up Michael Gaines, she'd been earnestly looking for the damned junonia shell.

And that at some point during the elapsed time, Rex had twined his fingers with hers and she hadn't protested.

Rex glanced up at the clouds gathering on the horizon. "Looks like a storm is blowing in. Guess we'd better be heading back."

Irritated with herself for blowing the entire afternoon and still being no closer to her goal, Lucinda was on edge during the ride back to the marina. Worse, she couldn't keep her eyes off Rex, couldn't help admiring the way he handled the boat and his body, how he negotiated the

wind and used the elements to his advantage. He was the entire package, she acknowledged— looks, brains, personality. And the money didn't hurt, either.

No wonder she was already half in love with him.

She inhaled sharply, remembering Eugenia's warning. *God, no.*

"You okay?" he asked. "You look like you got a sudden pain."

"It'll pass," she said, then muttered, "I hope."

At the marina, she helped him secure the boat and the sails.

"You're a fine first mate," he said, helping her out onto the dock.

"It was fun," she said, and meant it. "Thank you for taking me out, Rex."

Thunder boomed overhead and in the distance, lightning lit up the sky.

"Guess I'd better get going," she said.

"Uh, Lucy?"

She turned back. "Yes?"

"Would you like to come back to my place?"

*And have sex,* he might as well have added.

Lucinda was torn. If she went back to Rex's house with him, she had a good idea where things would lead, and making love with Rex could be hazardous to her emotional well-being. On the other hand, it was just what she'd been hoping for—an invitation into his house where she might find a note, a letter or a phone message from Michael Gaines that would tell her what she needed to know to maintain her one hundred percent success rate.

She inhaled deeply for resolve and to calm her nerves. As long as she kept her emotions in check, it seemed like a win-win situation.

"Yes, Rex, I'd love to go to your place."

## CHAPTER EIGHT

THEY MADE IT to the driveway of his house just as fat raindrops began to fall. He unlocked the gate with a keyless remote, then they dashed across the tiny yard and up the steps, soaked and laughing by the time they stepped inside and he closed the door behind them.

Gooseflesh rose on Lucinda's skin, both at the chill of the air-conditioning and at the opulence of his home, a home which she'd entered under false pretenses.

"I'm dripping on your floor," she said apologetically.

"Follow me," he said, then led the way upstairs to the top level with which she had become very familiar. But at close range, the quality of the construction, the finishing details and the furniture were so much more impressive. The hardwood floors were blackwood, the walls maple and cork, the fixtures pewter.

They walked through his spacious bedroom/office, where she cast a glance at his gargantuan platform bed before following him into the bathroom that was equally sleek and modern. He opened a drawer and handed her a warmed fluffy towel. "If you'd like to get out of those wet clothes and take a shower, I'll find you a robe."

She nodded absently, suddenly distracted by the sight of him in clingy, wet clothes, his dark hair dripping into his blue, blue eyes.

"Or," he murmured, fingering a lock of hair behind her ear, "we could take a shower together."

An electric current whipped through her body. Regardless of the reason they'd met, she'd never wanted a man so much.

She could control this. She could be with him and do her job. No one else had to know.

She tamped down all the misgivings rising in the back of her mind and reached forward to tug the hem of his T-shirt over his head.

They undressed each other, planting kisses on bare skin as it was revealed. When they were both naked, Rex wrapped his arms around her and kissed her savagely while backing her into the open shower area. He touched a sensor pad and three showerheads came on, blasting warm soapy water on their bodies.

As his hands roved over her body, lathering her skin and hair, she felt invigorated and alive and flush with anticipation to be made love to by this man. Another push of a button and they were being rinsed with cooler water. He kissed her hard, rounding his hands over her rear, drawing her against his erection, a sensation that sent vibrations through her. He lowered his mouth to her breasts, drawing on one, then the other, until she felt as if he were pulling an orgasm from the depths of her body.

The water switched off and a dryer fanned them. But their skin and hair were still wet when he lifted her and carried her to his bed.

He pushed his fingers into the tangle of curls between her thighs, and she opened for him. "Hurry," she whispered. "Get protection...I want you inside me...now."

He reached into a bedside drawer and removed a condom. She took it from him, tore it open and rolled it on. He sucked in a breath at her touch, and she knew it wouldn't take either of them long to lose control altogether.

Kind of like last night, she mused, as he lowered his body onto hers and kissed her, stabbing her tongue with his. He rubbed his erection over her sensitive folds, teasing her.

"Now," she urged, digging her fingers into his shoulders. He entered her in a thrust that tore a groan from his lips. She gasped and contracted around his considerable length, rocking her hips upward to bring them even closer together.

Rex didn't want to move, didn't want to diminish the full-body thrill of being imbedded in Lucy's sweet heat. God, she felt like wet silk wrapped around his cock. He withdrew and thrust into her again, incredulous when each stroke felt better...and better...and better. His body was being pulled toward such intense pleasure that he had to grind his jaw to slow down enough to bring her along with him. He stroked her with purpose, changing pressure when her expression or breathing prompted him.

"That's it," he whispered in her ear. "When you come, I want to hear it."

It was all the encouragement she needed to climax

in a bucking frenzy, crying out his name. Her clenching body catapulted his own body to a blinding orgasm that shook him to the core and left him drained, dozing on her chest.

LUCINDA WOKE to the exquisite pleasure of rain still falling on the roof and Rex's erection pushing against her from behind. She pulled his hand to her breast and shifted to allow him entry in one long, slow slide.

From this angle, he felt even fuller inside her. They quickly found a rhythm and the friction stroked at the nub of her desire. He kissed her shoulder and kneaded her breast, thrusting harder and harder until the bed shook. Her climax was more deeply seated this time, and even more satisfying. She released a long moan as her muscles spasmed around him. He came instantly, clutching her against him as his body shuddered with release.

WHEN REX AWOKE, Lucy's body was still spooned against his. His mind reeled from the passion they had generated. He had never bedded a woman with whom he was so sexually compatible. And after two intense sessions in a relatively short time, all he had to do was look at her lying nude on his bed and he immediately wanted her again.

He dragged his hand down his face, acknowledging that his relationship with Ginger was clearly over. Part of him mourned her companionship, but part of him stubbornly clung to the notion that fate had stepped in. It had to mean something, didn't it, that Lucy had so

accidentally dropped into his life, and that their connection was so effortless?

The only drawback to being with Lucy, he noted wryly, was that his desire for her might drive him to an early grave.

The mattress shifted and he felt her firm breasts press into his back, her warm fingers curl around his thickening cock. He groaned and climbed back into bed.

But what a way to go.

# CHAPTER NINE

THE NEXT MORNING dawned clear and sunny. Despite her lack of sleep, Lucinda was awake early. She stared into the sleeping face of Rex McCormick, struggling with the realization that she might be falling for him and how that foolish act could very well complicate things.

The case...her business...her life.

She would simply have to drop out of sight. Rex didn't have her real name, no address, no phone number. He wouldn't be able to track her down, and probably wouldn't want to.

She managed to slip from his bed without waking him and padded to the laundry room. Between their lovemaking sessions, he had gone to the kitchen to get them sustenance and had tossed her wet clothes into the dryer. Dressing quickly, she let herself out a back door of the house as quietly as possible and descended the stairs to the beach.

The sun was rising in a glorious, tie-dyed sky. The tide had left behind clumps of seaweed and other debris stirred up by yesterday's storm. Shell seekers were out in droves, some of them wearing matching T-shirts that identified a shelling club.

The full force of the magnificence of the ocean hit

her, making her pause long enough to draw the rain-washed air into her lungs. Had a morning ever been so beautiful, or was the beauty magnified by the sudden fullness of her heart?

"You're not leaving without saying goodbye?"

She turned to see Rex walking toward her, dressed in shorts and a T-shirt, his hair still sleep-tousled.

"No," she said quickly to cover her guilt. "I was just…going to look for the junonia, although I'm starting to think it's a hopeless cause."

"I'll walk with you," he offered, and she didn't see how she could refuse, considering how recently she'd shouted his name as part of the Deity.

She made a few cursory scans of the ground, pretending to look for the shell, but her brain was foggy, operating under duress and her recent realization.

"I had a great time last night," he said finally.

"So did I." The fact that she was leaving soon and wouldn't see him again was bad enough, but his morning-after geniality nearly made her knees buckle. "Your home is spectacular."

"Thank you." He smiled. "Listen, I thought we could go to the wildlife refuge today if you're interested."

She stopped and stubbed the toe of her tennis shoe in the sand, trying to decide if it was better to blow him off now, or to make plans and then not show. The former was more direct, but might raise questions. And the latter seemed liked such a cop-out.

She was out of her element here. She hadn't expected to develop feelings for him and didn't know how to extricate herself from the situation. In fact,

she hadn't expected to ever feel this way about anyone.

"Lucy, sometimes you find something as soon as you stop looking for it."

She lifted her head in surprise, wondering if she'd spoken aloud or if he'd read her mind.

Rex knelt down and inexplicably stuck his finger in the sand where she'd made a dent with the toe of her tennis shoe. He dislodged something from the sand and shook it off, then placed it in her hand with a smile.

A junonia shell.

## CHAPTER TEN

PERFECTLY FORMED, the junonia shell's solid creamy core gave way to a smooth brown-spotted exterior. Its simple shape and appearance stood out in sharp contrast to its rarity. Wonder flowered in Lucinda's chest.

"She found a junonia!" someone cried. "Over here!"

A crowd descended on her, chattering excitedly, craning to see the shell. A woman from the shelling club shooed everyone away and held up a camera. "I need to get a picture of you two for the local paper."

Lucinda opened her mouth to object, but a squeeze to her waist from Rex distracted her and when she looked back, the deed was done.

"Show me exactly where you found it," the woman ordered, then whipped out a notebook.

Lucinda pointed numbly and the woman made notations on the pad. "And I need your names for the record."

When Lucinda remained quiet, Rex piped up. "Rex McCormick of Captiva, and Lucy Bell of Orlando."

"Congratulations," the woman said, and waved goodbye.

Rex kissed Lucinda on the mouth, grinning ear to ear. "Are you happy?"

She nodded, still feeling a little dazed. "This is…unexpected. I don't know what to say."

"Say you'll have breakfast with me." An amused light shone in his eyes. "For some reason, I'm starving."

Warmth flooded her face as images of their lovemaking came back to her. Her chest was tight with warring emotions. She knew she should leave before things got more complicated, but the desire to spend more time with him was overwhelming. What possible difference could it make if she left now or two hours from now? She would be hurting no one but herself.

"I make a mean pancake," he said, wagging his eyebrows.

Lucinda laughed, bittersweet over a glimpse into what life with Rex might have been like if they'd met under different circumstances. As they walked back together hand in hand, she glanced at his handsome profile and wondered what his reaction would be if she told him the truth.

That her name wasn't Lucy Bell, that she wasn't a redhead, that she'd contrived a way to meet him and to continue to spend time with him in an attempt to extract information for a client, that she hadn't planned to fall in love with him.

The thought of confessing made her nauseous, but she allowed the idea to germinate while Rex put the makings for breakfast on the kitchen counter.

He grunted in frustration. "No eggs. Give me ten minutes to run down to the grocery?"

"You don't have to on my account," she said, feeling more and more nervous.

"I want to get a newspaper anyway. Do you need anything?"

*A dose of truth serum.* "No, thanks."

"Okay. I'll be right back." He grabbed his keys, brushed a kiss on her lips, then left whistling.

When the front door closed, Lucinda put her head in her hands and groaned. What had she done? Rex had been nothing but nice—more than nice. He didn't deserve this.

The sound of a phone ringing pierced the air, startling her. After the fourth ring, a machine turned on and she heard Rex's voice say, "I can't come to the phone. Leave a message."

"Rex?" said a woman, her voice echoing shrilly. "It's Ginger—why aren't you answering your cell phone, sweetheart? Are you mad at me?" The woman sighed. "Okay, I admit that I came on a little strong, forcing the marriage issue, but I want to talk, okay? Call me. I love you."

Lucinda sat frozen as the machine turned off. Rex was involved with someone else and they were talking about marriage? It sounded as if the woman had recently pressed for a commitment. And what had Rex done?

Gone to the beach and had a fling with a tourist.

She'd fallen in love with him, and he was using her to get back at his impatient girlfriend.

Emotional humiliation rolled over her in waves. She pushed to her leaden feet, angry with him for playing with her heart and angry with herself for becoming personally invested in what should've been just another job.

Lucinda set her jaw. She still had a job to do. Rex would be gone for a few more minutes—enough time to look around.

She jogged back to his bedroom and spied his cell phone lying on his desk. A few pushed buttons later she brought up a list of recently received calls: Ginger, Ginger, Ginger, Ginger, Ginger... The woman had called a dozen times! Did she suspect her boyfriend had found a diversion on the beach?

A couple of other names connected to Atlanta area codes told her they were business associates.

But one entry on the list stood out: Javitz Rehab Center, located in Orlando.

Hmm. Lucinda jotted down the number and returned Rex's phone to his desk. Then she let herself out the back door and started jogging down the beach toward her condo. Her achy muscles reminded her of last night's escapades with Rex, but she tried to put those memories out of her mind. Time to pick up and go. If her hunch was correct, she had what she'd come for.

She was drenched with sweat by the time she reached the condo building, but didn't want to take the time to shower. She called the rental office to let them know she was leaving, then began tossing clothes in her suitcase. She gathered up a pile of surveillance photos of Rex that she'd produced with her portable printer. The mounted shell collection she'd bought from the kid on the beach went into the trash.

As much as she tried not to think about Rex, fragmented memories of their time together kept sliding into her brain. Unbidden, tears welled in her eyes. She should

have heeded Eugenia's warning—Rex McCormick was
indeed a master at making women fall in love with him.

He'd conned a con artist, and that was hard to do.

A knock at her door sounded—the maid service, or
someone from the rental office, no doubt.

Lucinda sniffed mightily, then walked over and
opened the door.

Rex stood there, his expression a mixture of anger
and confusion.

# CHAPTER ELEVEN

AT THE SIGHT of Rex standing in her doorway, Lucinda gasped, panicked, then closed the door in his face and leaned against it.

"Lucy," he said, knocking again. "Lucy, what the hell is going on?"

She was trapped—now what?

"Lucy, I'm not leaving. You have to come out sooner or later."

Recognizing the truth, Lucinda heaved a sigh and opened the door to face him. "How did you find me?"

"When I was driving back from the grocery, I saw you running on the beach. I thought something was wrong, so I followed you."

He pushed open the door and saw her suitcase lying on the bed. "You're leaving, just like that? I know the shell was important to you, but—" He stopped when he spotted the tripod with the zoom lens camera and the binoculars. He looked up. "What's this?"

"Rex—"

He brushed past her and stepped onto the balcony, then leaned down to look into the camera lens.

Lucinda closed her eyes and when she opened them,

he was staring at her, his expression pure anger. "You've been spying on me?"

He spotted the pictures that she'd taken of him in the house and she shriveled inside. None of them were of him in the nude, thank goodness, but from the emotions playing over his face when he flipped through them, he was probably thinking of all the things she had seen.

He dropped the photos on the table and jammed his hands on his hips. "Either you tell me right now what this is all about, or I'm calling the police."

She held up her hands Stop-sign fashion. "Okay, okay. I'm a private investigator. I was hired by a client to get a particular piece of information that I thought I could get from you."

He looked incredulous. "What kind of information?"

She cleared her throat, then said, "The whereabouts of Michael Gaines."

His eyes widened. "Eugenia hired you?"

She hesitated, then nodded.

His mouth opened and closed, and he shook his head. "So all of this was planned—meeting you that day on the beach?"

She nodded.

He spotted the shell collection in the trash. "The junonia shell, that was just a ploy?"

She nodded.

"So that's why you were so interested in my friend Michael, why you asked so many questions?"

She nodded.

"So all of it, all the time we spent together, was just a sham?"

Her heart twisted in her chest, but she crossed her arms and nodded.

His mouth tightened. He walked past her out into the hall, then turned around. "Don't you have anything to say?"

Lucy bit down on the inside of her cheek, then angled her head. "Yes, I do. Your girlfriend Ginger called to say that she's sorry for pressuring you about getting married. You really should call her back." Then she slammed the door in his face again.

## CHAPTER TWELVE

LUCINDA SAT BACK in her office chair. "Eugenia, trust me on this. Michael is in a safe place and I suspect you'll be hearing from him in a few days."

"You know where Michael is, but you're not going to tell me?"

"That's right."

"But Lucinda, I *paid* you to find him!"

"I know. And I'm giving you a full refund."

Eugenia sputtered. "But that doesn't make sense."

"It will in a few days," Lucinda assured her, then hung up the phone. She scanned the information that an insider at the Javitz Rehab Center in Orlando had verified for her—that on the day Michael Gaines had fled his wedding, he had checked himself into a thirty-day program for alcohol dependency. And apparently the only person who knew was Rex McCormick.

A true friend who had kept Michael's secret.

Restless and bored, Lucinda stood and walked to the window, feeling landlocked in her small inland office, remembering the splendor of the sunrise the last morning she had been in Captiva.

She had woken up that morning in love. And had left

the island in disgrace…and brokenhearted. The look on Rex's face when he realized that she had deceived him was branded on her soul.

She idly toyed with the junonia shell she'd had made into a pendant and wondered what Rex was doing. Then a wry laugh left her throat. He had probably hurried home to Ginger—a true redhead, no doubt—and put an enormous diamond ring on her finger. Or maybe not. Maybe he was still in Captiva, collecting hearts.

"MR. McCORMICK!"

At the sharp tone of his assistant's voice, Rex turned away from his office window overlooking midtown Atlanta. "Yes, Linda?"

She pursed her mouth in frustration. "I said, here's your week's schedule, plus phone messages you need to return and your mail."

"Thank you, Linda."

When she left, he turned back to the window, where he seemed to be spending most of his time these days, lost in thought.

Michael had checked out of rehab, and he and Eugenia were on the road to reconciliation. As for himself, he had ended his relationship with Ginger with difficult words, but no regrets.

The regrets he saved for the time he'd spent with the woman who had called herself Lucy—in hindsight, it probably wasn't even her real name. He felt like an idiot, to have bought in to the emotion that they'd shared, or that he'd thought they'd shared.

He doubted that she'd faked the sex—those responses had seemed genuine enough. But it obviously hadn't meant anything to her. In fact, using sex to get information might be a common practice for her. He had found his cell phone in a mode that he rarely used. She apparently had snooped for information about Michael. The sex had simply been her entry into his house.

*No!* his mind screamed. Their time together, their connection, had been special. He had seen it in her eyes, had felt it in her touch. Their hearts had been in synch the night she'd spent at his house.

He massaged his temples, trying to banish thoughts of her from his mind. He'd been played, that's all. So why did it hurt so much?

Because he'd fallen in love with her.

He groaned at his own stupidity and dropped into his desk chair. He had to get back to work; he couldn't let this, this...*confusion of the heart*...sideline him forever.

With a sigh, he checked his schedule and messages, ridiculously hoping that one of them would be from Lucy, which made no sense whatsoever. Then he pulled his mail toward him and rifled through, stopping on the Captiva weekly newspaper.

He pulled it out and on the bottom of the front page was a picture of him and Lucy, the junonia shell in her hand. He was looking at the camera, squeezing her close. But Lucy was looking up at him.

With an expression of love on her face.

His mouth went dry with hope. Was it a trick of the

lighting, of the lens? Or had Lucy developed feelings for him against her will, just as he had for her?

If so, how had the voice message from Ginger affected her that morning?

Rex pushed an intercom button. "Linda, please get me Eugenia Sampson on the phone."

A few minutes later, Linda's voice said, "It's ringing on line one, sir."

He picked up the receiver just as Eugenia answered.

"Hi, Eugenia, it's Rex."

"Hi, Rex. To what do I owe this pleasure?"

"I need some information."

"About what?"

"Not what—who. I need the contact info for the private investigator you hired to find Michael."

"Lucinda Belvedere? So she wound up telling you, huh? Well, don't feel bad for telling her that Michael was in rehab—she never told me."

He frowned. "What do you mean?"

"She called me when she returned from Captiva and told me that Michael was fine, and that I would probably be hearing from him within a week or so. But that's all she would tell me, and she gave me a refund."

"She did?"

"Yeah. And she was right—Michael called me the next week to tell me that he hadn't felt right about marrying me knowing that he had this addiction hanging over his head. We're back on track. In fact, things have never been better."

"Glad to hear it," Rex said, but his mind was spinning.

"Lucinda's office is here in Orlando, Rex." She

rattled off the address and phone number. "Got some undercover business you need to take care of?"

"Something like that," he murmured, feeling almost giddy...and nervous.

## CHAPTER THIRTEEN

LUCINDA WAS STANDING over the shredder, flipping through the surveillance pictures she'd taken of Rex one last time. It was ridiculous to keep the pictures—they only prolonged her heartache and dredged up regrets.

She turned on the machine and fed them through one at a time, feeling as if her heart were being shredded, too.

"So am I only good for mulch?"

Lucinda turned and gasped to see Rex standing in the doorway to her office. He wore a dark suit and open-collared shirt. He was breathtakingly handsome.

"How…how did you find me?"

"It wasn't so hard, once I decided to do the right thing."

"What do you mean?"

"I had to find you."

Her pulse rocketed higher. "You did?"

He extended a newspaper to her. "I wanted to give you this. We made the front page."

"Oh." She swallowed and took the newspaper, her heart squeezing at the picture of them together. She reached up to touch the shell hanging on a chain around her neck, then felt self-conscious that he could see that the shell had meant something to her. "Thank you," she said primly.

"And there was something else I wanted to give you."

She steeled herself for whatever came next—a lawsuit, a subpoena, a restraining order. "What is it?"

"This," he said, then stepped closer and lowered his mouth to hers in a searing kiss.

Lucinda's mind flew in all directions. She wanted this, yes, but she was confused...and she didn't want to get mired any deeper in her feelings for this man if he wasn't available emotionally. She pulled back and took a deep breath.

"What happened to your girlfriend?"

"I ended it. I should've ended it a long time ago."

"You did?" she asked, daring to hope.

He nodded. "And I came here to find out if our time together was just a job for you."

Emotion swelled her chest and she shook her head. "No, it wasn't."

He picked up her hand. "So how do I know what was real and what wasn't?"

She splayed her fingers against his. "From the beginning, you really threw me off guard. The chemistry scared me. I've never had a case where I was trying to get next to someone, yet trying to resist falling for them." She placed his hand over her heart. "I didn't plan for this to happen, but I'm crazy about you, and that's real."

He exhaled and smiled. "I'm crazy about you, too, Lucy."

She went into his arms and kissed him fervently, her heart cartwheeling through her chest.

He lifted his head, but held her close. "You really blindsided me. I've never felt this kind of connection with anyone."

"Me, too," she admitted, toying with the end of his tie. "It happened so quickly. Do you think we can keep the fire burning?"

"I think we owe it to ourselves to try," he murmured. "You know, I've been thinking about opening an office in Orlando."

"Really?" she said. "That's funny, because I've been thinking about opening an office in Atlanta."

"I guess it doesn't matter, as long as we have the beach to get away to."

Lucy sighed happily, then pulled back and touched her dyed hair. "Oh…I should probably tell you that I'm not a true redhead."

He grinned, then nuzzled her ear. "I kind of figured that one out from…you know. And *speaking* of you know…"

She arched against him, her heart full to bursting. "Yes?"

He reached behind him and closed the door.

Lucinda melted into his arms. The future was a big, happy question mark, except for one certainty—lots of long, steamy nights with Rex on the beach.

\* \* \* \*

*If you liked this, you'll love Stephanie Bond's new book,* She Did a Bad, Bad Thing. *Available now from Mills & Boon® Blaze®!*

# Getting into Trouble

## Leslie Kelly

For Karen and Cheri, who have taken the word
"family" and truly enriched its meaning.
The past two years would have been absolutely
impossible without you...I so love you both.

# *PROLOGUE*

SEEING A shaggy brown camel drinking from a bucket on somebody's lawn would normally be surprising, at least to anyone *not* born in a country whose main landscape feature was sand. Damon Cole, however, could muster no surprise. Because here—in the Florida trailer park where his grandparents lived—the sight made just about as much sense as anything else.

And he suddenly found himself smiling.

His own reaction startled him. He hadn't had anything to smile about in a long time. Weeks. Months? Hard to remember the last happy, contented moment in his life. Yet, as he turned into the short gravel driveway fronting the typical single-wide mobile home, contentment was what he felt.

That could have been caused by the great memories he had of the place from his childhood, or by how much he'd missed his grandparents. Or even, simply, by the camel. Whatever the reason, he was glad. The emotions provided a respite from the more common feeling of helpless rage he'd experienced in recent weeks.

When he'd left Jacksonville that morning, he hadn't known where he was headed. He'd just had to get away—from his job, his life, his reality. So maybe it

wasn't at all unusual that he'd found himself in Gibsonton where he'd often enjoyed another type of reality altogether during his childhood. His grandparents' place had been his favorite spot on Earth when he was a kid. Both thrilling and a little frightening, it had provided many adventures and a whole lot of fantasies. *Of escape.*

"Yeah, not much of a surprise there," he muttered. Escaping had been all he'd been able to think about for weeks, since he'd hit rock-bottom professionally and emotionally. Since he was now officially unemployed, having quit his job as a counselor and caseworker with the Florida Department of Children & Families, he was ready to make that escape.

Swallowing, he pushed some ugly images out of his mind and cut the car engine. He looked around, trying to remember how long it had been since he'd come for a visit. Two years, at least. Grandson of the year, he was not.

The neighborhood hadn't changed much. The road signs were dull and hard to read, and the narrow street was pitted with potholes. Neatly trimmed, lush lawns competed for the small amount of rain with neighboring brown patches of weed. Pink flamingos and garden gnomes stood sentry over colorful flower beds.

At first glance it seemed a typical Florida retirement community for the blue collar people whose bones couldn't handle the northern winters, or whose social security checks couldn't deal with northern prices. It looked overwhelmingly normal. Except for the camel. And the man on stilts walking down the middle of the road. And the elephant grazing down the block.

"Damon!"

Glancing at the porch, he saw his grandmother, Nona, rushing out to greet him. As spry as she'd been a decade ago, she wore a typical old lady's flowery dress and a big hat. If not for the nearby menagerie and the sparkle of cunning mischief in her eyes, she could be mistaken for any snowbird wintering in Florida.

Few would recognize Madame Natasha, who'd told the fortunes of thousands of fair- and carnival-goers in forty-eight states. Not unless she took off that hat and unwound the waist-length hair, once jet-black but now an even more dramatic snowy white.

"Nona," he said as he got out. He braced himself for either a huge hug or a rap on the head because he hadn't been in touch.

He got the hug. She flew into his arms, her hat falling off as she kissed each of his cheeks. "I knew you were coming."

He laughed as he let her go. "Of course you did."

"You doubt me?" Taking his arm, she tugged him toward the house, giving the camel a wide berth. Seeing the line of drool dangling out of the animal's mouth, Damon did the same. Camel spit was one more knock he didn't need.

Once inside, Nona pointed at the table, neatly set for three with a platter full of steamy fried oysters and corn on the cob. "Papa went to get your favorite beer," she explained.

"Okay. You were expecting me."

"It wasn't my crystal ball," she admitted. "I read the latest article in the paper today and thought you might

arrive at my door." Her expression haunted, she added, "I'm so sorry."

Yeah. So was Damon.

"Did you really quit your job? Resign in grief like the article said?" She pushed him toward a chair while she spoke, putting a plate in front of him and filling it with food in her typical eat-no-matter-what-the-occasion manner.

"I couldn't do it anymore," he said through a throat that seemed too tight to inhale even enough air to keep his heart beating. Sometimes he wondered if he even possessed a heart at all, since his had felt pulverized that day five weeks ago. It had been wounded when he'd realized he couldn't keep his promises to a little boy who'd counted on Damon to keep him safe. It had been crushed—mangled—on the day he'd learned that boy's tragic fate. The image of him in his tiny casket was one that never left Damon's mind for long.

His grandmother shook her head and tsked, kissing a small St. Jude's medal that hung from a silver chain around her neck. "Bless his precious soul." Sitting opposite him at the table, she filled a plate for herself. "So where are you going?"

That was a good question. One he didn't have the answer to. He just knew he needed to *go*. To keep moving, until he figured out what he was going to do with his life now that he'd walked away from the career he'd been working toward since grad school. "Not sure. I packed up most of my personal stuff and let a friend move into my apartment for the summer."

Her vivid violet eyes widened. "That long?"

"It's a start." Three months hardly seemed long enough to figure out where he'd gone wrong, what he could have done differently—and what direction the rest of his life would take.

Then again, three months also probably seemed pretty self-indulgent to normal people raised on a traditional nine-to-five, two-weeks-vacation-a-year work ethic. He supposed having a carnival family background made the idea of dropping out of the real world for a little while not only possible but very appealing. If only he knew where he was going as a dropout.

*Cancún? Fiji?* Not on a former state employee's salary.

"You can afford this?"

Shrugging, Damon helped himself to more oysters, suddenly rediscovering his appetite. "For a while."

He was twenty-nine, mostly free of debt, except for one or two last tuition loans. His rent was covered for a few months and his car paid off. Yeah. He could handle a few months as a surf bum, even if Cancún or Fiji were beyond his means.

Not that he knew how to surf. His grandparents might live in Florida, but Damon had grown up in land-locked Indiana. His mother had been the black sheep of her family for marrying a quiet dentist and moving to Fort Wayne. She hadn't yet forgiven Damon for moving to Florida after college.

"You know, your cousin Paulie is having trouble lining up acts for this summer's Slone Brothers circuit. Things change so much—everyone has tattoos, so who cares about a man who is covered with them?" Shaking

her head dourly, Nona added, "And even if it wasn't so, what do they call it, 'politically incorrect,' no one would pay to see the *heavy woman*. Everyone is supersizing these days."

He almost chuckled at his grandmother's attempt to be PC.

"So. There you go."

The subject change had come so fast, Damon had to pause a moment before responding. They'd gone from talking about his decision to drop out of the real world to sideshow acts...*why?*

"There I go, what?"

She didn't even look at him. She simply sprinkled more pepper on her corn. "He needs help. You need a distraction."

He barked a quick laugh, finally getting it. "Sorry. I haven't learned to swallow swords since we last saw one another."

"You have gypsy blood in you, my boy."

Right. He'd wager his veins had as many drops of caveman blood as of the European gypsies his grandmother claimed as her ancestors. Not that he'd tell her that. She was as fierce about defending her heritage as she was about her psychic abilities. Which, Damon had to concede, he'd at least seen evidence of. He'd never been able to get away with anything as a kid when Madame Natasha was around.

"You know that hypnotizing thing, don't you? I remember how much you loved learning about it." She sounded so nonchalant, for a moment he was fooled into thinking she'd just thought of the idea. But she'd

probably been planning this since he'd first mentioned the class during his college days.

"Yeah, I studied hypnotherapy. Some therapists use it to help patients with addictions, that sort of thing."

His patients—the kids who'd been assigned to him by DCF—had more to deal with than quitting smoking or losing weight. Much more.

"So there is your gimmick. I see throngs of people crowding into a tent for a performance of…hmm, what shall we call you?"

"Surf bum," he muttered.

She ignored him. Lowering her corn and scrunching her brow in concentration, she fell silent for a moment, then suddenly snapped her fingers. Rising, she spread her arms up into the air, almost making him see the invisible banner she envisioned. "Come be enthralled and meet the world's greatest *mesmerist*."

She paused for a pregnant moment—the woman did have a flare for the dramatic. Then, with a glint in her eye, she introduced him to the person she wanted him to be for the next three months.

"Presenting Damon, the Gypsy King!"

Suddenly, he caught the vision. Saw the possibilities. And for some crazy reason, that person didn't sound so bad.

Not so bad at all.

# CHAPTER ONE

"THAT MAN could hypnotize me into doing *anything*."

Allie Cavanaugh hadn't really been paying attention to her friend, Tessa, until the awed-sounding pronouncement. Up to that point Tessa had been jabbering about the carnival cruising into town today and Allie had just zoned out.

Tessa wasn't the only one jabbering, either— everyone else had been just as giddy. Apparently, Trouble, Pennsylvania, had been off the lists of traveling shows for a long time, and the residents considered this a mark of their slow crawl back onto the world map. In fact, the town *had* nearly disappeared off the map until her boss, millionaire Mortimer Potts, had bought up most of it and brought it back to life.

Allie couldn't muster much interest in the carnival talk, though. She found laughing at her nine-month-old son, Hank—who was trying to lick a rogue Cheerio off the back of his sticky, pudgy hand—much more satisfying. "Almost got it baby-cakes," she said, nodding her encouragement.

"Oooh, it slipped," she said, wondering how he was going to get the treat, which had ridden a line of baby drool down his arm until it landed near his dimpled little elbow.

But her baby was determined. The way he bent his arm backward to find the cereal made her wonder if he had a future as a contortionist. Finally, with a grunt of effort, he got his prize and gobbled it, flashing her a gummy, two-toothed smile.

"Will you *look* now?"

Allie, tore her attention off Hank, who was busily searching for another treat that might be lurking on the tray of his high chair, or stuck to his arm. Fortunately, she didn't think he'd dropped any down into the front of his diaper. She knew from experience that he could get at those. "Huh?"

"Hello?" Tessa said, reaching across the table and grabbing Allie by the chin. She forcibly turned her head and made her look out the grubby front window of Tootie's Tavern, where the two of them had met for breakfast this hot June morning.

"Tootie needs to invest in some Windex." She moved her head, searching for an inch of clean glass through which to peek.

Tessa grabbed a napkin and wiped a spot. "Check *him* out."

At first she thought Tessa was talking about the guy changing a flat tire on his primer-speckled pickup right outside the restaurant. She couldn't say for sure, but she'd bet that unattractive half-moon salute appearing out of his too-low jeans belonged to Freddy, a guy who worked at the gas station. "Eww."

"Not *him*," Tessa said, gesturing to the left.

Allie immediately saw the line of dusty trucks and big rigs winding down Trouble's main street. One was

loaded with huge, glittering beams and arches of a Ferris wheel. Right behind it came a flatbed truck bearing concession booths—one marked tickets, another offering cotton candy and candy apples.

Her mouth began to water. She hadn't had cotton candy since she was a little kid. Probably not since she was about six years old—before her father had died. Because after that, she and her family had gone to live with her very strict minister grandfather, who believed sugar was a tool Satan had created to corrupt humans into decadence. So his grandchildren had gone usually without while living under his roof with their widowed mother.

"Mmm," she mumbled. She could go for some decadence. It wasn't as if she had to worry about what *he* thought anymore, that was for sure. Grandfather's prejudice against sugar was one more thing she'd left behind when she'd told him to screw off after he'd disowned her for her out-of-wedlock pregnancy.

She hadn't realized how much she'd missed cotton candy until she spied that puff of pink on the sign. "I want some cotton candy to go with my pancakes." She quickly changed her mind. Cotton candy didn't deserve to be sullied by Tootie's pancakes.

"Not that." Tessa sounded ready to pound her. Considering bubbly, blond-haired Tessa was five foot two and tiny, that'd be a feat. Allie had lost most of her pregnancy weight, but she still had a few extra pounds on her already curvy figure.

"Fine." Allie shifted her gaze to the next truck, a big grayish white one, its panel sides painted with crazy

clowns and funhouse mirrors. She hated the funhouse. Who'd want to look in a mirror and appear *bigger?*

"See?"

"Ick. Clowns. They're creepy."

"Not the clowns. Keep looking," Tessa said with a sigh, obviously knowing Allie would eventually stop yanking her chain.

It was their common routine. Over the past year, being pregnant and then raising her baby on her own, Allie had grown pretty pragmatic. Sarcastic, even. And very focused on the life she was building for her and Hank. So she wasn't easily dragged into Tessa's man-babble or her addiction to fashion magazines. Or carnivals, as enticing as cotton candy may be.

"I'm talking about *him!*"

Allie gazed at the next truck and suddenly found herself entirely sucked dry of all thought, all feeling, everything except awareness. And want. "Ho-ly…" she managed to whisper before her voice trailed off. Then she could only stare.

The vehicle was a typical carnival truck—oversized, road weary and a bit gaudy. Its graying paint matched the sad vehicles that had preceded it, but there the similarities ended. Because freshly painted on the side of this one was an invitation. Two invitations, really. One beckoned to the world to come inside and meet Damon—The Gypsy King: The World's Greatest Mesmerist.

The other invitation wasn't spelled out quite as directly. Instead, it was implied through the sultry stare of a man whose huge portrait stared down at the street below.

The painting had none of the distorted, freakish quality often depicted in sideshow displays. This one was actually very good. As for its subject? Well, he was to die for.

The gypsy king's tall, solid form was showcased to perfection in tight black pants and a silky black shirt, open almost to the waist. A red sash pulled tight across his lean hips provided contrast to the breadth of his shoulders and thickness of his chest. He was solid from top to bottom, shaped the way every woman wanted a man to be shaped. But the body wasn't the end of it, not by a long shot.

He had the kind of silky, jet-black hair that only seemed to naturally grace men and had to be stolen from a bottle by women. Its inky length, gathered at the nape of his neck and tied with a brightly colored ribbon, emphasized the man's dangerous—almost other-worldly—good looks. His chin tilted up in challenge, he dared any woman to resist him. The pose was punctuated by the high, carved cheekbones, strong nose and sensuous lips so perfectly curved Allie could almost feel them pressed on her own.

And the eyes. Oh, the *eyes*.

They weren't blue. Not exactly. And they weren't the dark brown or black she'd have expected with that ebony hair. No. They were purple. Vivid and clear, as bright as some exotic orchid she'd seen only in magazine photos of some movie star's wedding.

Which was when she realized the painting—the whole thing—had to be one big fat lie. Black-haired gods all dressed in silk didn't have purple eyes. And

they certainly didn't show up in dinky nowhere towns like Trouble, Pennsylvania. Not a chance.

"He can't be real," she muttered, tearing her gaze away from the truck, which had stopped on the street directly in front of the window. "He's an artist's rendering, right? He's probably really five feet tall, with a beer gut and bad teeth."

Her friend frowned, obviously not liking the idea. "I don't know," Tessa whispered, still staring out her own cleared-off circle of windowpane. "But I can tell you one thing. I'm going to that carnival opening, and I'm going to find out."

DAMON HAD BEEN TRAVELING the carnival circuit with his cousin Paulie's outfit for six weeks now, and his initial skepticism about the whole thing had definitely worn off. Because far from being greeted with jeers as an impostor, everywhere they went, his "mesmerist" act was the biggest moneymaker of the fair.

Every performance was sold out by the end of the first night in any given town. He'd even recently given in to Paulie's pleas to add another two to his already busy schedule. Most carnivals ran Sunday to Saturday, with two shows a night. Now, with another one each Friday and Saturday afternoon, he was standing up on stage masquerading as a gypsy king sixteen times a week.

"You need to wear a red shirt one of these nights," someone said from the doorway of his trailer, which served not only as his dressing room but his permanent home on the road.

Recognizing the voice, he didn't even look up from the mirror. He simply finished applying the most minute amount of stage makeup he could get away with to avoid looking like an anemic vampire under the bright spotlights.

Makeup. Unreal. He'd gone from running group counseling sessions for teens and helping abused kids get over their traumas to putting on face makeup every day of the week.

Not that he was complaining. In fact, he was having a damned fine time. No, he wasn't ready to throw away everything he'd worked for and become a permanent fixture on the Slone Brothers schedule. But for this summer—this painful, awful summer when he so needed an escape—it had proved perfect.

"Didja hear me?" his cousin—two years older, thirty pounds heavier and usually forty decibels louder—asked. Entering the tiny camper, he kicked the door shut behind him, then hung the plastic-wrapped clothes he'd been carrying on the back of Damon's closet door. "Gypsies were colorful, right?"

"I'm not a gypsy."

"Nona says we're all part gypsy."

"She also says we all have a destined mate who our souls will recognize at first sight."

"She was right in my case," Paulie pointed out. "Of course, since she and Bella's grandmother were friends for forty years, I think they played up that angle to force us together."

Damon wouldn't be surprised. But considering how happy Paulie was with his wife, who traveled with the

troupe as an on-the-road nurse, he didn't think that was such a bad thing.

Dropping onto the lumpy couch that had come with the equally lumpy trailer, Paulie sprawled out in exhaustion. "Just sold the last ticket for tonight's show. I had to step into the box office to help because they couldn't keep up with demand!"

Damon shrugged, not surprised.

"I'm telling you, that painting gets 'em every time. Women were lining up before we even opened the booth."

Shaking his head, Damon murmured, "Oh, great, another all-female audience, huh? Wonder if any of them will offer to let me hypnotize her right out of her clothes this time." His tone dry, he added, "Wouldn't *that* be original."

Paulie, who'd been happily married for eight years, wagged his eyebrows up and down. "Might be better if one of these times you said yes. Come on, man, you're getting ass thrown at you left, right and center. When are you going to catch some of it?"

Damon didn't even flinch at Paulie's crassness, because his cousin was right, and the terms he used pretty appropriate. The number of women offering easy sexual experiences to the gypsy king had become something of a joke among the whole outfit. Last he heard, there was a bet between some of the barkers about whether he'd hold out until the Fourth of July...and whether he'd go for a blonde, brunette, or redhead when he finally caved in.

*Brunette.* The word flashed in his head, though he didn't know why. There was no way he was taking up

with *any* woman this summer. Sex wasn't what this escape from reality was about.

Besides, carnival groupies were *not* his thing. He particularly disliked the persistent ones who followed the troupe from town to town. So far, Damon hadn't had to forcibly throw anyone out of his trailer, but he'd had to start locking the door at night. After one performance, a skinny redhead—with a tattoo of a bleeding heart on one shoulder and a rattlesnake on the other—had burst in on him while he was changing.

"Doesn't do a man any good to build up all that backwash," Paulie said, sounding as wise as only a man who'd spent his teen years fishing Ping-Pong balls out of goldfish bowls could. "You're gonna explode or something. I read it in a magazine."

Probably in one with pictures of naked women on every page.

Besides, if Paulie was right, Damon's head would have shot off his shoulders long before now. During the last few months at his former job, the stress of the tragedy and the investigation had made any semblance of a social life impossible. A sexual one, even more so. "Forget it. I haven't met a woman on the road who I'd consider sharing a cab with, much less take to bed."

"Doesn't *have* to be a groupie," Paulie said, obviously not giving up. "There's lots of women right here with us who'd be bouncing like Pogo sticks if you said jump." A sly smile curled his cousin's lips, and he suddenly looked very much like their grandmother. "That Rhoda's a nice girl. And she's single."

Damon's jaw dropped and he slowly shifted around

to face his cousin. "You mean the ring-toss barker who everyone says should start appearing as Flatulent Girl?"

Digging a dingy toothpick out of his front pocket, Paulie stuck it between his lips. "Beggars can't be choosers."

"I'm not begging." *Nor am I choosing.*

"Your decision," his cousin said as he sauntered toward the door. "But I'm still laying money that sooner or later you're gonna look out into the audience and find someone who makes those tight pants the ladies love fit a *little* tighter."

Considering *how* tight those pants were, that would be a very bad thing indeed. But he didn't worry. It wouldn't happen. What was left of his heart had finally begun to heal with this life of easy travel and he wasn't about to let anything interfere with that. He liked having no responsibilities, no personal interaction beyond the odd family he'd gained when he'd run off to join the sideshow. He didn't see that changing anytime soon.

But a few hours later, as he stood on the portable stage finishing up his first performance in Trouble, Pennsylvania, he glanced into the shadows, saw a woman who took his breath away…and suddenly began to wonder.

ALLIE HADN'T intended to do much at the carnival on opening night. She had to attend, since she'd volunteered to work a shift at the firehouse's bingo tent, but wasn't planning to stay afterward. Hank was at home with her landlady, and she almost never left him in the evening.

But somehow, after she'd awarded a gift certificate for a Thanksgiving turkey to the winner of a full-card match—finishing her shift—Allie found herself wandering the fairgrounds. "Just for cotton candy," she whispered as she explored the rides and walked through the maze of games.

Quickly finding the right vendor, she'd invested in a bag big enough to make an entire kindergarten class bounce off the walls for hours. But before she could grab a handful to savor on the way to her car, something else equally as irresistible had caught her eye. The gypsy king's show.

It was sold out. But it hadn't been hard to spot an untied flap in the rear of the tent. Which was how she had come to be standing in the shadows, watching a performance taking place on a small, portable stage a few yards away.

"Oh, my God," she whispered as she stared, unable to tear her eyes off him.

The painting hadn't lied. Not one bit. The Gypsy King was just as sexy, mysterious and devastating as his image had promised him to be. More, really, since she could so easily make out the power of his muscular body beneath the tight clothes, and appreciate the richness of his black hair—tied back in a short ponytail—beneath the shimmering spotlights. She honestly had never imagined just how hot a man could look in a pair of tight, silky black pants and a flowing shirt, equally as black. That dramatic red sash just emphasized his lean hips and taut butt…not to mention the ripples of muscle, and other *bulges.*

His profile revealed a hard, determined jaw and high cheekbones, with dark, slashing hollows beneath. A light beard, maybe two days' growth, gave him a slightly swarthy, dangerous look that was so damned sexy she could almost feel it scraping over her smooth skin. Though not prominent, his nose was strong, his mouth sinfully shaped and meant for kissing.

Unfortunately, from this angle, she couldn't see his eyes. A skeptical voice inside her said they wouldn't be purple—no man could be *that* perfect. But she found herself hoping she was wrong.

She also found herself breathing faster. Leaning toward the stage, she could feel her heart tripping over itself in her chest.

"I'm going to count backward from ten, now, Mr. Fitzweather," the performer said, addressing a balding, middle-aged man who stood facing the audience. "When I reach one, I want you to be the ten-year-old boy you once were and tell us why you didn't do your homework assignment."

Allie snorted, wishing somebody would hypnotize nasty old Mr. Fitzweather into keeping his clothes on. The man was a weekend nudist, as Allie knew from firsthand experience. There wasn't enough soap in the world to wash away the mental image of Butch—her sister's poodle—dangling between the inn owner's chunky, hairy legs. Butch had accidentally mistaken the man's family jewels for a pair of kiwis.

"I did the report, honest," Mr. Fitzweather said. He remained in place, but his body had changed. He was hunched over, his arms crossed tightly over his chest

and his foot scuffing the floor of the stage like a nervous kid. He even stuttered a bit before adding, "B-but a big gust of wind blew it out of my hands on the way to school today. Can I use the bathroom?"

The audience laughed, Allie along with them, acknowledging this was meant to be entertaining, not humiliating. She'd heard of Vegas hypnotist acts where audience members made fools of themselves by stripping, quacking like ducks or crawling like babies. This gentle ribbing wasn't like that, which made her appreciate the hot-as-sin performer even more.

But, gentle or not, it was still pretty darn funny, especially since Mr. Fitzweather wasn't a particularly good sport. She suspected he'd only gone up on stage to prove he *couldn't* be hypnotized, which made his sudden transition to nervous schoolboy even better for the crowd.

Though she told herself she needed to slip back out of the tent the same way she'd crept in, she couldn't help standing there for a few more moments. She couldn't stop staring at the so-called mesmerist… Damon—at least that's what the sign had said his name was.

*The name's probably as fake as his eyes.*

When, she suddenly wondered, had she become such a skeptic? She didn't wonder for long. It had been when she'd been used and dumped by a guy who'd only been out for payback against her sister. Still, she couldn't hate Peter-the-prickface too much anymore, for two reasons. First, because he'd given her Hank. Second, because he'd since stayed away from *both* of them, which was exactly the way she wanted it.

Suddenly realizing she no longer heard the tittering of the audience or the boyish stammerings of an out-of-it Mr. Fitzweather, she shook the bad thoughts out of her brain and peered toward the stage again. And immediately found herself staring into a pair of intense-looking eyes.

Even from here, she could see they were not the stormy purple from the painting, but rather a clear, brilliant violet that were somehow even more disarming. Beautiful. Intelligent. And they were looking right back at her.

# CHAPTER TWO

TRAPPED BY the captivating stare of the mysterious gypsy king, Allie could do nothing but remain frozen in place, whispering the word crap a few times under her breath.

She'd been busted. She was a carnival crasher, sneaking into a sold-out show like a horny kid trying to get a peek at the hootchy-kootchy girls. Mr. Fitz-weather had obviously snapped out of his daze and gone back to his seat, and the audience had gone silent. As had the main attraction, who was, at this moment, staring at her with such powerful intensity that she felt almost magnetically pulled to him.

She sent a message to her feet. *Move. Backward. Now.*

But they didn't listen. Instead, she edged forward.

"Come out here," his strong voice demanded. His hand rose as he beckoned her toward him.

*No way, bud.* But her feet continued to ignore her, edging forward an inch at a time.

She hadn't gone too many inches when suddenly Mr. Mysterious was right before her eyes. He'd obviously gotten tired of waiting and had come to her. "No need to hide in the shadows," he murmured. "I don't bite."

The black clothes and hair, swarthy face and brilliant

gleam of his white teeth as he smiled made her question that assertion under her breath. "*Sure* you don't."

His eyes glittered. She obviously hadn't spoken as quietly as she'd thought. "Well, maybe just a little bit, when I'm asked. And only very carefully."

Gorgeous, sexy, with a hint of kink? She'd found her dream man. *Forget it. Peter was your dream man once, too.*

Allie had to give herself a pass on that one. Hank's father had never been her dream man. He'd just been her first *adult* male, ever.

And because of her experience with Peter, she definitely clung to the motto Once Bitten, Twice Shy. No matter how attractive the biter.

"Sorry, not in the market for a vampire."

"Well, then, don't ask me to bite you."

No problem, even if she could think of a few places she'd like him to nibble.

With that sheen of mystery enhanced by an enigmatic half smile, he added, "And definitely don't invite me into your bedroom. I think vampires have to be invited in, don't they?"

"I'm not up on vampire lore," she responded softly.

Who, she wondered, was that weak-voiced, sappy girl? Surely not her, who'd once bluffed her way aboard a Greyhound bus with a poodle disguised as a service dog. This guy truly did have some gypsy magic because he'd turned her into an imbecile.

"What's your name?"

*Gone. Outta here.* She opted for the most basic. "Allie."

He touched her arm, a fleeting scrape of his finger-tips against her elbow, yet she felt completely overpowered. "Come on." With just a slight tug, he led her out to the center of the stage and stood facing her. Close. But not touching. "Let's show Allie some support," he said to the audience.

They began to clap. The whisper of her name raced through the crowd, and she heard Tessa's voice call, "You go, girl!"

The warm response melted some of her inhibitions because she knew everyone in this tent would look out for her. Funny, after living here for only a brief time, she already felt so safe. She'd been completely accepted.

Maybe it was just because she was related by marriage to—and worked for—the town savior, Mr. Potts. Even so, the warmth she'd felt in Trouble for the past year had somehow eradicated all the dark memories of the judgmental criticism she'd grown up with in Ohio.

"Relax," he murmured, his mouth so close to her ear, she felt his breath on her hair. "Everything's going to be fine."

Hmm. Hadn't that been what Hank's father had said right before he'd relieved her of her virginity and nearly ruined her life? Not that this guy in any way reminded her of Peter. He wasn't a sniveling pretty boy. Oh, no. He was all sexy-pirate-or-vampire-in-a-romance-novel *man*.

"Now, Allie, do you want me to hypnotize you?"

She suspected he already had. Because though she

tried to make her mouth say "No," she couldn't do it. Instead, she only managed to reply with a slow shake of her head.

"You don't?" he asked, looking surprised, as if he didn't believe her. "Then why were you hiding in the shadows?" His eyes sparkled, which was appropriate. After all, his body seemed to emit some kind of electrical current that gave off incredible heat and had made her incapable of moving.

"I was just…passing by," she finally mumbled, wondering if her face was really candy-apple red or if the heat she felt in her cheeks was caused merely by the spotlights.

"Taking a shortcut through the back of my tent, hmm?"

Hearing the skepticism in his voice and chuckles from the audience helped her shake off some of the brainless lethargy.

Tilting her head and cocking a brow in false bravado, she said, "Yeah. I mistook it for the animal tent, there's so much crap being shoveled around in here."

His dramatic eyes flared and he barked a surprised laugh. So did several people sitting close enough to have heard her.

He recovered quickly. "You don't believe in hypnosis?"

Regretting being quite so snarky, she lowered her eyes. "I guess it's a cute trick for the fair, but that's about it."

The performer shook his head. "She doubts me. Shall I prove her wrong?"

The audience roared. "Do it!"

"I don't think so." Glancing toward the audience,

Allie squinted against the spotlights, memorizing the faces of the people in the crowd who were ready to sacrifice her like some virgin to a hungry god of lust. Tessa was number one on the list.

Then she thought about it. *Mmm…hungry lust god.* Interesting. True, she wasn't exactly a virgin, but she wasn't that far from it. She could honestly say it had taken longer for Hank to come out of her during childbirth than his loser father had ever spent going in her.

"I could help you with your addiction," he said, the words almost cajoling.

She gave a surprised little yelp, wondering if he'd seen something in her face that had indicated just where her thoughts had temporarily drifted. Near virgin plus hungry lust god equals lots of great sex for lonely Allie. "My addiction?"

He pointed down to her side, where the huge, almost-forgotten bag of cotton candy hung limply between her fingers. "You obviously like cotton candy. A lot." His voice remained soft, melodic almost. As if he was already hypnotizing her.

Man, he was good. *He'd be* very *good.*

She nodded. "Who doesn't?" Some deep, impish impulse made her lick her lips and add, "It's so delicate—pink and soft."

Ignoring the crowd, keeping her voice low, she focused only on the man who obviously didn't know who he was dealing with. If he thought he was going to take control of this conversation and make a fool out of her in front of all these people, he was about to find out otherwise. Allie didn't give up control easily, and

she definitely wasn't a brainless twit, despite doing a pretty good impersonation of one for the past few minutes.

If the man wanted to play a few sexy word games, however, she would most certainly accommodate him. Hey, innuendo was about as much sexual interaction as she was likely to get for the next twenty years or so, until Hank grew up. She wasn't about to bring random guys around her little boy.

Her voice now a throaty whisper, she added, "I just love taking tiny tastes of it, almost kissing it into my mouth until it melts into a warm pool of sweet liquid. Mmm."

There. Let him try to maintain that calm, in-charge tone when she'd thrown some pretty blatant sexual suggestion at him.

His jaw tightened. His thick muscles—easily visible beneath the satiny shirt—tensed. And his breathing slowed, as if he were focusing on drawing each breath in and then expelling it out in a determined effort for control. "I like picking it apart, piece by piece, morsel by morsel. That way it gets all over my fingers and my lips," he murmured.

Oh. Wow. He was coming back at her. Verbally and—judging by the subtle shift of his body forward— physically. She reacted immediately to his words, her breath catching, her pulse skittering. A warm flow of awareness began to ooze through her body, already hot under the lights.

"It's sticky," he added. He was close enough now that his chest brushed hers. "And I like to lick off every tasty bit."

Nearly unaware she was doing it, Allie lifted her hand to her mouth. She brushed the tips of her fingers against her lips, almost tasting the cotton candy she hadn't even opened yet. Almost tasting what she suspected he was *really* talking about—the delectable flavors two bodies made when making love.

"And maybe bite it, very carefully."

She instantly remembered his comments in the shadows about biting and the lazy river of warmth flowed a little further, a little deeper. All the places on her body that wanted to be tasted by him as if they were sweet, spun sugar on a stick awakened and sang with anticipation.

There were a lot of them. And the overwhelming theme of their chorus was "Yes, yes!" with a few "Hallelujahs" thrown in. She needed no hypnosis to desperately want this man. Yet she felt as if she were under a spell, anyway.

"So should I cure you of this need you have?" he asked. He spoke softly, intimately, for just the two of them.

"What if I don't want to be cured of it?"

"You merely want it satisfied, is that it?"

"Maybe."

He looked down to where their bodies touched...his chest to hers, their hips a whisper apart, his black pants against her capris. "I think there's enough to satisfy you."

She followed his gaze, saw the tightness of his pants and suspected he could absolutely satisfy her. "Definitely."

"I was talking about the cotton candy."

"I wasn't."

It was crazy. They were complete strangers. They were also in full view of a bunch of people—on stage, under the spotlights no less. Yet all she wanted was to throw herself into this man's arms and see if his mouth was as magical for other things as it was for those sweet, sultry, seductive whispers.

*You can't.* No. She couldn't. Unless…. "Are you wearing a microphone?" she asked, still remaining close—so close.

He shook his head.

"So they haven't heard much of what we've said?

"No."

Allie could have backed away. Grabbed some sanity while she was still able. But that glint in his eyes—a glint that asked just what she was up to—wouldn't let her.

"Well, then," she finally said, leaning closer, until her body was pressed hard against his, no suggestive whisper about it. "For all they know, you've been hypnotizing me into doing…all sorts of things," she said with a smile.

Then, giving him no chance to evade her, she slid her arms around his neck, tangled her fingers in his thick, dark hair and tugged his face to hers. She saw his eyes widen the tiniest bit in surprise just before she pressed her mouth to his.

But she was soon too busy kissing him to care.

As IF the place were truly under some gypsy spell, the audience slowly began to fade away. So did the

lights...all other sound, all other sensation. Damon could see, hear, feel nothing except her.

When Allie wrapped her arms around his neck and made it clear she was coming in for a landing on his lips, he didn't hesitate for one second. He merely opened his mouth on hers and took what she was offering. Gave what she was demanding. Indulged in both.

After all, kissing her—putting his hands on her—was what he'd wanted to do from the moment he'd seen those big blue eyes and that magnificently sultry mouth in the shadowy recesses of his tent.

With her sultry whispers and sexy playfulness, he would have expected nothing less than a mouth as addictive as sin. That's what he got. Delicious, irresistible sin. Her pouty lips welcomed him and her warm tongue invited him home. She tasted not like cotton candy but like mint...sweet, spicy. Yes, she was a stranger, but her kiss seemed familiar all the same, the way anything really good always felt.

And it *was* really good. The kind of kiss that wasn't particularly going anywhere but was a destination in and of itself. Deep. Hungry. But not desperate. They tasted and explored, gave and took, completely oblivious to everything except the ever deepening well in which they were drowning.

Damon groaned in the back of his throat at the feel of her soft thigh slipping between his legs. Her hands tightening in his hair, she arched against him, crushing her full breasts against his silky shirt until he burned. His hands rose, as if of their own volition, desperate

with the need to cup her, to toy with the pouty nipples he could feel burrowing into his chest.

A shocked gasp pierced the cloud in his brain, stopping him. Everything quickly snapped back into place as the audience returned. Reality returned. And with it, some measure of sanity.

Slowly—gradually—he ended the kiss, drawing back from her with crushing regret.

She stared at him, her big blue eyes enormous, the pupils merely a pinpoint beneath the bright spotlights. Her lips remained parted, and he watched the pulse in her throat flutter, then finally slow.

They both began to breathe.

And the audience began to clap. Slowly at first. Then louder. Someone yelled, "Hypnotize me next!" That was followed by a male voice shouting, "Introduce me before you wake her up."

At which point Damon realized that the entire audience truly believed the most impressive kiss he'd ever experienced had only occurred because he'd hypnotized his way into it. He almost laughed. He would have, if not for the wide-eyed, nearly desperate look on the face of the woman whose mouth he wanted to dive into again. Her lips trembling and her cheeks flushed, she grabbed his arm and whispered, "Snap your fingers or something."

"Wha…"

"Quick."

Not thinking about it, he did as she asked. Then the sexy siren turned into an adorably disconcerted young woman. She lifted a hand to her face, shook her head

once, then turned to look out at the audience, appearing entirely bemused. "What happened?" She was talking to them. Not to him.

"You've just made your Oscar nomination tape, that's what happened," he whispered with a grin as he stepped beside her and joined her for a bow. The woman wanted to play the innocent, hypnotized bystander. So be it. "I'd vote for you for Best Supporting Actress in a kissing role," he added, keeping his voice low, just for her. "Just as long as this isn't one of those fade-to-black movies that stops at a kiss."

She licked her lips. That was her only response. So he pushed a little more. "Why don't we discuss it further after the show? I'll be finished in a few minutes." Taking her hand and squeezing it as the audience continued applauding, he ordered, "Wait for me and I'll let you pretend to be hypnotized so you can do any outrageous thing you want to me."

He had just propositioned a near stranger on a stage in front of dozens of people. But he didn't care. Not even when she kicked his ankle. She had a hard foot, but for some reason, Damon found himself smiling… like he hadn't in a very long time.

He didn't smile for long, though. Because ten minutes later, when he'd taken his last bow and looked over in the shadows, certain he'd see her waiting there for him, he discovered his mystery woman was gone.

## CHAPTER THREE

"HOW MANY WOMEN named Allie can there be in this tiny town?"

Damon thrust a frustrated hand through his hair. It had been five days—*five*—since a sexy siren named Allie had turned him inside out and then disappeared. And with every day that passed, the intrigue ratcheted up…as did his desire for her.

With just one kiss and some sexy innuendo, she'd practically had him ready to tear off their clothes and take every bit of wicked, delicious pleasure she'd whispered about. If the audience hadn't been there, he might have done it then and there. If she hadn't run away, he might have done it every single night since.

"Still no luck, huh?" Paulie asked from the other side of the trailer where he'd been digging into Damon's tiny fridge. Paulie was trying to avoid the diet food Bella was forcing on him. "What I wouldn't give for a sausage sandwich with peppers."

"I'll sneak you ten of them if you find her for me."

Paulie looked up, amusement making his angular face appear elf-like. "Guess that betting pool's about to pay off."

"Not if I can't find her before we leave here."

"You kissed her and she ran. Priceless." His cousin snickered as he gave up and slammed the refrigerator door.

"*She* kissed *me*," he muttered, mostly to himself.

Paulie's laughter got a little louder.

"*What?*"

"Some hot babe kisses you and you mope about it for a week."

"Only because she disappeared right afterward."

"That's what's so great about it. One kiss and she went into the witness protection program. You losing your touch?"

Paulie's comment rankled. It did seem as though Allie, the brown-haired beauty, had disappeared. If not for the way he smiled when he pictured her "snapping out" of her hypnotic spell, he'd have wondered if he'd imagined the whole thing.

"I better go." Paulie's sigh could have been heard from the next town. "Bella's making meatless hamburgers. Why not just call it a hockey puck on a bun and be done with it?"

Damon barely paid attention as his cousin left. He still couldn't get over how clever the stranger had been—how quick to take what she'd wanted. A hot kiss that he could still taste. In public. With absolutely no repercussions. At least not for her.

Oh, he felt pretty certain some of the townspeople had been whispering about *him*. He suspected he'd been cast as a manipulative carny, hypnotizing an innocent young woman from their town into carrying on like that.

They were protecting her from *him*. Even though

*he'd* been the innocent party. Well, pretty much. He hadn't remained a bystander once her arms had encircled his neck and her curvy body had melted into his. Oh, no. He'd participated in that kiss big-time.

He didn't suppose the townspeople would feel any better hearing that, however, since nobody would tell him one thing about his mystery woman. All his queries had been met with blank stares, innocent shrugs and some type of frown.

The frowns told him he was being had. The pursed lips and disapproving scowls on the faces of the older ladies told him why: the wagons had circled around one of their own.

Carny prejudice wasn't unusual. His own grandparents had been accused of any number of crimes when they'd been on the circuit, simply by virtue of their professions. Stranger equaled criminal in a lot of places. Including, apparently, Trouble, Pennsylvania.

Finally, unable to stand staring at the walls of his trailer any more, he decided to get out for a while. The run ended tomorrow night. By this time Sunday, the caravan would be setting up at another fairground, in the next state, and he could move on.

The carnival grounds were right by a small park. Grabbing a paperback from his camper, he headed out. He'd kill an hour or two in the bright June sunshine, and be back in plenty of time for tonight's first show.

But the moment he reached it, he realized he'd chosen a lousy place to relax. "Bad idea," he muttered. The park was busy, crowded with mothers pushing their children on swings. Normal. Happy. *Unbearable.*

The sound of children's laughter stinging his ears, his body tensed. When one boy with white-blond hair ran past with a cheery grin, a stab of regret cut through Damon with the power of a blade. Closing his eyes, he immediately saw another face—the face of the child who'd trusted him to keep him safe, even from his own parents. The child he'd failed. "God, Tyler, I'm so sorry," he whispered.

He almost left, but stopped himself. Because he slowly realized that the laughter of the children did hurt but not as much as it had a few months ago. Maybe this road trip actually was doing what his grandmother had assured him it would do—help him heal.

No, he wasn't ready to work with children again—nor, even, spend time with them. And he never wanted to be *responsible* for one again as long as he lived. The guilt over his one deadly failure was all he could handle during this lifetime. But at least he'd gotten used to the sounds of laughter and childish voices at the carnival, so hearing them elsewhere didn't instantly send him walking the other way.

Slowly lowering himself to the bench, he forced himself to stay. It wasn't as if he could hide from the world forever. And frankly, he'd realized it wasn't the world he was trying to hide from, anyway. It was his own helplessness. His own guilt.

At first, nobody seemed to notice him. But he'd only been reading for five minutes when he realized everything had gotten quiet. Too quiet. When he looked up, he realized why.

*She* was there. Just a few feet away, watching him

from the sidewalk. And everyone else was watching her watch him.

Damon didn't care. For a second, he just stared back, wanting to make sure she wasn't some phantom rising out of his heated imagination.

"Hi," she said, offering him a tiny smile. The twinkle in her eyes and the way she nibbled the corner of her mouth told him she was still embarrassed about their last meeting. The way she licked those lips told him even more…like maybe she wanted to repeat what had happened at that last meeting.

"Hello," he replied, continuing to devour her with his eyes. On the stage the other night, he'd been too captivated by her face and her outrageous behavior to truly look at the rest of her. Oh, he'd known she felt amazing in his arms, but he hadn't realized just how lush and curvy her body was. Not until now, when he saw the deep V of cleavage revealed by her tank top, and the fine hips outlined beneath the tight jean skirt. Not skinny, she was beautifully curved and soft—incredibly feminine and so damned appealing he forgot to breathe for a few seconds.

"I was just passing by, on my lunch break," she said. "Sure didn't expect to look over and see you here."

"Am I going to get tackled by your concerned friends and neighbors if I ask you to join me?"

One of her brows shot up in confusion, and she quickly took stock of the situation around them. The confusion changed into a frown when she realized they were being watched. "Small town."

Rising to his feet, he stepped close. "Every resident of which seems to be on vigilant guard of your virtue."

She laughed, the light sound matched by the sparkle in her eyes. "My *virtue?* Maybe you *are* straight out of a pirate romance novel." Then she lowered her gaze, her smile fading as her eyes noted his Jacksonville Jaguars T-shirt and his tight, faded jeans. "Though you do the contemporary look pretty well, too."

There was that forthright honesty again. No game-playing, no flirtation. No pretending she hadn't practically kissed his lungs out last weekend.

She was attracted to him, as much as he was to her. "Maybe you should tell me your last name and phone number now, before someone whisks you away from the big, bad carny man."

She rolled her eyes. Opening her mouth to reply, she was interrupted. "Allie, come join us," one of the mothers called, her tone more commanding than cajoling.

She sighed. "Okay. Apparently some of my friends and neighbors are a bit overprotective." She waved nonchalantly and told the woman that she'd catch up later.

"Have they had you tied up and hidden since last week?"

"Sorry. Not into bondage."

A reluctant laugh crossed his lips. "I guess I shouldn't be surprised but considering you faked hypnosis to steal a kiss from a helpless man, I have to wonder what your limits are."

"Handcuffs and chains are definitely outside my limits."

"Aw, shucks."

She gave him a sharp-knuckled punch to the

shoulder and even that contact felt so good coming from her that he wanted to grab her hand, open his mouth on her palm and devour her.

As if sensing his thoughts, she stepped away. "Let's walk."

To the nearest hotel would be good.

She didn't head for a hotel. Instead, she led him through the tiny downtown area of Trouble. Ignoring the looks of everyone they passed—most of whom greeted Allie with a smile and Damon with a glare— they talked about the weather. And the lousy coffee in the local restaurants. And the carnival. And her job as a secretary to a local millionaire. And nothing important at all.

One surprise was her age. Allie was twenty-two. Not *too* young for his twenty-eight, but it still took him by surprise. She looked young, of course, but there was a wisdom—an air of experience—in her tone, and her matter-of-fact outlook. It intrigued him, made him wonder what the rest of her story was, why she seemed older than her years.

"So where *have* you been?" he asked after they returned to the park. The crowd had thinned out, with only one or two moms watching their kids.

"Have you really been trying to find me?"

He could have kept things easy, come back with a flirtatious answer, but he didn't. The truth was, a deep want had existed within him since the moment he'd seen her. The reaction wasn't shocking, considering his sex life had been so dormant lately. But the power of his interest in only *her* surprised him. He'd never

been immediately hit by such intense attraction for any woman before now. Her shadowy silhouette, those amazing eyes and incredible mouth had created a powerful first impression. Her actions…the determined way she'd taken what she wanted, and how damn *good* the kiss had been, made her unforgettable.

And their simple walk today made him realize one thing more—he liked her. So he didn't try to pretend, and he held nothing back. Not his interest. Not his intensity. Not his intentions. "I've been searching for you every single day since the night we met."

"Oh," she whispered. Her full lips parted and she breathed deeper. Stepping in until her mouth was close to his throat, he felt her soft exhalations as well as the warmth of her body. His responded with typical heat, and Damon realized just how much he'd missed his previously healthy interest in sex.

"Have you been hiding?" he asked, reaching up to touch her arm. A mere stroke of his fingers on her elbow, it was loaded with sensation just the same. "Purposely staying away from me?"

She shook her head, thought better of it, and slowly nodded a yes.

"Embarrassed because you went for something you wanted? A lot of people would love to have the guts to do the same thing."

"I wasn't embarrassed. I was afraid."

"Afraid?"

"Afraid next time even an audience won't stop me."

His muscles reacted to her words before his brain did, growing tense and aware. His skin suddenly

seemed electrified—reacting with lightning intensity to her nearness, the smell of her hair, the brush of air her whispers created on his neck.

"Come to the fairgrounds with me." He forced the command out of his throat rather than doing what he really wanted to do—kiss her senseless again and see if she meant it. But their daytime audience was more impressionable than last Sunday's, so he stifled the impulse. His hand still on her arm, he turned, intending to lead her to his trailer. Not a four-star establishment, but it was the nearest private place he knew of. At least, the nearest private place with a bed. Which was exactly where the two of them were going to end up—he knew it as sure as he knew he was ready to start living *this* part of his life again. Emotion might have been dead to him for a while, but his libido had woken up and it had this woman's name imprinted on it.

She didn't budge. "You don't really know me."

"I know you grew up in your minister grandfather's house, have lived here for a year, you love your boss." Brushing a strand of hair away from her eyes, he added, "I know you like cotton candy."

"I repeat, you don't know me."

"Are you married?"

She shook her head.

"Then I know enough."

"No," she insisted. "Look, I like you. Really. But I'm not in the position to have a one-night stand with a stranger. My life's not as… simple as it might appear."

"My full name's Damon Cole. And our walk—not

to mention the kiss—says we're no longer strangers. Besides, I don't like *simple*."

A tiny smile appeared. "Mine's Allie Cavanaugh."

He noted the name, just in case she managed to slip away again. "I don't want a one-night stand with a stranger, either," he said. "But we've established that we're now officially not strangers." He looked up and pointed at the brilliant blue sky. "And it's not night."

Snagging her bottom lip between her teeth, she fought a visible battle not to laugh…or agree. He could almost see the mind working behind her eyes as she gave it some serious thought.

He knew what she was thinking. They were on the verge of being wild. Crazy. Reckless. All of the above.

But it came down to chemistry. They had it. For whatever reason, they sparked off one another in a way few people did, even those who proclaimed everlasting love and fidelity. He didn't necessarily believe his grandmother's stories of soul mates and love at first sight, but he definitely believed in chemistry.

"I'm sorry," she finally said, her answer clear. "I guess I should have kept on walking when I saw you there."

His jaw tightened. "You're saying no?"

She nodded, though her frown told him she didn't want to.

"When I know you want to say yes."

With a helpless shrug, she tugged her arm free. "Maybe I do. I'll be honest with you, right now, I don't know *what* I want."

He tried to coax a smile. "Other than cotton candy?"

Her lips didn't even twitch. "I ate too much and got

sick. I think I cured myself of giving in to silly cravings for a while."

His chin lifted in challenge. "Including your craving for me?"

A typical female might have become indignant, denied his claim and tried to pierce his supreme confidence. Allie didn't. "Yes. Including my *craving* for you." With a sigh, she lifted a hand to his cheek and rubbed her thumb along his jaw, the brush of her smooth fingers cool and hot all at once. "I'll regret it," she said. "Believe me, I already know I'll regret it."

Without another word, she began to walk away. Because of the hungry helplessness in her voice, her obvious regret and their audience in the park, Damon had no choice but to let her go.

"WHADDAYA MEAN, you don't know what you want? Any woman with a drop of estrogen in her body would want that man!"

Allie glanced over at Tessa, who was working with her at the library bake sale Saturday night. Already mourning the carnival's imminent departure, all of Trouble's residents appeared to have turned up to gorge themselves on candy apples and get dizzy on the Tilt-A-Whirl. "I can't afford to want him."

"Come on, what woman can't afford a night of booty-shaking, rock-til-you-drop sex with a hot stranger you'll never have to see again?" She rolled her eyes. "Imagine one night with a dream man who you'll never have to watch scratch himself or get a beer gut or snort when he tells his nephews to pull his finger."

Allie grinned, knowing the kinds of guys Tessa dated.

"You can do *anything*…have your own personal fantasy come true, a night to remember the rest of your life," her friend said. "As the years go by, he'll become sexier, stronger, more dangerous in your mind. When you're old, you'll get a secretive smile on your face when you think of that one amazing time when you went for something incredible."

Fanning herself with her hand as her vividly painted words sunk in, Tessa fell silent. Reaching for a plate of cellophane-wrapped brownies, she tore one open and began to shove it into her mouth—every woman's first substitute for great sex. "Who wouldn't go for that?" she mumbled around the chocolate.

Allie's legs were still shaking at the picture Tessa had put into her head. "One whose last experience with irresponsible sex made her a single mom by the age of twenty-one." She hadn't even mentioned her son to Damon during their walk, knowing any sexy guy would be unnerved by a woman who'd gotten pregnant the first time she'd had sex. Maybe if she'd actually planned to sleep with him, she would have told him. But it was a moot point now.

"Allie, there is such a thing as protection."

Yeah, and she owned stock in it, never going anywhere without condoms in her purse, not that she expected to use them. "There's also such a thing as my reputation. Do you think I don't know the way some people look at the unwed tramp who wormed her way into Mr. Potts's good graces?"

"That's *so* twentieth century."

"It's also *so* true."

Tessa frowned, but she didn't deny the accusation. How could she? She knew as well as Allie that there were a few holdouts in Trouble who had only accepted Allie and her little boy because of their connection to the town patriarch. Not only did Allie work for the man, but her sister was now married to his grandson. She was, whether the old-timers liked it or not, a member of his extended family, so they'd grudgingly accepted her. But if she slipped up and made a scandal of herself with some traveling gypsy, she'd lose all the ground she'd gained with them.

Last week's kiss had been whispered about, she was sure. But Damon's act was so good, even the most scurrilous old gossips—like the Feeney sisters—couldn't be certain she hadn't been under his spell.

Well, hadn't she? And wasn't she still?

"All I'm saying," Tessa continued, grabbing another brownie and then a handful of chocolate chip cookies, "is that if you don't go after what you want, you're never going to get it."

"But what if I'm not sure what I want?" A good, stable, old-fashioned home where she was loved and re-spected—enfolded into a community family—was what she *thought* she'd always wanted.

Now sin in the arms of a violet-eyed stranger was all she could think about.

"I think I know someone who could help you figure it out," Tessa said. She pointed toward the crowd pouring into the Gypsy King's tent, anxious to attend his last show of the carnival.

"Oh, yeah, he could help me figure it out while relieving me of my clothes one piece at a time."

"Yum."

"Forget it."

Tessa wasn't giving up. "Seriously, you need *professional* help." Smirking, she added, "That, or a dildo."

"Very funny."

"Well then, go to the professional. Hypnotists are good at getting to the heart of people's innermost desires, right?" Tessa reached into her pocket and pulled out two tickets for tonight's show. "I think it's time you go to the expert and let him help you figure out what it is you *really* want."

# CHAPTER FOUR

DAMON IMMEDIATELY spotted Allie in the audience. Seeing her face in the crowd two rows back from the stage explained the tension he'd been feeling. His body had known she was there, even though his brain had told him all day that she wouldn't show. He was glad his body had won out over his brain. If only hers would.

Nodding to let her know he'd seen her, he began looking for volunteers. He knew better than to try to get her onstage—she'd bolt. There were plenty of others to choose from. Dozens of people's hands were up as they offered to be hypnotized.

For the past week, Damon had avoided selecting any young women—the most vocal about wanting to be chosen. Since the night he and Allie had kissed on stage, his show had been packed with females with low-cut shirts and high expectations. It wasn't just the young, on-the-make ones he had to look out for. On Tuesday he'd chosen a middle-aged blonde from the audience, whose husband had been sitting beside her, making her a safe choice. Uh…wrong. She'd barely stepped onto the stage before she'd thrown her arms around his neck and yanked his face to hers for a slurpy kiss.

After that, he'd picked men and old ladies, or, on occasion, a few people together. Multiples generally proved susceptible to suggestion due to group mentality. And three people wouldn't be diving on him with lips puckered all at the same time. He hoped.

It was when choosing another group for his last session of the night that he noticed the woman sitting beside Allie. She was young, maybe twenty, with frizzy blond hair and a loud laugh. Her arm waving frantically in the air, she almost fell out of her seat in an effort to gain his attention. "We want to be part of the group!" she said, jerking Allie to her feet.

"You'd better be talking about you and the mouse in your pocket when you say 'we,'" Allie snapped, making Damon and the closest audience members chuckle.

The woman was already pushing Allie over the legs of those sitting between them and the aisle. "There's safety in numbers."

Damon didn't say a word. If Allie's friend wanted to get them together again, even in front of an audience, he wouldn't argue. Tonight was probably the last time he'd ever see the woman who'd awakened something in him that he'd thought was dead. Several somethings. Not just his sex drive, but his sense of humor, even a bit of his optimism.

"Okay, we're ready," the blonde said when they reached the stage. Her arm was wrapped tightly around Allie's, almost holding her captive, and a married couple who'd volunteered stood between them and the stairs, blocking any escape.

He should have offered her an out. Maybe if he hadn't been dressed up as a gypsy he would have. But frankly, the Gypsy King persona sometimes lowered his inhibitions. So he didn't give her a way out. Instead, he met her eye, daring her to go for it.

She did. Stiffening her spine, she lifted her chin and forced a tight smile. "Fine."

"Good girl," he mouthed, then turned to the others in the group. "You're all willing to participate in this experiment?"

They nodded, even Allie. But before Damon could continue with one of his standard routines, such as having the group perform a Beatles song or act like characters from a popular movie, Allie's frizzy-haired friend spoke up. "Do you take requests?"

Allie's eyes widened.

"I mean…can you hypnotize us all into thinking about—revealing—what we truly want? Our secret wishes and desires?"

The married couple each shrugged, apparently having no problem with the idea. Allie obviously did. "Forget it."

Damon quickly realized what the friend was up to. Hadn't Allie said something about not knowing what she wanted? Or, at least, she hadn't had the courage to *own up* to what she wanted.

"You're saying you want to explore your own hopes and dreams?" he asked, his voice low and even, already gaining the trust of his test subjects with his soothing tone.

"Beats hopping around like a frog," the male volunteer said.

The audience murmured their approval. With one last glare at her friend, Allie said, "All right. Go ahead."

"It won't work if you hold yourself back. You have to let yourself go, open up to me," Damon said, moving close to her.

Her eyes closed, as if she were striving for some control. But when she opened them again to meet his stare, he saw calm acceptance and realized she *was* ready. For…whatever.

He began, and this time, he had no doubt. Allie wasn't playing any games. He recognized the slowness of her breathing, the slight easing of the muscles in her body. He'd seen enough people genuinely hypnotized to know that she, and the rest of tonight's volunteers, were in a very susceptible state.

Some thought hypnosis could be used to force people to do things they wouldn't ordinarily do. It couldn't, of course. It only worked on willing subjects, sometimes releasing inhibitions, capturing lost memories or allowing one the freedom to do something they secretly wanted to do anyway. Though he hadn't thought of this particular shtick before, he had to admit, Allie's friend's idea had been a good one. Who didn't have secret dreams and desires that a little coaxing might help them reveal?

The blonde, whose name, he discovered, was Tessa, was the first up. She soon had the audience clapping when she talked about how badly she wanted to win the lottery.

"So what else would you do, other than telling your boss he needs to get laid by someone other than Angie

the Blow-Up doll?" Grinning, he held the microphone toward her.

"I'd pay to get my nose smaller and my boobs bigger. I'd go live with Jake Gyllenhaal and the entire male cast of *Lost* on some desert island that had 24-hour delivery of pizza and Ben & Jerry's ice cream. And condoms."

He snapped his fingers. She fell silent and lowered her head, not hearing the audience's roars of laughter.

The older couple was up next. While Tessa and Allie remained motionless, deep inside their minds in self-imposed isolation, he asked the pair what it was that they wanted.

The husband answered first. "I want my wife to stop eating Doritos and watching *Days Of Our Lives* while I'm out working my ass off all day." The women in the audience began to grumble.

The wife didn't respond to her husband, only to Damon, who put the question to her next. "I want my husband to stop thinking of me as a fat, useless house-wife and treat me as romantically as we did when we got married." Her voice still soft, vulnerable, she added, "And I want to stop feeling like he's right."

For a woman her age, Damon thought she looked great, especially in comparison to her potbellied husband. Her spouse had obviously done a number on her self-confidence.

"When you wake up," he said to the husband, "you'll be overcome with passion for your wife. From now on, no other woman will look as good to you. Every time you see her, you're going to see the beautiful girl you married."

Damon faced the wife and took her hand. "From now on, you will not only see the passion in your husband's eyes...you'll believe you're worthy of it. Because you *are*."

Soon it was Allie's turn. He led her to a stool on the stage and helped her onto it. "You're good at hiding what you want."

"Yes," she mumbled, not opening her eyes.

"But you do know what it is. You just need to admit it."

Under the spotlights, her hair glimmered and her smooth, creamy face appeared even more beautiful. Vulnerable. She shifted a little, arching her back, dropping one shoulder so that one strap of the low-cut sundress she wore slipped off her shoulder.

From here, standing above her, he could easily see the curve of one breast, cupped by a lacy strapless bra. Soft, pink, as tempting as cotton candy. Both the bra...and her skin. Only the presence of the audience prevented him from lifting his hand and scraping the tip of his finger from the vulnerable pulse point in her neck, across her throat and down between those lush breasts.

He forced the impulse off and got back to business. "I want you to stop hiding your dreams and say what you most long for."

He held his breath, half expecting her to say, "True love," or even, "World peace." He *didn't* expect what he actually got.

"I want to be touched."

Damon stiffened.

"Intimately. Sexually." Her words were slow, almost dreamy. "I want a fantasy lover come to life."

Damon shifted away from the audience, focusing entirely on Allie, whose sultry tone had shot through him like an electrical current.

"I want a man's strong, powerful hands on me. Thick arms to hold me, a hungry mouth to devour me." She sighed audibly, the sound amplified by the microphone.

He was tempted to stop her, knew that he should because of the audience. But something—perhaps his own heated reaction to her throaty whispers—made him let her go a little further. Though he did have the presence of mind to pull the microphone down a few inches, making the moment slightly more intimate, as if she spoke only to him.

"I want to know what it's like to have a man so desperate for me he can barely control himself. No games, no ulterior motives. Just pure, undiluted want."

Such as what he'd felt for her since the night they'd met.

"I want him so aroused when he looks at me that his hands shake as he strips off my clothes, piece by piece. He'll handle me tenderly, as though I'm fragile, then more aggressively because he simply can't help himself. He has to touch me, feel me…experience me absolutely *everywhere*."

She moaned, a feminine sound of arousal and anticipation that made Damon think of rumpled sheets and wild nights.

"I want to do things I've never done with someone I trust not to hurt me—physically, or emotionally. To

be wild and wicked. To make love for hours under a starry sky, with a strong nighttime breeze blowing over our hot bodies. To be with someone who doesn't have any other agenda than the pleasure we can make each other feel. And to finally sleep in his arms, knowing we'll start all over again when we awake."

She fell silent, her pose entirely relaxed. Damon stood beside her, unable to speak, her whispers echoing in his head. Silence surrounded him, broken only by the distant ding of bells and the cries of barkers hawking the games on the midway.

Finally, someone in the audience whistled. A whisper rolled through the crowd—"Who is she?"— picking up speed and volume as the wide-eyed onlookers continued to stare at the still hypnotized young woman on the stage. Damon bit back a groan, realizing what had just happened. He'd been so captivated by Allie's erotic fantasies that he'd allowed himself to forget dozens of other people were hearing them, too. He had let her go too far.

He couldn't, however, turn around. He was still too hot himself. God, her voice was like audible sex, and his whole body had reacted to it with pulse-pounding power. He was hard for her—dying for her—ready to give her every single little thing she asked for.

Unfortunately, he realized, every other man in the place probably felt the same way.

*But she was talking to me.* He was certain of it.

Finally, unable to ignore the groundswell of applause rising from the crowd behind him, he drew Allie—and the others—out of their trance. They all snapped to and

were drowned by the crowd's enthusiasm, none of them realizing why the men in the audience were whooping and the women staring at Allie in shocked envy.

He understood their reaction. After all, it wasn't every day a woman was free to tell a man exactly what she wanted him to do to her, in great detail, and bear no responsibility for the telling. He'd wager any number of women would give a lot to have the chance to freely tell the men in their lives exactly what they wanted and how they wanted it.

"Was it okay?" Tessa asked, wide-eyed and a little pensive, as if suddenly wondering just what she'd revealed under hypnosis.

"As long as your boss isn't here, you did just fine," he murmured as he led his volunteers forward to take a bow.

"Uh-oh," she muttered.

Allie snickered. "Serves you right."

He didn't have the heart to tell Allie that her revelations had been much more shocking than her friend's. At least not now, surrounded by curious onlookers.

He'd tell her later. When he got her alone.

Then, if he had his way, he'd grant every one of her whispered desires.

ALLIE WASN'T SURE *when* she began to suspect she was being talked about, but by the time she saw a third woman pull her husband away to avoid her, she knew it was true.

"Why is everyone staring at me?" she whispered to Tessa as the two of them exited the tent with the rest of the audience.

Tessa didn't reply, apparently still focused on her own performance. "What did I say about my boss?"

"I have no idea, but I think we both need to find out."

Unfortunately, since a lot of out-of-towners had poured into Trouble for the last night of the carnival, Allie recognized a few people but didn't personally know any of them. So why on Earth did they all seem so fascinated by her? "I'm definitely being stared at."

"You don't think he made us take off our clothes or anything, do you?" The hint of a grin on Tessa's face didn't quite match her concerned tone. "I mean, I know he'd like to get *you* to take off your clothes, but I doubt he'd have included me. Unless he's into kinky stuff. Threesomes. Exhibitionism."

Oh, wonderful. Tessa spoke at high school gym teacher volume, so if they hadn't been stared at before, they certainly were now. One scruffy, rough-looking carny worker was positively leering at them from a game booth a few yards away, and a trio of teenage boys appeared to be egging each other on to come talk to them.

"Would you shut up?" Allie said from between clenched teeth. "We're already getting enough attention—and I want to find out why." Just not from any scruffy-looking men or cocky teens.

"There's one person you could ask. I bet he's waiting for you in the back of his tent right now."

Her friend was probably right. Allie didn't have to hear the words to know Damon hadn't given up on the idea of something happening between them. The heated stare he'd laid on her as she'd left the stage had said a lot.

*Come to me. Give yourself over to it. I know what you want.*

And, oh, boy, did she suspect he was right.

"Actually, I know better than to wait for her," a silky voice said from behind them. "She has a habit of disappearing."

Allie jumped, instantly realizing who had overheard. "You."

"Me." Never taking his eyes off her—as if afraid she would leave—he addressed her friend. "Tessa, you talked about winning the lottery and made one crack about your boss."

"Kind of a take-this-job-and-shove-it thing?"

Damon's lips curved up the tiniest bit with a hint of amusement. "Something like that."

"Whew," Tessa said. "I mean, who doesn't fantasize about winning the lottery and quitting their job?"

Judging by that enigmatic sort-of smile, Damon hadn't revealed everything Tessa had said, and probably for a reason.

"Okay. What about me?"

His smile immediately faded. In the colorful glimmer of light provided by the carousel lazily turning nearby, his expression suddenly appeared intense. Dangerous, even.

"You…talked quite a lot."

"About what?"

"I think we should go someplace private to discuss it." Taking her elbow in his hand, he steered her away from Tessa, away from the tent. Toward the perimeter of the fairgrounds and the long line of trucks and campers beyond.

"I'm not going to march to your trailer with you right in front of all these people." She tugged her arm away, frantically looking around to see if they were being watched.

They were. By what looked like every person who'd attended the show.

He followed her stare. "Damn." Letting her go, he crossed his arms over his chest and leaned a shoulder against the side of a game booth, as if it had been his destination all along.

She liked him for that. "Thanks." Turning, she slid her heels against the booth and leaned her back against it as well. She was fully visible, facing out, so any busy-bodies could clearly see her and know she wasn't making out with a sexy stranger in public. Even though a naughty part of her wished she were.

She hadn't realized quite how intimate even this casual position could be until she looked up at Damon, standing perpendicular to her shoulder. He was staring at the deep *V* of her sundress with outright lust in his eyes, which suddenly made her very grateful indeed that she had retained some serious curvage after she'd stopped breast-feeding Hank a few months ago.

"You are so hot," he muttered.

He meant it. The sex god really meant it...about *her*, mouthy, silly little Allie Cavanaugh, the college dropout and inexperienced single mother who'd grown up in the shadow of her tall, perfect, blond-haired older sister.

Her legs shaking, she pressed her hands flat on the wall behind her. She was *so* out of her league here. Because instead of getting all seductive and flirtatious

like a normal, experienced woman might, she wanted to do a happy dance that this amazing man wanted her. Then she'd rip off her clothes and let him *have* her.

Obviously realizing she had no idea how to respond, Damon cleared his throat and looked away. "Okay, we do need to talk, but I don't want to give anybody anything more to say about you."

Right. So ripping off her clothes was definitely out.

"Why don't you go to your car, then come through the back gate of the lot. My camper's the fifth on the left."

His camper. His *bed*.

He might say he wanted to talk to her, but Allie was no fool. If he wanted merely to tell her what stupid, idiotic thing she'd done on stage, he could do it right here. They were a dozen feet away from the nearest wide-eyed, nosy onlooker, so they could be seen but not heard. Yet he didn't do it.

"You want me to come to your camper *just* to talk?"

He shook his head, stepping closer, so that his silky shirt brushed her bare shoulder and his pants caressed her leg. Her skin sizzled in both places as her head filled with his scent.

"No, I don't just want to talk." He leaned down, as if to whisper in her ear, but instead pressed a deliberate kiss on her temple. Light. Soft. But still so damned erotic that Allie almost slid down the side of the booth and melted onto the dusty ground.

"I want you to come so that I can touch you," he whispered, the words flowing over her as smoothly as warm water.

Oh, God.

"So I can use my hands and my mouth on you. Take your clothes off slowly—piece by piece—almost shaking as I try to keep myself from ripping them off and having you immediately."

Allie did start to sink then, sliding down the wall. Her feet probably would have gone out from under her if Damon hadn't reached out and grabbed her hip, his arm stretched across her stomach as he tugged her back up. Inflaming her.

"Say you'll come."

Oh, she had no doubt she'd come if he did what he promised to. She'd been on the verge of climax since seeing his face on the side of that damn truck a week ago. Now she was almost out of her mind with the need to explode with pleasure in his arms.

"*Say* it."

She shouldn't, she knew that. How foolish would it be to have a one-night stand with someone totally out of her realm? A traveling carny who probably picked up a woman in every town.

But oh, was it tempting. Hank was safe at home with Miss Emily, her landlady, who absolutely adored the little boy. She'd already told Allie she would put him to bed in the crib she used when she babysat him during the day, and to not bother waking him up if she came in late. So she *could* come in late. Very late.

Damon's warm hand rose, sliding from the curve of her hip up to the indentation of her waist. Then higher, until he was cupping her midriff, the tips of his fingers almost brushing the bottom of her aching, hypersensitive breast.

*"Come."*

He was using that hypnotist voice on her, the command weighty and deliberate, accepting nothing but full capitulation.

And suddenly she couldn't resist it anymore. She might only have one night, but that would be enough. Enough to sate the hunger. To fill the emptiness. To perhaps even begin to eradicate the memories of the last man who'd touched her intimately, then not only abandoned her but had tried to hurt her and her sister.

"I'll come," she whispered, hearing the throaty want she couldn't possibly disguise. "I promise."

As if not trusting himself to speak, he stepped back. Spinning around, he walked away, in the direction of his camper, so sure she'd show up that he didn't even say, "See you soon," or "I'll be waiting." He demonstrated his certainty of her with every sure step he took in the opposite direction.

Overbearing. Cocky. But, God, that confidence was sexy.

Allie knew she should find Tessa, but she didn't want to deal with the knowing look she'd see on her friend's face. Instead, she headed toward the parking lot, feeling as if she were floating over the ground rather than walking on it. Even the stares and whispers of a few people she recognized from the show earlier couldn't deflate her mood or dampen her excitement.

Only one thing could do that. And three minutes later, when her phone rang, it did. When Miss Emily called to tell her she was taking Hank to the emergency

room in the next town, Allie didn't pause, didn't consider one thing other than getting to her son.

It wasn't until many hours later, when the doctors had declared her baby boy just fine despite having sampled a bar of soap at Miss Emily's, that she even remembered the promise she'd made to the dark-eyed Gypsy King. And realized it was too late—much too late—to fulfill it.

# CHAPTER FIVE

*Two weeks later*

HAVING LIVED in Florida for the past several years, Damon had grown to love the beach. At home, in Jacksonville, he lived a short five-minute drive from the ocean and had spent a lot of his spare time there—swimming, running, catching an occasional beach volleyball game with friends. So this latest appearance with the carnival, in a small ocean town in Delaware, should have felt like coming home. It should at least have improved his mood.

No such luck. His mood had been pure crap for a couple of weeks now, ever since he'd been aroused to the point of madness by a sexy little brunette, then stood up by her that same night. Allie Cavanaugh's sultry whispers and helpless sighs had gotten him hotter than he'd ever been in his life.

Damn her for not following through.

"Hey Mr. Gypsy King, how's it hanging?"

He stiffened, wishing he hadn't been seen by Jonesy, one of the old-time barkers who ran the ring-a-knife game. Jonesy was hard-core all the way and lived up to every negative carny stereotype ever created. From

the stringy, graying hair, to the scars and prison tattoos, he was the kind of guy parents warned their kids about when they let them go off alone at the fair.

"That little cock tease still got you tied up in knots?"

"Shut the hell up," he snarled.

"I mean, she was hot, I give ya that, but nothing unique. I'd swear I saw a skank looked just like her on the beach this morning."

Allie and *skank* were not two words that went together, nor did Damon think there was any way the woman had followed him here. She'd had her chance with him two weeks ago in her own backyard and she'd made it clear she didn't want it.

"You know, some other carnival ho would do just as well."

"Go away." He shot the man a glare, not slowing his pace as he maneuvered through the gauntlet of games lining either side of the midway. It was mid-afternoon, the second day of their appearance in Dalton Beach, a small town near Rehoboth, and the crowds hadn't started pouring in yet. So the barkers were busy calling out insults to each other—and whoever passed. Lucky him.

"Hit a nerve, huh?" Jonesy said with a phlegmy chuckle.

"Not even close."

The barker left his booth and followed him. "You know, if you're still all het up, I know a couple of the sideshow girls who'd take care of you. I could arrange it...for a small fee."

Damon knew the sideshow girls would take care of

him for free, given their many offers. "Don't you have kids to fleece?"

"Too early. Kiddies are waiting for Daddy to get home from work," Jonesy replied. Damon noted the absence of any denial by Jonesy about the fleecing part.

Paulie prided himself on running a clean operation, but Damon wasn't sure everyone had gotten the message. From bottle caps behind the woven slats of baskets—which would cause any ball landing in them to pop back out—to hoops too small for a basketball, some shady carnival traditions managed to stay alive.

"Now, about my offer…"

"Forget it." Finally, knowing how to shake the other man off, Damon stopped. "I'm going to the security trailer for a meeting with Paulie and the local police. You coming, too?"

Bingo. Without another word, Jonesy made a sharp U-turn and went back to his booth. Feeling as if he'd just scraped something from the pony ride off the bottom of his shoe, Damon made a mental note to talk to Paulie about the man.

But for all his distaste of the messenger, the message had hit home. Damon spent the rest of the day thinking about the fact that his sex drive had returned with a vengeance. He was dreaming wild, erotic things every night—waking up hard and sweaty, reaching across his bed for someone who wasn't there. Winding up frustrated, with her face in his brain and her name on his lips.

He needed to get laid. And while he couldn't see himself getting it on with the multi-pierced sideshow

manager, or one of her girls who liked to dance on glass or lie on beds of nails, he didn't imagine it would be hard to find someone to help him slake the urge. This was a beach town, during Fourth of July week. There would be lots of bikini-clad vacationers just as anxious to make a sexy mistake they would regret later but couldn't bring themselves to care about now. Surely *someone* would appeal to him.

With that in mind, once the sun went down and the midway lit up, he kept his eye out for any interesting woman who might suit his needs. Unfortunately, none did. Because in his head, he kept seeing the one woman he truly wanted. Allie.

He had a bad case for her. Bad enough that he was considering going back to Trouble at the end of the run to confront her. He wanted to know why she'd led him along, then not followed through. Especially when he *knew* she'd wanted him just as much.

She was so much on his mind that night that even while he was on stage, performing, he glanced over the crowd and thought he saw her face. That wasn't unusual, though—hadn't he been seeing it every place he looked? Especially in his bed, staring at him with ravenous hunger in those big blue eyes, begging him to take her, to put her out of the misery she'd caused them both.

As he chose his next volunteer, a strange tingling started in the back of his neck. He felt as if he were being studied. Stared at. By someone interested in more than the performance.

He kept going, but glanced around, his eyes sliding

over the crowd, not betraying his keen interest. And then he saw her. The woman he'd caught a brief glimpse of earlier. The one he'd thought looked a little like Allie Cavanaugh, of Trouble Pennsylvania. Now, having a better look, he realized something and the stage almost dropped out from beneath his feet.

It *was* Allie Cavanaugh from Trouble, Pennsylvania.


ALLIE KNEW the instant Damon spotted her. In the time it took her heart to beat twice, he segued from his smooth, sexy-and-dangerous Gypsy King persona to a dark, scowling, betrayed man. "Oh, hell, he's still mad," she muttered under her breath.

She almost stood up and left, cursing the crazy impulse that had driven her here tonight. But it had seemed so *destined*. As if fate had decided they weren't finished yet. How could she leave?

To say she'd been surprised when she'd seen the Gypsy King's truck parked at the fairgrounds near her oceanfront hotel this morning would have been like saying she'd be surprised if she found Elvis Presley in her house eating a peanut butter sandwich. She'd been stunned. What were the chances that she'd go on a business trip and bump right into the man who'd occupied her every waking thought for weeks?

Slim. To. None. "You're *sure* you didn't plan this?" she asked her boss, Mortimer Potts, who sat beside her in the crowded tent. As usual, his shoulder-length white hair and prominent features, including a pair of blazingly intelligent eyes, had drawn the attention of everyone around them. Not to mention his extreme

height and unusual dress—he was in cowboy mode this week, right down to the chaps hugging his skinny thighs.

"I don't know what you mean." Mortimer was focused on the stage, fascinated, as always, by anything mysterious and exciting. Maybe because they reminded him of his own life which, from the sound of it, had been those things and more.

"I mean," she muttered, still feeling the seer of Damon's disdainful stare from several feet away, "did you know this carnival was going to be here when you decided we simply had to come down and check out this condo building this week?"

It wasn't impossible that her boss had set her up with this impromptu trip to the Delaware shore to look at some potential investment property. The old man was an incorrigible matchmaker, having taken delight at his role in bringing together his grandson, Max, and Allie's sister. But how could he have known anything about what had happened between her and Damon Cole?

"Well, don't these quaint seaside communities often have carnivals to celebrate the Independence Day holiday?"

Frankly, his innocent tone made her *more* skeptical rather than less. The man was a prankster who liked to get his way. Still, she didn't think he'd set her up to be hurt. So maybe she was wrong and it *had* been fate. Fate that she'd be able to see Damon again, and hopefully explain why she hadn't shown up. Maybe she could also question him about exactly *what* she had said to

so shock her neighbors, who'd been whispering about her since the last night of the carnival.

Nobody else was volunteering the information, that was for sure. It was driving her batty, knowing something she'd said had made women whisper about her and men come on to her as if she'd suddenly grown Pamela Anderson's boobs and Angelina Jolie's lips.

"He's very dramatic, isn't he?" Mortimer nodded in approval. "Cuts a dashing figure. A young Errol Flynn, I'd say."

Allie didn't even know who Mortimer was talking about, but there was no doubt Damon looked enticingly hot. As usual. Maybe even more so because of the dark shadows beneath his eyes and the tension so obvious in his tightly coiled body.

"I might have to dust off the clothes given to me by that sea captain during my brief pirate excursion."

She didn't know where to begin. With the clothes, the captain, the pirates. One never knew with Mortimer whether he was existing entirely in reality…or merely part-time. That was one of the things she liked best about him: his wild stories *might* actually be true…but they also might be a figment of the man's brilliant imagination.

"I think you'd look wonderful," she murmured.

He squeezed her hand. "I do believe that gypsy man is looking straight at you, m'dear."

Not even having realized the show was over, she glanced up and met Damon's blazing stare. Most of the people in the audience were heading toward the exit, though a few had stopped to talk to him. Several of them

women, she noted with some disgust. But he was barely responding, he was too busy watching *her*. Angrily.

"Oh, dear," Mortimer said, obviously noticing. "Is there something I've missed? Do you know that man?"

"I do. And I don't think he's very happy with me right now."

"Shall we go?"

She could be a coward and slip away with Mortimer's escort. Could avoid facing Damon's anger and his disappointment. But she wouldn't. She owed him an explanation. And he owed her the truth.

"Thank you, but no. I need to talk to him."

Mortimer rose, his straight posture showing no signs that he was in his early eighties. "Very well. I'm sure Roderick's patience is just about gone anyway. I should get back now."

Roderick, Mortimer's majordomo, had refused to enter the carnival and was sitting in Mortimer's air-conditioned limousine. The prissy Englishman's loyalty to Mortimer was stronger than his dislike of such low things as carnivals, and he'd insisted on chaperoning, if only from the car.

"You enjoy yourself, young lady, and call when you're ready to return to the hotel. I'll have the car pick you up."

"I just need a minute to speak to him. You can stay," she said, suddenly panicked at the idea of being alone with an angry gypsy who could hypnotize her into doing all sorts of things.

Hmm. All sorts of things. That suddenly didn't sound so bad.

*No.* She needed to apologize and get the truth. Nothing else.

"Don't be silly, it's early. Stay. Have some fun since I've dragged you here and forced you to work during a holiday."

"But Hank…"

"Do you really think Mistress Emily has taken her eyes off that child for one moment since we left the hotel?"

No, she probably hadn't. Ever since the soap incident, for which Allie's seventyish landlady felt entirely responsible, she'd been incredibly protective. "It was very nice of you to invite her along to babysit so I didn't have to leave him."

"Wouldn't dream of leaving him behind!" Mortimer smiled and gave her a wink. "Besides, though he denies it, I think Roderick has developed a bit of a tendresse for the lady."

Allie chuckled. "I think it's reciprocated." Shrugging, she added, "You know, I once thought I'd try to set her up with you."

His chest puffed out as he laughed. "Me? Goodness, no, she's much too nice, too quiet for the likes of me."

Considering Mortimer had liked being kidnapped and held as a sex slave by two old ladies last year, he might be right.

Before she even really had time to prepare herself, much less figure out what to say, Mortimer had left, following the last audience members out. Now, just she and Damon remained in the tent. He didn't say anything. Not a single word. The man was obviously going to make this very hard on her.

"Hi," she mumbled, mustering the courage to approach him.

He stared down at her from the stage, a few feet above, looking big and remote—powerful—like some sea captain on the deck of a ship. *Okay, enough with the romance novel images!*

"Miss Cavanaugh." Ignoring her, he headed to the prop box on the side of the stage.

"I guess you're wondering what I'm doing here."

"No, I'm not." He didn't even look over, instead reaching for the top button of his silky shirt and slipping it free.

Allie had just inhaled a breath of air, but when she saw him slowly strip the shirt off his hard, golden body, that air turned into a lump in her throat. She choked on it, coughing into her fist, looking down—looking anywhere—but at that taut, rippled chest, sprinkled lightly with dark, wiry hair. Not to mention those broad shoulders, flexing with muscle and slick with sweat under the hot lights. "Wh-what are you doing?"

He didn't even look at her. "Changing."

"Don't you have a dressing room or something?"

Shrugging, he snagged a T-shirt out from amid the props and walked over, holding it in his hands. He took his damn sweet time putting it on, too, stretching it over his head, lifting his arms up and tugging it down over those impossibly broad shoulders. Each moment he delayed gave her another chance to drool over the incredible body. While every bit of him flexed and rolled with power, every bit of her went soft and gooey with want.

Once he'd pulled the shirt on, he muttered, "Makes

it easier to get from here to my camper if I'm not as easily recognizable."

Oh, sure. A tight T-shirt was going to disguise that hard form, that handsome face, those amazing eyes. It'd be easier for Leonard Nimoy to go incognito at a *Star Trek* convention.

"Well, bye," he said, hopping off the stage and heading down the aisle toward the exit. He sounded so completely unaffected, uninterested, that she almost believed it was true. Almost.

But the tension illustrated by his clenched fists and his rigid, hard steps away from her told her he was lying. He was affected. He was interested. He was just too angry to admit it.

"Stop. Please. I want to talk to you."

He glanced back over his shoulder, raising a bored brow. "You don't have to say anything. I've had plenty of *ladies* follow me from town to town. Frankly, it seems kind of desperate. Especially because, once I leave a place, I always lose interest. In it…and in the people."

Direct hit. She flinched, as if he'd thrown a rock at her rather than just some harsh words. "Wow, you're really angry at me for standing you up."

That got a reaction, and he spun around and stalked back until he towered directly over her. A blast of heat enveloped her, sparked by his tense form and his electric anger. "Don't flatter yourself. I get offers every night of the week."

Yeah. He probably accepted a lot of them, too. Which meant she should be giving thanks she hadn't just been

one of his harem. Somehow, though, looking at his handsome face and stormy eyes, feeling the almost magnetic pull that urged her to wrap her arms around his neck and slide closer—just a bit closer—so that her breasts rubbed against that broad chest, she couldn't manage to be grateful. All she felt was an indefinable sense of loss.

The sadness over what might have been colored her perceptions of this man and her time with him—it probably always would. Men like Damon Cole weren't used to women saying no, and they definitely weren't the type who were stood up. Allie had done both from the minute she'd met him and he had obviously run out of patience. And interest.

She could try to explain, tell him she'd been called to the hospital for her baby. But she sensed it wouldn't matter. He'd moved on—to the next town, to the next woman. No second chances. The only thing left to do was get the information she needed to reclaim her normal life back in Trouble.

"I'm sorry I stood you up. But I need to talk to you," she finally said, blinking away a hint of moisture in her eyes, a product of regret for something that might have been. "I didn't come here to stalk you."

A disbelieving smirk told her how much he believed that one. "Right. I guess you were just passing by…like you were that first night in my tent."

Lifting her hands helplessly, she said, "I know it sounds crazy, but it's true. My boss is thinking of investing in some condos here and needed me to come along."

"Sure."

"You probably saw him—the old man sitting beside me?"

He thought about it for a second, and she thought his clenched arms relaxed the tiniest bit.

"I was stunned when I saw the carnival set up here. I swear to you, Damon, I'm not a psycho, game-playing woman pulling some *Fatal Attraction* stunt."

The jaw clenched. "I don't think the woman in *Fatal Attraction* went nuts until *after* the guy had nailed her in every way known to man and then dumped her."

Her mouth opened and she sucked in a quick breath at the hot look he raked over her, as if he knew he was being aggressive—threatening—but didn't give a damn. Both anger and awareness dripped off him. Sex—thick and raw—hung in the air between them. They were both thinking about it, hinting about it.

"Tell me what you really want, Allie, I've got things to do." A thin smile widened his mouth, completely devoid of humor. And warmth. "I've been on the lookout for the local woman I'm going to spend *this* week with."

She shivered. Damon was different tonight…a little rough. A little mean. This wasn't the nice guy she'd walked with in Trouble. She'd liked that man…but *this* one made her shiver in pure, primal hunger. This was the dangerous Gypsy King she'd fantasized about from the minute she'd seen his image on the side of that truck. And she wanted him desperately. Whether he had a woman in every town or not.

*Too late, too late, too late,* a voice screamed in her head.

Licking her lips and mentally reminding herself it wasn't polite to leap onto a guy and ride him like a pony unless he asked you to, she focused on her mission, the reason she'd come here tonight. "I need something from you."

A half smile curled that sultry mouth up on one side, and he crossed his arms, watching her. "Oh, yeah?"

*Not your body. Well, yes your body. But something else, too.* "I need to know exactly what I said that night."

His sudden start proved she'd taken him by surprise. "What night?" he asked warily, shifting back, creating more distance between them, which was probably just as well for her sanity but didn't do her tingling breasts or quaking thighs any good.

"That night on the stage, when you hypnotized me. Strange things have been happening since then, and people are talking about me. But I don't know why—I don't know what I said."

His eyes shifted away. "So ask them."

"I *have*. Nobody will tell me a thing." Grunting in disgust, she added, "Women whisper about me and I've been propositioned by more men than a prison nurse."

Grabbing her arm, he asked, "Has anyone hurt you?"

He said it as if he cared, which made an absurd gurgle of optimism leap around in her stomach. "No, of course not."

He nodded. "Good." In a move so blatantly casual it had to be calculated, he shrugged and moved away. Damon didn't like that he was reacting to her again. He didn't like it one bit.

She liked it a lot.

"I...well, I wouldn't want something that happened during one of my shows to cause anyone problems."

"But it has. I'm being whispered about."

His remoteness—his refusal to unbend as much as an inch—infuriated her and she stuck an index finger in his chest. "Tell me what you did to me."

That finally did it. He not only unbent, he stepped in close and kept stepping until Allie had to back up for fear of being knocked down. It was only when her butt hit the edge of the stage that she could stop, and then she found herself entirely trapped. Blocked by the stage behind, by his hard body ahead. And by his strong arms, which snaked around either side of her to rest on the stage floor behind her. "What *I* did to *you?*"

Allie somehow found the strength to nod, even though every molecule in her body was firing and exploding. Her fight-or-flight instinct kicked into high gear, though fighting him was the *last* thing she wanted to do. No. If he put his hand on her—his lips, his mouth—she'd do anything but fight or run.

She'd *take*. Have. Indulge. She'd grab whatever she could get and be grateful for every bit of it.

"Tell me," she urged, wanting him to go over the edge.

"You know, maybe I will," he whispered, his voice throaty, almost a purr. His mouth was beside her temple, his breaths brushing her hair. He was crowding her, touching her with every part of himself except his hands. If she were so inclined, she could lift a leg and wrap it around his thighs, tug his sex to hers and rub against him like a feline in heat. Could use his strength and his arousal to gain her own satisfaction.

Then give it back to him.

But before she could do it—do anything—he started to talk. And Allie realized she might very well get the climax she needed just from the hot, sultry words he whispered in her ear.

# CHAPTER SIX

"YOU WANT to be touched. Intimately. Sexually."

As Allie's eyes widened in shock, Damon steeled himself against falling yet again into their fathomless blue depths. Her eyes lied. Allie Cavanaugh, despite her sweet face and innocent smile, was as dangerous as a piranha. She'd bitten him, hard, with her game-playing. Her showing up here tonight—despite her claims of being on a business trip—could only mean more scars for him.

That didn't mean he couldn't give her a little taste of her own medicine...by giving her *exactly* what she'd asked for.

Leaning down, he scraped his teeth along the edge of her ear, nibbling...threatening to bite. His every move was calculated to heighten the tension—the sense of danger. "You want a man's hands on your body and his mouth devouring you. Someone so aroused he'll shake as he removes your clothes, piece by piece." He didn't say the words so much as growl them.

"Damon..."

He crowded closer, crushing his body against hers. Demanding her silence and her acquiescence. "You want someone who will be sweet and tender at first,"

he said, trying to focus on the point of this—a bit of payback—and not on the way her softly whispered words had been pinging around in his brain for the past two weeks. It was easy to throw them back at her because he hadn't forgotten a single one. "But who will eventually lose control and go wild with his intense need to have you."

She was hauling in deep, choppy breaths now, her pupils dilated, her lips wet and parted. Her full breasts pressed into his chest, her erect nipples stabbing at him, telling him he was getting to her. "You want him to touch you, taste you. Experience you absolutely *everywhere*."

"Oh, God." Sagging slightly, her legs growing weak, she braced her hands on the stage behind her, right beside his.

"You want someone out of control in his hunger for you, with no games, no agendas." His own heart beating faster, Damon strove to regain his anger, which was oozing away, sucked out of him by her closeness. Unable to manage it, he wondered if he'd already lost this battle of wills when his tone segued from angry to seductive. "You need a strong man taking you on a steamy night when your hot bodies are cooled only by a gentle breeze."

Her eyelids fluttered, and she whimpered.

"Admit it. It's what you want."

"Yes." She whimpered helplessly. "It is."

Pulsing desire now surged through his body, in his blood, settling in his groin. He ground his rock-hard erection against her until she began to pant. Then she

arched against him, taking the heat, rising on tiptoe to fit him more intimately between her soft thighs, beautifully bared by the short, filmy skirt she wore.

Through their clothes—his pants, her barely-there panties—he felt her warmth and nearly lost his mind with the need to plunge into it. He reached for her waist, lifting her until she wrapped her legs completely around him. She jerked and gasped in pleasure as she rode his erection toward her own release.

She was magnificent...wanton. Her hair fell from its clips to hang around her face as she twisted and writhed. Damon watched for a moment, getting off on seeing *her* get off, but he couldn't take it for long. Damned if he'd remain an observer.

Lowering her to sit on the edge of the stage, he twined his hands in her hair and tugged her mouth to his for a deep, ravenous kiss. She opened to him immediately, kissing him back with frantic thrusts of her warm tongue. Her cries of delight burst against his lips as she rocked up, tugging him down to lie on top of her. He memorized the taste of her, explored her mouth and gave himself at least a full minute to savor the feel of her body beneath his and her legs wrapped around him.

Ending the kiss, he moved his mouth to her jaw, tasting the softness of her skin, licking a path to her vulnerable throat. Her breaths growing shallow and a flush rising through her body, Allie signaled her approaching climax. Damon knew he could make her come by going down a little further, to her breast. Or going down all the way. And he almost did it.

Sanity, however, said he couldn't. They were under a spotlight on a stage. From right outside came the laughter of fair-goers catching one last ride for the night. Anyone could walk in on them. Anyone could *already* have been watching them.

He slid off her, dropping to the dirt floor at the base of the stage. She followed, shimmying close, her legs still parted in a blunt, unmistakable invitation. He couldn't accept it, even though his mouth immediately went wet and hungry at the sight of her dusky curls hidden behind her silky white panties.

*Not happening.* Even if they weren't risking exposure, he knew better than to proceed. Whether Allie had come here to finish what she'd started two weeks ago or not, he didn't know that he wanted to travel that road with her again. To get involved with a woman who'd played games with him, led him on, stood him up, then possibly stalked him from another state.

A voice deep inside told him she wasn't that person, that there was a reason, an explanation for her hot-and-cold behavior and her multiple disappearing acts. But he wasn't sure he could trust his instincts about *anything* anymore.

"Enough," he murmured. Dropping his hands to her soft thighs, he forced himself to push them closed. What he really wanted to do was reach between them and sink into all that sweet wetness that had dampened his pants and filled the air with her musky, feminine scent.

"Damon?" Allie whispered, looking confused. Still panting, her eyes wide and her face flushed.

He shuffled back. "I gave you what you asked for."

"Well, you came close." She hopped off the stage and followed him, as if unwilling to end their physical closeness.

"You didn't ask for *that*," he said, not sure whether to laugh at her determined expression, or groan at his own weakness, which urged him to drop to the nearest chair and pull her down on top of him. "You asked what you'd said on stage that night."

As understanding washed over her, the color fell from her cheeks and her mouth opened in dismay. That finally got her to stop her pursuit. "I said…all those things?"

"And more."

"That's…why you said them to *me?* You didn't mean it?"

He steeled himself against the hint of hurt in her voice, telling himself she'd only gotten what she'd asked for. But still feeling like an ass for giving it to her the way he had. "Look, I'm sorry. I should have just come right out and told you what you said when you were hypnotized."

She met his eyes, hers bright and moist, then looked away and lifted a hand to her brow. "My God, no wonder everyone was looking at me like I was a sex addict."

If the townspeople had seen her three minutes ago, they would have concluded she was a sex *goddess*. Though he suspected she could become addictive. Which was why he needed to get out of there before he did something stupid, such as dragging her by the hair to his camper and doing her all night long.

*Well, why not?*

Because, he reminded himself, she was dangerous. Trouble. She was also a coward—having to be hypnotized before admitting what she wanted, and not having the guts to act on it. Plus, judging by the way he hadn't been able to drive her out of his brain in the past few weeks, she was already someone to whom he could be too susceptible. He needed to get back in the saddle—*not* tangled up in any kind of relationship. His heart could end up crushed just when it had finally started to heal. Falling for the wrong woman could be as dangerous as letting himself care too much about a kid again whose fate he couldn't control.

His decision made, he still wondered if he'd really be able to walk out on her. He still gave it his best shot, heading toward the exit. And though he heard her softly call his name, he somehow managed to walk out into the night and leave her behind.

IT TOOK Allie a good ten minutes to pull herself together enough to leave the tent. Not only did she have to bring herself back under control sexually—since she'd practically been a walking orgasm a little while ago—but also emotionally, because Damon's rejection had hurt. A lot.

She'd blatantly offered herself to him and he'd walked out. *But isn't that exactly what he thought you did to him two weeks ago?*

Yeah, he might see it that way. After all, she'd only mumbled an "I'm sorry" tonight, not any explanation. At the time, she'd been convinced it didn't matter, that

he didn't want her and had moved on. Now, though, she knew better. He wanted her, all right, despite what he said. He was letting his anger and hurt pride determine his actions.

She needed to tell him the truth. Now.

Frankly, though, she wasn't sure she was strong enough to do it to his face and risk getting tossed out on her butt. *Reject me once, shame on you...reject me twice, I might just shoot myself.*

Reaching into her purse, she grabbed an old receipt and scratched a quick note on the back of it. It was simple, to the point: "I have a ten-month old son. The night I was supposed to meet you, my babysitter called to tell me she'd taken him to the E.R. That's why I didn't come. I'm sorry."

At the bottom, she scrawled one more thing—her cell phone number, then crammed in the letter A; it was all the signature she had room for. Hopefully, Damon wasn't the kind of man to immediately be turned off by a woman with a child. If he was...well, better that she find out now, anyway.

Exiting the tent, she made her way through the fair, which was shutting down for the night. A few last, thrill-seeking kids were getting their stomachs turned inside out on the Volcano ride, and some weary-looking parents were dragging their high-on-candy-apple kids toward the parking lot. Most of the games were closed and dark, the concession stands offering late-night specials on popcorn that would be stale in the morning.

Searching for the mobile homes where the perform-

ers and workers slept, Allie soon found them on the other side of the grounds. The long line of vehicles backed up to the dunes, close enough to the beach that she could hear the lapping of the waves over the sounds of soft laughter and conversation. She had no idea which camper was Damon's, but planned to ask someone.

As she cut between the first camper and a tractor trailer painted with bizarre images of sideshow oddities, a short, dark-haired man emerged from the darkness ahead of her. "Oh, jeez," she muttered, immediately clutching her chest in surprise.

"Sorry, lady, didn't know anybody was back here. Fair's closed, though, and this area's for cast and crew only."

Stepping out of the shadows, into an open area lit by a string of lights, she took stock of the man. He wasn't tall, had thick, black hair, and an elvish face with deep dimples. Not exactly threatening. "I'm looking for Damon Cole's trailer."

The man's brow shot up. "Why?"

Lord, this was embarrassing. She felt like a school-girl passing a note in class. *Do you like me, yes or no?* As tempting as it was, she would not compound the feeling by asking this guy to deliver it for her. "I just need to tell him something."

He frowned. "Why don't you tell me and I'll let him know?"

"Look, I'm not some stalker. Damon and I met a few weeks ago in Pennsylvania. I wanted to tell him… to let him know…"

A huge grin appeared. "Are you the broad from Trouble?"

*Broad.* Not a word she'd ever heard in connection with herself. But the guy looked as if he might be inclined to help her, so she wasn't about to argue with him. "Yes. I'm Allie."

"I'll be damned." That grin never fading, a sparkle appeared in his eyes. His *violet* eyes.

"Are you related to him, by any chance?"

Walking briskly away and beckoning for her to follow him, he said, "Yeah. His cousin." As they reached a small, dusty camper, its white color now spotted with primer and rust, he pointed. "That's Damon's." With a wink, he spun around and walked away.

She eyed the camper doubtfully. It was hard to believe a man as big and vibrant as Damon lived in such a place, even if only while on the road. It certainly hammered home the reality of what she was doing...chasing after a poor traveling carny who claimed he had a woman in every town. *That was his anger talking.* She knew that and wanted him to admit it.

Beyond that, though, what could she hope to gain by trying to work things out with him, other than a few nights of incredible sex? Hmm. Incredible sex. That sounded like enough.

But even if it wasn't—if the crazy emotions she'd been experiencing about the man signaled that she felt *more* for him than just lust—well, his modest lifestyle didn't matter. She was no snob. She lived in a tiny

apartment herself and would never judge anyone by their salary or the home in which they lived.

Decision made, she proceeded with her admittedly rather lame plan. Mentally calling herself a chicken for not knocking on the door and dealing with Damon face-to-face, she forced herself to remember how it had felt to lie on that stage, legs spread, lips parted, hair wild around her face…and be turned down.

The note idea sounded better all the time.

The camper was lit from within, meaning Damon was probably inside. She had to be quick, or else risk being caught and having to admit she really *was* stalking him. A sizable sliver of light was visible along the edge of the door, and there was more than enough space to slide the note through it. So she did.

Then, feeling like the kid who'd once liked to sneak out and play knock-and-dash on neighbors' doors, she tapped once. And then she dashed. Over the dunes and toward the beach.

It wasn't until she reached the sandy shore, panting for breath and laughing at herself for being such an idiot, that she realized something. Something that made her wonder if she'd just done something a whole lot more *dangerous* than silly.

She'd been followed. A man stood watching her from the shadows of the dunes, a few yards behind her…and he wasn't Damon.

As DAMON made his way back to his home on the road after a visit to Bella to get some aspirin for his headache, he ran into his cousin. Paulie was finishing

up his nightly rounds and heading to his own camper. When he saw Damon, he gave him a curious look. "Didn't think I'd see you until morning." He wagged his brows. "Unless you, uh, had to bum some protection?"

"What?"

"Don't play innocent. I saw your cutie with my own eyes."

Immediately glancing toward the line of quiet, darkened campers, he asked, "You mean Allie Cavanaugh?"

"She the one from Pennsylvania, had you all tied up in knots for the past few weeks?"

Yeah. That'd be the one. He nodded.

"I led her to your door not ten minutes ago."

She was at his camper, waiting for him? Which meant…what, exactly? That she'd come to tell him off, to finish what they'd started? He had no idea. He only knew he was tired of fighting the attraction he'd been feeling for her since they'd met. Maybe it was time they stop fighting or making out and just do some talking about what they really wanted and what was happening between them.

"I wasn't there, I was visiting your wife." Noting Paulie's deep frown, he added, "For some aspirin."

Looking a little mollified, his cousin peered toward Damon's camper. "I don't see her outside. You still locking the place?"

"After the biker-chick-from-hell incident in Jersey? Yeah."

"Maybe she gave up."

Damn. Maybe she had. He took a step toward it, half hoping he'd forgotten to lock the door and that Allie was waiting for him inside. Naked would be good. Better than armed, considering how he'd walked out on her a half hour ago. But he stopped abruptly when he heard an unexpected sound. "Did you hear that?"

His cousin cocked his head. "Yeah. What was it?"

They both fell silent, listening.

Then the sound came again, from the direction of the beach. It was faint, almost indiscernible. The high-pitched keening might have been written off as a product of the wind. But Damon knew by the way every muscle in his body tensed with adrenaline that it wasn't. It was a scream. "Someone's in trouble," he snapped, racing through the darkness toward the beach, Paulie keeping up with him step for step, despite his shorter stature.

They tore through the sea grass and across the wind-battered crossover, pounding down the steps to the sand on the other side. The last of the carnival lights hadn't gone off yet and the beach was awash with the reds, greens and golds of the Ferris wheel, plus the starry sky above. He could easily make out the waves, and scanned them, looking for the flailing arm of someone who might have gotten into trouble while taking a late-night swim.

Then he heard Paulie mutter a foul word, and swung his head around, seeing a couple a few yards down the beach.

There was no mistaking the figures for anything but a man and a woman wrapped in an embrace, and at first

glance, they might have been assumed to be sharing a passionate moment. But the woman wasn't crying out in pleasure, and she wasn't twisting in passion. She was struggling. She was fighting.

He didn't think twice. Running the short distance to the couple, Damon took the man at a flying leap. The guy had been so intent on what he was doing, he obviously hadn't heard Damon coming, so he put up absolutely no resistance.

As the woman stumbled away, Damon and the attacker flew onto the sand, rolling over and over into the thorny scrub. He lifted a fist back to pound the man in the face, recognized who it was, and checked his swing. "Jonesy?" he choked out, shocked—but somehow not entirely surprised.

"Get off," the carny said, his eyes shifting crazily back and forth, like a cornered rabid animal. "Mind your own business. We were just having some fun."

Judging by the screams, Damon didn't think the woman agreed. He looked over for confirmation—or denial—and his heart stopped. Because he recognized that brown hair, that soft face, the vulnerable mouth. And saw nothing but red.

Mindless with rage, he let his fist fly, hearing the satisfying crunch of Jonesy's nose, and maybe the snap of one or two of his own fingers. But he couldn't bring himself to care, not even when blood from his own knuckles mingled with the blood pouring out of Jonesy's face.

The man howled in pain. "You hit me! I'll sue!"

"You miserable son of a bitch!" Grabbing the man

by the collar, he hauled him to his feet, then drew his fist back again.

Paulie grabbed it with both hands and held tight. "I'll see to him. Go take care of the lady."

Noting the stricken look on Allie's face—the tears, the red marks on her skin and what looked like blood on her neck—he felt his rage shift to concern. Giving Jonesy one last bone-rattling shake, he thrust him toward his cousin who, despite his size, was dangerous as hell, as only the dirtiest of fighters could be.

Jonesy was moaning, but Damon couldn't hear him. He was focused only on the woman who'd been in his arms a short time ago. Slowly walking to her, he held his hands out, making sure she didn't feel threatened, not sure how bad things had gotten.

*Not that bad.* It couldn't have gone that far. Not in so short a time. *Please.* "Allie, honey?"

She flew into his arms. "Thank you, thank you, thank you," she whispered. Curling into him, she burrowed her face in the hollow where his neck met his shoulder. Keeping her arms tucked self-protectively against her body, her hands fisted below her chin, she almost bored her way into him. She shuddered twice, as if racked with cold, but said nothing more.

Damon gently rubbed her back, his touch meant to soothe and comfort, to calm and to let her know it was over. She was safe.

Finally, she drew in a slow, deep breath, and he felt her heart rate slow to a normal rhythm. "Okay now?"

She nodded. "Yeah. He didn't…"

"Thank God."

"I fought, but the bastard had a knife."

"Are you hurt?" His stomach lurched. "The blood…"

"It's his. He nicked himself while cutting my blouse."

Damon started to let her go, his feet already turning around so he could go back and cut Jonesy's nuts off with his own knife.

She stopped him. "Don't leave. Please."

It killed him that Paulie was the one gaining the satisfaction of beating the crap out of the scumbag who'd just tried to rape a woman—a woman Damon already considered his. But he wasn't about to leave her alone, not when she needed him.

"What's going on?" someone called.

Glancing up, he saw several carnival workers and troupe members descending the wooden stairs. They were staring with avid curiosity from him—with Allie in his arms—to Paulie, who was now holding Jonesy in a death grip, one arm across his throat, the other hand tangled in a fistful of his greasy hair.

The group's strong man, a barrel-chested guy who doubled as a security guard on the road, lifted Paulie away from the would-be rapist. "I guess I don't even need to know what happened here," he said with a look of disgust at Jonesy.

The others, including three women who worked in the sideshow, murmured their agreement. "Glad somebody finally *nailed* the slimy bastard," one of them said.

"Is the lady okay?" somebody asked. "We heard screams."

Allie murmured against his neck. Though he wanted nothing more than to keep her safe in his arms for hours, Damon slowly let her go. Clutching her torn blouse in front of her, she turned to the others and offered them a shaky smile. "Thank you all for charging to my rescue, but I'm fine. Really." Glancing over at Jonesy, she added, "I was about to kill him, just so you know."

Damon didn't doubt it. She sounded dead serious. He suspected that if Jonesy hadn't had a knife, he would have been the one to come out bloody after a fight with this feisty young woman.

After a quick discussion, three other women in the troupe lodged complaints against the carny. They felt safe coming forward as a united front, since his threats had kept them individually quiet before now. And, again as a group, they all decided to handle things their own way and not bring in the law.

Damon, though he traveled with them, wasn't entirely one of them. He was still a bit of an outsider. So he had no vote…nor did he quite understand what they meant to do. Frankly, that was probably just as well. He didn't want to know. He just wanted to get Allie out of there, and take her someplace safe, someplace private.

Finally, with two of the big workers taking Jonesy by the arms, they all shuffled away. Paulie was the last to leave, but not before offering Allie a sincere apology.

"Thanks, but I don't blame you for your employee's actions."

"Maybe not, but I will make sure he never does it again."

Carny justice. Damon noted the steely look in his normally affable cousin's eye. The two of them exchanged one long stare, then Paulie walked away, leaving Damon and Allie alone.

Alone…and finally ready to stop playing games.

# CHAPTER SEVEN

"COME ON," Damon said once they were alone. "Let me get you safely back to your hotel."

Still shaken over her close call, Allie picked up her purse and sandals from where they'd landed on the beach during the struggle. She slid her arm around Damon's waist as they started walking. They didn't speak, both lost in thought, hearing only the soft crunch of their feet in the sand and the churn of the waves breaking on the shore. His arm draped across her shoulder, he kept her close beside him, as if afraid to let her go.

With every quiet step, and the cool caress of the night breeze, she regained her calm. Her sense of security. Safety.

She liked the idea of being safe. But she didn't need to go to her hotel to feel that way. Since the moment Damon had come charging across the sand, tackling the pig who'd attacked her, she knew she'd be okay. "That's my hotel," she said, pointing to the lights of the closest building past the fairgrounds, which was still a good hike away. "Let's just keep walking."

"You sure you're up to it?"

"I'm fine, really. He scared me…he didn't hurt me." Rubbing her cheek against his cotton T-shirt, she

murmured, "I was *ready* to kill him, you know, but I'm not sure I would have been *able* to. So I'm really glad you showed up."

"Paulie told me he'd seen you and then we both heard you scream." He pulled her tighter against his side. "I didn't stop to consider it at the time, but I think subconsciously I came running because something told me it could be you."

She was suddenly very thankful she'd left him the note, figuring it must have sent him out looking for her. If she hadn't, he might still be locked in his camper, falling asleep, out of earshot of her screams. And she could be…. She didn't want to think about it. Not for one more second.

A big part of her wanted to know what he thought about her explanation of why she'd stood him up, including his reaction to her baby. But the fact that he was here, close and protective, told her everything she had to know right at this moment. He'd obviously understood and wasn't the kind of jerk who'd hear a woman had a child and instantly find her less attractive.

She stopped walking, turning to look up at him, his handsome face shadowed and mysterious in the moonlight. "What's happening between us, Damon?" Even to her own ears, the confusion in her voice was obvious.

Why was she so crazy about a man she didn't know very well? Why had he occupied her thoughts every day for three weeks? Why did something deep inside keep urging her to go after him, even after he'd so thoroughly rejected her?

"I don't know," he admitted. "But you're not the

only one feeling it. I've been telling myself it's just sex—the need to get you into bed." Shaking his head, he added, "But when I saw you tonight—your shirt torn, the marks on you—hell, Allie, I haven't felt that terrified about anything in a long time."

Behind them, the lights of the distant Ferris wheel finally went off, cloaking them in a more intimate darkness. They were far from the crossover now, and still far from her hotel, on a secluded stretch of beach. Completely alone but for a few nighttime sea birds crying out as they flew overhead.

Lifting a hand to his cheek, she traced the line of his jaw with her fingertips. In this midnight-blue light, his eyes had gone from violet to almost purple and they glittered as he turned his face to press a kiss in the center of her palm. An open-mouthed kiss…it sent a rush of warmth up her arm.

Dropping her shoes and purse, she snaked her other arm up and over his shoulders, tunneling her fingers in his silky black hair. She leaned into him, rose on her tiptoes and whispered, "Thank you." Then she touched her lips to his, sweetly, underscoring her thanks.

Not letting her go, he dropped his hands to her hips. Circling her waist, he gently stroked the small of her back as he licked her lips apart, then slid his tongue between them. She sighed, tilting her head to deepen the kiss, savoring the slow strokes as he explored her mouth.

For all the crazy feelings she'd had about the man since she'd first seen his image on the side of a truck, Allie hadn't expected that it would be pure tenderness and

emotion that would finally bring them together. But it was. Without saying a word, without even ending the kiss, they slowly reached for each other's clothes. He slid her torn blouse off her shoulders and Allie let it fall to the sand. She tugged his shirt free of his pants, pulling away from his kiss only long enough to push it up and off.

Flattening her hands, Allie stroked Damon's thick shoulders, then caressed her way down his hard chest, delighting in the textures of his body and the warmth of his skin. Continuing to press those crazy-sweet kisses on her lips, he let her explore every bit of him.

He delicately felt his way from the sides of her neck down each of her arms, the tips of his fingers barely touching her, providing just enough pressure to drive her mad with the need for more. When he reached her hands, he twined her fingers in his. "You're sure you're all right?" he murmured as he moved his mouth to her cheek, then her jaw.

She shivered in delight at the feel of his tongue on her pulse point. "I'm fine. I want this. I am ready for this."

"Me, too."

Then he moved lower, kissing his way down her throat, to its hollow, where he stopped to take a deep breath, as if inhaling her very essence. Allie arched back, offering herself to him. When he lowered his mouth to the curves of her breasts, only half-covered by a sexy, lacy bra, she felt her legs go weak.

He wrapped his arms around her shoulders and leaned her back, kissing, tasting his way across both breasts. When he covered one taut nipple with his

mouth and sucked it through the fabric, she groaned. "Please, Damon, I need more."

He didn't pull away, merely reached up and unclasped her bra with one hand, then tugged it down. "Beautiful," he mumbled as he pulled away to look at her breasts in the moonlight. Then he filled his hands with them, plumped one toward his mouth and covered her nipple again. Licking, sucking, nibbling a little until Allie was almost crying at how good it felt.

As if knowing she couldn't take much more, he dropped to his knees, tasting his way down her stomach, not caring about the tiny bulge she'd never been able to get rid of after her pregnancy.

Without even pausing, he pulled her filmy, elastic-waist skirt down, letting it pool at her feet, and kept right on tasting. He tugged at the hem of her tiny panties with his teeth. As he had with the bra, he tormented her, licking her through the fabric. But he couldn't manage it for long. She felt the tension in his shoulders and knew he needed more. Now.

So did she. Pushing the panties down, she thrust away her lingering embarrassment. She hadn't experienced anything *this* intimate before. But she wanted it. Badly.

Damon took hold of her bare hips, squeezing her bottom, then tilting her closer to his waiting mouth. She tensed the tiniest bit, then all tension slid away and she became a boneless heap of sensation as he licked her most sensitive spot. "Oh, my," she whispered, overwhelmed by the pleasure of it. "I never imagined... never knew..."

He paused only long enough to murmur, "Then your other lovers were imbeciles."

Ha. If only he knew that there'd been only one. And he'd been worse than an imbecile; he'd been a rotten bastard.

But Damon's incredible mouth drove those thoughts away along with any others. He toyed with her until she trembled, then licked lower, tasting the wet folds of her sex. Dipping in, teasing her, driving her wild.

She gasped. "I can't…"

"Yeah. You can."

Sliding a hand around between her thighs, he reached up, readying her with the tips of his fingers, then plunging one into her. Her legs did give out then. Damon caught her as she came down, immediately pushing her onto her back on the ground. As if he couldn't stand the brief interruption, he immediately returned to what he'd been doing, free now to use both hands—and his mouth—to pleasure her fully.

Allie hardly felt the rough sand on her back, didn't process the sound of the waves crashing near their feet, barely saw the stars shining brilliantly above her. She couldn't think, couldn't do anything but lie there as he devoured her like a starving man at a banquet. Until finally all the sensations came together and her senses took in every bit of it—the stars, the sand, the lapping waves, the unbelievable ecstasy of his mouth—and she shook into a shattering climax.

"Oh, my God."

She hadn't even finished her high-ptched moan before he was there, catching it on his mouth. It was

strange—tasting herself on his lips—but still so incredibly erotic, she grabbed his hair and held him so she could thrust her tongue against his.

Reaching down, she unfastened his pants, pushing them over his lean hips. She stroked his taut butt, arching up in delight at the feel of his warm skin between her thighs.

He kicked out of the rest of his clothes, and when he moved over her again, she could feel his erection—hot, huge—pressed against her belly. She started shaking again. In pure, unadulterated want.

"Tell me you're on the Pill," he muttered, his body tensing.

She shook her head, watching his eyes close and his jaw clench in frustration. "But I came prepared, anyway," she said with an impish laugh. She reached for her small purse, which lay near her clothes and sandals, and grabbed a condom from it.

Damon muttered something that sounded like a grateful prayer, then took it from her hands and tore it open, his hunger and need rolling off him in almost tangible waves.

Allie wanted to touch him, wanted to feel that throbbing heat, so she said, "Let me help you."

He looked into her eyes and must have seen the appreciation and curiosity there. Rolling onto his side, he guided her hand until they were both touching the tip of his erection. Though shaking, Allie was able to roll the protection down, her fingers lingering, her touch obviously driving him wild.

"Allie," he warned when she slid her hand lower, to

the base of his shaft…and beyond. When she cupped him, toying with him in his most vulnerable spot, he let out a guttural groan. "If you don't want me coming right in your hand, you'd better let me set the pace," he said. He immediately pushed her onto her back, settling again between her thighs.

"Set the pace, take control, do whatever you want," she said, now nearly desperate to feel all that rock-hard flesh buried inside her. "Just do it *now,* Damon, *please.*"

He didn't hesitate, driving in, driving hard, driving deep. He stretched her, filled her completely. And it was such a relief, after so much waiting, she wanted to shout out loud. So she did. She shouted, she groaned, and when he began thrusting, short and quick, then long and so deep she thought she'd split in half, she actually screamed.

"You're gonna have the troupe down here again," he said between choppy breaths. Then he covered her mouth with his, kissing her deeply to shut her up, which made her laugh against his lips. Twining her arms around his shoulders, she arched up to meet every slow, deliberate thrust, taking all he could give her and demanding more.

Damon tried to keep it that slow, and at first, she let him, loving the lethargy and the sweetness of it. But soon her body caught the pounding rhythm of the waves. The tide was coming in, and suddenly the water lapped over their feet. Warm, silky…splashing a little bit higher with each subsequent wave. It soothed their hot skin, as did the ocean breeze. The caress of the water and the stroke of the wind enhanced the pleasure.

"Allie?" Damon finally said, his voice throaty and strained.

"Yes?"

He stopped moving, buried to the hilt inside her. Bracing himself on one arm, he cupped her face in his other hand. "It was right. Whatever we've been feeling, whatever's been driving us…this was meant to happen."

He didn't have to say another word, she understood completely. "I know."

Then they couldn't speak anymore. They could only stroke and caress, kiss and touch, give and take. And soon, when the water had reached their thighs and Allie had almost gotten dizzy from staring at the stars, feeling as if she were climbing toward them, Damon cried out his release, bringing her with him as he flew.

DAMON DIDN'T KNOW how long they stayed on the beach. After the first time they made love, they moved a little farther from the surf, which had gone from cooling off their naked bodies to chilling them. But they remained curled together on the dry sand for a long time. They didn't talk much at first, just exchanged soft, slow kisses and easy strokes. He couldn't stop touching her, even after the initial frenzy was spent. Running his hand over her arms, her throat, her breasts, her stomach, he marveled at the texture of her skin. She was soft everywhere, not skinny, not plump, but beautifully rounded and so damned feminine she took his breath away. The moonlight caught the highlights in her hair and he ran his fingers through it, plucking out the sand, laughing softly when she complained he was pulling it.

Eventually they started to talk. Mostly about what had just happened, but also a bit about their romantic pasts. When he found out he was only her second lover, he was pretty surprised. And when he found out her first lover had been a ruthless bastard who'd seduced her just to get back at her older sister, who'd dumped him, he wanted to hurt the man.

Instead, he focused on doing sweet things to *her*, as if he could erase those bad memories. They made love again—slow and easy—with her riding him, taking whatever she wanted. She wanted a lot. He was happy to lie beneath her, looking up at her beautiful, full breasts and her lovely face framed by moonlight.

Afterward she'd collapsed on his chest. He took a couple of deep breaths and muttered, "I'm *so* glad I ended up in Trouble."

"Pun intended?" she asked, sounding just as breathless.

"Yeah. Strange name."

"Strange place."

She rolled off him and tucked herself against his side. Damon still didn't have the energy to move a muscle. "Why do you stay?" he asked, wondering—as crazy as it seemed since they'd known each other only a few weeks—if she would consider leaving Trouble. Say, perhaps, for Florida.

"It's become my home in the past year," she said with a yawn. "The small town I always wanted, without the criticism and constant judging of the one I grew up in."

"What brought you there?"

"My sister. I'd just been officially 'thrown out' of the

family by my grandfather, and was living with Sabrina. When she went to Trouble on business, I got bored and followed her. I never left."

He wasn't sure where to start—on the sister, Trouble or the thrown-out-of-the-family part. Allie's tone was casual. There was probably no situation more open to honesty than one such as this, when they were completely exposed and vulnerable. And sated. So he went for the tough part. "Your family disowned you?"

"Oh, yeah. My grandfather hated that Sabrina got out from under his thumb. When I did, too, just a couple of years later, he threw a fit. And the fact that I got myself into *way* more trouble than anyone ever expected," she added, suddenly sounding sarcastic, "was the last straw. He disowned me. The rest of the family and everyone else in town followed suit."

Damon squeezed her shoulders, stunned at how cruel her family could have been to someone so adorable. He was, of course, curious about what kind of trouble she'd gotten herself into, but figured if she wanted him to know, she'd have said so. Then he remembered something she'd said on the day of their walk in Trouble. "He's a minister, right? Your grandfather?"

She nodded.

"Whatever happened to love thy neighbor?"

"In Bridgerton, Ohio, people don't ask, 'What would Jesus do?' they ask, 'What would Reverend Caleb Tucker do?' And what he did was call me a whore and kick me to the curb."

"Unbelievable." She'd had one lover—had been

taken advantage of by a ruthless pig—and had lost her family because of it. The woman was about as far from a whore as he was from a real gypsy. His body clenched and tight with anger, he forced himself to relax, not wanting her to stop opening up to him.

"My mother has finally come around, though. She took my younger sister and brother and moved out of his house. She even came to Sabrina's wedding to Mortimer's grandson last Christmas."

"Mortimer...that's your boss?"

"Yes. The one sitting beside me during your show tonight."

He laughed softly, certain now, after what they'd shared, that she hadn't been making an excuse for her presence here. "You really came here on a business trip, didn't you?"

She tilted her head back and gave him an indignant look. "I told you I did."

"Come on, you gotta admit, it's pretty coincidental."

"Tell me about it." Nibbling her lip, she added, "Mortimer's a big-time meddler and matchmaker. I don't suppose it's impossible that he heard something about my involvement with a hottie Gypsy King and found out where you'd be."

"Well, remind me to *thank* him."

She smiled broadly, obviously pleased, and he wondered again at her life, that she'd be so happy at a little compliment. But she changed the subject on him, groaning about the state of her hair, and her clothes, so he couldn't press her on it.

Knowing it had to be two in the morning, he reluc-

tantly helped her up and scoured the beach for their things, watching with a smile as she tried to brush the sand off her body and shimmy into her underclothes.

"This is impossible," she said, staring at the blouse. "I can't go walking through the hotel lobby in this."

He grabbed his T-shirt and helped her put it on. "Doesn't match, but it'll keep anyone from leering at you."

A half hour later, they reached Allie's hotel, and he walked her into the lobby. Shirtless, yes, but after what had happened to her tonight, he was taking no chances.

"You're not going to walk all the way back to the carnival grounds, are you?" she asked.

He didn't answer at first, waiting to see if she was suggesting she just stay with him. She didn't, which was probably just as well. If she was on a business trip with her boss, the last thing she'd want was to bring a man to her hotel room. But he couldn't help feeling a stab of disappointment, already missing the way she'd felt in his arms out on the beach. "I'll be fine. It's not that far," he murmured. Then he brushed his lips against hers. "Spend the day with me tomorrow. I mean…today."

"You have to work."

"Spend *part* of the day with me tomorrow."

"*I* have to work," she said. "Mortimer is meeting with a condo developer, and I need to be available for him. But I think I could manage another visit to the fair in the evening, Mr. Big Bad Carny Man."

Carny Man. She still believed him to be a traveling performer, living in a camper. Well, at least no one could accuse her of wanting him for his money.

He'd tell her everything tomorrow. Get it all out in the open—his past, why he'd left his job. How what had happened had changed his views about himself—his life, his future.

If he was getting involved with the woman, she deserved to know where he stood on the issue of children. No, he didn't want to scare her off, but she ought to know right up front that he couldn't see himself raising a child. Not anytime soon, at least.

But Allie was young, only twenty-two. If things did go the way he thought they might, given the depth of his feelings for her already, they'd have time to deal with that in the future.

Plenty of time. Maybe he'd change…someday. Maybe his fear of failing another child would gradually ease, allowing his heart to open up again. But in case it didn't, Allie deserved to know up front.

As he walked off down the beach toward the fairgrounds, Damon couldn't help thinking of his grandmother. Her stories of soul mates and love at first sight.

He had the feeling that wherever she was, she knew what was happening. And was laughing.

## CHAPTER EIGHT

THE NEXT MORNING, Allie got up early, somehow not at all sleepy despite her late night. She felt energized, excited and very happy. It seemed impossible to believe that last night had really happened—that she'd been in the arms of her dream man who'd been both incredibly hot and beautifully romantic.

"You're going to like him, baby-cakes," she said to her son as she dressed him for the beach. His bathing suit hung to his dimpled knees like a pair of surfer's board shorts and she laughed in delight when she looked at him. As always.

A tiny part of her wondered why Damon hadn't seemed more interested in Hank—why he hadn't even asked her his name or anything about him. She could only figure one thing—last night had been a big step, introducing Hank into the equation would be another one. That was all.

"You ready to go play in the waves, like we did yesterday?"

As if knowing what she meant, Hank clapped his pudgy hands together, then tried to roll away.

"Huh, uh. More lotion," she said, grabbing him before he could struggle to his feet and toddle away.

He'd started walking at nine months and had become one motoring little guy. As Miss Emily had discovered the night of the soap incident.

She covered him with a thick coating of the highest SPF lotion the hotel carried, then grabbed a diaper bag and headed for the beach. She had to work later, which was okay since she couldn't keep Hank out in the blazing sun too long, anyway.

He toddled in the sand—got it in his diaper, his hair, his mouth. Chased a crab. Barreled through another kid's sand castle, leaving Allie to apologize to the crying little girl, all the while chuckling over her bruiser of a son.

God, she loved him. It overwhelmed her, sometimes, how much she loved him. And she *knew* that Damon would love him, too.

She kept telling herself that, throughout the day, but as the hours wore on, the doubts crept in. Nodding her way through the business meetings, where she took notes for Mortimer, she couldn't help going back to the same subject. Why *hadn't* Damon even mentioned her baby? Okay, so he didn't want to talk about it. He'd wanted only to take care of her after the attack, then to make passionate love to her. Another man's baby wouldn't be high on the conversation list for either of those situations.

But afterward, when she'd told him about Peter, that would have been the perfect moment for him to ask about what she'd revealed in her note. Yet…nothing.

"He had to have found the note, right?" she kept asking herself as she finished feeding Hank in the room that night, then got him ready for bed. As usual, once

his tummy was full, his eyes started to drift closed, and by seven o'clock, he was sound asleep in his portable crib. Miss Emily, the first friend Allie had made on her arrival in Trouble, was right there watching him.

"You're sure you don't mind me going out again?" Allie asked doubtfully. She'd spent more evenings out in the past few weeks than she had the entire first nine months of Hank's life.

"Go, go, go," Emily said. "Go find your gypsy man."

Allie's jaw dropped.

The curly-haired woman, whose round face exuded warmth, chuckled. "Oh, everyone knows. You haven't figured out that you were dragged here on a matchmaking mission by your employer?"

"I knew it!" she snapped, not knowing whether to laugh or groan. "I'm going to have a talk with that old man." But not now. Now she was heading over to the fairgrounds to enjoy whatever time she had with Damon Cole.

She found him easily, showing up just as his first show was starting. Obviously he'd left word because the carny at the entrance winked, not asking for a ticket when she arrived. Seeing the pleasure on Damon's face when he spotted her would have made paying for one worthwhile, though.

Allie remained in the back, standing behind the audience. She'd seen Damon do this show several times now, but his natural abilities as a performer continued to impress her. He wasn't a showman—there was no grandstanding, no overacting. He simply exuded a quiet confidence, a sense of calm, that made everyone in the room

trust him. It was an interesting talent for someone who traveled the road, and she wondered where he'd gotten it.

After the show, when they were alone, she asked him.

"There's a lot you don't know about me," he said. "We should probably talk about that."

Allie wondered if there was a *lot* he didn't know about her, too. But she still hadn't figured out a way to find out if he had actually read her note, short of asking him straight out. If he hadn't, it would be a good opening to the whole I-have-a-baby conversation. If he had, it might force them into a conversation he wasn't ready for yet. So she kept her mouth shut.

After he'd changed out of his pirateish shirt, looking just as delicious as he had when doing it the previous night, he hopped off the stage. "What do you want to do?"

"Hmm." Allie's mouth curved up in a Cheshire cat grin.

"I have another show in an hour."

"I think the second time took less than an hour last night."

He threw his head back and laughed. "Maybe your town was right and you are a sex fiend."

"You started it."

"And I finished it."

"So finish it again."

He tugged her into his arms, dropping a quick kiss on her mouth. "Eleven o'clock. My camper. I'll finish it so many times you won't even be *able* to walk back to the hotel tonight."

Allie stumbled a little at the very thought. He kept his arm around her, leading her out into the fair. "You know," she said, "I haven't ridden a single ride. Not here, and not in Trouble."

He tugged her toward the Ferris wheel. "Well, let's go."

"Not that one. I don't do heights."

"Oh, come on, I won't let you fall."

She knew that already. "Huh uh."

"I'll buy you some cotton candy…"

"I told you the last time I ate cotton candy, I got sick."

"It's not for you to eat," he murmured. In a growly whisper, he added, "It's for you to *wear*…and *me* to eat."

Her legs wobbled again. "You're so bad." *And irresistible.*

Following him onto the Ferris wheel, she tried to remain focused only on the warmth of him sitting beside her in the bucket seat. Not on the sky into which they were climbing—or the ground where she would get smashed like a bug if they fell.

He obviously sensed her nervousness. "Okay. What should we do while we're going around?"

She dropped her hand on his lap.

"I don't think my cousin would be too happy if one of his featured players gets arrested for public indecency," he said, laughing, yet also groaning as her hand crept higher.

"You got me up here, wicked man. I thought you traveling types lived for danger."

Damon's smile slowly faded. "Allie, there's some-

thing I should tell you right now. I'm not what you think I am."

"A hot, amazing man who saved me last night and then made love to me the way every woman dreams of being made love to?"

He wasn't distracted. "I'm not really a Gypsy King."

"No duh. Are there even gypsies anymore?"

"I mean," he explained, shaking his head in reluctant amusement, "I'm not a mesmerist. I'm not a professional carny. I don't live on the road. This summer is the first time I've ever traveled with Slone Brothers, and I only did it because I needed to escape my real life for a little while."

Allie carefully shifted in the seat to face him. "Explain."

And he did. Speaking slowly at first, gazing out at the ocean, almost lost in his own thoughts, he told her.

The fact that Damon was a professional therapist came as no surprise, given his people skills. But when he told her why he'd quit his job—what had driven him to take on this carnival life—she felt tears prick her eyes and understood his haunted look.

"How old was he…the little boy?"

"Four."

She closed her eyes briefly, still not fully able to comprehend the horror of it. "And the courts gave him back to his parents, after everything you did to keep him away from them?"

Still not looking at her, Damon nodded. "Yeah. Despite the medical records—the trips to the E.R., the photos of the bruises and X rays of the broken bones—

they gave him back." His voice broke. "I had sat by that little boy's hospital bed and promised him nobody would ever hurt him again. And not eight months later, some judge decided the sanctity of the family took precedence over the child's own welfare." Shaking his head in disgust, he added, "The parents had gotten off drugs and alcohol. They played nice in court. The judge was sure everything would be *fine*."

"You knew it wouldn't."

"Hell, yes, I knew it wouldn't," he said, his mood shifting and anger underscoring his every word. "I *knew* them and it wasn't drugs that drove them, it was pure meanness. They were bad, for themselves, for society. Especially bad for their little boy."

"I can't imagine how hopeless you felt."

"Hopeless. Helpless. No matter how much I fought it, short of kidnapping him myself there was nothing I could do."

She seriously suspected he wished he had. "How long after they got him back did it happen?"

"Three weeks. As his caseworker, I was the one they called when the mother reported him missing, claiming he'd been kidnapped. But they found his body in her car. The police got her to admit she put him there after her husband had lost his temper over Tyler spilling a glass of juice." His body hard, taut as a wire, he shook his head in disgust. "A damn glass of juice."

He fell silent, as did Allie. She was crying now, unable to picture that poor child without immediately picturing Hank.

The Ferris wheel paused occasionally to let people

on and off, but not *them*. The operator obviously knew Damon and allowed them to go round and round, until Allie felt her tears finally dry and the tense rage slowly ease out of Damon's body.

"What will you do at the end of the summer?" she asked softly, wanting to know if he was getting over what had happened.

"I don't know. I won't go back to work for DCF, that's for sure. Not even sure I'll return to Florida." Leaning his head back on the headrest and staring up at the stars, he murmured, "Is Pennsylvania a lot like Indiana in the winter?"

Her heart tumbled, knowing what he meant. "Yeah," she whispered. "I guess it is."

He didn't say anything else. He didn't have to. They were both thinking the same thing—that as crazy as it sounded after such a short time, they were involved in something big here. Something that might involve a future.

"There's one more thing I have to say," he said, clearing his throat. Lifting his head, he met her stare, his gaze unflinching. "I know how early this is and that I probably have no business even going here so soon, but I want to get this out in the open now. Because it might be a make or break thing."

She held her breath, wondering what on earth there could be left to say, and how it could possibly be that bad considering what he'd just revealed. When he spoke, however, she understood.

And it wasn't just bad. It was the worst thing he could ever have said to her.

"After what happened, I don't ever see myself being able to get close to another child again. I can't handle it, the guilt, the fear of failing another helpless little person."

Her heart stopped. Even though they'd been on the Ferris wheel forever, she just now started to feel queasy.

"I'm falling for you, and if it wouldn't terrify you and make you think I'm a wacko, I'd admit that I think I'm in love with you," Damon said, so matter of factly. So seriously she couldn't even enjoy the little thrill his words gave her.

Any thrill she might have felt dissipated on the sea breeze when he finished. "I can see a future with you. Which is why I have to tell you now…I don't ever want children."

LATER THAT NIGHT, back on stage for his second performance, Damon had a hard time keeping his mind on what he was doing. He couldn't stop thinking of Allie—the look on her face when they'd talked about his past life. The silence that had descended when he told her how he felt about children.

He didn't regret telling her. She was a young woman and deserved to know whether a man she was getting involved with wanted the same things she wanted. To be honest, he didn't know *what* she wanted. Because she hadn't said much. After the Ferris wheel had gone around twice more, she'd simply murmured, "Thank you for being honest with me." Then something strange. "I guess that answers my question about the note."

But before he could ask her about it, the ride operator

was stopping them. A quick glance at his watch confirmed Damon only had a few minutes to get over to his tent and change before the late performance. Promising Allie they'd talk more later that night in his trailer, he went back to work.

She didn't come to the show, which made him nervous as hell. So nervous that when it was over, he left with the audience, scanning the crowd outside for her. She wasn't there either.

"You looking for your friend?" a passing worker asked.

Damon nodded.

"She went that way." The man pointed toward the line of campers and Damon breathed a quick sigh of relief.

She hadn't left. She was just meeting him where he said he planned to take her at eleven o'clock. Still, he didn't shake off all of his concern until he walked past the last of the rides and concession stands, and saw her standing outside his place.

"You had me scared for a minute there," he murmured when he reached her side. "I thought you'd run out on me."

She shook her head. "I wouldn't do that to you again, not without letting you know why. I promise."

Unlocking the door, he helped her up the metal step into the old camper. It had been through a lot of years on the road and the only reason he felt comfortable bringing Allie here was because he'd replaced the mattress when he'd taken it over.

Once inside, rather than looking around the place, Allie stopped and looked at the floor.

"What?"

"I left you a note, last night, before I went down to the beach. I slipped it through your door."

Damon's eyes widened. "After our fight?"

"Yes. I wanted to apologize. To explain."

She'd tried to reach him. Again. Even after the way he'd left her in his tent. "You're a strong woman."

"Not strong enough," she whispered. Then, her gaze shifted to the floor mat just inside the door. She bent down and retrieved a small, white piece of paper, which was sticking out from the edge of it. "I found it."

"Still want me to read it?"

She didn't answer. Instead, she balled it up and shoved it in her purse, which she then dropped to the floor. Then she wrapped her arms around his neck and tugged his face to hers. "I want you, Damon. Now." She seemed desperate, kissing him hungrily, reaching for the buttons of his shirt and almost ripping it as she unfastened them.

Last night had been sweetly passionate. *This* was frenzied. Wild. Allie's fingers raced over him, touching him everywhere. Where her hands went, her mouth followed, tasting, devouring.

He didn't even have time to get her to the bed before she was on her knees, tugging his pants open and freeing his engorged cock. Before he could even prepare for it, her mouth was on him, driving him into madness until he had to clutch the door frame.

He gave himself over to it for a few minutes, but knew things would be over much too fast if he didn't stop her now. So he wrapped his hands in her hair and

pushed her head back. She looked up at him, wide-eyed, her lips wet and parted, and he couldn't stand not tasting them. He dropped down in front of her, covering her mouth with his, then pushing her onto her back.

"Now, Damon, please," she urged, still frenzied as she lifted her skirt and pushed her panties off, not even bothering with the rest of her clothes. "Take me *now*."

He couldn't deny her. Her feverish demand only ratcheted up his own need to lose himself inside her.

Testing her and finding her drenched with readiness, he grabbed a condom from his pocket and covered himself. Then he thrust into her, sinking into her heat, feeling her wring every bit of pleasure from him she could.

They thrust and pounded. She scratched him, bit him. And he loved every minute of it. Right up until he exploded into her, unable to even wait to see if she was ready to join him.

As they gasped to regain their breath, and their sanity, Damon tugged her into his arms and stood. Carrying her to his bed, he dropped her onto it, then climbed in with her, curling his arm possessively around her waist. "More. Soon."

She didn't reply, just kissed his jaw and ran her hand over his chest as if she were memorizing his body. And that's how he fell asleep—with the feel of her hand, the brush of her lips.

He dozed briefly, for minutes, an hour at most. When he opened his eyes, he found himself alone in the bed. Beside him, on the pillow, was a small, dirty piece of paper, crumpled and torn. He instantly knew what it

was. Her note. The one she said she'd left for him. Something told him he didn't want to read it.

"Allie?" he called, not believing she'd left without waking him. She had to be in the tiny bathroom of the camper. *Had* to be.

He was greeted with nothing but silence. So much for promises that she'd never again leave without telling him why.

Left with no other choice, he reached for the note. As he read the few words, his heart pounded and his vision swam, everything becoming brutally clear.

"Oh, my God," he whispered, groaning as he thought of everything he'd said to her a few hours ago on the Ferris wheel. He'd crushed her—pushed her away without even realizing it.

She'd kept her promise. She'd explained to him why she was leaving. He knew where she'd gone. He knew why she'd gone.

And he knew one more thing…he couldn't go after her.

# CHAPTER NINE

*One month later*

"YOU'RE SURE you won't change your mind and stay?"

Allie glanced up at Mortimer, who'd popped his head into the small office she used when working at his enormous house. He'd invited her to stay for dinner, since one of his grandsons—the youngest one, the sexy New York cop—was coming into town. Allie had met the guy last year at Sabrina's wedding and, like every other woman there, had melted over the groom's two brothers. Especially Mike, the gruff cop, who looked as if he'd rather be beating up bad guys than wearing a tux.

She wasn't swooning over other guys now, though. She greatly feared she'd been ruined for life, having found the man who was perfect for her in every way but one.

He didn't want her child.

"No, thanks. I really just want to get home to the baby. He's cutting another tooth and he was very cranky last night. I'm sure Miss Emily's had her hands full today."

"I doubt she minds, my dear," Mortimer said as he

entered the office, closing the door behind him. He watched her, remaining silent, which wasn't like him at all, since the man was usually very talkative, telling stories of his adventures if there was nothing else to talk about.

"Is there something else you need?"

He cleared his throat. "Your forgiveness."

"What on Earth for?"

His hands clasped behind his back, he paced the room. "For pushing you at someone who's hurt you," he finally admitted.

She and Mortimer had already talked about his matchmaking efforts. He had, after all, been the one in whose arms she'd cried that night after she'd left Damon sleeping in his trailer.

As the weeks had gone by, she'd thought more and more about that last night. She'd been frenzied and selfish, desperately taking whatever she could get from him sexually. Already mourning what she knew would happen, she'd been determined to capture one more moment in his arms before she walked away from him for good.

Maybe she'd been a coward to just leave the note, rather than telling him herself. But it wasn't cowardice or nervousness that had made her do it. It had been the certainty of his reaction. She knew what she'd see in his face the moment she told Damon she had a son—disbelief, anger and, ultimately, rejection. And she couldn't bear to witness those awful feelings, not in *his* eyes. Not when they were caused by her perfect, beautiful little boy.

Knowing her original note to him would be all the explanation he needed about why she'd left, she'd slipped away while he slept, crying with every step she took. She had no doubt he'd gotten the note this time. His silence had confirmed it.

"Allie? Do you forgive me?" Mortimer asked.

"You apologized weeks ago."

"But when I did, I honestly didn't know how deeply you'd been wounded. And I am so terribly sorry."

Wounded. Was she wounded? Hurt, yes. Lonely, yes. But wounded to her soul?

Oh, yes.

"It's not your fault. You didn't make me fall in love with him. You didn't make him the wrong man for me."

"But if I hadn't dragged you to the shore, you'd never have seen him again and wouldn't have gotten in quite so…deep."

Perhaps. But perhaps not. Something in her had awakened from the moment she and Damon had met. She didn't know that she'd be quite as desolate now if she'd never made love with him, but she knew she'd still be mourning what might have been. Even if she'd never seen him again after he'd left Trouble.

"I'm fine. But I hope you won't try any more matchmaking."

He shook his head, sending his snow-white hair bouncing on his shoulders. "Of course not." Then, a glitter of mischief making his blue eyes sparkle, he added, "Though I can't help hoping Michael will meet someone interesting while he's here. Trouble certainly was lucky for Max."

"As long as you leave me out of it," she said vehemently as she got up and straightened her desk for the night. Grabbing her purse, she walked over and leaned down to press a soft kiss on Mortimer's smooth, finely veined cheek. "Thank you," she whispered. "I don't know what I'd do without you."

Touching her hand and smiling, he rose to escort her out.

As Allie drove home, she couldn't help feeling a bit sorry for Michael Taylor. He might not know it, but he was entering the lion's den. His grandfather wanted great-grandchildren, and since Max and Sabrina lived in California, Mortimer was probably willing to do just about anything to marry off his remaining two grandsons. Looked like the younger one was on the block next. "Better you than me, buddy," she muttered, having had enough matchmaking to last her whole life.

When she arrived at Miss Emily's house, which was divided into two apartments—Allie and Hank living upstairs—she noticed a strange car parked out front. She didn't think much of it, though she briefly wondered if Miss Emily's nephew had come for a visit. God, she hoped not. He was a nice enough young guy and he'd made it clear he wanted to take her out.

Allie wasn't interested. Hadn't been B.D.C.— Before Damon Cole—and certainly wasn't now.

Pulling into the driveway, she reached over to the other seat, grabbed her purse and stepped out. To her surprise, she noticed that the other car was occupied. A man was stretched out in the front seat, which was tilted back in a reclining position. It wasn't until he sat up, ap-

parently hearing her car door slam, that she realized who it was.

"Oh, my God," she whispered, recognizing the black hair, the violet eyes.

He stared at her through his open window, unblinking, devouring her with his stare. It seemed like forever before he finally opened the door and stepped out.

She'd forgotten how tall he was. How lean, how hard. How utterly masculine. Unable to do anything but stand there, Allie watched him approach, racking her brain for something to say. Unsure what, exactly, this meant.

Finally, he reached the driveway and crossed it, until he stood directly in front of her. Even before he said a word, she swayed a little, as if magnetically drawn toward him. "What are you doing here?" she whispered.

"Taking my life back."

He didn't say anything else. He merely put his hands on both sides of her face and tugged her toward him for a sweet, warm kiss that said everything else there was to say.

Allie sighed, dropped her purse, forgot the world existed and fell against him. Wrapping her arms around his shoulders, she tangled her fingers in his now short hair, so different from his wicked Gypsy King look. But perfect for Damon, the guy she'd fallen in love with.

The slow, sweet and drugging kiss both asked for forgiveness and offered understanding, and Allie answered it with every bit of emotion coursing through her until they broke apart, each breathless.

Lowering his hands to her waist, Damon picked her up off the ground and buried his face in her hair. "God, I've missed you."

"I've missed you, too."

Slowly—very slowly—he let her slide down his body to stand on her own two feet. It felt as if she'd landed on a new planet. One where everything was perfect and where the future stretched out in a magnificent lifetime of love and happiness. And family.

"I'm okay, Allie," he said. "I'll never stop mourning what happened, but I am certain of this—I can't live my life under the shadows of an ugly past or worries about what *could* happen in the future. I can't close my heart off completely unless I want to spend my life entirely alone."

"Bad things can happen to *anyone,* not just a child," she murmured, thinking of the long, sad life her mother had lived after the death of her father.

"Exactly," he said, looking relieved that she'd instantly understood. "Nobody can keep someone else entirely safe. Trying to protect myself against being hurt or from ever feeling such tremendous guilt again isn't worth the trade-off of never opening my heart to another person. Be that a child…or *you.*"

Closing her eyes, she let herself believe that this was really happening. He was here. He was ready. "I can't tell you how happy I am to hear that."

He kissed her again, sweetly, tenderly, then whispered, "Now, introduce me to your son." Smiling, with no trace of hesitation in his voice, he added, "I can't wait to meet him. Tell me he has your blue eyes."

Smiling, laughing, even crying a little, she nodded.

"He does. And two-and-a-half teeth. And the sweetest smile. His name is Hank—after my father. You're going to love him."

"I have no doubt of that since I already love his mother."

He'd given her the words, for real this time, with no qualifying, no questioning of how soon it was. She could do nothing less. "I love you, too."

His hands tightened on her hips and he smiled, so content, so absolutely happy, she knew that what they were doing was right. That it was meant to be.

"My grandmother can't wait to meet you. She somehow knew I'd met you even before I went back to Florida and told her. She claims to have a little gypsy blood."

"I think it's true. You had me mesmerized…under your spell from the minute I saw you."

"Ditto." Brushing a kiss on her temple, he asked, "So are you ready to start?"

She didn't have to ask what he meant—she knew. They were starting on *everything*. Their future. Their life together. Everything that mattered.

"Oh, yes. I am definitely ready to start."

Grabbing her hand and turning toward the door, Damon said, "Then let's go. I can't wait to meet the little guy who's about to become one of the two most important people in my life."

Allie heard the warmth—the tenderness—in his voice, and knew he meant it. He had healed. He was ready to move on—with her and with her son.

Overwhelmed by pure happiness, she led the man

she loved to the child she lived for, silently acknowledging that falling under the Gypsy King's spell had been the luckiest moment of her life.

\* \* \* \* \*

*Don't miss Leslie Kelly's next red-hot read*
Overexposed
*Available from Mills & Boon® Blaze®*
*in November 2008*

# Shaken and Stirred

## Heidi Betts

To Shannon Maines (and Sierra!) –
two of the best neighbours ever. This one's for
you, and you know why. *grin*

And a very big thank you to Amy J Fetzer,
friend and fellow author, who helped me
with the USMC details for this story. Amy's
knowledge is impeccable, so any mistakes are
entirely my own. Thanks, Amy!

# CHAPTER ONE

"OH, COME ON. Give me one good reason why you wouldn't want to get away from this place for a couple of weeks for some fun in the sun."

Abigail Weaver snagged a chip from the platter on the table between them and dipped it conservatively in the bowl of chunky salsa on the side. She fought the urge to roll her eyes at her best friend's wheedling, concentrating instead on the sweet and spicy flavors mingling on her taste buds.

"I'll give you two good reasons," she said after she'd swallowed the chip and taken a sip of her watermelon margarita. Loud fiesta music filled the Mexican restaurant and made them have to nearly shout to be heard. "Red hair and milky white skin that burns if I get too close to a light bulb."

It was true; she was one of those natural, strawberry blond redheads with pale, pale skin and freckles that only got worse when she was in the sun.

Her friend had no such worries. Rachel Stanford was a tall, leggy brunette who tanned beautifully and looked spectacular in a bikini. She looked spectacular in everything, which usually made Abby feel like an ugly stepsister whenever they were together.

The only reason Abby could tolerate being friends with Rachel without becoming suicidal was that Rachel had absolutely no affectations whatsoever connected to her looks. She knew she was attractive, but Abby didn't think she realized just how drop-dead gorgeous she was.

Unfortunately, the same couldn't be said for the dozen men who were even now drooling in their drinks and stealing sidelong glances at her companion. No one paid the least bit of attention to her.

"That's what big hats and SPF 30 are for," Rachel teased, toying with the straw in her own lime margarita. "Come on, Abby. You have vacation time coming, and you need a break. We both do. You need to get away from this provincial little Ohio burg for a while and remember what it's like to be single and carefree—and have fun."

Rachel didn't mention his name, but Abby knew she was talking about her recent breakup with Kirk. Kirk the Jerk, her boyfriend of three years, who had dumped her just as she was beginning to think they were marriage-bound.

It had been the shock of her life, to be mentally planning her wedding, then come home one day to find Kirk packing his bags. He'd announced that he was feeling trapped and that she wasn't the woman for him, after all.

She suspected that the peroxide blonde with the big boobs and tight skirts who worked at the coffee shop down the street might have been, since she'd seen them together only a week after he'd moved out.

"I don't like the beach, Rachel," she said in a low voice. "The crowds, the sun, all those people looking better in their bathing suits than I do."

"How do you know?" Rachel asked. "You've never even been to the beach, not really. This is Fort Lauderdale, Florida, we're talking about. And you have got to get over this whole quiet recluse thing you've got going on. You're young and beautiful."

Abby rolled her eyes at that.

"Stop it!" Rachel chastised. "You are, and just because Kirk was too blind and stupid to see it doesn't mean all men will be. But this trip isn't about finding a man, it's about us. It will be a girls-only vacation. We'll get a great room with an ocean view, go shopping for sexy new beach outfits and laze around on the sand all day, reading steamy romance novels and sipping umbrella drinks."

She leaned forward, her blue eyes striking and intense. "Come *on,* Abby. Please? We'll have such a good time, you'll never want to go back to your basement lab with all those test tubes and microscopes."

Abby took a deep breath, holding her friend's earnest gaze. Her stomach clenched just thinking about leaving her safe, comfortable apartment and safe, comfortable routine, but a little voice in the back of her head was telling her to do it. Telling her life was too short, and that she *had* been keeping too much to herself since Kirk left.

Not that she'd exactly been a party girl while they were together, but she hated—absolutely *hated*—the idea that she might someday look back at her life and

have to admit that she'd let Kirk's actions affect her own—in any way, but especially negatively.

"Okay," she said slowly, "I'll go."

"Whoo-hoo!" Rachel threw up her hands and leaned back in her chair to cheer, drawing even more stares from interested males. Then she reached across the table top to clasp Abby's hands. "This is fabulous! We're going to have the best time, Abby, I promise."

She wasn't as confident, but if Rachel was right about being able to just sit on the beach and read or do a bit of sightseeing, then maybe a trip like this was exactly what she needed. She was even starting to almost look forward to it. Maybe.

"I'll take care of all the arrangements, don't worry about a thing," Rachel continued, her voice even more animated now that she'd gotten what she wanted. "And after that, all we need to do is take you shopping for a bathing suit that will make men choke on their own tongues."

With a groan, Abby let her head fall to the table, where she buried it in her folded arms. She wasn't sure why she'd let Rachel talk her into this, but she was regretting the decision already.

FOUR WEEKS LATER, Abby was packed and ready to go. She'd *been* packed for the past three days, but wished now that she'd left the task until the last minute to eat up some of the restless energy boomeranging around in her system.

As many times as she'd contemplated backing out of this over the past couple of months, Rachel had kept

her in line, and it was too late now to do anything but go.

She'd taken two weeks of vacation time from the lab where she worked, stopped her mail and paper delivery, and used up all the food in the refrigerator that might spoil. In her two suitcases and carry-on bag, she had everything she could possibly need for a girls-only trip to Florida with her best friend—including a frighteningly skimpy bikini Rachel had talked her into during one of her more excited and less lucid moments.

The very idea of wearing it outside the hotel room and without a bathrobe to cover every inch of exposed skin nearly made her break out in hives.

*Reading on the beach, reading on the beach...* That's all they were going to do. No one would even have cause to see her in the scraps of glittery material.

The phone rang, and she paused in her contemplation of the luggage on the floor by the bedroom door to race across the room and answer it.

"Hello?"

"Abby," Rachel said on the other end of the line, "please don't hate me."

A ball of dread started to form at the base of her stomach. "Why would I hate you?" she asked softly. "What did you do?"

"It's not what I did, it's what I can't do. I can't leave tomorrow."

"*What?* What do you mean you can't leave tomorrow? This trip was your idea!" Her voice went up two octaves, her fingers tightening on the handset pressed to her ear.

"I know, I'm so sorry. All hell just broke loose over here on the Bryant case, and there's no way I can take my vacation days until we get things straightened out."

In Rachel's defense, she did sound miserable and extremely apologetic, but all Abby could think was that she'd gotten worked up, spent a bunch of money and taken time off work for a trip they weren't even going to take.

"But I still want you to go," Rachel continued. "It should only take a couple of days to get this mess cleared up, then I'll fly down and meet you."

Abby's eyes went wide and she shook her head as though her friend could see the frantic gesture. "No. No, no. I barely wanted to go *with* you, I'm certainly not going to go *without* you."

"Oh, yes, you are," Rachel said, her tone turning sharp. "I'm not going to let this fiasco ruin your vacation, or mine. You're going to go down there, check into the hotel and start having fun. And as soon as things settle down here—the minute I can get away—I swear I'll follow and we'll *both* start having fun."

"Rachel—"

"Abby," Rachel cut her off, using her best attorney-for-the-prosecution tenor, "everything's set. You have to go. I won't take no for an answer."

Glancing at her suitcases and the travel itinerary printout lying on the bed in front of her, Abby gave a resigned sigh and said, "All right. You'd better show up *soon,* though. I mean it."

"The very second I can get away, I promise. Enjoy yourself, Abby. Just relax and *enjoy yourself.*"

ENJOY HERSELF. That's what she was supposed to be doing, but she wasn't quite sure where to begin. Not here in this unfamiliar place.

If it hadn't been for Rachel's phone call first thing this morning, and Abby's subsequent agreement to get out of the hotel room, she probably would have simply stayed in, ordered room service, and started one of the half dozen paperbacks she'd brought along for entertainment.

Because of her promise to her friend, though, she was now dressed in her gold lamé bikini. She felt as on display as a Victoria's Secret lingerie model.

It *was* pretty. The bra-like top was fitted to give her a little extra lift. Rhinestone circlets added flare between the two cups and on either side of the hip-hugging bottoms. And the color did seem to make her normally pale skin glow, which had been Rachel's strongest argument in convincing her to buy it.

She had a matching sarong and sandals, a big, floppy hat and sunglasses. Every inch of her body was already slathered with sunscreen. Rachel might have joked about her using SPF 30 on her delicate, easily sunburned skin, but she'd gone one better and packed 45 and 50.

A giant orange mesh tote bag pulled at her arm. It held a huge beach blanket, a towel, a few snacks and a book to read. And in her other hand, she had a small cooler filled with ice and assorted beverages.

For better or worse, she was ready for her first day on the beach of Fort Lauderdale. All she needed to do

now was rent one of those extra-large umbrellas from the hotel when she got downstairs.

Taking a deep breath, she pulled open the door, then elbowed her way into the quiet, carpeted hallway. The door hit her as it swung closed, bumping her forward a couple of steps.

She caught and righted herself, sighing with the realization that she wasn't cut out for this fun-in-the-sun vacationing bit. Everyone else made it look so easy, so effortless.

But she'd promised Rachel she would at least try to have a good time, so she would. Even if she looked ridiculous doing it.

MICHAEL MASTRIANI'S chest heaved, the muscles in his calves and thighs burning, straining as he pounded the surf. He focused on regulating his breathing, pushing himself to reach the halfway point of his daily ten-mile run.

Five miles up the beach, five miles back, the hot Florida sun beating down on him the entire time. If he was lucky, a slight breeze would blow in off the Atlantic Ocean and offer a modicum of relief. Otherwise, he simply pushed through, used to the heat, humidity and exertion, and to pushing the limits of his body.

His sneakers dug into the wet sand, kicking up thick divots behind him. Sweat poured down his face from his hairline and soaked through his USMC T-shirt. His pulse was good, his heart pumping at maximum efficiency.

Being on leave was no excuse to let himself go or

slack on his daily routine. Especially when his mother was forcing him to eat enough big, home-cooked Italian meals to feed his entire platoon. He'd be lucky if he didn't return to base twenty pounds heavier, with a roll around his middle it would take a month to work off.

The lifeguard tower he used to mark the midpoint of his run came into view, and he kicked it up a notch, racing to meet it.

At this hour of midday, the beach was already littered with people. Colorful suits and towels dotted the sand, and both children and adults played at the edge of the water.

He was used to blocking out the noise they created, as well as skirting them when somebody inadvertently stepped in his path—usually a giggling kid with a pail and shovel or water wings strapped to his arms. He just smiled and jogged around them.

When he reached the lifeguard station, he kept up his pace and circled until he was headed back in the opposite direction.

To his right, he caught a glimpse of a woman coming down a path from one of the towering beachfront hotels. He couldn't see much of her, covered as she was by a big, floppy hat, large-framed sunglasses, a fabric tote, small cooler and the oversize umbrella she was struggling to carry along with everything else.

She looked like a harried mother of six, taking her brood to the beach for the day, except this woman didn't seem to have any children. In fact, from what he could tell, she was completely alone.

He slowed a fraction, watching her as he drew closer.

She dropped the cooler, then when she bent to retrieve it, dropped the umbrella. The umbrella, once she'd picked it up again, brushed the side of her face, knocking her glasses askew and pushing the wide-brimmed hat off her head.

She made a grab for the hat, but missed, and he could all but hear her muttering under her breath as she crouched to get it while juggling the rest of her load.

Mike chuckled and altered his course slightly to head in her direction—even before he saw the cascade of long, red hair that fell across her back and shoulders without the hat to both hold it in place and hide it from view.

His gut clenched and his step faltered as he swallowed hard. He was a sucker for redheads, though this woman barely qualified.

Where he was usually attracted to ladies with deep copper or auburn tresses, her hair was significantly lighter, almost a blondish-red that screamed "all natural." If the shade of her hair hadn't convinced him of that, her light skin and sprinkling of freckles would have.

His intention had been simply to help a young woman in need, one who was obviously trying to carry more than she could handle. But now that he'd caught a glimpse of that hair, and was close enough to see she had an adorable little body to match—strapped into a sexy gold bikini that would make a monk break his vow of silence—his libido was kicking in and sending all of his Good Samaritan objectives straight out the window.

"Hey," he called out lightly, using his arm to wipe sweat out of his eyes as he jogged to her.

She jerked and spun around, both the hat and cooler falling from her grasp again, and the umbrella teetering dangerously.

"Sorry." He offered a small smile to let her know he didn't mean her any harm. "Didn't mean to scare you. I was just out for a run and thought you might need some help. You look a little overwhelmed."

Her eyes were green behind the lopsided sunglasses, he noticed. And not just any green, but a startling emerald specked with bits of gold. They drew him in, deep and unfathomable.

She bent to collect her things again, and he swooped in to grab them before she could.

"Here, let me get that." He set the hat back on her head with a grin, then reached for the large umbrella. "Where to?"

"Oh, you don't…I wasn't…you don't have to do that."

He was amused to hear her stumble over her words and see her face blaze with color. "It's all right, I needed a break anyway."

It wasn't true, but the little white lie served its purpose.

"I was going to try to find a spot away from everyone else to just sit and read."

He scanned the beach, knowing that as the day and season progressed, the beach was only going to become more and more crowded.

"How about over there?" he asked, pointing with the cooler toward an area closer to the hotel than the shoreline where no one had staked a claim yet.

Still looking uncomfortable, she turned and started across the sand in her flimsy gold sandals to match her suit and sarong. He couldn't keep a grin from stretching across his face as he followed, enjoying the slinky swish and sway of her hips and the long line of her shapely legs. She might be tiny, but everything about her was in perfect proportion.

When she reached her destination, he quickly wiped any signs of amusement or appreciation from his face. She seemed skittish enough without knowing he found her attractive.

She dug a big, square beach blanket from her bright orange tote and shook it out while he stuck the end of the umbrella deep in the sand, arranging it so that it was both steady and protected as much of the blanket from the brutal summer sun as possible.

Not waiting for an invitation, he plopped down on the edge of the blanket, leaned back on his elbows and crossed his legs at the ankles. She'd been digging in her bag, pulling out a paperback novel, a smaller beach towel with a pattern of tropical fish, and a couple bottles of sunscreen, but when she noticed that he'd made himself comfortable, she stopped, staring at him in confusion as she knelt on the other side of the blanket.

"What are you doing?" she asked, eyes narrowed and voice suspicious.

Keeping it light, he said, "Hope you don't mind. I just need a bit of a rest before I start back."

She considered that for a few seconds, but didn't look any happier about his presence. "How far do you have to go?"

"Five more miles."

"Five *more* miles?" she asked, goggling. "How far have you run already?"

"Five miles."

Her voice rose and her eyes widened even more. "You run ten miles a day?"

He grinned at her wide-open mouth and the expression on her face. "For starters."

"For God's sake, *why?*"

"Babe," he said, as though the answer should be obvious. Then he patted his chest where his shirt said it all. "I'm in the Corps."

Her gaze flicked down to the bold yellow letters on a background of olive-green cotton before she quickly looked away, a hint of color staining her cheeks once again. "You're a Marine?"

"Yes, ma'am," he said with a nod, straightening with pride, even in his relaxed position. With a small, informal salute, he said, "Gunnery Sergeant Michael Mastriani, at your service. You can call me Mike. I didn't catch your name."

One light brow winged upwards. "I didn't throw it."

He threw his head back and laughed at her snappy retort. It was the first thing she'd said so far to show a little brass, and he liked it.

"Right. Well, why don't you toss it at me now…I promise not to miss."

Her other brow rose, and for a minute he thought she might refuse to share even that much information. Then she sighed and scooted around on the blanket until she was sitting cross-legged, facing his direction.

"Abby Weaver."

"Nice to meet you, Abby." He held out a hand and was delighted when she leaned forward—after only a short pause—to take it in her own and give it a quick shake.

Her hands were as petite as the rest of her, with long, slim fingers and pretty nails painted a soft, glossy peach. And there was no wedding or engagement ring on her left hand, he was happy to note.

After letting go, she reached into the small cooler he'd carried across the sand for her and pulled out a bottle of Diet Coke with lemon.

"Would you like one?" she asked.

Since she no longer seemed annoyed that he was sticking around, he wasn't about to pass up the opportunity to stay and get to know her a little better.

"Sure, thanks." He twisted the cap and took a long drink while she got one for herself and did the same.

"So what are you doing at the beach all by yourself?" he asked by way of making conversation and getting some much-needed information out of her.

Pulling the hat off her head, she ran a hand through her long, straight hair, then finally slipped the dark sunglasses off her nose to reveal those sparkling emerald eyes.

"I'm on vacation. A friend was supposed to come with me, but she had to stay and work on an important case. She's going to fly down as soon as she can get away."

"Where are you from?"

"Ohio. I'm a researcher for Carlisle Pharmaceuticals, and Rachel, my friend, is a prosecuting attorney for the county where we live."

Mike gave a low whistle. "Nice. Is your friend as attractive as you are?"

She coughed and nearly choked on a mouthful of Coke, her eyes going wide and damp as she struggled for air.

He leaned forward to pat her on the back, amused that she could be so easily flustered.

"Okay?" he asked once she was breathing normally again and her eyes no longer threatened to bug out of their sockets.

Hand at her throat, she nodded. Then she screwed the cap on her bottle of soda and set it aside.

"My friend is very attractive," she told him, pointedly refusing to meet his gaze. "You'd like her. If you want, when she gets here, I can introduce you."

It was his turn to almost choke. Could she really believe he was more interested in her faceless friend than the flesh and blood beauty sitting right in front of him?

"So what does she look like?" he asked, just out of curiosity.

Abby licked her lips, glancing anywhere but at him. "She's tall, with a great figure. Brown eyes, long, wavy brown hair. She's witty and confident, and men love her. Not that she dates a lot," she added quickly in a bid to defend her friend's reputation. "Her work keeps her busy."

"And you think I'd be more attracted to her than I am to you," Mike said, making it more of a statement than a question.

She shrugged one slim, bare and adorably freckled shoulder, finally raising her gaze to his. The lack of light and energy in her eyes made his gut twist.

"Most men are."

*Then most men are idiots,* he thought to himself. And the one thing he'd never been was an idiot.

"Good," he said brightly, shifting an inch or two closer on the giant blanket. "I'm an excellent competitor, but the time I don't have to waste beating other guys off with a stick is time I can spend getting to know you better."

# CHAPTER TWO

HE FLASHED A SMILE that showed his straight white teeth and had his chocolate-brown eyes glinting.

The butterflies that had been swooping and swirling in her belly since she'd first raised her head to find him staring down at her were trying their best to escape.

Why was he here?

She understood his desire to come to her aid; she even appreciated it. But why had he taken a seat on her blanket and made himself comfortable when he could just as easily have returned to his ten-mile run?

Maybe it was the bikini. Because normally, men didn't stick around to talk to her—not men like this, at any rate.

Mike Mastriani. Gunnery Sergeant Michael Mastriani, United States Marine Corps. She liked the sound of that.

The guys she usually attracted, or hung around with, were the brainy types—lab geeks, computer geeks, geeks in general. That sort of thing was right up her alley, so she didn't take exception to the trend. She even enjoyed the conversations she got into with those kinds of men.

But she enjoyed the looks of this one.

She was shallow enough to admit it, she thought,

with only a small flutter of guilt. Shallow enough to admit that his broad shoulders and humongous arms made her heart catch. His six-pack abs, visible beneath the tight, sweat-damp material of his sleeveless T-shirt, and thighs as strong as tree trunks made her mouth go dry.

And that was before she ever got to his face, with its sharp lines, strong jawline and intense brown eyes, all framed by dark black hair in a close-cropped military cut.

He was the kind of guy girls went gaga over…the kind she'd never been very comfortable around to begin with, and who would normally be farther down the beach, playing in the waves with those big-breasted, bleach-blond, thong-clad women.

Even her gold lamé bathing suit couldn't compete with those skimpy neon-colored numbers—and neither could her God-given, but far from impressive, breasts.

Which only made her wonder again—what was he doing here with her when he had other, more obvious and enthusiastic options within shouting distance?

She kept her head down, toying with the label on her bottle of soda. "Why do you want to get to know me better?"

"Is there some reason I shouldn't?" he countered, one brow quirking upwards. "Are you married? Engaged? Seriously involved?"

"No." Not anymore.

"Then what's the problem?"

At that, she lifted her head and met his direct gaze. "Wouldn't you rather finish your run or go flirt with

someone like—" she caught sight of a gorgeous brunette from the corner of her eye and waved a hand in the woman's direction "—her?"

Mike turned to examine the woman she'd pointed out, but only for a fraction of a second before returning his attention to her with a lopsided grin. "Nope."

She shook her head and laughed, finally succumbing to the ridiculousness of the situation.

"I'm not going to get rid of you, am I?" she asked, though she wasn't sure that was even the objective any longer.

His grin widened as he rolled to his side, facing her, and propped his head on his bent arm. "Nope."

With a sigh, she gave in to the inevitable. "All right, but if I tell you about myself, you have to do the same."

"Fair enough."

From there, they started talking about their respective lives, and Abby was surprised to find herself quite intrigued by the stories Mike told about his career in the military, and time overseas and in combat. He explained that his father had been in the Marines at one time, before meeting and marrying his mother, and that he'd grown up wanting to join, too.

He was currently on leave and visiting his parents, who still lived in the home where he'd grown up, right here in Fort Lauderdale. From the sounds of it, they were a very close-knit family, and he came home to see them as often as he was able.

Then he told her about Camp Pendleton, where he was currently stationed, and about some of his friends and daily duties.

In return, she told him about the pharmaceutical company in central Ohio where she worked with an R & D team to develop new medicines for everything from the common cold to cancer and heart disease. New or sometimes simply more advanced formulas of current ones. And when he probed into her personal life, she even found herself confiding in him about her three-year relationship and subsequent breakup with Kirk.

She didn't tell him everything…like how crushed she'd been, or that Rachel had planned this trip primarily to shake Abby out of her lingering funk…but she shared more than she would have expected after knowing him for such a short amount of time.

He also made her laugh, which was another side benefit of their conversation. She hadn't thought he'd be so funny, or that anyone could ever make her see Kirk's abandonment as amusing. But with a few well-placed remarks—albeit of the four-letter variety—and some comical faces cracked at just the right moment, he actually helped her put the whole situation into better perspective.

It had been a short-lived romance with a man unworthy of her affections that she'd let herself believe was more serious than he'd ever intended. Now it was over, and she should be moving on with her life. Learning a lesson, putting it behind her, and moving on to bigger and better things.

She tucked a strand of hair behind her ear and tapped the base of the soda bottle against her bare ankle. Mike was still stretched out on his side across from her, while she sat with her knees tucked up to her chest. Every

once in a while, she would toy with the tiny daisy charm hanging from the chain of her anklet or take a sip of cola, but mostly she just listened and answered his questions.

Should she be so arrogant—or was it naive?—as to think that Mike might be one of the "bigger and better" things she needed to invite into her new and improved lifestyle?

A little thrill stole through her chest and tingled its way down her spine. My goodness, she certainly hoped so.

And Rachel would be so proud of her for hooking up with such a gorgeous male specimen on her first day on the beach.

"So," he said, sitting up and stretching forward to pop open the lid of the cooler and toss his empty soda bottle inside to be disposed of later, "what do you say to dinner tonight?"

She was startled by the invitation, as well as the sudden segue from chatting about their backgrounds and personal lives. Licking her lips, she took a breath, waiting for her nerves to stop jumping like downed electrical wires.

"You want to take me out to dinner," she said slowly, not quite believing things were progressing so quickly.

He chuckled. "Don't sound so surprised. I like you, Abby. I've had fun talking with you and would like to see you again. Dinner seems like a logical next step."

*Step toward what?* she wondered, but was delighted at the prospect of finding out.

"All right," she responded, not giving herself a chance to over-think or talk herself out of it.

"Great." He offered her a warm smile. "How about I meet you in the hotel lobby at nineteen hundred— sorry," he said, lips twisting wryly. "Seven o'clock. Then we can either eat right there at one of the hotel restaurants, or I can take you out to one of the popular local spots. Your choice."

She nodded, first-date jitters already beginning to tap-dance low in her belly.

Tilting his left wrist, he glanced at his watch. "I'd better get going," he said with a regretful sigh. "I promised my mother I'd help her clean out the garage as soon as I finished my run, and I've been gone a lot longer than usual."

He flashed her a grin as he pushed to his feet. "It never fails. Every time I'm home, she puts me to work. Guess she doesn't think the Corps keeps me busy enough."

Abby laughed, lifting a hand to shade her eyes from the sun as she looked up at him.

For a minute, he stood staring down at her, an odd expression on his face. She swallowed hard, almost afraid to believe it was a reflection of the same peculiar attraction she was feeling for him.

"See you tonight," he said. "Seven sharp."

"Yes, sir." She raised a hand to offer her own salute and earned herself a hearty laugh as he turned to jog off.

A second later, he glanced back over his shoulder, lifting an arm to wave one last time. She returned the gesture, feeling her mouth curve up at the sides in a grin she couldn't seem to control.

As soon as he was out of sight down the beach, she jumped to her feet and started gathering her things,

stuffing them in the oversize bag as fast as possible, then yanking on the giant umbrella pole until it came out of the sand. The items gave her just as much trouble getting back to the hotel as they had on the way out, but she made it, returning the umbrella to the rental place, then racing to her room on the eighteenth floor.

She was out of breath by the time she arrived, and dropped everything on the floor just inside the door in her rush to get to the phone on the bedside table. Dialing Rachel's work number by heart, she waited impatiently for the law firm's receptionist to answer, then transfer her to Rachel's personal assistant.

The young woman told Abby that Rachel was on the other line at the moment, but if she wanted to wait, Rachel should be with her in just a couple minutes. So, of course, Abby waited.

Her stomach was doing somersaults, her pulse beating so erratically, she wondered if it would ever again return to normal, and her fingers were clamped so tightly on the handset, the knuckles ached. The seconds ticked by like minutes, the minutes like hours.

"Come on, come on," she muttered, beneath her breath, mentally urging her friend to finish her business and get on the line.

Just when Abby thought she'd scream from frustration, she heard a click, and then her friend's voice.

"Abby, hi. How are things in sunny South Florida?"

"Ohmigod, Rachel, you have to get down here. Now. Hurry. Help."

"What's wrong?" Rachel asked sharply. "Abby, what happened?"

Like a tape recorder stuck on Fast Forward, Abby told her everything, from struggling to carry her things out to the beach after promising Rachel she wouldn't hide out in the hotel room all day, to meeting Mike when he offered to give her a hand, and then spending a large part of the morning with him, just talking. She finished by relating Mike's invitation to dinner, and her near-panicked state after accepting.

"Help!" she wailed again. "What do I do?"

"Good lord, Abby, I thought you'd been mugged," Rachel said, blowing out a relieved breath. Then she started to chuckle. "All right, relax, you can handle this. First, congratulations, I'm very excited for you. This guy sounds hot, capital *H-O-T*."

Abby's throat tightened as the memory of Mike's well-sculpted and even more well-muscled body popped into her head. "He is very…"

"Yeah, I got that. You go, girl."

Abby wished she could share her friend's enthusiasm, but she was just too darn nervous.

"Are you coming down here or not?" she charged.

"Not yet, things are still a mess on that case. But I hope to get there in a couple of days. In the meantime, I'll talk you through."

"I've never gone out with anyone like him before," she said softly.

"I know," Rachel said in a chipper voice that completely contradicted Abby's own glum tone. "It's great."

Abby snorted. In theory, maybe, but going through with it was a whole other story.

"What's the big deal?" Rachel continued. "You've

already spent a couple of hours with this guy, talking and flirting—"

"I didn't flirt."

"Well, you sure as hell should have," Rachel said dryly. "But you can make up for that tonight. My point is that dinner is more of a second date…the same as today, but in a different setting. It's no big deal."

Her skyrocketing blood pressure begged to differ, but she listened as Rachel compiled a checklist of things for her to do. Abby scribbled them down frantically, determined not to overlook any of them.

Taking deep, calming breaths was number one, followed by grabbing a bite to eat for lunch so she wouldn't be either starving or nauseous by the time she met Mike in the lobby. She was also supposed to take a relaxing bubble bath and use any lotions or perfumes that would make her feel sexy and feminine.

If she had any qualms about doing her own hair or nails, she was to call the hotel salon immediately to set up an appointment. And while they were still on the phone, Abby went to the closet and described each of the dresses hanging there—most of which Rachel had convinced her to buy just for the trip in the first place, so she knew what they looked like—bowing to her friend's wisdom when she told her to wear the black one.

She finally hung up after promising to call Rachel with a full report as soon as she returned from her date later that night. She wasn't feeling a hundred percent confident after her friend's pep talk, but she was definitely feeling better.

She could do this. She was even…she shivered… looking forward to it. To seeing Mike again, and having him look at her with that intense brown gaze that made her warm and tingly all over.

Several hours later, she was dressed and ready to go ten minutes before she needed to head downstairs. Taking Rachel's advice, she'd visited the hotel's salon to have her hair and nails done, so now both her finger and toenails were painted a deep wine color, and her long strawberry blond hair was swept up in a loose French twist.

She'd done her own makeup, as well as dabbing a touch of perfume behind each ear and at all her pulse points. And the black dress Rachel had encouraged her to wear did look good.

It had a light, flowing, knee-length skirt, then cinched at the waist where the gathered sides of the bodice began. The two edges traveled over her breasts to hook behind her neck, the deep vee leaving an almost obscene amount of her chest bare, and drawing the eye even more quickly because of the row of rhinestones between her breasts.

She almost didn't recognize herself in the full-length mirror that ran along the front of the hotel room closet. And in her mind, that was okay. She looked sexy and confident, which she considered a nice change.

Now, to find out if Mike would agree.

Schooling her breathing, she collected the small clutch purse that contained a lipstick, compact, her room key, and a few dollars, just in case, and started for the lobby. They hadn't agreed on a particular spot to

meet in the large, wide-open lobby, so she simply strolled slowly down the middle, hoping she would find him when he arrived. And with a man as tall and broad as Mike was, he would be hard to miss.

She felt a tap on her bare shoulder at the same time someone murmured her name behind her, and turned to find Mike standing not a foot away. He smiled, and she felt her heart flip over in her chest.

Oh, my. He'd looked good in running shorts and a sweaty tee earlier, but he looked even better now, in a pair of black chinos and black dress shirt. The snug fit of both showed off his extremely muscular form, his arms nearly busting the seams whenever he moved.

"You look great," he said, taking the words right out of her mouth. His gaze raked over her appreciatively, from head to toe and back again. "Better than great. Amazing."

She smiled a little self-consciously. "Thank you. So do you."

"What? This old thing?" he said with a wave of his hand, grinning.

She laughed, knowing the same couldn't be said of what she was wearing. Everything, right down to her underwear, was brand spanking new, thanks to Rachel. She really might owe her friend for talking her into turning over this "new leaf" if things continued to go as well as they had so far.

"So," Mike said, running a hand from her elbow to her wrist, then taking her hand in his.

Her stomach dipped at the familiarity of the gesture, but she liked it. It felt good and right.

"Would you rather eat here in the hotel or go out somewhere else?" he continued.

"It's up to you," she told him, starting to lick her lips, then remembering that she didn't want to smear her lipstick. "Either is fine with me."

He started forward slowly, his hand still gripping hers so that she was forced to fall in step beside him.

"Well, that is a dilemma," he drawled. "If we stay here, I won't be able to show you parts of Fort Lauderdale that you might not get the chance to see on your own. But if we go out, with you in that dress, I may end up spending the whole night trying to keep other guys off of you."

They'd reached the bank of glass doors at the front of the hotel lobby by then, and she stopped both to let him push open one of the doors and because his words had startled her to a halt. She tilted her head to glance up at him, and before she could guess his intentions or brace herself for it, he leaned down and pressed a quick kiss to her lips.

"I think I'll take my chances," he said, pushing the door open with his hip and tugging her outside, into the balmy evening air.

From that point on, Abby felt as though she couldn't quite catch her breath. It wasn't the fact that Mike whisked her into his car and drove her around town for a while, pointing out some favorite spots while also keeping up a steady stream of conversation. Or even that when they finally stopped for dinner, it was at a lovely, upscale Italian restaurant with tiny white lights sparkling in the front windows and at every table inside.

It was simply being with him, and realizing that she'd never met anyone before who made her feel the way he did—so anxious and out of control, yet at the same time easy and safe.

They were seated at a small round table in a far corner where it was quiet and more shadowed than the rest of the room. She wondered briefly if Mike had planned it that way, then decided she didn't care. Rather than question and second-guess every little thing that happened tonight, she was going to remember what Rachel had said about relaxing and enjoying herself.

Once they'd gotten settled, the waiter brought them a wine list, but Mike suggested they have cocktails instead.

"I'm not much of a drinker," Abby confessed. "What would you recommend?"

"How about a couple of martinis," Mike said, smiling up at the waiter, who quickly jotted the note on his pad. "I'll take an olive in mine, but she'd probably prefer a cherry."

Then he leaned forward conspiratorially and lowered his voice, as though he was imparting some big secret. "Don't tell James Bond I said this, but I prefer mine shaken *and* stirred."

She chuckled, thinking that James Bond—no matter how suave and sophisticated—had nothing on the man sitting across from her. Mike was double-oh-*ooh-la-la*.

Only a few minutes later, they had their drinks, and she took a first, tentative sip. It was stronger than she was used to, but she liked it.

Taking a drink from his own glass and then setting

it carefully aside, Mike said, "Whatever you do, don't tell my mother I brought you here. She believes that if anyone is going to eat Italian cooking, it should be at her house, where she's made everything from scratch."

Abby chuckled, thinking his mother must be quite the character.

"She thinks I'm taking you to a French restaurant—which she thoroughly disapproves of, since she believes snails belong in the garden and not on a dinner plate."

She knew she was supposed to laugh at that, too, but she was too distracted by the thought of him talking to his parents about her.

"You told your mother about me?" she asked in a tight voice.

He leaned back in his seat as the waiter brought a plate of mushroom ravioli appetizers, then shifted forward to focus his attention on her once more.

"Sure. Not much. I just said I'd met a girl on the beach and was taking her to dinner, so I wouldn't be eating at home tonight."

"And what did she say?"

He shrugged one massive shoulder. "She wanted me to bring you home for supper, but that's only because she thinks it's her responsibility to feed the world, and also because she doesn't think anyone should be forced to eat French food. But other than that, she just said, 'Have a good time.'"

Swallowing hard, Abby reached for her drink to wash down the sudden lump in her throat.

"Why, did you want to meet my folks?"

She nearly choked at that. God, no! Things were

moving quickly enough as it was, she certainly didn't need the added pressure of meeting Mike's parents to send her blood pressure into the stratosphere.

"No, I was just curious," she managed. Then, because the devil must have been sitting on her shoulder, she asked, "Do you often pick up girls while you're home on leave?"

Even in the dim lighting around their table, she saw his eyes darken almost to black. "You would be the first," he said in a low, serious tone.

Wow. She didn't know what to say to that, but the intensity of his gaze had her shivering and breaking out in gooseflesh.

"Are you cold?" he asked in that same soft near whisper.

She shook her head, unable to speak at the moment. She was anything but cold. Heat streaked through her body like a forest fire, making her want to pant and cross her legs where an itchy dampness began to throb.

He didn't say anything more, but from the narrow line of his lips and tick of a muscle in his jaw, she suspected he was well aware of the battle being waged by her hormones—and was possibly fighting his own sudden and overwhelming case of lust.

The meal passed quickly and in relative silence, almost as though they had crossed an invisible line into some forbidden area neither knew quite how to navigate away from.

There was no more talk about their families or jobs, no more idle chitchat designed to fill the empty spaces and help them get to know one another better. There

was only the tense, sexually charged air of want and need and…things Abby wasn't sure she could identify or had ever before experienced.

She choked down her last bite of tiramisu, barely tasting it, even though it was normally one of her favorite desserts. Mike seemed to do the same, then silently got out his wallet and paid the bill.

As soon as the waiter returned his credit card, he stood and circled the table to pull her chair out for her while she did the same.

"Ready?" he asked.

She nodded and started toward the door ahead of him when he waved her forward. Where he'd had no qualms about reaching out and taking her hand as they'd been leaving the hotel earlier, he now made a point of *not* touching her.

Her stomach took a dip when she noticed the difference in his behavior, and she wondered if she'd said or done something to turn him off. She thought the evening had been going well, that there had even been a moment when things had gone from casual to smoking.

But now she wasn't so sure.

He helped her into the car, then got behind the wheel and headed back to the hotel, all without touching or speaking to her.

She worried the small clutch bag on her lap, trying to think of something—anything—to say to put things back the way they'd been. Back when they had been chatting and having fun.

When they arrived at the hotel, he parked and got out of the car at the same time she did.

"I'll see you to your room," he said stiffly, and as much as she wanted to tell him it wasn't necessary, she couldn't seem to make her mouth form the words.

Tears pricked behind her eyes as they walked through the lobby to the bank of elevators and waited for a car to take them up to the eighteenth floor. She blinked her eyes and breathed through her nose to keep them at bay.

The elevator doors slid open and she stepped into the carpeted hallway, Mike following behind as she dug the key card out of her purse and found the door to her room.

She slipped the card into the lock and waited for the light to flash green, then twisted the knob and opened the door a fraction, bracing it with her foot while she turned back around to wish Mike a good night.

"Thank you for dinner," she said, licking her dry lips. Taking a deep breath, she stared at the rhinestone-studded clip on the front of her sling-back heels. "I'm sorry if things didn't go the way you'd hoped. I still had a very good time."

Right up until the end, at least.

"What are you talking about?" he asked sharply, bringing her head up to meet his hard, coffee-brown gaze.

She swallowed and licked her lips again, not sure what had caused the ire in his expression.

"It's just that…we seemed to be enjoying ourselves at first, then you got quiet and we stopped talking. I don't know why, and if it's something I did—"

He cut her off with a harsh curse that had her eyes going wide because she didn't hear such language very often.

"You didn't do anything," he said through his teeth. "It was all me. I clammed up because watching you from across the table made me hard, and instead of talking, I was concentrating on not grabbing you and making love to you right there in the middle of the restaurant."

His hand snaked up to wrap around the back of her neck and tug her closer as he swooped in from the front.

"But we don't have to worry about drawing unwanted attention anymore," he muttered just before his mouth crashed down on hers.

# CHAPTER THREE

WITHOUT BREAKING THE kiss, he shuffled her backward, walking her into the hotel room with his feet on the outside of hers. His hands stroked her back, her waist, her arms, everywhere he could reach.

The door clicked closed behind them at the same moment they ran into the edge of the bed. The mattress hit Abby in the back of the legs, and she would have fallen if Mike hadn't caught her, finally pulling away to gasp for air.

"Damn," he breathed, chest heaving.

His fingers clenched in the flesh at the top of her right buttock and the side of her waist before sliding up to skim her neck and cup her jaw. He tipped her head back a fraction and took her mouth again, soft and light this time, just a brush of lips against lips.

"You kill me," he whispered, his breath dusting her cheek as he continued to nibble at her mouth. "And this is all moving really fast, I know. If you don't want to go any further, tell me now, and I'll leave. Otherwise…"

He exhaled a shaky sigh. "I can't promise I'll be able to maintain control much longer."

Abby's insides tightened, her throat going dry at the

realization that he was asking her quite frankly to sleep with him.

He was right, things were moving fast. At warp speed, considering they had only met that morning.

But was it *too* fast?

The common sense sector of her brain said yes. She'd never done anything like this before in her life, never let things move forward nearly so quickly.

But her gut…her gut and her heart were telling her no. As crazy as it was, everything about this—about *him*—felt very, very right. His offer to walk away only reinforced those instincts.

"I don't want you to leave," she said, her voice only slightly less than firm and even as she clung to his forearms.

A shudder rippled through him, vibrating all the way from his body into her own a second before he grabbed her up and began to once again devour her.

She'd been both in love and in lust a couple of times—or at least she'd thought she had—but she'd never experienced passion like this. Hot, eager desperate. Every nerve ending was electrified, jumping and sizzling in her veins.

His mouth was in constant motion, nipping at her lips, tangling with her tongue. He gave and took, and consumed her as he might a particularly decadent dessert.

Although his attention seemed entirely focused on the kiss, his hands remained busy. They dropped from her face to her shoulders, arms, back and waist. When he found the zipper at her spine, he slowly slid it down,

the *snick-snick-snick* of the teeth sounding louder than normal in the quiet room.

He caressed her smooth, bare back for a moment before reaching up to the strip of material behind her neck that was all that still held the dress in place. It took him a few seconds to realize there was no snap or fastener holding the two edges of the bodice together, but that it would have to be lifted over her head.

With a groan of frustration, he tore his mouth from hers, wrenching the strap up and off, knocking a few hairpins loose in the process. Rather than apologize, he plucked the remaining pins, with their sparkling rhinestone tips, free and tossed them to the floor.

Despite her decision to go all the way with him tonight, she was still shy and held her hands over her breasts to keep the dress from falling and leaving her nude from the waist up.

If he noticed her timidity, he didn't say so. He simply stepped back—less than an inch, so that the heat of their bodies still met and mingled—and started removing his own clothes.

Unbuckling his belt, he pulled the narrow strip of leather from its loops and let it drop at his feet, then opened the hook at the top of his pants.

She swallowed hard, her gaze locked on the bulge pushing out the fabric of the black chinos. But instead of taking the slacks the rest of the way off, his fingers moved to the buttons of his shirt, releasing them one after another in quick succession until he was able to yank the tails from his waistband and shrug out of the garment entirely.

Her lungs hitched at the sight. His chest had looked impressive enough beneath the dress shirt and the sweat-dotted tee from that morning. But bare, it was a true work of art. If there was a muscle in his body that could be made bigger, harder, better, she was hard-pressed to find it.

His biceps were so large, she didn't think she could span them with both hands—a theory she fully intended to test at some point during the night. His pectorals were firm and extremely well-defined, leading down to six-pack abs that could have been carved by a master sculptor.

It was enough to make her mouth water. And from the look in his eyes, he knew it.

Brushing his palms down her arms, he wrapped his fingers lightly around her wrists and gave them a gentle tug, silently urging her to drop her hands and let him see what was beneath her dress. Her heart stuttered for a moment as she worked up the courage to loosen her hold and let the flowing black material flutter to the floor.

She stood in her high, sparkling heels with the dress spread in a pool around her feet. Since the dress was strapless, she hadn't worn a bra, but she had donned peek-a-boo French-cut panties and a garter belt—both black to match the dress—and silk stockings. They had been Rachel's idea, and Abby was glad now that she'd let her friend talk her into so many items that she would never have bought on her own.

The heat in Mike's expression let her know how much he appreciated the sexy, feminine articles, and that made her appreciate them, too.

"I hope you know how beautiful you are," he said in a low voice, his thumbs drawing circles on the soft insides of her elbows while he studied her intently from head to toe. "I'd like to spend hours telling you just how beautiful, waxing poetic about every inch of you. But I'm just too damn frantic to get inside you."

His words had her knees going weak, her bones turning liquid. She'd never known anyone to be so blunt and honest about what he wanted, or anyone who wanted her as blatantly and eagerly as he seemed to.

That knowledge, and the steady, unflappable conviction pouring off of him in waves, made her feel incredibly confident, too. And just like that, any shyness, any inhibitions about being here—in this room, with him, doing what they were doing—disappeared, leaving her completely, one-hundred-percent certain and self-assured.

"That's all right," she murmured, surprised she could manage to form words, let alone coherent thoughts with the maelstrom of emotions stirring to life inside of her. "You can tell me later."

One corner of his mouth lifted. "Count on it."

Driving his fingers into her hair, which now hung loose around her shoulders, he tipped her head and kissed her again. This time, he pressed himself flush against her body, his hard chest flattening her bare breasts between them, his erection nudging her low in the belly.

She felt every callus on his big, wide hands as they ran down the line of her spine, just skimming the top of her panties where they covered her bottom. His touch

then trailed around the sides of her waist and up to the swells of her breasts. They weren't large, but that didn't seem to bother him in the least as he cupped them in both hands, covering them, weighing them, running his thumbs over the taut nipples.

She moaned into his mouth, her own hands lifting to clasp the nape of his neck and scratch through his hair. The short, buzz-cut ends tickling her fingertips was a new, unique sensation. One she quite enjoyed.

Bending her knee, she raised one leg to wrap around his calf and thigh, clinging to him like a vine of ivy. With a groan, he dropped a hand to her behind and lifted her straight off her feet.

She tensed for a moment in surprise, then relaxed as she realized she liked the higher position, the sensation of towering over him for a change. And he seemed to have no trouble whatsoever holding her that way while they continued to kiss and caress.

The next several minutes convinced Abby that she could be completely happy spending the rest of her life doing nothing more than kissing this man. His fingers teasing her breast and his arm propped beneath her buttocks were nice, but his mouth was pure heaven, and as skilled as any she'd ever known.

If it felt this good just to stand and kiss for a slow, sultry half hour, she could only imagine what it would be like to finally have him inside her, making love to her fully.

Apparently, he was thinking along the same lines, because he stepped forward until his own knees bumped the edge of the bed, and bent to deposit her on

the wide, firm mattress. He followed her down, his mouth moving to her throat to lick the pulse point, then gave a light bite that had her arching beneath him.

She unclenched her teeth and the nails digging into his upper arms to complain, "You're taking too long."

He lifted his head, staring down at her with a black brow arched high over one eye. "I'm enjoying myself. Aren't you enjoying yourself?"

Oh, yes. Too much.

"I'm ready for the grand finale," she said.

His lips turned up in a wicked smile. "So am I."

Sliding slowly off her and the bed, he got to his feet, making short work of discarding his shoes and pants. Before tossing the slacks aside, he reached into one of the pockets and pulled out a couple of square foil packets.

He stood at the end of the bed, hands on hips, looking down at her in all his naked glory. Propped on her elbows, she reveled in the magnificent picture he made, all flat planes and gently rippling muscles.

His erection was as impressive as the rest of him, standing out from his body at a stiff, upward angle. While she watched, his penis twitched, and an amused giggle rolled up from her throat.

"You think it's funny, huh?" he asked, his voice vibrating with mock anger. "How would you like to be stuck with one of these?"

Something about this place, this situation, this man, made her feel bold and uninhibited enough to retort, "I'm hoping to. Very soon."

His eyes went wide a split second before he growled

and took a flying leap for the bed, landing right on top of her. She gave a squeal of delight, laughing and wiggling as he worked to pin her down by her wrists and ankles.

Given his size, it didn't take him long. His legs wedged against hers. His hands held her arms above her head. And his lips moved mercilessly across her mouth and down her neck to her breasts.

He circled the puckered, sensitized tips, licking, sucking, nipping lightly with his teeth. And he didn't seem to be in any hurry to get to that "grand finale" she'd thought they both wanted so badly.

"Mike." His name hissed through her lips on a panting breath. "What are you doing?"

*Why aren't you inside me already?* she wanted to ask.

"Relax," he told her, not missing a beat in what he was doing. "Things are just getting good."

She moaned in both frustration and ecstasy, knowing he wouldn't stop until he'd carried out whatever delicious, nefarious agenda he had in mind.

And she was right. Taking his own sweet time, he finished squeezing and laving her breasts, his mouth making a slow, damp trek down the center of her stomach. His tongue flicked around and inside her navel, then lower still.

His fingertips delved into the top of her panties, dragging them down just ahead of his roving lips. He slipped them over her hips, down her thighs and past her feet, pressing kisses to her flesh, even through the silk of her stockings.

While he was near her feet, he peeled off her heels

and dropped them to the carpeted floor with first one and then a second muted thump. Grinning, he reached for the snaps of the garter belt, carefully releasing them from the tops of the sheer stockings and rolling them down her legs.

The entire ordeal had her panting with need, squirming with eagerness. She thought if he took much longer she might scream.

His rough palms circled her ankles, then ran with agonizing slowness up her calves, behind her knees, inside her thighs. He pushed them apart gently, spreading her wide and open for him.

He rose over her, and as soon as she could reach him, she grabbed his shoulders, digging her nails in and doing her best to tug him closer. She was making pathetic little mewling sounds, but she didn't care. She wanted him, *needed* him. Now.

"Please," she whimpered. "Stop teasing me. You're being cruel."

He kissed her lightly on the mouth, rubbing his chest seductively across her breasts. "What happened to women wanting foreplay?"

"Later," she gasped as the tip of his heated erection nudged the damp folds between her legs. He could do all of that later, once they were worn out, and this desperate, pulsing longing was no longer tying her in knots.

"Yes, ma'am," he replied dutifully.

Gathering one of the condom packets from the bedspread where he'd dropped them earlier, he tore it open with his teeth and made quick work of covering himself

with the thin latex. Then, taking hold of her hips, he lifted her slightly and drove inside.

She rolled her head back and bit her lip at the tightness, the friction, the amazing sensation of being filled by such a large, substantial man. It had been a while since her last sexual encounter, and Kirk could only dream of being as well-endowed as Mike, so it took a moment for her body to adjust.

And he gave her the time, holding himself perfectly still above her, his chest heaving and his biceps quivering with the effort. He seemed to understand that a woman her size would need a second or two to accommodate a man so much larger.

It didn't take long, though, and soon she was canting her hips, her slick inner muscles clenching around him.

Blowing a slow breath through his teeth, he bit out a rough, "Okay?"

She nodded, lifting both her arms and legs to wrap more fully around him. Brushing her cheek along his coarse jaw, she drew the lobe of his ear into her mouth and nipped gently.

He moaned, his fingers digging more deeply into the flesh of her buttocks as he pulled back just slightly, then moved back in. His strokes lengthened, his motions picking up speed. Their bodies moved together naturally—hot, wet, amazing.

Her blood pulsed through her veins, pounding in her ears as tension built, gathering like a tidal wave low in her belly. She bit her lip to keep from crying out, then gave up when the pleasure became too great.

Beneath them, the mattress quaked, the bedsprings

squeaked. The wide mahogany headboard banged against the wall in time with Mike's hammering thrusts. Then suddenly, almost without warning, stars burst behind Abby's closed eyelids, every muscle in her body seizing with an orgasm of epic proportions.

It was all-encompassing, mind-blowing, like nothing she'd ever experienced before in her life. A heartbeat later, Mike groaned above her ear as he plunged forward one last time, then collapsed atop her.

They panted in tandem, chests heaving, their labored breathing filling the room. His massive weight pinned her in place, and would have been smothering if the heat and intimate contact hadn't felt so darn good.

Her hands smoothed over his back and up through his short-cropped hair. He was still inside her, but she could have sworn she felt him stirring to life again.

Before she could tell for sure, he pushed himself up on his forearms, holding the position for a moment to stare down at her.

"I'll be right back," he said, kissing her briskly on the lips. He slipped off the bed and headed for the bathroom.

She heard the water running, and a minute later he returned to the bed, still blessedly naked. He crawled onto the mattress and over her, hovering there while he tugged at the covers above her head. Yanking them down, he propped the pillows against the headboard.

Turning his attention back to her, he lifted her around the waist one-handed and moved her bodily from the middle of the mattress to the top. She shrieked at the momentary sensation of being airborne, the shriek turning into laughter when she landed and bounced.

Mike threw himself down beside her, sending the mattress recoiling like a trampoline. He was grinning right along with her as he pulled the sheets up to cover them both, propping himself against the pillows with one arm behind his head, the other draped around her shoulders.

"That was pretty good," he said, his chest puffing out with smug self-importance. "We should do it again real soon."

Abby reached out and pinched him in the rib cage, just beneath his tight right nipple. She chuckled when he jerked, yelped, and rubbed at the abused area.

"If you can keep from being too obnoxious and unbearable," she said with a haughty note to her tone, "maybe we will."

"Oh, okay. Good to know the ground rules," he replied stoically.

But a second later, he ruined the mock serious mood by smiling and swooping in for a toe-curling kiss.

"How many of those condoms do you have left?" she asked breathlessly when they finally came up for air.

He slanted his gaze toward the end of the bed, jiggling his foot under the covers until the square blue packets came into view.

"Two," he answered.

She arched a brow. "Do you always run around with a handful of condoms in your pocket?"

"One, almost always. Just in case," he responded matter-of-factly and without the least hint of chagrin. "Tonight, I grabbed a couple extra." It was his turn to raise an eyebrow. "Let's just say I was hopeful."

"Men live in a constant state of optimism when it comes to getting lucky, don't they?" she teased.

"Oh, yeah," he agreed wholeheartedly.

"And I made it pretty easy for you, didn't I?"

He rolled closer, brushing his lips across her temple and sliding a hand over her hip beneath the sheets. "Not easy, no. If it had been easy, we'd have wound up here as soon as I arrived at the hotel, instead of having to fake our way through that terrible dinner."

"I thought dinner was delicious," she said, tipping her head back and trying to keep her mind on track as his mouth continued to do wicked things behind her ear and near the curve of her neck.

"Not as delicious as this," he murmured, slipping a hand between her legs, where she was already wet and waiting for him.

She moaned, sinking deeper into the mattress as he covered her body with his own and began doing things that were more than just delicious.

After giving her two sharp, amazing climaxes with only his hands and mouth, he twisted around, searching amidst the rumpled covers for one of the condoms. She couldn't help but laugh as his grumbles turned to curses, and his curses grew darker and more foul the longer the tiny packets remained MIA.

He was sitting up now, leaning forward to claw through the sheets and bedspread. With the miserable tangle they were in, and only a single low-watt, overhead light still on near the hotel room door, she didn't think his chances of finding what he was looking for were all that great.

As much as she wanted him to find that condom so she could feel him inside her again, the broad span of his bare back was entirely too tempting.

Climbing to her knees, she knelt behind him, flattening her hands near the base of his spine and running them both slowly upwards. His muscles bunched and clenched the minute she touched him, going even harder beneath her seeking fingers. He slowed in his search for only a fraction of a second before uttering another vile expletive and redoubling his efforts.

When he gave the quilted coverlet another vicious flick, something caught her attention, and she reached out to grab one of the elusive plastic packets.

"Is this what you're looking for?" she asked, squeezing the roped muscles of his shoulder and leaning into his back as she held the square out in front of him where he could see it.

He muttered another creatively masculine invective and snatched the condom from her fingers. "Finally, thank God."

She chuckled. "You seem to have an extensive vocabulary when it comes to bad language. I'm learning a lot."

"Marines know all the best curses," he said offhandedly, tearing a corner of the small packet open with his teeth. "Stick around, and you'll learn even more."

Everything inside of her went still for a moment at the unintentional invitation. She could certainly see herself sticking around, getting to know all his habits and idiosyncrasies.

But this was just a summer fling. Shorter, even—a vacation fling.

The fact that things were moving so quickly was astounding enough. She wasn't going to ruin it, or limit herself and their pleasure, by expecting too much or letting her imagination get the better of her.

Taking a breath to jump-start her heart and lungs again, she pushed any heavy thoughts out of her brain, replacing them with a voice similar to Rachel's, reminding her to have fun, enjoy herself, live in the moment.

And with Mike turning to face her, swooping in for a soul-stealing kiss, it wasn't difficult.

His arms snaked around her waist, yanking her close as her own locked behind his neck. His mouth was a conduit for heat and electricity, numbing her lips and sending tiny shock waves rocketing through her system.

He started to press her backward, down to the mattress, but she stopped him, pulling away just enough to whisper, "I want to be on top this time."

She felt him shudder, heard his sharp intake of breath. And then he was shifting, stretching his legs out in front of him and getting ready to let her take control.

"I may end up regretting this," he said in a low, grated voice, "but I'm all yours. Do your worst."

Surprised by her own boldness, a bevy of luscious options swirled through Abby's head. She couldn't partake of them all without burning them both down to ashes, but she could certainly try the top two.

"Lie back," she said, placing a hand in the center of his chest and giving a little shove.

He went without protest, holding the open condom packet out to her, to make use of when she decided they needed it.

"Thank you," she said, taking the plastic square from him. But she wasn't ready for it just yet, so she set it on the bed near her left leg, in easy reach.

She leaned forward to kiss him, her breasts brushing his chest, his rampant erection nudging her belly. Their mouths meshed, tongues tangling together for several long minutes until they were both panting and writhing with need.

Abby's fingers were balled into fists around the sheets on either side of Mike's head, but his were clamped on her hips, holding her tight, kneading her soft flesh. Before she could succumb to his urgings to lower herself only a couple of inches and take him fully into her body, she broke away and sat up.

"Not yet. There's something else I want to do first."

He groaned, but let her go. Settling back a bit more, he folded his arms behind his head in a relaxed pose that directly contradicted the erotic tension radiating off of him in waves.

"Good boy."

With a small smile, she caressed his chest, taking her time as she traced his pectorals, the tiny, bronzed circles of his nipples, and the square, taut muscles of his abdomen. Beneath her, his thighs jerked, along with his stiffened member, pointing skyward.

The dark tower of his penis caught her attention, and she took great delight in the silky texture covering that otherwise hardened flesh as she wrapped her fingers

around the base. Mike hissed a breath through his teeth as she rhythmically tightened, then loosened her grip.

His pelvis tilted off the bed, straining for more of her touch. And she gave it to him, covering him with her mouth.

She kissed and licked, nipped and swirled. He bucked beneath her. His arms had moved from behind his head to lie straight at his sides, and his hands clawed at the sheets beside his hips.

"Abby." Her name tore from his lips, harsh and edged with desperation.

She continued to tease him, enjoying the taste and texture of him, as well as her ability to drive him to distraction. But before another minute had passed, he was gripping her shoulders, pulling her up and away.

"Stop," he bit out. His breathing was ragged, his entire body quivering with need. "I'm too close. I can't take any more."

Licking her lips, she sat back slightly, stretching out her left arm to pat around for the condom packet.

"*Any* more?" she asked, tearing the plastic open the rest of the way and removing the latex circle, "Or not much more?"

The air stuttered from his lungs as she covered him with the thin layer of protection, then positioned herself above him. She could feel the heat and hardness of him at her opening, pressing forward just a bit.

"Not a hell of a lot more," he barely got out through his locked jaw.

His nostrils flared as he looked up at her, his hands balancing her breasts, his thumbs running gently over the

puckered nipples. Laying her hands overtop his, she arched her back, shook out her hair, and slowly let herself down until he slipped inside her welcoming warmth.

Her eyes slid closed as delightful sensations swamped her. His hands at her breasts, his swollen length filling her, his amazing, well-formed body beneath her and at her disposal…they all merged and mingled, drowning her in an almost indescribable pleasure.

Her internal muscles contracted around him, and she sighed.

Mike didn't. The sound he made was more predatory, quivering through every cell of her being and straight to the marrow of her bones.

"Move," he grated, his fingers flexing at her breasts. "Please."

She opened her eyes to gaze down at him, and another stab of excitement flashed low in her belly. His jaw was clenched, the muscles of his neck standing out in stark relief as he held himself perfectly still, rigid as a plank of wood.

Rising higher on her knees, she let him slide nearly all the way out of her before lowering herself and absorbing him completely once again. Over and over, she took him to the hilt. Over and over, she thrilled to the strain in his expression, the tension in his arms and legs as he fought to maintain control.

She didn't want him in control. She wanted him crazed and frantic and spinning out like a greased sled on a sheet of ice.

Dropping her hands to his chest, she leaned forward,

taking his mouth with her own and changing the angle of their connection. With a grunt, he grasped her hips and bent his legs, working actively now to speed her movements and bring them both to a quick, earth-shaking, shattering completion.

When it was finished, leaving her wrung out and exhausted, she draped herself across his chest, let her head drop to the crook of his shoulder and fell into a deep, contented sleep.

# CHAPTER FOUR

IT COULD HAVE BEEN hours or only minutes later when she next stirred awake. She was lying on her side, facing the right direction on the mattress this time, with her head on one of the pillows near the headboard and her feet tucked under the covers near the foot of the bed.

She vaguely remembered Mike turning them around and drawing the sheets up before pulling her close and drifting off to sleep. Now, though, he wasn't beside her, and she sat up to see if he was elsewhere in the room.

The same single entry light was still on near the door, and in its dim yellow-orange glow, Mike stood shrugging into his pants and shirt.

Clutching the sheets to her chest, she sat up. "Where are you going?" she asked, sounding as groggy as she felt.

"I need to get home," he said softly.

Finished tucking the tails of his shirt into his slacks, he stepped into his shoes, then walked toward her. At the edge of the bed, he bent over and pressed his lips to the top of her head.

She watched him, stunned disbelief lying like a stone at the bottom of her stomach.

*He was leaving? Already?*

"Meet me on the beach in the morning," he

murmured, his fingers toying with the ends of her hair. "Same place as before, okay?"

Relief poured through her so strongly, she nearly wilted. Finally, she managed a weak nod.

He smiled in the darkness, kissed her again, then turned and left. As soon as the door clicked shut, she fell back against the pillows and stared up at the ceiling.

He wanted to see her again, which meant he hadn't been leaving-leaving, as in *escaping*. That had to be a good sign. But then, he hadn't stuck around until morning, either.

She didn't know what to think about that, or what to feel. This was all too new to her, too fast and incredible and unbelievable.

Rachel would know, though. Rachel understood men and relationships way better than she did.

It was late, and Rachel was probably sound asleep, but since it was her fault Abby was in this mess to begin with, she didn't feel a shred of guilt at waking her best friend in the middle of the night.

Rolling across the rumpled mattress, she reached for the phone on the nightstand and dialed her friend's number.

MIKE DIDN'T EXACTLY feel like a gentleman of the first order as he drove away from Abby's hotel.

He should have stayed until morning…had *wanted* to stay until morning…but the longer he'd lain there, with her head on his shoulder and her arm draped across his waist, the tighter his chest had become. His heart had beat so fast, he'd been afraid it might explode.

It was still pounding like the drum set at a heavy metal concert, and damned if he could figure out why.

Being with her had been amazing. The sex alone was incredible—and about a hundred other words he couldn't even think of to describe it.

But it was more than that. Something about Abby Weaver drew him, called to him.

It should have bothered him that things between them had developed so quickly, that *everything* was moving so fast.

Should have, but for some strange reason, didn't. Not in the least. If anything, it all felt perfectly normal.

It felt…right. Real. Substantial.

And that was what made him uneasy. Because as much as his emotions were getting tied up with thoughts of Abby, there were people in his life who might not be happy about him making time with a new woman.

So before he could spend the entire night in Abby's bed, before he could wake up in the morning with her in his arms or make more permanent plans where she was concerned, he had to take care of that one, small issue.

REMAIN CALM. Assume nothing. Be patient and see where things lead.

That had been Rachel's sage advice, once Abby had woken her enough for lucid thought and some good old-fashioned girl talk.

Rachel had been almost giddy to learn that Abby had spent the night making love with her gorgeous, ripped Marine sergeant. And she hadn't been nearly as concerned by Mike's leaving as Abby.

"Maybe he has an early appointment in the morning," she suggested. "Maybe Mommy and Daddy would worry if he wasn't home by curfew," she'd teased. "Maybe he's as freaked out by you as you are by him, and he needed some time to think," she'd added rationally.

It was that last possibility that actually helped to calm her fears. Rachel was right. If she was this…confused…nervous…excited…overwhelmed…by what was happening between them, then it was only natural that he would be, too.

And weren't guys supposed to be even more gun-shy than women when it came to this sort of thing?

Her friend had also reminded her that Mike *had* asked her to meet him on the beach in the morning. That had to be a good sign, since blowing her off as a one-night stand would definitely *not* include making arrangements to get together again.

By the time they'd finished, Abby was breathing much easier and already thinking about changing into her bikini and heading back down to the beach. To "their" spot, she thought with a secret grin.

Even Rachel's news that she was still swamped at work and wouldn't be able to fly down to Florida any time soon couldn't spoil Abby's buoyant mood.

She hardly slept at all the rest of the night and bounded out of bed at the crack of dawn. Changing into her suit and sarong, she spent a little extra time on her hair and makeup, then slipped into her sandals and headed out.

She decided not to rent one of those giant umbrellas today, but made sure she had an adequate amount

of sunscreen in her tote, along with a towel, book and a bottle of water.

Her main intention was to be on the sand when Mike showed up, but she didn't want to just sit there, looking like a dolt. She would read and pretend to be getting some sun, and hope to be acting casual when he finally arrived.

The sun was high in the sky and shining brightly when she heard his sneakered footsteps in the sand. She lifted her gaze from her open book, absently sticking a bookmark between the pages to mark her place as she watched him through the tinted lenses of her sunglasses.

"Morning," he said, smiling even though he was breathing hard with exertion.

She returned the grin, admiring his physique in sweat-dampened shorts and shirt, similar to what he'd been wearing when they first met. "Hi."

Dropping onto the corner of her beach blanket, he reached for her water bottle and took a long swig. After quenching his thirst and drying his face with the sleeve of his T-shirt, he said, "I'm glad you're here. I was a little afraid you wouldn't show."

She fought not to laugh. If he only knew.

For the next few minutes, they made small talk, avoiding the topic of the night before altogether. And as they talked, Mike moved around, shifting his body until he sat at her side, facing the ocean just as she was.

"So I've been thinking…"

Sucking in a small breath, she slanted a glance in his direction from behind her shades. "Yes?"

"I want you to come to Sunday dinner at my parents' house."

She blinked, trying to process what he'd just said.

"Your parents?" she asked, relieved when the words came out more steady than they felt.

"Yeah." He leaned back on his arms, his legs crossed at the ankle. "Sunday dinner is a big deal at their house, especially when one of us kids is home. Unless I'm lying comatose in the hospital or am abducted by aliens, I'm sort of required to be there. I'd like you to come with me so we can spend the day together."

"And meet your folks," she said slowly.

A hint of color tinged his high cheekbones. "Something like that. Don't worry, they won't bite. You may need a couple antacids after my mother practically force-feeds you enough food for an elephant, but you won't shed any blood."

She chuckled only because she knew it's what Mike expected, while in reality her insides were knotted and pulled tight.

*Remain calm. Assume nothing. Be patient and see where things lead.*

Meeting a man's parents might normally be a big step and mean something important. In this case, however, it might be completely innocuous.

It could be no more than exactly what he claimed—he needed to have dinner with his parents on Sunday and also wanted to spend the day with her. Mixing the two seemed like a logical solution.

Deep down, she suspected there was more to it than that, but was willing to play along. She would remain

calm, assume nothing, and be patient enough to see where things led.

Taking a breath, she nodded. "All right."

"Great," he returned, sounding relieved. "Dinner is at one, so what do you say I pick you up around twelve, twelve-thirty?"

"I'll be ready."

She was already beginning to wonder what she should wear. Definitely something closer to her normal wardrobe and farther away from Rachel's choices for her. Her first time meeting Mike's mother and father was not the occasion to show a lot of skin and cleavage.

"That takes care of Sunday," he said, his feet rolling back and forth in front of them on the brightly colored towel. "But it still leaves us with Thursday, Friday, and Saturday. Any chance you'd care to spend those days— and every remaining day of your vacation—with me, too?"

He wiggled his brows, his mouth tipped up at the corners, and she couldn't help but smile. How was she supposed to resist such an endearing expression teamed with such a cajoling voice?

And, she had to admit, she simply didn't want to resist. She *wanted* to be with him every free moment she had for the next two weeks, as long as he was willing.

"Okay. You may get tired of me after a while, though."

He met her gaze, and his brown eyes were nothing but sincere. "Not a chance."

Leaning in, he brushed his mouth over hers, startling her with the sudden kiss. Then he returned to his relaxed

position as though he hadn't just sent her pulse skipping into a samba beat.

"So what are you up for today? Shopping? Sightseeing? Dancing?" He turned his wrist to look at his watch. "Maybe lunch in a couple hours?"

She imagined doing any of those things with him and felt her chest swell with anticipation.

"How about all of the above?" she asked boldly.

He let out a deep chuckle that caused his six-pack abs to jump beneath the strained cotton of his dark green USMC T-shirt.

"I say we spread them out over the next couple days, but other than that, I'm game. What do you want to do first?"

She thought about it a moment, then shrugged a shoulder and said, "Surprise me."

"All right. When do you want to leave?"

"Whenever you're ready. I'll need to go up to my room and change first, though."

Turning sideways, his warm breath dusted her shoulder, neck, the curve of her ear as he moved closer. He nipped at the lobe of her ear with his teeth, pressing his lips to her throat, down to her collarbone and the upper swell of her breast.

"Think I could come with you?" he asked seductively.

The air caught in her lungs, but she forced herself to say, "You want to watch me change clothes?"

"Uh-huh."

His tongue flicked out to lick just above the line of the gold lamé bikini top while his index finger slyly

worked its way under the elastic bow on the right hip of the bikini bottoms.

"I humbly volunteer my services in helping you get out of this sexy little swimsuit. I'm very good with knots and zippers and hooks."

A thick, strangled laugh rolled up from her diaphragm, goose bumps breaking out all along her skin. "I'll bet you are."

She swallowed hard, letting her eyes fall closed and her head fall back as his extremely talented mouth drifted first over her other breast, then up to the arch of her throat and jawline. His hand spanned her waist, his thumb brushing back and forth along her bare abdomen…back and forth, back and forth, slow and mesmerizing.

With a moan, she clamped her fingers into the broad expanse of his shoulders. When he slid one knee between her legs, she let her muscles go lax, welcoming him into the cradle of her body.

He accepted the invitation without hesitation, shifting until he covered her from head to toe, limbs twined and tangled. His mouth aligned perfectly with hers, and he wasted no time kissing her senseless.

She had no comprehension of time or how long they made out on the hot sand, with the midday sun blistering down on them. All she knew was that when he kissed her, the rest of the world fell away and ceased to exist.

They were both panting heavily when they broke apart, chests heaving, blood thick and pooling at their extremities. Mike's erection pressed at the juncture of her thighs, rampant and pulsing.

When he lifted himself away from her, she whimpered and dug her nails into the solid meat of his upper arms. Swooping back in, he kissed her again, quickly, brutally.

"Not here," he grated, "but soon. Believe me, it's going to be soon."

He pushed off of her and to his feet, extending a hand to yank her up beside him. The fabric of his olive-green running shorts did nothing to hide the evidence of his arousal.

Following the line of her gaze, he cleared his throat and tugged unsuccessfully at one leg of the shorts. She snickered and dropped her forehead to the center of his chest.

"Go ahead and laugh," he grumbled in a mock threatening tone. "I'll be making good use of this tent pole soon enough."

Because her head was still tilted toward the sand and she didn't have to meet his eyes, she had the courage to venture, "Will I still be laughing then?"

He reached around to spank her lightly on the rear end, growling low in his throat. "Not if I have anything to say about it."

Releasing her, he bent and started to gather her things. She helped him until they had everything picked up and tucked away, and she didn't miss the way he draped her towel over his arm so that it hung low, covering any questionable physical responses.

"Ready?"

Stifling a grin at the knowledge that she had the power to do that to him, she nodded and headed through the warm sand toward the hotel entrance.

"This isn't helping," he muttered as he followed a few steps behind.

She tossed a glance at him over her shoulder. "What isn't?"

His gaze cut pointedly to her bottom. "Watching you sashay in front of me in that little scrap of gold whatever."

"I didn't mean to sashay" was the only response she could think of.

He arched a brow and fixed her with an intense stare. "I know. To you, it's just the way you walk. To me, it's a punch straight to the gut."

Her mouth went dry at his stark confession, and a fist of pure lust seemed to squeeze between her legs.

Swallowing past the lump in her throat, she inhaled a bolstering breath, then turned back toward the hotel and started walking again. And this time, she made sure to put just a hint of extra swish in her hips as she moved.

Behind her, she heard Mike groan, and a flair of feminine awareness bloomed in her belly. She was definitely beginning to enjoy this.

If she was lucky, she thought as they wandered through one of the hotel's side hallways toward a bank of elevators, she would get the chance to tease and torment him every day for the rest of her vacation.

And if she was very, *very* lucky, she would get the chance to let him tease and torment *her*.

THEY SPENT the first couple of hours after returning to the room making love, starting with some heavy petting

in the elevator on the way up to the eighteenth floor. It was everything Abby could have imagined for a torrid vacation-time affair and more.

Afterward, they'd showered together, which only led to more hanky-panky. Then they redressed and headed out for a day of strolling along chic Las Olas Boulevard.

They strolled along narrow alleyways and brick walkways, browsed through trendy boutiques, did lunch, grabbed an ice cream cone, and even stopped for a short time at a popular jazz bar.

The next day, he took her to the Secret Woods Nature Center, and followed that up with dancing in the evening, just as he'd promised.

The music at the hot Latin club was loud, the dance floor crowded, and the lights frenetic enough to induce a migraine.

She loved it.

Even though she recognized none of the songs, and knew none of the dance steps, being pressed that tightly to Mike's tall, muscular form, with the incredibly sensual beat throbbing through their veins, made it feel natural and right.

The day after that, they started out at the gigantic Swap Shop Flea Market where she saw dozens of things she would have loved to buy, but resisted them all because she knew she couldn't lug them all back to Ohio with her on the plane. Next was a Jungle Queen Riverboat ride on the other side of town, and they ended the evening dining on a nearby island amid tropical foliage.

It was more than she ever could have expected of her vacation—with or without a handsome Marine as her tour guide. Every day, she seemed to grow more content, more comfortable, and more confident, both with herself and with Mike. And to top it all off, they spent every night wrapped in each other's arms, making love until neither of them had the strength to stand.

She tried to deny it, but she was very afraid she was starting to fall in love with him.

Not tiny, insignificant infatuation. Not mere lust.

But real, deep, genuine affection.

It scared her, and made her palms sweat. Because she knew it wouldn't last. Couldn't last.

She only had another week before she would return to her job and life—however mundane it all seemed now—back in Ohio.

At about the same time, Mike would be flying back to Camp Pendleton and his career military life in California.

They couldn't be more different, couldn't be farther apart, both literally and figuratively.

There was no future for them, no matter how much she might wish otherwise. Her only option was to take everything she could get for the rest of her time in Florida and absorb it, store it all away in her memory banks for the long, cold days ahead.

So that's what she did, enjoying every single minute she got to spend with Mike.

Rachel would have been proud.

And before she knew it, Sunday rolled around. The moment of truth, when she would go home with Mike and be introduced to his parents.

A panicked phone call to the still-absent Rachel didn't help as much as she'd hoped, since her best friend insisted a visit with Mr. Tempting-But-Temporary's family was rarely included as part of a hot summer fling.

Her best advice was to not let his parents catch her playing grabsies under the table with their son while they were eating, which wasn't much help at all.

An hour before Mike was scheduled to pick her up, she dressed in a pair of jeans and low-heeled hemp sandals, with a light pink ballerina-style tee. The jeans weren't too tight, the heels weren't too high, and the neckline of the top wasn't too low.

She added a simple gold chain necklace, gold filigree earrings, a watch and a small charm bracelet before doing her makeup and running a brush through her hair. Except for a small clip to hold the sides up, she opted to leave it hanging long and loose down her back.

The knock on the door came as she was finishing up, dabbing a bit of perfume on her wrists and behind her ears. She rushed to answer it, pressing a hand to her stomach in an effort to still the battery of butterflies flying around down there.

Mike was smiling when she opened the door, one hand resting above his head on the jamb.

"Ready to go?" he asked.

"Just let me grab my stuff," she said, leaving him to prop the door open while she ran back to the bed for her purse and key card. Stuffing the key into the front zippered pocket of her handbag, she met him in the hallway and let the door lock behind them.

"I hope you like lasagna," he told her as they weaved their way through the hotel lobby and out to his car. He saw her inside, then rounded the hood to slide behind the wheel. "It's one of my mother's specialties, and as soon as she heard I was bringing a friend to dinner, it went to the top of the menu."

"I do." She waited a beat before finding the courage to ask, "What did you tell them about me?"

He slanted a glance in her direction before returning his attention to the road. "I told them we met on the beach during one of my runs. And that you're the reason I haven't been home much this leave," he added with a grin.

She felt her face flush. "You didn't tell them *how* you've been spending your time, did you?" she choked out, thinking of the half-used box of condoms that now resided in the nightstand drawer beside her hotel room bed.

"Oh, sure," was his quick response.

The air strangled in her lungs, coming out as a hiss through her wide-open mouth.

He caught her mortified expression and laughed. "Relax. I mentioned a few of the places we've gone in the past week, but nothing more. There are some things my parents don't need to know."

At his admission, relief poured through her.

Several minutes later, they pulled up in front of a nice little two-story house with a fenced-in yard. The white siding was trimmed with black shudders. A kaleidoscope of bright, seasonal flowers lined both the concrete walk and filled boxes along the front porch railing.

"Don't worry," Mike murmured as he held the gate of the waist-high chain link fence open for her, taking her elbow as they walked the rest of the way together. "They'll like you. And it's just dinner."

Just dinner—with his *parents*. Talk about pressure.

At the front screen door, Mike paused with one hand on the knob. His other lifted to frame her face, the side of his thumb brushing evocatively over the swell of her full bottom lip as he pinned her with a dark, meaningful stare.

"Even if they don't like you," he said slowly, and low enough for only them to hear, "I certainly do."

## CHAPTER FIVE

HURDLE NUMBER ONE had been cleared, and Mike felt he was well on his way to winning the race.

Dinner had not only been delicious—with his mother at the controls, there wasn't a chance of it being anything else—but Abby fit in like a long lost family member.

His parents loved her almost on sight. For the first few minutes after introductions had been made, they'd been wary and she had been visibly nervous. But after she'd started to talk, complimenting his mother on the house's decor and his father on his collection of ships in bottles, any sense of caution on either side flew out the window, and the three of them became fast friends.

That was good, Mike thought, watching Abby now, seated beside his mother on the living room sofa while they flipped through the family photo album. As usual, his mom couldn't wait to show pictures of him as a child to anybody who stepped into the house—including ones of him naked in the sink, naked in half a cowboy costume—hat and holster, and not a damn stitch more—naked in the yard with the garden hose.

It was good, because if he had any say in the matter, Abby was going to be in his life for a while, and he wanted her to get along with his folks.

That had been a major concern, since he knew how fond his parents were of Diana. Diana had been his high school sweetheart, and he knew that just about everyone—his parents, her parents, all their friends and relatives—had expected them to marry and start a family. They *still* expected it, even though they'd been out of school for years now.

His mistake, he realized now, was never really breaking things off with her. He'd enlisted soon after graduation, but stayed in touch. Whenever he was home on leave, he gave her a call or she dropped in, and they ended up going out. Occasionally, they spent the night together.

It was nothing serious, nothing they'd discussed. Instead, it was casual and convenient.

And now he was very much afraid that he'd unintentionally led her on. Let her believe that some day they'd end up together.

Explaining the reality of the situation to his parents hadn't been easy. They thought of Diana as another daughter and a very-much-desired future daughter-in-law.

Thankfully, they'd handled the news well. They'd been disappointed, which he understood, but as soon as he'd told them about Abby, about wanting her to come for Sunday dinner and get to know them a little bit, they'd both brightened right up and wanted to know all about her.

He was sure they were already getting ahead of themselves, and him, in the revised "future daughter-in-law" department, but he'd deal with that later, if need be.

The next hurdle would be talking with Diana. He'd been avoiding that, he admitted, but it would have to happen soon.

"Here you go, son." Coming up behind him from the kitchen, his father handed him a cold beer.

"Thanks, Dad."

Mike took the bottle, twisted off the top, and took a long swallow as his father wandered into the living room and took a seat in his favorite chair. He followed at a more leisurely pace, enjoying the sounds of the women's cheerful, mingled voices.

There was barely enough room for him between Abby and the arm of the couch, but that didn't keep him from sliding into the tight space. They were pressed together snuggly from hip to knee, just the way he liked it.

Her body heat soaked through both layers of their jeans, sending a low-level hum of desire into his bloodstream. If he wasn't careful, he'd end up alerting his folks, in no uncertain terms, of just how attracted he was to Abby.

She looked down at where they touched, then up to meet his gaze, her green eyes filled with interest and pleasure.

A jolt of arousal, like lightning making a direct hit, blistered him from head to toe, and he had to bite his tongue to keep from groaning aloud.

As though she could read his distress, Abby turned her attention back to the photo album, half on her lap, half on his mother's.

"You were a very cute baby," she said.

He took another sip of his beer before attempting to speak. "One who apparently never wore clothes. Unless Mom just didn't bother to get the camera out unless I was doing something cute in the buff."

Abby chuckled with amusement, and his mother made a clucking noise, reaching past Abby to give him a swat. He pretended to duck, hiding a grin.

"There are plenty of photos where you're not naked," Abby offered, then ruined her conciliatory tone by adding, "but those are my favorites."

He growled playfully, catching his arm around her neck and pulling her close so he could press a kiss to the crown of her head. She flushed and tried to get away, but even though he loosened his hold, he kept his arm draped lightly across her shoulders.

They were past his pictures and on to those of his brother and two sisters when there was a tap at the back kitchen door.

"Knock, knock," the visitor called out as the door opened and Diana sauntered in.

Mike felt his stomach plummet and swallowed hard. The arm around Abby's shoulders tightened, but Mike was otherwise unable to move.

It wasn't unusual for Diana to drop by and make herself at home, but he certainly hadn't expected her to stop in today, of all days.

"I brought some of my famous double chocolate brownies," Diana sang out, marching through the house and setting the platter in her hands on the dining room table. "They're Mike's favorite."

Everyone in the living room froze, watching as she

bustled around, a wide smile on her face. Diana was an attractive woman, there was no doubt about that. She had short, stylish blond hair and a nice, curvaceous shape, even if her clothing choices were sometimes a little too snug for Mike's personal tastes.

Diana hadn't yet noticed Abby—or his arm slung around her in a very familiar, very possessive manner. Mike might have been trained to react in crisis situations, but at the moment, his mind was a total blank. Beside him, he could feel Abby's tension and confusion.

Diana finished uncovering the tray of brownies and straightened away from the table, still smiling. She turned in their direction, her gaze flitting quickly over the entire scene, then coming back to land on him and Abby. Her eyes flickered, and the cheeriness on her face began to fall.

Finally finding his voice and reclaiming the use of his limbs, Mike pushed slowly to his feet. He didn't want to let go of Abby, felt a certain loyalty to protect her while she was in his parents' home, but he was the one who'd created this state of affairs, and it was his responsibility to make sure no one got hurt.

From the looks on both Diana's and Abby's faces, though, he didn't think that was going to be possible.

"Frank," his mother said pointedly, standing as she addressed his father, "let's go out to the garage and see if we can find that bird feeder you promised to hang for me."

As excuses went, it wasn't bad—unless someone happened to glance outside and see the same bird

feeder his mother was talking about hanging from a tree in the backyard, where Mike had hung it only a couple of days ago.

Still, he was glad to have his parents out of the room while whatever was going to happen happened. He would be busy enough just trying to handle the two women who remained.

"Diana," he said, clearing his throat, "this is Abby Weaver. Abby, this is Diana Hartman. We went to school together."

At that less-than-inclusive explanation, Diana arched a brow. "We did a little more than just go to school together, didn't we, Michael?"

The query sounded friendly, but was edged with enough meaning to let Mike know he wasn't going to be able to sweep anything under the rug or leave it for another time. Not today.

Abby rose and held out a hand, either not comprehending or choosing to ignore the underlying friction hovering in the room like a thundercloud. "Hello."

Diana returned the gesture, hesitant but polite. "I didn't know Mike had company. I probably should have called before dropping in, but I'm just so used to coming and going like family."

She reached out to stroke a hand down Mike's arm, bare except for the short sleeves of his snug black T-shirt.

He recognized the action for what it was—marking her territory. It was a side of Diana he'd never seen before, and even though this whole thing was his doing, he couldn't say he liked it.

The room fell into awkward silence once again, and Mike knew he had to come clean. It might get ugly. He may end up pissing off both women beyond forgiveness. But it had to be done.

Sliding his hands into the front pockets of his jeans, he took a deep breath and hoped for the best. "The truth is, Abby, Diana and I dated all through high school, and have been on and off ever since."

Turning to the other woman, he added, "Diana, I know you were probably expecting things between us to become more permanent, but Abby and I recently started seeing each other."

He didn't go into detail, didn't want to make matters any worse than necessary.

"You didn't tell me you were already involved," Abby murmured quietly.

Despite the calm of the words, it was an accusation all the same. And when he met her gaze, the pain and hurt shimmering in the emerald depths felt like a punch to the gut.

"It's always been very casual. More for convenience than anything else," he explained, knowing that only made him sound like more of a heel.

"A convenience," Diana snapped, and her tone was definitely not calm. Jamming her arms across her chest, she glared at him, one toe tapping on the carpeted floor in agitation. "Gee, that's nice, because I thought we were going to be married."

Mike's head snapped up. *Whoa*, he thought. That was news to him.

"We never said anything about getting married," he

insisted, pulling his hands out of his pockets and holding them up in front of him as though to ward off any more of Diana's audacious claims.

Turning to Abby, he said, "The topic never came up, I swear to God."

On his other side, Diana half growled, half shrieked in fury, spun on her heel, and stormed out of the house the same way she'd entered.

Mike watched her go, then glanced back at Abby, torn between staying with her to let her know how much he cared about her, or running after Diana to repair what he could of their relationship.

"Dammit," he swore, running a hand over his short-cropped hair.

The dejected expression on Abby's face clawed at him, but twenty years of friendship did the same. He'd made this mess and now he had to clean it up.

"I'm sorry, Abby, I have to go talk to her. It won't take long, I promise, then I'll come back here so we can straighten things out."

Grabbing her by the arms, he squeezed her tight and pressed a kiss to her cool cheek. She didn't move, didn't respond.

"It's not as bad as it seems, Abby. Just give me a chance to explain."

With a sigh, he let her go and stepped away. "Don't go anywhere," he commanded. "I'll be back."

THIS, MIKE THOUGHT as he walked back into the house an hour later, had to be one of the longest days of his life.

He was exhausted. More worn out and tired to the

bone than he could ever remember, even including his days at boot camp.

Breaking up with a girlfriend he hadn't realized he was seriously involved with, and then hashing things out so that they could at least part as friends, really took it out of a man.

And he wasn't finished yet. He still had to sort things out with Abby.

He could only hope she was willing to listen to reason and forgive him for not telling her about Diana from the beginning.

Scowling, he let the back screen door slam shut behind him and headed for the dining room.

In his defense, they hadn't exactly gotten around to discussing dating histories and past relationships. Not all of them, anyway. He thought that should at least count for something.

"Hey," he said when he found his mom and dad in the living room, a game show playing on the television screen. "Where's Abby?"

A frown marred his mother's brow. "I'm sorry, sweetheart, but she left."

"Left?" The already bunched muscles in his back and shoulders knotted even tighter.

"As soon as you went after Diana, she came out to the garage and asked if we would call her a cab. We didn't want to," she rushed to assure him. "We begged her to stay until you got back, or to at least let your father take her wherever she needed to go, but she refused."

Mike raised a hand to pinch the bridge of his nose

where a massive headache was beginning to throb. He managed to hold back a curse that would have had his mother boxing his ears.

There was only one place Abby could have gone—back to her hotel—so that's where he needed to be, too.

"It's all right," he said calmly, seeing the regret in his mother's eyes, and a similar concern in his father's. "I know where she went."

Turning on his heel, he headed back the way he'd come.

"Good luck," his mother called out to him.

With a wave, he said, "Don't worry if I'm not back for a while," then pushed open the door and stalked to his car.

Twenty minutes later, he decided that either Abby was very good at ignoring his pounding and yelling through her door, or he'd been wrong about her returning to the hotel.

But where the hell else could she have gone? She wasn't from around here and was only familiar with some of the local spots he'd shown her, none of which would make good hiding places when she was upset.

Well, even if she hadn't come back to her room right away, she had to return eventually. He'd bunked down in worse places.

Leaning close to the door one more time, he raised his voice enough to be heard and said, "I'm not going anywhere, Abby. If you don't want to talk to me yet, that's okay, but we *are* going to talk."

Then he turned around, braced his back against the flat panel, and slowly lowered himself to the carpeted hallway floor. Resting his arms on his knees, he

checked his watch before laying his head back and making a concerted effort to relax.

FOR THE TENTH or fifteenth time in as many minutes, Abby peeked through the peephole, but didn't see any signs of Mike. He'd said he wasn't leaving, but that was apparently exactly what he'd done.

She didn't know whether to be sad or relieved.

What had started out as such a nice day with him and his parents had turned into the closest thing to a nightmare she could imagine. The whole time he'd been seducing her, making love to her, he'd had a *girlfriend*. Dear God.

She believed his claims that the relationship hadn't been serious—or at least that *he* hadn't considered it to be. But her reaction to Abby's presence made it obvious that Diana strongly disagreed.

Abby wondered what Mike had said to Diana once he'd caught up to her. She wondered what he'd planned to say to her.

As soon as she'd gotten back to the hotel, she'd tried calling Rachel, only to get her friend's voice mail. Abby had left a message telling Rachel to call her back as soon as possible, but was otherwise on her own to deal with this catastrophe.

Never mind that it was her friend's fault to begin with for sending her to Florida all on her own.

She'd been pacing the floor when Mike's first knock had sounded on the other side of the door, and a part of her had wanted to open it immediately, desperate for an explanation that would make some sort of sense and erase the pain and confusion of the past few hours.

But another, wiser part of her knew it was better to leave things as they stood. She would finish out the rest of her vacation and then return to Ohio to get on with her life.

Eventually, she would forget him. She hoped.

Releasing a breath, she turned the locks on the inside of the door and yanked it open. She expected the hall to be empty, but almost before she could register the movement, Mike popped up from a sitting position on the floor to full attention, spinning to face her.

With a gasp, she jumped back and tried to shut the door again, but his big foot wedged into the opening and blocked her attempt.

"Abby," he said in a calm voice that didn't quite mesh with the foot he had lodged in her door. "You have to talk to me sooner or later."

Her first instinct was to deny it, maybe threaten to call hotel security. But she recognized that for the over-reaction it was.

She also trusted that all he wanted to do was talk. After he'd had his say, if she asked him to leave, she knew he would. And if she refused to let him in, there was a good chance he'd still be camped outside her room this time next week when she tried to leave for the airport.

"Fine," she grumbled, releasing her hold on the door and moving back into the room.

She avoided the bed, instead taking a seat on one of the wide armchairs in the far corner, between the bed and the air-conditioning unit. Crossing both her arms and her legs, she sent a foot swinging and waited.

Mike stopped several feet in front of her, legs apart, hands on his hips. She thought he would look better down on his knees, groveling. That definitely wasn't a position that suited a man like Mike.

"I'm sorry," he said, holding her gaze with his dark, intense brown eyes. "What happened back at the house was definitely *not* what I had in mind for today. I didn't know Diana had planned to stop in."

"Maybe you could have avoided it by telling me about her ahead of time," she tossed out. "Or telling her about me."

He shook his head. "I know. I know I should have handled things differently, and I know how it sounded, but I swear to you, we weren't seriously dating. We'd dated in high school, but after I enlisted we hardly ever saw each other. The times I came back, we'd go out and enjoy ourselves, but we both saw other people. I thought we were just friends." He shrugged a shoulder. "Friends with benefits, maybe, but still just friends. If she expected us to get married anywhere down the road, that was entirely on her. I never mentioned the M word and I definitely never proposed to her.

"We talked about that after I caught up with her," he admitted, "and I think she realizes now that what she thought and what she felt for me was more fantasy than reality. We're better off being just friends."

Blowing out a breath, he ran a hand over the top of his head. "From the moment I met you, *you* were the only woman I thought about, Abby, I can promise you that. And I brought you home for dinner today because I wanted my parents to meet you, to know that you're in my life now."

He took another step forward, rounding the edge of the bed and lowering himself onto the bottom corner, his knees only inches from her own. Holding her gaze, he said softly, "I don't know where this is leading. I don't know if it will only last until we both fly back to our respective homes, or if we can make it work long-distance. The only thing I am sure about," he stressed, reaching out to grab the arm of her chair, "is that I want to find out. I want to keep seeing you, keep touching you. I want to go as far as we can and see how it all works out."

His hand slipped from the chair to one of her wrists, wrapping his long fingers around the delicate bones and tugging her arm away from where she had them both linked beneath her breasts. She'd started out tense, holding her entire body stiff and immovable, but the more he'd talked, the more she'd softened, inside and out.

Bringing her hand to his mouth, he kissed it, then continued to cling to her, toying lightly with her fingers. "I'm hoping you want that, too."

His words filled her heart, sending warmth and anticipation through her veins.

Moments ago, she hadn't thought anything could repair the damage he'd done by not telling her about his old girlfriend. But she believed him when he said his relationship with Diana hadn't been serious since high school. Believed him when he told her he hadn't been seeing anyone else this past week while they'd been together.

And as much as she could have used her friend's

good sense and support, she didn't need anyone to tell her what she felt or what she wanted.

She wanted him…for as long as it lasted, just as he said.

They weren't talking about forever or happily ever after. They were just talking about getting to know each other even better, spending as much time together as possible before they each had to head home, and then maybe doing their best to maintain a long-distance relationship until they decided what the next step should be.

It was a big move for her, but then, this seemed to be her week for them. Flying to Fort Lauderdale on vacation, alone…hooking up with the first man she met on her first day on the beach…tossing aside her usual caution and reticence to take a chance with that same man.

Despite the nerves skittering down her spine, it felt right.

Uncrossing her legs and leaning toward him, she turned her hands over in his so their fingers linked. His skin was warm and slightly rough, and she could feel the apprehension in his touch.

"You're sure Diana is all right with this?" she asked, watching his eyes carefully for the truth of his response. "There are no more hidden emotions or miscommunications lurking beneath the surface?"

He gave his head a quick shake. "Everything is fine, I promise. You're welcome to talk to her yourself, if you don't believe me. I'll give you her number."

He looked as if he'd rather face a firing squad, but she appreciated the offer.

"No, that's all right," she replied quietly. "And your parents? Are they okay with all of this?"

"My parents think you're great," he assured her with a sexy half smile. "They're still fond of Diana, of course, and she'll probably still come around from time to time, but they trust me to live my own life and choose my own women."

His voice went even lower, the brown of his eyes sparking to near black. "I choose you."

With a small, secret smile, she slid off the chair and into his arms, loving the way he pulled her tight and held her close.

"I choose you, too," she whispered against his ear.

Turning his head, he covered her mouth with his own for a passionate, toe-curling kiss, his arms wrapping around her like steel bands.

Beside the bed, the phone rang, but they both ignored it.

This was one decision she didn't need her friend's advice on. To the depths of her soul, she knew it was right.

For now, at least. Maybe forever, maybe only for a while.

But for as long as it lasted, she would have Mike.

# *EPILOGUE*

"WILL YOU PUT sunscreen on my back?" Abby asked, twisting slightly from her position on her stomach to hold out the bottle of SPF 45.

"With pleasure." Clapping his hands together and giving them a rub, Mike climbed to his knees with a lascivious grin on his face. "This is my kind of mission."

As he straddled her hips and began rubbing the thick lotion into her skin, she rested her head on her folded arms, closed her eyes, and relaxed. Every once in a while, the firm, seductive strokes of his hands caused a moan of pleasure to roll its way up her throat.

This, she thought dreamily, might just be her favorite spot on Earth.

A year had passed since they'd first met, on this same beach, in this exact spot.

A year since they'd begun their whirlwind courtship and agreed, rather on the spur of the moment, to meet here twelve months later for a sort of unofficial anniversary of that day when she'd been making her way awkwardly through the sand, carrying everything but the hotel's kitchen sink, and he'd jogged to her rescue, helping her with her load and stealing her heart in the process.

Not counting the few hours of upset they'd experi-

enced after the blowup at his parents' house concerning his former girlfriend, they'd spent almost every minute of that last vacation together—sightseeing, making love, getting to know each other.

Climbing on a plane and flying back to Ohio had been one of the hardest things she'd ever had to do, and she remembered vividly standing at the gate, waiting for her flight to begin boarding, and clinging to him as if she would never let him go.

She'd managed not to burst into tears, but just barely, and only until she was out of his sight on the plane.

Thank God they'd agreed to keep in touch. Mike had flown back to California a couple of days later, when his leave ended, after which they'd both spent a good deal of time and money on phone calls, e-mails and the occasional cross-country weekend trip.

Those had been amazing, and worth every penny and every hour flying in cramped, noisy coach class.

This, though, was so much better. Two weeks of uninterrupted vacation, back where it had all begun. They were going to have to spend a lot more time with his parents than they had before, but that was okay—she was lucky enough to truly like her in-laws.

"All done," he announced, flopping back over to his side of the blanket. "Care you return the favor?"

She opened her eyes to find him wiggling his brows at her and dangling the sunscreen enticingly. Chuckling, she pushed herself up and climbed over him, using the delectable curve of his firm behind to sit on.

He gave a huff, pretending the weight of her straddling him was too much to bear. She happened to know

better, but added a pinch to her first application of lotion for good measure.

As she stroked and caressed, the small diamond on her left ring finger glittered in the bright Florida sun. Beneath it was a beautiful gold band that matched the one on Mike's left hand, exchanged only three months earlier at a small ceremony in the chapel at Camp Pendleton.

Having a husband who was career military man took a lot of getting used to. They were living on base, and Abby had found a job in the lab of a local pharmaceutical company that was very similar to the one she'd left back in Ohio. And she knew there could be frequent moves in her future as Mike's rotations came up. Months spent alone when he was deployed overseas— if she didn't go with him—or, God forbid, if he was sent into combat.

But nothing about her relationship with him had been normal or expected, so she would handle those situations the same as she had everything else since meeting him—enthusiastically and by rolling with the punches.

In fact, there was one rather major shake-up that she'd been waiting to spring on him. It might be her only chance to catch *him* off guard for a change, and she was quite looking forward to it.

"Mike," she said slowly.

"Hmm?"

He was as relaxed as he was going to get, his eyes closed, every muscle in his incredible body warm and loose beneath her fingers.

"You like being married, right?"

With a groan, he lifted his head and rolled over, grasping her hips to keep from dislodging her. Now she was straddling his front, which she knew must look much more suggestive than their previous position.

"You know I do," he answered, his clear gaze locking on hers while his thumbs danced back and forth over the bare expanse of her stomach just above the edge of her bikini bottoms.

She was wearing the same gold lamé suit as when they'd first met, since he'd declared it his "favorite" and made her promise never to get rid of it.

"And how do you think you'd feel about parenthood?" she asked casually.

He shrugged. "I'd be okay with it eventually, I suppose. When the time is right, after we're both settled and ready."

It wasn't exactly the ringing endorsement she'd been hoping for, but decided not to hold it against him.

"What about seven or eight months from now?" she pressed.

"That seems a little soon. Besides, it generally takes nine months once—"

He trailed off in midsentence, his eyes widening as the point of her question sank in.

"Wait a minute. Are you saying…" His eyes darted to her still flat abdomen, then back up to her face. "You mean… You're…"

Laughing, she leaned forward and gave him a quick, hard kiss. "I love seeing a big, brave Marine speechless for a change. And, yes, I am. I just found

out last week, but was waiting for the right time to tell you. Are you happy?"

His head bobbed up and down, his words still more garbled than clear. "Yeah, of course. I'm just... Wow. A baby. My folks are going to be over the moon."

"I know." She rolled her eyes and chuckled. "They've already been threatening to move closer to California, and I have a feeling this will get them out there within the year. Maybe I can rope them into baby-sitting for us."

"The problem won't be getting them to help out. It will be getting them to leave."

She started to laugh again, but he smothered the sound by covering her mouth with his own.

"I love this bikini," he said a few minutes later when they finally came up for air. "I love this beach. And I love you."

"I love you, too." She ran her hands over the ticklish top of his short-short black hair. "I also think we should come back here every year as an anniversary of sorts, even if it means dragging along a stroller, diaper bag, water wings...the works."

He reached up to tangle his fingers in the long strands of her hair, flipping some of it back over her shoulder and some forward to trail along his bare chest.

"Sounds like a plan to me," he murmured, drawing her down for another long, slow kiss. "Ooh-rah."

\* \* \* \*

*Look for Heidi's next book,* Christmas in His Royal Bed, *coming in December 2008 from Mills & Boon® Desire™!*

# Summertime Blues

## Kate Austin

For Mary Louise and Susan –
who happily spent time at the aquarium with me.

# CHAPTER ONE

*Weedy scorpionfish (Rhinopias aphanes):*
*Disguises itself as seaweed and*
*waves in the current, waiting*
*to snag any unsuspecting prey*
*that might float by*

Ardella wondered if brides or mothers-to-be felt this unbearable combination of sheer, unadulterated panic and mind-blowing joy. And if they did, she couldn't understand how so many of them managed to make it down the aisle or give birth without bolting.

She could barely walk. Her legs felt like limp spaghetti and her ankles and knees didn't want to support her. If she'd been behind the wheel of a car, she'd have killed someone. Nothing, not a single thing over the difficult years, had made Ardella feel this way.

She was a coper—she coped with illness, with bureaucracy, without her dreams. She could do anything. Really.

Except maybe not this.

Her heart pounded—a deep, almost painful thumping—in time with her footsteps on the pavement.

But all the stresses and strains of the past twenty years vanished in the joy of walking toward the *employee* entrance of the place that had been her true home for as long as she could remember.

The aquarium had saved her sanity—and maybe even her life—and now she was going to work here. She hurried down the path to the door and then stopped when she caught a glimpse of herself in the mirrored windows. She wore the aquarium's royal blue employee shirt with the logo—a white starfish and the name— over her left breast.

It wasn't quite warm enough for her white walking shorts—not in Vancouver at the very beginning of June—but Ardella had worn them anyway.

She'd imagined wearing these exact clothes, imagined herself striding through the back passages of the aquarium, mistress of all she surveyed.

And now here she was.

Starting at the bottom of the heap.

But one day soon Ardella Simpson was going to be a force to be reckoned with. Every single one of those fish, and the mammals for that matter, would listen to her.

Twenty years ago she'd been on her way to a degree in marine biology when her mother got ill. Twenty years of home nursing, of cooking and cleaning and ne- gotiating with health-care providers and Ardella had wondered—sometimes still did wonder—if she might not be too old or too tired to start all over again.

Not that forty was old, she thought. After all, didn't the magazines say that forty was the new thirty and surely thirty wasn't old?

This summer as a volunteer was a test.

She missed her mother, had never once begrudged the time or energy spent caring for her, never regretted giving up her dream, but now it was time to see if it was possible.

She sold the condo to pay their debts and her tuition. She'd packed up her mother's belongings and Ardella was on her way.

She wasn't sure whether she actually felt twenty again but that's what she was aiming for. Lighthearted yet committed to her future. Friendly and open instead of closed off. Willing to take risks.

That was going to be the hardest part of this experiment.

Ardella had spent the last twenty years—through no fault of her own—being extremely risk-averse. But if she wanted to become the woman she'd dreamed of being, she would have to take all kinds of risks. She squared her shoulders, smiled at the woman—in royal blue and white—reflected in the window and pressed the buzzer on the door. She was ready. At least she thought she was ready.

The flight instinct—once again—reared its ugly head, making her heart pound, her palms sweat and her face red. She took a step back from the door. And then another.

"Careful," a voice said behind her. "You're going to step on my brand-new sneakers.

"Not," the voice continued as if musing to herself, "that it really matters. They'll have fish guts and slime all over them within a week. It doesn't matter what de-

tergent I use, and I've used them all, nothing gets that slime out. I don't know why I bother, but I love the look and feel of new sneakers.

"I buy five or six pairs a year. Have to. It's not so hard on your clothes—they wash better. But the shoes? Two months, tops, and then they look like I've worn them for a two-week vacation on the seventh level of hell.

"I'm Marney. Marney Kenner. I've worked here forever. You know, narrate the shows, talk to the kids, make sure they don't fall into the water?"

Ardella, whose flight instinct had been suppressed by the outpouring of unrequested information, simply nodded, then feeling the nod not quite enough, said, "Yes. I've seen you, I think."

She paused for a minute, checking out her heart, palms and face. All normal. Maybe the flight instinct had vanished, maybe she was going to be okay. She still wavered between turning around and heading for the exit or talking to Marney so she could get herself to walk in the door. Ardella chose the latter.

"I'm Ardella Simpson."

"Your first day? I can tell by the look on your face, a lot nervous and a little excited. I remember—" Marney pushed open the door when the red light on the handle turned green "—my first day. I spent almost all of it trying not to puke."

"Have you worked here long?" Ardella felt a bit nauseous herself as she hurried through the back corridors after Marney who never, not even for a moment, stopped talking.

"Ten years this summer. I volunteered during high

school and college—my degree's in communications—
and just never left. There are lots of us like that. Not
many like you, though. Not first timers."

Ardella endured Marney's careful perusal of her.

"You're a little older—" Marney giggled "—than our
usual new recruits."

Ardella had to smile back at that carefully judged
*little*. She expected she was a whole lot older than the
rest of the new kids; she expected that *kids* was the op-
erative word.

"Lunchroom's over there. Showers—not that they
help, even with the soap we use, if you're spending your
days preparing breakfast, lunch and dinner for our in-
habitants. Helps even less if you add cleaning tanks to
your repertoire."

"Do you do that?" Ardella leaned forward a little and
sniffed. No fishy smell, just soap and shampoo.

"Not anymore. But I used to. My first couple of
summers? The only people who'd come near me were
the kids who were doing the same job. The only people
I talked to those summers were people at the aquarium.
I didn't have a date for two whole summers except
casual ones with the other volunteers, and those were
my prime dating years."

Ardella smiled to herself at the thought of a date. She
basically hadn't had a serious one for almost twenty
years. A slight exaggeration, maybe, but close to the
truth.

She'd had dozens of first dates but as soon as those
men found out that she might have to hurry home if her
pager went off, she might as well have been gone already.

Years of being on call twenty-four hours a day had put a dent not only in her dating but in her friends. Missing out on them because she smelled like fish seemed like a step forward rather than back.

"I think," Ardella said, taking a risk with her pride, "I'm going to be doing just that. Lowest of the low—cleaning tanks and preparing meals." She smiled, mostly to herself. "Not much different than what I've been doing. Just in a much more beautiful place."

Marney, towing her along behind, had just popped out of the windowless concrete corridors into the office space laid out above the aquarium's great hall.

Ardella stopped in her tracks. She'd been here for her interview but had been too nervous to enjoy the view. Besides, it had been gray and raining all those weeks ago.

Now the sky was the pure, clear blue of a early June day, a few white fluffy clouds adding texture to its beauty. The sun shot sparks off the belugas' pool and the tall cool green cedars in the background added depth.

*Home,* her heart said. *You're finally home.*

And when one of the belugas surfaced—and soon, Ardella promised herself, she'd know which one it was at first glance—its head tilted as if to say *hello.* Ardella, for only the second time in her life, fell in love.

# CHAPTER TWO

*Jellyfish (Cnidaria Scyphozoa):*
*Fish-eating animals that*
*float in the sea. They have soft*
*bodies and long, stinging, poisonous*
*tentacles that they use to catch fish.*
*A jellyfish is 98% water.*

The first time had been as a teenager. She'd grown up on the great plains of Saskatchewan—big blue bowl of a sky, winter and summer. The horizon so far away that most days it just vanished into the haze of forever. The prairies had no discretion; they exposed themselves to everyone.

Ardella grew up in a place where the bones of the land were right there to be seen, no mystery, no clothing. Beautiful, yes, and she still missed those crystal-clear nights, something unheard of in this city's clutter of light pollution.

She'd been thirteen when her mother brought her to the coast for a vacation. A summer holiday in Vancouver was a rite of passage in the small towns of the prairies, something to brag about for the following school year, and Ardella had planned to do just that.

They did the usual tourist things—Stanley Park, the ferry over to Vancouver Island, which mostly scared Ardella to death. She'd never imagined so much water all in one place.

They walked down Robson Street, marvelling at the shops and restaurants, but gawking at the number of people in one place, on one street, at one time. They'd picnicked on the beach at English Bay, even swam in the salty cool water, so different from the tiny lake back home.

And then it happened. On the day before they were to leave for home, Ardella fell in love.

"What do you want to do today, Della?" her mother asked. "We can take the gondola up to Grouse Mountain or we can go to the aquarium. Doesn't matter to me."

It didn't matter to Ardella, either, so they flipped a coin and the aquarium won.

Ardella still thought about how odd love was, still pondered the meaning of that coin toss. What if she'd gone to Grouse Mountain instead? Would she have spent all her life pining for something she couldn't define? Or would she have found something else to love?

Her mother never did. She'd married Frank Simpson on her twenty-first birthday. He died ten months later in a stupid accident—that's what her mother always called it.

But Sylvia loved Frank until the day she died, having lived more of her life loving him than not, having spent two years with him and almost sixty without.

Ardella supposed that her ability to sustain love without having its object around came to her naturally. She never did decide whether that was a good or a bad thing.

Yet she would never forget, or regret, that summer day in the July of her thirteenth year.

They drove through Stanley Park—as they'd done every single day of their trip—making goo-goo eyes at the trees, taller than any buildings they'd seen before this visit to the big city. They stopped, as always, to stare at the mountains overwhelming the water. They smiled at the lighthouse, the people on their wobbling bikes, the flowers and the fountain in the lagoon. They laughed at the big old farm horses hitched to a wagon of tourists and stopped to admire the police on their tall bays, the horses as calm and dignified as their riders.

Ardella had no indication that morning that her life was about to change forever, no warning at all. No magpies flying overhead, no black cats crossing her path, no ladders to walk under. They walked from the car park through the zoo to the entrance of the aquarium.

Looking up at the mountains on their way in, she even felt a pang of regret. "Maybe we should go up to Grouse Mountain," she said.

"We're here now, Della. Let's try it for half an hour and if we don't like it, we'll go up the mountain later."

The entrance to the aquarium held no sign of what lay within, it was simply a door with a seller of tickets, like a ticket booth at a movie house, Ardella thought at the time. The entrance to the aquarium was through the gift shop—interesting, maybe, but certainly not memorable.

But then it happened. They turned right out of the entrance hall, walked through a dark corridor into an even darker space and there it was.

Ardella's world.

Backlit tanks of brilliantly colored tropical fish swimming through forests of coral. Octopi clinging to the glass so only their round tentacles were visible. Seahorses standing as still as sentries. Green stickfish hiding among the waving water plants.

She couldn't tear herself away, not even for lunch. Her mother finally left her standing in front of a tank of almost translucent jellyfish, her nose pressed against the glass, mesmerized.

They were the last people to leave the aquarium that day, Ardella's arms piled with every brochure, every pamphlet, every piece of free information they had to offer, along with two books—the cheapest ones—and a souvenir that still sat on her dresser twenty-seven years later.

It was a dried starfish. Not very big, not much wider across than the palm of her hand, and the palest of golds. Even dried, Ardella could feel the texture of it, imagine it clinging to the rocky shore of the Pacific Ocean as it did in its tank.

She spent the next seven years preparing for university, preparing herself to spend a life with her first love.

Well, that life was a little—Ardella laughed at that so she wouldn't cry—delayed, but here she was.

Her first day working at the aquarium. She tried not to think about how her stomach responded to all this excitement, and thanked heaven she'd remembered to

buy, and wear, extra-strength deoderant. Not that the smell of her sweat was going to be noticed, not if what Marney had told her was true.

Ardella looked down at her pristine white shorts, socks and runners and shrugged. She'd happily smell like fish for the rest of her life. She'd happily give up dating—she, unlike Marney, wouldn't have the option of dating her fellow newbies—forever.

She didn't care. She was here, looking out over her new world.

It felt like a fairy tale, one with a very happy ending.

# CHAPTER THREE

*Arapaima (Arapaima gigas):*
*Largest scaled freshwater fish in the world.*
*Newly hatched fish take refuge*
*inside the adult's mouth.*

Ardella had completely forgotten about Marney standing next to her on the balcony, she'd forgotten about everything except her joy at finally being in this place. But she could already tell that Marney wasn't the kind of woman you could forget about for long.

"I'll drop you off at the director's office," Marney said. "She's a sweetheart and one of her favorite things is giving the whole orientation speech and tour. I think there are four or five new people starting today. Half of the summer students are going to be back again from last year but there are a few new ones.

"I'll just leave you here."

And off she went, leaving Ardella in a small waiting room with three babies. Okay, maybe they weren't babies but she'd be surprised if they were more than twenty—any one of them.

"Hi," she said, deciding that this was another test—of her lightheartedness and courage this time. "I'm Ardella."

"Joe," the tall lanky blond boy said. "I'm from New-foundland."

Ardella smiled. His provenance had been obvious the minute he opened his mouth.

"Terry," the tiny redhead offered. "I'm from here, just over the bridge, really."

"Nick," the dark boy in the corner said. "I'm from Winnipeg."

She smiled at all of them, imagining herself at their age, eager, excited, without a worry or concern. Just a whole summer full of fun to look forward to.

Maybe that's what Ardella should aim for, maybe this could be her vacation—the only one she'd had since—well, since forever.

She thought about that for a while. The trip to the coast when she was thirteen, then the rest of her high school summers working, saving for college. Then her mom got sick and since then? A few weekend trips when her mother was feeling well enough to travel, but never on a plane, never more than a few hours from home. Never far because it was too hard on her mother to be away from her doctors, her safety net, her home.

They'd moved to Vancouver after Ardella finished high school because her brother couldn't bear the cold winters of the prairies. The city had become their home—and the aquarium Ardella's refuge.

So right there and then, as soon as she got the letter telling her she had the job, Ardella decided that this summer would be her gift to herself, a vacation to make up for all the holidays she'd missed. And this was the perfect place for it.

She'd visit the tropics, the Queen Charlottes, the Arctic. She'd spend time in the jungle with the butterflies and the scarlet ibis and the caiman. She'd see exotic bugs and even more exotic fish.

It was her idea of the perfect vacation.

She thought she'd probably spend most of the next three months smiling and she couldn't wait to get started.

The door to the director's office opened and Ardella, along with the others, stood up to greet the woman who'd interviewed her.

Except that wasn't who appeared from behind the door marked *Denise Allen.*

"Hi," a laughing voice said. "I guess I'm not who you expected to see."

He sounded as if he were used to surprising people and looked as if it didn't matter a bit.

"I'm Greg Angus," he said, "the new co-director. Denise is spending most of the summer on various expeditions so I'll be your guide. And if you need anything at all—" he smiled around the room, his eyes lingering, Ardella thought with a flash of pique, on her "—my door is always open."

"Except this morning." Ardella opened her mouth and out it came, bringing a flush along with it. *That's it,* she thought, *antagonize the boss on your very first day.*

GREG ANGUS LAUGHED. "This isn't my door. I don't have a door." In fact, he wanted to point out to the woman who had to be Ardella Simpson, he'd never had an office door. He'd worked for the aquarium—volun-

teer and paid—for almost twenty years and he'd never had a door of his own.

Tents, yes. Hatchways, yes. Kayaks and canoes and icebreakers filled with equipment, but never a door.

But this year he'd been forced into it. The powers-that-be had spoken. "Greg, you've been in the field for twenty years, it's time for you to share some of that expertise with our staff and our visitors."

He'd said no, said it as many different ways as he could think of, but they won. So here he was, shepherding a crew of inexperienced, young—except for Ardella, which was how he'd already begun to think of her—volunteers. Shepherding them through tasks he knew nothing about.

He shook off the unhappiness he felt about being grounded and continued. "I don't close the door or the blinds, either." Would he tell them about why *he* was supervising and not Denise? *Hell,* he thought, *why not?*

"I've been grounded for this summer so I'm borrowing Denise's office for a few months while she's away. And then I'll be back out in the field." He hoped he wasn't lying—to them or to himself.

"I'm nosy and I'm social. I like to know what's going on and I like to talk. To everybody."

GREG ANGUS WAS NOT at all the kind of boss Ardella had expected, not at all who she anticipated spending her summer with. He scared her with his big, booming voice, his sunburned face and eyes—the green of the ocean on an October day—cradled in a network of laugh lines.

He scared her because in some ways he had the face

she'd always wanted for herself, a face radiating the confidence and skill she craved.

Denise would have been the perfect boss. She was a woman her age, who would understand Ardella's goals. Greg Angus was going to be much more difficult.

She tried to hide herself at the back of the pack of newbies, hoping he'd give up with his handshakes and his conversations before he got to her. No such luck.

"Ardella Simpson?"

"Yes," she said, stirring up her courage and holding out her shaking hand.

He grasped it, his hand big and warm and callused, its deep brown almost shocking against the winter paleness of hers.

"I'm glad you're here," he whispered. "The others are all so young." The laugh lines around his eyes wrinkled when he grinned at her. "And they're already tiring me out. And the biggest part of my job this summer…"

Ardella closed her eyes, hoping she was wrong about what he was going to say.

"Open your eyes," he said, patting the hand he still held clasped in his, "you don't want to miss anything, not after all these years."

Of course he'd read her résumé and the impassioned letter she'd sent along with it. Of course he knew every boring detail of her life to date. Things couldn't get any worse.

They did.

"The biggest part of my job this summer—" he

smiled right into her eyes "—is making sure that all of you work your asses off and learn everything you need to take to school with you.

"Come on," he said, grabbing her hand and towing her—in shock—after him. "It's time to take the tour."

Like Marney, Greg Angus was a talker. Ardella wondered if that was a result of working for too long on the water or in this amazing place, if it was a response to the deep silence of most of the creatures housed here. She wondered if her long silence was about to be broken and if her voice could cope with a sudden influx—or would it be outflux?—of speaking.

The tour took in the public areas—the Great Hall, the outdoor pools. The underground viewing areas, Clown-fish Cove, the childrens' section—and then it took in lunch.

One big table, outside on the patio next to the UpStream Café, sandwiches and salads and desserts waiting for them when they arrived.

"You won't get free food again," Greg Angus said, "but they've told me it's a tradition with brand-new volunteers so here." He gestured and swept an over-blown bow at the four of them, his eyes once again lin-gering—once again agitating her—on Ardella.

And then, to anger her even more, he obviously ma-neuvered the seating so *he* got to sit beside her. She, equally obviously, turned away from him to talk to the others and watch the crowds enjoying the aquarium and the early summer sun.

Greg made certain she was right with him during the whole tour, though Ardella gave him the benefit of the

doubt—he only wanted her to hear and see everything and he wasn't so solicitous because she was old. And old she felt with this group. Any one of them could have been a child of hers.

Except Greg, who was her age, maybe a few years younger. Or older. The deep tan and the lines of a man who'd worked outdoors most of his life made his age hard to peg with any accuracy.

The afternoon tour went deeper into the hitherto unseen parts of the aquarium, places Ardella had dreamed about for most of her life. Engineering, maintenance, the feeding stores—all of the nuts and bolts, the *real* life of the aquarium, the places visitors never saw.

The joy of being there, being a part of it, came close to overpowering her. She fought off the sting of tears half a dozen times, ignored the chill accompanying the goose bumps riding her spine.

She kept her eyes firmly on the sights and even more firmly off Greg Angus's face, tempting though it was.

Because she'd spent much of the time since she first saw him wondering how long it would take her to have a face like his. She wanted the deepwater tan, the lines carving his face like a paddle through the sea. She wanted the calmness he wore like a cloak. And, most especially, she wanted the knowledge, the bright sense of competence that shone from his eyes.

She could do without the inability to stop talking, but she wanted everything else.

# CHAPTER FOUR

*Giant Pacific Octopus*
*(Octopus dofleini):*
*Lives in caves in the rocky reefs*
*of the north Pacific coast. Comes out*
*at night to hunt prey of crabs and fishes.*

The first real day of her dream job. Ardella again arrived at the door with Marney right behind her and braced herself for the onslaught.

She'd gone home the night before, tired and excited and somehow even more frightened than she'd been before she started the job. But the hours of silence—no radio, no TV, she'd even turned off the phone though the chances of it ringing were slim to none—soothed her enough that here she was. Again.

"How was your first day?" Marney asked but didn't wait for an answer. "I remember that tour. Neither Denise nor Greg were here then so the Old Man took me around. I was the only summer student that year and I'd worshipped him forever. I was scared to death."

"Me, too." Ardella finally got a word in and took advantage of it. "I've imagined this day for so long and now that it's here, that I'm here? I'm not sure I can do it."

"Of course you can. I did. Hundreds of us since then have. And you've got experience—"

"Age, you mean," Ardella interrupted.

"No," Marney insisted. "I mean experience, life experience. When I got here I knew whatever I did—from cleaning a tank to dropping a bucket of fish on the Old Man's shoes—would change my life forever. Now I know it's not that serious, but I sweated every single decision I made that summer, worried that any move I made would mean life or death to me."

"And it didn't?" Ardella's question was at least half serious.

"Of course not and that's the big advantage you have over the others. You know if you drop a bucket of fish on Greg's feet, it won't change your life forever."

"It won't?"

But this time Ardella knew exactly what Marney meant. Decisions could be changed—one could quit a job, divorce a husband, sell a house or cancel a vacation. Changing these decisions might have a cost, but they could be changed. Decisions had to be made but they didn't always have to be stuck to.

And any decision was often better than no decision at all. At least that way you felt at least partly in control of your life.

The same thing was true with mistakes.

Marney dumping a bucket of fish on the Old Man's shoes was a mistake she'd obviously overcome. Ardella took heart from that thought—if she made a mistake, she'd get over it or past it or around it. Somehow.

"You're right," Ardella finally admitted to Marney.

And to herself. "When I was twenty I believed every-thing—from what shirt to wear or whether to get my hair cut—was of the absolute importance, so much so that at times I was paralyzed, couldn't make any decision at all."

"I remember once," Marney laughed, "when I can-celled a date with a boy I wanted so badly I dreamed of him every night for a year."

"Why?"

"Because I couldn't decide whether to wear a bra or not. Would it be too obvious if I didn't? Too awkward if I did? Stupid. But that kind of thing happened to me all the time back then."

"Me, too. But it won't happen to me now." Ardella crossed her fingers behind her back for luck and pushed open the door into her brand-new kingdom.

The smell already seemed familiar to her, as if she'd spent years of her life living with it in her nostrils, as if her brain welcomed it. The aromas rested at the back of her tongue, a little less obvious than their scent in her nose, but she tasted them.

The rich saltiness of the ocean, distilled down in the tanks to its essence. Wet concrete, reminiscent of summer rain on asphalt after a long dry spell. Brine and fish. You couldn't smell the live ones, but the scent of the feed overlay everything in the working tunnels of the aquarium. From the tiniest of shrimp to pieces of thirty-pound salmon, the smell of fish was everywhere.

And then there was the smell of the lush tropical greenery, faint under the stronger aromas. It blew in

whenever the door into the Amazon rain forest opened
or shut.

Ardella inhaled it as if it were life to her and she
thought it might be, this particular combination of
scents and flavors.

Then there was the light, filtered through glass, reflected off water, rippling through the air, turning it
into something she could almost touch.

Ardella's heart pounded in her chest, an unman-
ageable grin on her face. She was here and today she
was going to work.

And she did.

She learned how to filet fish, to weigh shrimp, to read
the feeding schedules and lists. She learned how to shift
fifty-pound buckets from trucks to freezers. She learned
how to use her shoulder to scratch her nose after half a
dozen times of smearing fish guts on her face and
sneezing scales for an hour afterward.

She learned that her body contained muscles she'd
never used before and she learned that blisters could
and did reform in places where they'd only just burst.

She learned that while white shorts and running
shoes were standard garb, they didn't last long at this
job and she resolved to buy a dozen pairs of shorts—
the five pairs she bought before she started work would
never see her through the summer.

She learned that Terry and Joe and Nick were funny
and cheerful enough that she could—at least temporarily—ignore the blisters and aching muscles and she
learned that even hidden in the dungeons—Joe's term—
Ardella could think of nowhere else she'd rather be.

The day, and the ones following it, passed so quickly she could barely keep track. She knew when Fridays came because the four of them—usually accompanied by Marney and occasionally by Greg Angus—treated themselves to fish and chips and a beer or two at Lumberman's Arch.

GREG ANGUS WORKED very hard at that *occasionally*. He didn't want to scare Ardella, didn't want her to know how quickly he'd fallen for her. He'd seen her standing with the other volunteers and the look on her face reeled him in, hook, line and sinker.

He'd gone home that night and couldn't remember what color her hair was, or her eyes, but the look on her face? It killed him. She looked excited and scared and nervous all at once. And on top of all those emotions rolling over her face in waves, one emotion stood out. Greg recognized it because he'd felt it himself the day he started work at the aquarium. Love.

And for the first time in months, for the first time since they'd forced him away from the ocean, he felt grateful to be on dry land.

Ardella had to know he was interested, how could she not? No matter what he was doing, no matter what she was doing, he made sure to run into her every couple of hours. He laughed at his strategy. He used all the skills he'd learned working with dolphins and sea lions in the wild. He wanted her accustomed to his presence before he moved in, before he got close enough to study her, to get to know her.

At first, she acted just as the sea creatures did, turning

away when he showed up, but as she got used to his presence, she began to look forward to visits. Sometimes she even talked to him.

But Greg Angus hadn't spent twenty years with wild creatures for nothing. He knew exactly how often to show up, when he needed to back off, when she was uncomfortable with his presence, and when he needed to push—just a little.

Fish and chips at Lumberman's Arch was a perfect example. She seemed to be fine with him showing up *occasionally* but she wasn't ready to see him every Friday night. That would be too much like a date. And she wasn't ready for that. He could tell.

ARDELLA LOVED Friday nights, especially the ones when Greg Angus wasn't around to make her uncomfortable in her own skin. It didn't matter if it was sunny—they ate on a blanket on the grass—or raining—they huddled at one of the few picnic tables under the sloped roof of the fish and chips shop. The fish and chips and the beer were their treat for making it through the week.

It was the only time she left her apartment except to go to work. She even ordered her groceries online and had them delivered. She was just too tired—and too smelly—for anything else.

And showers didn't help at all. She'd come home on Friday nights, thanking her landlord for having those monstrous hot water tanks in the basement. By Sunday night, she could almost bear herself, but the rest of the time she had to force herself into the shower.

The heat and humidity pulled the fish smell out of her pores until she felt as if she were standing in a pile of three-day-old dead fish. Breathing through her mouth helped only a little.

If she couldn't bear the smell, no one else should have to.

She wondered about Marney and Greg who, not spending their days in the dungeons slinging fish, weren't quite as aromatic as the four volunteers, but decided in the end that they'd lived with it so long they were used to it. She saw no hint of disgust on either of their faces.

Joe, though, didn't worry about the smell at all.

"My wife—" Ardella had been shocked the first time he said those two words, thinking him far too young to be married "—my wife," he'd said, a smile lighting his face, "grew up in a fishing village. The smell doesn't bother her, not a bit."

Ardella envied him having someone besides a goldfish to talk to. Even when she was very sick, her mother had been a talker. She talked about the books she'd read, the TV program she'd watched, the radio interview she'd heard in the middle of the night. Ardella missed that running commentary on life.

But the aquarium and—as much as hated to admit it—Greg Angus helped make up for the silence of her apartment.

## CHAPTER FIVE

*Belugas or Arctic white whales*
*(Delphinapterus leucas):*
*Small flippers and tail flukes*
*help them stay warm in*
*cold Arctic waters.*

The long summer days rolled into each other and Ardella settled into her new home. Her muscles still ached at the end of the day but now a long shower was enough to soothe the worst of it.

A good night's sleep on her clean linens completed the rehabilitation.

Ardella couldn't remember ever enjoying the mornings so much. She'd thought of herself as a night person, watching the late late show and dragging herself out of bed around ten or ten-thirty and then taking another hour to be human.

But that was no longer true.

She jumped out of bed at six, showered, cooked bacon and eggs and hash browns—she'd had to learn how to make breakfast because she was sure she'd never done it before. She and her mother always planned lunch as the first meal of the day.

Ardella wondered how much of her behavior—behavior she'd always considered as much a part of her as the color of her eyes—was really *her's* and not her mother's.

She guessed this summer would go a long way toward finding out.

When her mother had finally—after twenty years of coping with her illness—given up the struggle, it had taken Ardella months before she'd changed a single thing.

*Mourning,* Ardella thought of those months. The Victorians had the right idea, forcing survivors to take the time to get over their loss before moving on with their life. Because those months of sameness had worked for Ardella.

One day, almost eight months after her mother had died, she woke up. Not in the morning but in the middle of the afternoon. Not in bed but out in the world. She woke up as if she'd spent the last months in some sort of dream state.

She was walking along the Seawall when she looked up and saw her future. It came to her in a roar, an almost unbearably intense cascade of desires and thoughts and plans.

She'd walked halfway around the park—and far past her usual turning-around point—before she'd sorted it all out.

She walked and the sky was bluer, the air more exhilarating, the water more inviting. She took off her shoes and socks to walk on the beach, to stand at the water's edge and feel the rough sand scraped away beneath her feet by the power of the ocean.

Ardella ignored the risk to her clothing and sat on a damp log while she planned her life, not noticing the cold or hearing the voices of the people walking or running or cycling the Seawall behind her.

The planning didn't take long because it was all there, as if it had been percolating for the previous eight months and was now brewed to perfection.

She knew what she would do, how and when she would do it. She could see—for the first time since she was a teenager—what she wanted her life to be and how she was going to get there.

She'd sell the condo, pay off all the bills and still have a nest egg, albeit a very small one. She'd rent an apartment downtown, close to buses for school and close to the aquarium for everything else.

She'd work at the aquarium in the summers and maybe at term breaks—she'd use her nest egg to live on, for books and tuition, to get to her dream job.

She'd get her degree in marine biology and then she'd work full-time at the aquarium for the rest of her life.

Ardella sat on a log that cool winter day and saw the rest of her life spread out before her, just as the ocean filled the world in front of her, right to the horizon. Sure it might be rough at times—storms and rain and wind—but the ocean was big enough to roll right over those things and so was she.

She was prepared to do whatever it might take to live her postponed life, work as hard as necessary, sleep as little as required, study harder than every other student.

This was her chance, her shot, and she would do whatever it took to make her dream come true.

There was just one little problem.

# CHAPTER SIX

*Sea otters (Enhydra lutris):*
*Have thick fur to keep them warm*
*instead of fat or blubber. They*
*spend a lot of time floating*
*at the surface grooming their fur*
*or sleeping.*

Ardella's years so far had ill-prepared her for a social life, even the limited kind of one involved in a job where she worked mostly with three kids young enough to be her sons and daughter.

Applying for a place at university was simple in comparison, though the requisite interview—needed if she applied as a mature student—was the tiniest bit hair-raising. But it was nowhere near as tough as her first few weeks at the aquarium had been.

Every morning she had to convince herself to walk up to the door. Every morning she had to fight her in-grained shyness to carry on conversations with her co-workers. Every morning she had to resist the urge to quit, to walk up out of the dungeons and into Greg Angus's office.

Every time she saw him she'd been tempted to say,

"I can't do this," and every time she resisted the temptation. She'd also been tempted to say, "What are you doing after work?" but she resisted that as well.

And now, weeks into the summer, she no longer thought of quitting, no longer had to work to talk to even complete strangers, no longer struggled with shyness.

In fact, she thought with a grin, if I keep this up, I'll soon rival Marney or Greg in the talking department. Soon *they* won't be able to get a word in edgewise.

Because the real Ardella had shown up, shining through the facade, the wall of double-wide bricks and dense mortar, that had built up over those twenty lonely years. The real Ardella was a whole new person.

Or maybe a new and improved version of the person she'd almost been at twenty. A person tempered through sorrow and caring and hard, sad work.

Take this week, for example.

She'd spent her first weeks at the aquarium in the kitchen, named so, once again, by Joe, who'd shared her duty. Though the aquarium called it the fish house, the four of them ignored the others and called it the kitchen. It took Joe and Ardella six hours every day to prepare the food for all the creatures in this huge space.

Then it took them many more hours each week to offload the supplies that made their continuous way to the loading ramp. Running the aquarium was a much bigger and more complicated job than Ardella had imagined.

But today was celebration day.

This Monday she and Joe would switch jobs with Nick and Terry. They would move further up in the tunnels and begin the round of cleaning and refilling the

tanks. There was an ongoing schedule, ensuring that every tank, every pool, every rock and piece of glass got cleaned regularly.

Ardella could hardly wait. Even with the extra hours she put in on the weekends watching the sea otters or seals or belugas in their outdoor pools, she missed the dazzling light that seemed visible only in the aquarium. Now she'd get to spend almost all her day as part of the light she'd fallen in love with.

GREG HAD BEEN DELIGHTED when it became time to switch the volunteer duties. Now he wouldn't have to search out Ardella in the back alleys and dungeons of the building. She'd be visible all the time. Much easier to find her in the upper part of the building, much less obvious when he showed up at her side.

He'd found her, as he often did, leaning over the sea otter pool, the sun lighting up her hair, her grin as big as the Pacific.

He couldn't blame her. No matter how unhappy or worried he was, watching the otters made him smile. They played with each other, played *to* the audience, played with their food, just like seagoing puppies. Or babies. Everyone loved them.

Especially Ardella.

"Hey," he said, warning her of his arrival.

"Hey, yourself," she said, without turning her head away from the pool.

Greg surprised himself. He'd come out to see her face, talk to her about her new job, but found himself talking about something he never spoke about.

"It's my mom's birthday today," he said. "I miss her, you know, all the time."

"How long?" Ardella's voice was as steady as his was not.

"Since forever. I was almost nineteen. Now there's just me and my brother, Bobby. My dad lives in England, moved there right after Mom died. We never see him."

"Where does Bobby live?"

Greg shook off the lingering sorrow and smiled at the interest in her voice. "He's a vagabond, a musician. He travels all over, looking for the next gig. No money in it, but he's happy. So between me being somewhere on the ocean and him being wherever it is he's interested in this year, we don't see much of each other. But we talk a lot, use e-mail and phone calls."

"It's nice to have family."

"You don't have any?"

"No, just my mom and she's gone now."

He watched as she wiped a tear from her eye and then turned to face him. The smile on her face…God, he wasn't sure he could stop himself. But he did.

"Tell me about your brother."

"I'll do even better," he said, once again surprised at himself. "I'll bring him with me on Friday night."

## CHAPTER SEVEN

*Black ghost knifefish*
*(Apteronotus albifrons):*
*A jet-black eel-like fish,*
*it can swim backwards and*
*forwards. Some believe these*
*fish hold the souls of their ancestors.*

Being in the light was great, though there were days…

Days when every time she turned around, she found Greg Angus. Days when he forced her to talk to him—about her life, about her dreams, even about her mother. The one thing she didn't talk about.

And then he talked to her—and she wanted to hear him. This was not going well. Or it was going too well. She wasn't sure which.

She had a pat answer for any questions about why she was going back to school at forty. "I've been busy," she'd say, "but mostly," with a grin that fooled almost everyone, "I've just figured out what I want to be when I grow up."

That made everyone who asked that question laugh and they let her go. They didn't just let her go, they

grinned back at her. Ardella was used to that response, she'd come to expect it.

So when she tried the line on Greg Angus she knew exactly what he'd do. He'd grin that big gorgeous grin of his and he'd laugh that belly laugh and then walk away.

Except he didn't.

"I read your application, remember? I know why you're doing this now and I really respect that. Most people—" he paused for a minute as if remembering something he didn't like "—don't have the courage to start something this late in life. Most people—" he paused again, looking down at the Steller sea lions in the pool in front of them "—just give up."

Ardella wasn't sure what to say to that. So she reached out and touched the back of his hand. He looked up from his contemplation of the sea lions and shook his head, slightly. Ardella recognized that gesture, having often made it herself. She needed to remember that Greg Angus wasn't only the happy guy she'd seen at work, that he, too, had a past, a complicated one.

She turned his hand over and tucked it into hers, squeezing it for reassurance. And she wasn't sure whether the reassurance was for her or for Greg. *Maybe both,* she thought.

SHE'D FINALLY DONE IT, finally begun to see him as a man and not just another problem she had to solve to get to her goal. He'd been waiting weeks for that touch and now that it had happened, Greg had absolutely no idea what to do about it.

He was pretty sure Ardella didn't know what it

meant, but he did. And he'd played out all kinds of scenarios for what he'd do when she finally touched him.

None of them were going to work. He was just going to have to go with his instincts. And Greg Angus had great instincts.

He tugged on her hand to pull her a little closer, not close enough to scare her, just near enough that he could feel the warmth from her body, smell the scent of her.

And then he took a big risk. He took the hand she'd given him and raised it to his lips.

"Thank you," he said. And kissed it again, savoring the taste of her.

He started counting—one, two, three. He figured he'd get to ten before she pulled away, but he was wrong again. Ardella Simpson was ignoring all of his plans. He made it as far as five, enjoying the blush on her cheeks and the warmth of her skin on his lips, before she moved back, taking her hand and her warmth with her.

And then she ran. Right across the courtyard and—he guessed—right down to the fish house.

He grinned. She didn't know it, but today's touch was just the beginning.

# CHAPTER EIGHT

*Steller sea lions (Eumetopias jubatus):*
*Highly gregarious, they spend time*
*on rock shelves, ledges, boulders*
*and beaches for resting and breeding.*
*They eat about six percent of their*
*body weight every day.*

Greg Angus had kissed her hand as if he didn't even notice the smell. And she'd bet he didn't. He'd spent all his life around sea creatures—he probably liked her aroma.

This job gave her an excuse to indulge her favorite passion—baths. She bought cinnamon scented candles and placed them around the tub and then picked bars of soap from the baskets.

She laughed and thought of her bathroom counters piled high with baskets full of soap. Sweet soap. Glycerin soap. Soap made specially for mechanics. Soap with granules of some harsh substance to get grease off. Soap with deep-cleaning properties. Goat's milk soap. Honey soap. At least one bar of every single brand of soap sold at her local drugstore.

Once she'd picked the soap—or soaps—of the day, she turned off the light, turned on the CD player—usually Bach or some kind of new age water music—and lay back in the water, dreaming of Greg Angus. Okay, okay, she had to admit it, when he told her about his mother and his brother Bobby, she'd fallen. She'd been hanging on by her fingernails up until then, but now? She was in love.

She shrugged her shoulders, rolling them backward and forward to eliminate the tension she felt just thinking those words. It didn't mean that she had to do anything about it, did it? It didn't mean she'd have to give up her first love for her second, did it?

Ardella had planned her life so carefully, so perfectly. She wrote it down, she put a copy of the list on her fridge, on her bathroom mirror, inside her locker at work. Affirmations. Proof she would make it.

Volunteer at the aquarium.

School.

Study.

Full-time employee of the aquarium.

Happy.

No relationship in that plan, especially not a relationship with the *co-director*. That would be a very bad idea.

Ardella had reheated the bath water half a dozen times before she made a decision. She would stick to her plan, to her first love. She'd be fine without Greg Angus, she'd been fine without a man this far, she could do it. Really.

SHE RAN INTO Marney on Monday morning as she hurried down to the security door—Marney running

because, as usual, she was fifteen minutes behind schedule.

"Hmm, let's see," she said. "I smell apple and jasmine." She leaned in closer and took a whiff. "Is that Ivory soap?"

Ardella nodded, embarrassed.

"And Chanel No. 5 soap? Where did you get the money for that?"

"I didn't buy it. Mom gave it to me for Christmas years ago. I just hadn't used it before."

"Okay, and then there's some kind of drugstore brand for men, right? Irish Spring or something like that?"

"I admit it. Last night I took half a dozen bars of soap into the bath with me and I used all of them."

"And bubble bath? I used to try all kinds of bubble baths. From the cheapest ones in the drugstore to the expensive ones from Holt Renfrew. None of them ever worked."

"No bubble bath, not last night. I took the soaps, cut them up into tiny slices—I'm getting really good at that—and then put them under the spray. Lots and lots and lots of bubbles.

"And then I bundled up all the leftovers into a single bar and used that this morning."

Marney laughed. "You're much more ingenious than me, though—" she leaned in to smell her again "—you don't smell much better."

Ardella loved the smell of her bathroom in that moment before she turned on the shower, when all the aromas were still distinct, and then she loved it even

more when they all mushed together into something new and precisely *Ardella*.

And despite the perfume and her determination to go with her first love instead of Greg, he still followed her around. She often found him waiting for her at the summer students' table at lunchtime or trolling the dungeons for her in the middle of the afternoon.

She wasn't sure what to make of him, of his obvious interest in her, except to suppose it was that she was practically the only person in the entire place who was close to his age. There were a few administrative people who had probably been there for a while, a few of the senior staff who were his age, but she was the one he followed.

She couldn't be falling in love with him. That would ruin everything.

Ardella had her life mapped out and she wasn't interested in taking any more detours. The route was all laid out, day by day, year by year, and nothing was going to interfere this time.

Not even Greg Angus.

GREG COULDN'T HELP HIMSELF. Every morning he got out of bed and spoke to his rumpled self in the bathroom mirror.

"You have to stop following her," he said. "It doesn't matter that she used to talk to you. She doesn't anymore."

He scraped the hair from his chin, puffed out his cheeks and spoke around the puffs. "And she has a plan." The crease between his eyebrows—the one that meant *huh?*—deepened. "How do I know that? Because she talks about it every single day.

"Because she spends every single spare minute and at least one day every weekend following the aquarists around. We've never had a volunteer who's more committed to her job than Ardella. *That's* how I know she has a plan."

She hadn't talked to him about it. She hardly spoke to him at all anymore. She smiled at him but she *spoke* to the other volunteers, just not when he was in the group. Occasionally, and he cringed at the thought of his foolishness, he sat at the table behind the volunteers, his back to Ardella and he listened to their conversations.

He knew, and not just from the résumé he'd pulled from her file, that she was going to university in the fall. He knew that she'd wanted to be a marine biologist since she was a teenager, for most of her life.

He understood that desire. He'd never wanted anything else. Or anything more. Until he met Ardella Simpson.

He knew as much about her as it was possible to know until he somehow convinced her to talk to him. He knew she lived in a tiny, relatively cheap—in Vancouver there were no cheap rents—apartment so she could spend the summer working at the aquarium for nothing, knew she hoarded every penny in her savings account so it would get her through four years of school.

But they had a connection. He knew it. He knew too much about her not to realize that she'd backed off once she saw that connection.

He knew she liked burgers, loved fries with salt and vinegar, drank beer from the bottle. She smelled like all

the perfumes of Araby—Greg laughed at that image because he was sure that when he'd started volunteering at the aquarium he'd probably smelled exactly the same way—on Monday mornings.

The rest of the time she smelled like home to him. She smelled like the ocean.

# CHAPTER NINE

*Brooding anenome (Epiactis prolifera):*
*These long-lived flowerlike creatures are*
*predators. They have no skeletons, live attached*
*to sea floor, rock or coral but can*
*slide around very slowly.*

The next few weeks passed so quickly Ardella was as-tonished when she looked up from her book one Saturday night to find it would soon be August and her stint at the aquarium was winding its way down to the end.

After the incident—she couldn't think of anything else to call it—at the sea lion pool, Ardella had backed off even further from Greg. She gave up the Friday-night fish and chips because he was always there. She stopped eating lunch in the courtyard and took her lunch out of the aquarium and onto the grass opposite the pools.

It slowed him down a little, she thought, though it didn't exactly stop him. He had an uncanny ability to find her, no matter what tank or pool she was cleaning.

She'd be hidden in the back of the Treasures of the

BC Coast and he'd walk by. Or she'd be hiding out in the kitchen and he'd find her there. She wondered if he'd put a secret transmitter in her sneakers or something, but seeing as she had to change them every few weeks, that probably wasn't it.

Even when she went down into Clownfish Cove, braving the screams and giggles of the dozens of kids who loved the place, he wandered in. He smiled at all the children, bending down to answer their questions, often getting caught up in some game they were playing.

He was like a big kid himself.

And she felt that big kid right behind her. He'd followed her out of the aquarium and into the shade of the huge cedar she'd chosen as her lunchtime retreat.

She wasn't safe from him even out of the aquarium.

But when he sprawled on the grass beside her and grinned, she smiled back at him and passed him the cardboard container of fries.

"I know, I know, there's probably too much salt and vinegar on them."

"Nope, never too much for me," he said, and proceeded to eat the whole top layer of fries, the ones with the most salt, most vinegar, the best ones.

"You could at least pretend you didn't want them," Ardella said. "I bought them for myself."

"I'll buy you some more, I promise. But it's been a rough week and I need the sustenance."

The dark circles around his eyes matched the black T-shirt he wore. Ardella hadn't seen much of him—at least in the daylight—in the past week what with hiding

out in the dungeons. And when he did find her, it was pretty dark back there and she ran as soon as she could.

"Everything okay?" she said against her better judgment. She shouldn't be talking to him, he was just too tempting.

"Hmm," he said, "delicious," licking the salt and vinegar from his fingers.

Her eyes followed the fingers and then darted away. "I mean other than the fries." She wanted to add the words *you idiot* but restrained herself, not because he was the co-director, but because it was too personal.

She'd spent her grown-up life with an ill mother and not many other people. Teasing was something she was still working on and she'd still only managed it with a few people. Marney, Joe, Terry, Nick. They were it.

So she quelled the impulse to do it with Greg and waited to see if he'd answer her. If not, she'd pick up her blanket and head back to work.

"Busy," he said, sprawling back on the grass, his arms over his face.

"Nope, it's not just that. You *like* to be busy."

"Could I ask you not to ask?"

"You could, but I won't listen. You could tell me that you don't want to talk about it."

A smile appeared from beneath his crossed arms. "I could, but the trouble is I do want to talk. To you. And if this is my only choice…"

She interrupted him. "It is." Ardella thought about running and then thought, *what the hell.* "Come on, Greg, tell me what's up. You look terrible."

He sat up and rubbed his fingers through his hair.

Now instead of a serious co-director, he looked like a little boy who'd been caught in a hedge while playing tag.

She reached out to smooth down the wayward hair, but stopped herself just in time. She remembered how it felt the last time she touched Greg Angus. Better not to try it again.

"Is it work?"

Ardella didn't have all day. Even if she was out here playing *tell me if you can* with the co-director, she still had a whole pile of things on her schedule before the end of the day.

"Not work."

"Okay, that's enough. I don't have time to drag this out of you. You want to talk to me, try saying more than two words at a time. I have to get back to work in—" she looked at her watch "—half an hour. Get your mouth in gear and tell me the damned problem."

HE SAT UP, crossed his legs, settled his forearms on his thighs and squared his shoulders. This wasn't going to be easy. Social he might appear, but he was a pretty reserved kind of guy about stuff that really mattered.

"You know about my brother Bobby. He's ten years younger than me and I practically brought him up after Mom died. Menopause baby, I guess. Mom called him her miracle baby."

Ardella nodded encouragement when he slowed down. "And?"

"He's sick. And they can't figure out what it is. Some kind of virus, they say. But he just keeps getting weaker

and weaker. He's on super-strength drugs, getting fed through a tube, and he's still losing weight. I swear, Ardella, he's lost twenty pounds this week alone."

She reached out her hand and rested it on his arm. "What are they doing next?"

"They've sent samples to be tested. They think it's some kind of African virus, but they have no idea how to treat it. And there's nothing I can do."

There was the crux of it, he thought. He couldn't help his baby brother and he'd always looked out for him. Always. That had been his job since the day Bobby was born.

He tucked Ardella's hand into his and felt comforted by the warmth of it. He felt the calluses she'd acquired over the past couple of months, the deep indentations growing on her soft skin from immersion in salt water, from cutting up herring and squid and mackerel.

In lots of ways, he missed the last time he'd worked on dry land, when he'd worked on the floor of the aquarium instead of in the executive offices. He missed the daily contact with the kids, missed the feel of the water on his hands, missed… Well, he missed a lot of it.

But most of all, right now, he was sick to death with worry about Bobby.

"That's why I haven't seen much of you this week," Ardella said, her voice low and sweet. "You've been at the hospital."

"Yes."

"Why don't you go now? Meet me at the bar in the Sylvia at seven o'clock, I'll buy you a drink and you can tell me how he is today."

ARDELLA COULDN'T BELIEVE she'd offered to buy him a drink but it was too late to take it back. And the look on Greg's face was worth whatever qualms she'd suffer until seven o'clock.

He looked as if she'd given him a gift. And she guessed that maybe she had.

# CHAPTER TEN

*Reid's seahorse (Hippocampus reidi):*
*These small fish have armored plates*
*(not scales). The female seahorse*
*produces eggs but they are held*
*inside the male's body until they hatch.*
*This is the only animal in which the*
*father is pregnant.*

Ardella ran into Marney on her way back down to the dungeon, literally ran into her.

"Oh, God, sorry. I'm just not paying attention."

"Obviously not." Marney laughed. "And why is that?"

Marney had spent a fair amount of time over the past couple of months teasing her about what she called "Greg's obvious crush." And Marney knew everything Ardella did, in or out of work. She just *knew*.

Two weeks into her new job, Ardella had begun to wonder whether Marney had ESP or some sort of highly trained spy network. Because she knew *everything*.

She knew Ardella never went out, except occasion-

ally to buy new kinds of soap. She knew Joe and
Kathleen spent every weekend at Kathleen's parents'
house in the valley. That was one thing, but she also
knew that Joe and Kathleen were trying to get pregnant.
Ardella hadn't known that, and she spent hours a day
with Joe.

She knew that Nick and Terry were dating, but that
it wasn't serious, both of them too wrapped up in their
careers to get involved at this stage of their life.

"Who do you think is going to be happier?"
Marney asked her.

"Who are you talking about?"

"You know. Nick and Terry totally focused on their
careers and ignoring the fact that they really care about
each other. Or Joe and Kathleen. Yeah, they're keen on
their careers but they're making a family."

Ardella didn't really want to answer that question
because she didn't know the answer. She'd started the
summer with one thing in mind—working for the rest
of her life at the aquarium. Sure, she had to go university to do that, but it was all about the aquarium for her.

The summer hadn't changed her mind about that, but
she had realized a few weeks ago that work wasn't the
only thing she was thinking about.

Damn that Greg Angus, getting into her head like
that.

"Ardella? What's going on in that complicated brain
of yours? You thinking about Greg?"

Ardella shook her head and ignored those questions,
forced by her own distraction to answer the first one.

"I don't know about Nick and Terry, but you only

have to look at Joe and Kathleen to see how happy they are. I mean, they don't have any money, they're both going to school and working two jobs, they must be exhausted all the time, yet they light up when they see each other."

"They do, don't they? I'm just worried that Nick and Terry are too focused on the future to be enjoying the present. I loved being twenty—and I don't want them to miss all that fun."

Ardella waited for the punch line. Marney wasn't just talking about the kids, she was talking about Ardella. She didn't wait long.

"You, too."

"Me, too, what?" Ardella didn't really think that it would stop Marney but it couldn't hurt to try. Even though nothing ever stopped Marney once she was on a roll.

She hurried down the back corridor. Maybe going right back into the tank would stop her? No; not even a good try.

Marney stood just barely inside the tank—making sure she didn't touch anything and not because she didn't want to mess up the tank but because she didn't want to mess up her white shorts and brand-new sneakers. Ardella threw her best get-over-yourself look at her.

Marney replied with, "Hey, don't get snarky about my fastidiousness. That's the reason I have a new car. I just put all that money away that I'd spend on shorts and sneakers if I weren't careful and voila. Brand-new bright red Toyota Prius."

Ardella grinned and threw a damp sponge her way,

making sure to miss her by a couple of feet. "Yeah, yeah, yeah. Quit gloating, okay?"

"It's almost the end of the summer," Marney said out of nowhere. "Pretty soon your clothes will stay clean and you'll smell nice all week instead of just on Sunday nights."

"I'm trying not to think about that." Ardella's mouth opened and the words popped out before she could stop them.

Marney didn't need any help coming to conclusions. She was the queen of jumping to them and she'd long ago jumped to the Greg and Ardella conclusion.

"It's not about anything except that I'm going to miss this place."

Ardella looked around at the empty tank, at the piles of stones and other accoutrements just outside the entrance. She stared out the front wall of the tank at the pale light of the Tropic Zone, knowing she'd miss this moment for months.

"I'm meeting him for a drink tonight," she finally said. "I don't know if it's a good idea or not."

"He asked you?" Marney's disbelief was almost insulting.

Ardella sniffed. "I asked him."

"Oh," Marney said. "Oh, I see."

Ardella sniffed again. "You do? Because I don't. It was a stupid idea, even if I did it for a good cause."

"Look," Marney said, stepping firmly into the tank, "it's obvious the two of you are crazy about each other. He follows you around, you watch for him every minute of the day. What can it hurt if you go on a few dates?"

"But my plan—"

"Plans can be changed."

Ardella had been forced to change her plans once and she didn't know if she could do it again. A little shift one way or the other might be okay, but Greg Angus would be a quantum leap, not some little, easily assimilated shift in her lifetime plan.

She had enough to worry about.

She still didn't know whether she'd be able to come back for a few hours a week while she was going to school. It wasn't going to be easy but she'd put in her request and was waiting—waiting for Greg to make a decision about it.

He'd already told Joe and Terry that they could work as many hours as they wanted during the school year, except Terry didn't want to and Joe wasn't sure what he was going to do, but Greg hadn't said anything to her.

Working as a volunteer at the aquarium was the thing that was going to keep her sane during the school year. She wasn't any too keen on being in a classroom with a whole bunch of eighteen-year-olds.

"You're going to miss us," Marney sang from the side of the tank where she'd retreated as soon as she'd made her point, her voice echoing around the glass. "You're going to miss me."

"I am going to miss you."

"Has Greg told you whether you can work weekends in September?"

"Nope. But he's told Joe and Terry that they can so I bet he's going to say no to me."

"But they don't want to work during the school year. I think he's just worried that it's going to be too much. You have to make at least a little money, don't you?"

"I redid my budget this weekend. If I cut back on everything—" she grinned over at Marney's gleaming white sneakers "—including clothes and eating out—not that I do much of that—I can make it through the four years."

"You can?"

"Yep. Just."

Ardella thought about the twenty hours she'd spent over the weekend balancing her new budget so she could work at the aquarium for the whole four years and not have to work anywhere else. The four years were possible without having a part-time job—just—but she'd have to get one the minute she finished school. And she wasn't kidding about that minute. She suspected she wouldn't even be able to pay her rent that final month if she didn't get a job.

But this was what she wanted, what she'd wished for her whole life. It would be worth it.

"You'd better tell Greg that. I think he's worried about you going to school, working here and having to get another part-time job. He'll probably tell you no for your own good. You know, so you'd get at least a little sleep over the winter."

"I'll tell him later on."

Ardella went back to cleaning the glass and the concrete floor, feeling the muscles she'd developed over the past couple of months. She felt good, both physically and emotionally, in a way she hadn't in so long she'd forgotten what feeling good felt like.

She was exactly where she wanted to be. She was happy right here in this smallish tank, a few kids watching her out of the corner of their eyes, Marney harassing her from the back. She was happy every night, even when she could barely stand the smell of herself as the heat of the shower intensified the aroma of her workday.

She was happy every morning, even when she woke up—despite the Advil—with sore muscles in places she didn't know she had them.

The only problem she could see was Greg Angus. And she had no idea how she was going to solve it.

# CHAPTER ELEVEN

*Picasso triggerfish (Rhinecanthus aculeatus):*
*Eats just about anything that comes along,*
*swims constantly and protects territory*
*against intruders, including divers.*

Ardella loved the bar at the Sylvia Hotel. That's why she picked it. She'd feel safe, it'd be her territory and it wasn't at all romantic.

Okay, maybe it was slightly romantic, especially in the summer. The huge windows looked out over English Bay, at the freighters, sailboats, sea kayakers and windsurfers, to where the sun was just starting to lower itself down to the mountains across the water.

The bladers and the bikers and the just-plain-wanderers filled the sidewalk and bike path across the street with color and energy.

Everyone was out on the beach. Teenage girls in giggling pods, seniors in smaller groups but just as loud, serious runners, their shorts and T-shirts matted damply to their bodies.

Seven o'clock. Seven-thirty.

Ardella finally ordered herself a glass of wine at

eight o'clock and tried to concentrate on the excitement on the beach.

Family picnics, romantic dinners on a blanket for two. A handful of drummers and their fans. A man carving tiny stone bears and a woman selling a row of paintings.

Couples strolling, hand in hand, their attention on each other and not the scenery.

No Greg Angus.

Nine o'clock and another glass of wine.

"I'll wait for a few more minutes," she said to her reflection in the window. "Maybe his brother is worse and he can't leave the hospital."

Ardella still waited but now the sun was below the horizon, leaving just the faintest glow of light reflecting off the water. She waited, but mostly she worried.

Her wineglass sat empty and her stomach growled. She didn't move.

She knew herself to be a fool. It didn't matter, that foolishness, because if Greg Angus needed her, if something had happened to his brother, she wanted to be here for him.

"ARDELLA?"

Greg couldn't believe she was still waiting for him. He looked at his watch. He was three hours late and she still sat, alone, at a table by the window, an empty wineglass in front of her.

He stopped on his way over to the table and ordered a bottle of champagne. He had a lot to celebrate, not the least of which was Ardella's patience.

"Hey," he said, sliding into the chair opposite her. "You're still here."

"I was worried that something—" He saw the concern on her face change to surprise. The grin he'd been wearing for the past several hours must still be glowing at full wattage.

"He's okay, isn't he? Bobby's going to be fine."

"He is. They got the test results back, found out what it was, and he's going to be coming home in a week or so. They want to feed him up, make sure he doesn't have an adverse reaction to the new drugs, but…"

He leaned over the table and kissed her cheek. "Thanks for waiting for me," he said. "I need to wind down a bit."

"Looks like you need to wind down a whole bunch," Ardella replied, smiling. "But my boss is an ogre—" another smile "—and I have to be at work pretty early tomorrow morning, so we can't stay too long."

"All right, but at least help me drink this bottle of champagne. I'm celebrating tonight."

ARDELLA STOPPED after the champagne and moved on to food. It was late and she was tired, but she couldn't pull herself away from the attraction she felt toward Greg. Especially now, when he was so impossibly happy.

She never thought she'd think this, let alone say it out loud, but she did.

"I wish I had someone to worry about," she said. "I miss having my mom around. I miss making sure she got to her appointments. I miss making sure she took her pills. I miss having someone…"

She had to stop or she'd cry, and that was the last thing she was going to do in front of Greg, the very last. Life was complicated enough without adding *that*

complication. Men always felt uncomfortable around crying women.

At least, Ardella thought to herself, that's what the movies and books all said. So she sniffed, ignored the one tear that managed to escape, and took another sip of the glass of water in front of her.

"I think I need to get a cat. Or a dog."

She contemplated. "Okay, not a dog. I won't be home enough. But a cat would be good."

"You have fish, don't you?"

"How'd you know?"

"You told us one Friday night a few weeks ago. Nick was talking about his tank and you…"

"Oh. Well, yes, I have fish, not many, just a small tank, but I love them. Do you think the cat would eat them?"

"I don't know. But cats love movement. I mean, these are animals that chase string—fish would be ir-resistible. Maybe you could put the tank in your bedroom and keep the door closed?"

"I can't do that. If I get a cat, I want it to sleep on my bed. Okay, so no cat."

"But I do miss having someone to care about. Still," she brightened, "starting in a few weeks, I'll be so busy I won't have time to worry about it. Especially if—" Ardella paused and then blurted it out "—you let me work part-time during term."

Greg didn't look so happy about that, his brows almost meeting between his eyes and the lines around his mouth deepening.

"I don't think you're going to have time to do that," he said.

"I don't have anything else to do." Ardella hated admitting that to Greg. "And besides, I know the first-year material—" she didn't mention the second and third and fourth-year material "—by heart. It's going to be a snap and I don't want to leave."

She didn't want to leave the aquarium. It was home to her, not her tiny apartment.

She looked across the table at Greg Angus, at the way he cradled the glass of scotch in his hands as he looked out into the darkness. She loved his face, wanted more than ever for her face to look like his. She knew it would take years—years of working on the ocean, years of squinting into the sun, years of knowing who she was and what she was meant to do.

But she knew, too, that she'd make it. And she hoped that some day, some volunteer would walk into the aquarium and see her, and say exactly that same thing. "I want to look like her."

But even more than his face, she'd learned to love him.

She'd discovered over the summer that he was the hardest worker in the aquarium, almost never leaving before the building closed to visitors. He was there when Ardella arrived in the morning, often still there when she went home.

If she came in on the weekend—and she almost always did—Greg was there. Seldom in his temporary office, he took the opportunity to fill in for anyone who needed help or time off or who he thought looked tired. He helped with the training, he manned the volunteer carts, he worked in marine mammal rescue, he worked

with the aquarists, he worked as a spotter at the beluga shows.

He loved the place as much as she did, Ardella thought. And that love was compelling as well as scary. Because he, like her, was completely focused on his work.

And if she ever had a relationship, she wanted to be first.

# CHAPTER TWELVE

*Chilean rose tarantula (Grammastola rosen):*
*A nocturnal hunter who*
*finds a shelter to web itself into*
*at dawn.*

Two weeks to go and Ardella, promoted out of the tank cleaning brigade, was now working with a volunteer cart.

She'd wanted the dolphin cart—outside in the sun, with the skull and the teeth found in the aboriginal dump—she'd ended up in the dark with the tarantula and the cockroaches.

She suspected Greg of putting her in this place. He had control of the volunteer scheduling—at least as much control as he wanted—and she thought the cockroaches might be in reprisal for her insistence on working during term.

But she'd gotten her way—and she'd barely seen him since the night at the Sylvia. They'd closed the bar, he'd walked her home, and then he'd disappeared.

He was still at work, but he didn't show up for lunch or the ongoing Friday nights at the fish and chips stand. He didn't follow her around the aquarium, didn't show up in the fish house or the dungeons.

When she did see him, he was always off in the distance somewhere, avoiding her. He was *so* obvious.

GREG WATCHED Ardella from the back of the Tropic Zone, keeping his distance. He wouldn't be surprised if she threw one of the cockroaches at him, except she was too professional to do that.

He couldn't remember another volunteer who was so committed, so professional, so knowledgeable. When she insisted that she wanted to work during the school term, there was no way for him to tell her no.

Because he couldn't tell her the real reason he didn't want her to work while she was at university. He didn't want to tell her that he worried she'd be too busy for him.

He'd resolved to wait until September before he asked her out. And there were only two weeks to go.

He wasn't sure he could wait that long.

He smiled as he watched Ardella with the kids clamoring around the cart. She laughed and chatted with them as if they were her best friends, and maybe they were.

She was much more comfortable with them than she was with him. All summer she'd been avoiding him, except for that one day when he told her about Bobby.

And that one night they'd spent in the bar at the Sylvia Hotel, Ardella sitting across the table from her, her eyes shining in the candlelight, laughing with him, drinking champagne to celebrate.

*That* was a perfect night.

But before and after that night? Nothing. A big fat zero. He knew she was aware of him, could feel her

breath catch, her body tense, when he came up next to her. But she fought it, fought it big-time.

It was almost September. If he could wait that long.

ARDELLA KNEW he was watching her, she always knew when he was watching her. Greg was somewhere at the back of the room, just out of comfortable reach of her eyesight in the dim light of the big fish room.

She could see the caiman, sleeping as always. She didn't think she'd seen that creature move more than two or three times in the past couple of months. He loved the water, but he didn't swim in it, or if he did, it was at night when the building was closed to visitors.

Maybe he was shy, she thought, maybe he just didn't like people. Or maybe, she laughed inside at the thought, he liked people too much. Maybe he saw them as food. All those kids had to be mighty tempting, their giggles and their warm little bodies.

She wouldn't want to be a caiman in this world. No way. Except that he got fed regularly and he got to be as lazy as he wanted to be. Maybe that made up for the excitement of the real world.

"What's up?"

Ardella jumped and almost dropped the tarantula— and that would be the equivalent of dropping a bucket of fish on the director's shoes. Marney had snuck up on her while she was watching out for Greg.

"I just about lost the bloody tarantula. Don't scare me like that."

"Sorry, I didn't realize you were so engrossed. And what were you engrossed in?"

Marney turned until she saw—and Ardella saw that she saw—the door heading out of the Tropic Zone closing behind Greg Angus.

"It all makes sense now. And get that bug out of my sight. You know I hate bugs."

"You don't like Rose?"

Ardella held the tarantula, its legs long and covered with silky hair, out to Marney, who shuddered and backed away.

"No. I don't."

"What about the cockroaches?"

Ardella put Rose back in her case and reached for the cockroaches. It had taken her a few days to get used to holding the big shiny black bugs in her hand, but now they just tickled and didn't scare her.

"I'm outta here. Right now."

Ardella watched Marney practically run for the exit and then listened for a minute, tuning out the soft laughter of the kids drooling over the tarantula she'd picked up again.

She heard the soft sounds of the scarlet ibis in the room next door, the drip-drip of the pipes on the roof of the rain forest room.

She didn't hear Greg's booming laugh—which was unusual because wherever he was, she usually heard him laughing. He laughed all the time. And she was trying to follow his example.

This summer had been a real revelation. She'd expected hard work. She'd expected excitement. She'd expected the fear of trying something knew. She'd expected anxiety.

And she'd felt all of those things.

What she hadn't expected was the joy. And the friendship.

She hadn't expected the happiness and comfort she felt in this place, with these people.

And more than anything else, she hadn't expected the temptation of Greg Angus. Well, she was just going to keep resisting it.

She had her plan and she was sticking to it. It had taken her twenty-seven years to get here—from her thirteenth summer to her fortieth—and there was no way she was going to give up everything she'd ever dreamed of for a *man*.

Even a man as attractive and funny and perfect as Greg Angus. Not even for him.

## CHAPTER THIRTEEN

*Spectacled caiman (Caiman crocodiles):*
*Caiman is a Spanish term for alligator. They are*
*large, meat-eating reptiles that spend most*
*of their lives in the water, including the Amazon*
*basin.*

"One week to go," Marney said as she pressed the buzzer for the security guard to open the back door. "And then you'll be at school every day. Looking forward to it?"

She didn't let Ardella answer that question.

"Of course you are. But I bet you're going to miss being here every day. You're going to miss me, right?"

"Yes, I'll miss you, but we've already decided that you'll meet me every Tuesday for dinner. So I won't miss you *that* much."

Ardella laughed at the expression on Marney's face. She'd expected her to say… What? She'd expected her to talk about Greg, she guessed. Well, that topic was out of bounds.

"You're going to miss the kids, too. Joe and Nick and Terry. And Kathleen."

Ardella and Marney had gotten to know Kathleen over the summer. She met them—really, she met Joe—for fish and chips every Friday night. Mostly because the two of them couldn't wait to see each other.

When she and Joe walked home together during the week, Ardella could see from a block away Kathleen sitting, her head swivelled to watch the street, on the stoop of their apartment building. She could have waited for Joe in the apartment, but that would mean another few minutes without him.

And when she saw him? When they saw each other?

Joe didn't even bother to say goodbye, he just took off running down the street, Kathleen doing the same from the stoop, and they'd meet in the middle, arms reaching for each other as if they hadn't seen each other for days, instead of only ten hours.

Ardella watched this same scene enacted four days a week for the whole summer and she still loved it. Loved the way Kathleen screamed when she finally spotted Joe, loved the way Joe ran, even at the end of an excruciatingly hard day, as if he couldn't wait another minute to have Kathleen in his arms.

"I'm going to miss the kids, but I'll see Joe and Kathleen over the winter. Joe and I might hit a few shifts together and we've already decided to have drinks or dinner together when we can fit it in."

"It's going to be hard, you not being here every day," Marney said. "I swear I spend more time here than I do at home and I loved you being here."

Ardella smiled and waited for the next Marney on-slaught, hoping she wouldn't mention Greg, because

she had absolutely no idea how to respond to any questions about him.

"The new food services people are doing a pretty good job, but it's all too healthy. I'm going to miss the fish and chips. Once they close down the Lumberman's Arch stand, there isn't a place around for *real* food."

Marney's idea of real food was plenty of grease and salt. Ardella suspected their weekly dinners would consist of burgers, beer, fish and chips, maybe the occasional stop at KFC. Both of them were addicted to grease and salt, though Marney wasn't a real vinegar fan.

"We can find a place that serves fish and chips downtown somewhere."

"It won't be the same. You need to eat them outside for the perfect effect."

Marney smiled, ruffled Ardella's hair and said, "I'll see you at lunchtime. Have fun with the cockroaches."

Marney had come by that once to see the cockroach show and then conspicuously stayed away the rest of the time. Bugs were not on Marney's list of fun things to see or do.

Marney's favorite things? The belugas in the big pool at the aquarium. She loved them and Ardella was willing to swear they loved her back.

When she passed the pool, all of them followed her, their heads out of the water, their eyes following her every move. When she leaned down over the blue water, they were there, waiting for her.

If she was down in the underground viewing area giving her spiel about the belugas, it was hard for the trainers to convince them to do their routine. They

wanted to be where they could see Marney. Splashing the customers wasn't anywhere near as entertaining as following Marney around the pool.

Ardella wondered why Marney hadn't become an aquarist or a trainer. The belugas loved her—they'd do anything she asked of them. And so did the sea lions and the sea otters. Even the sharks seemed to accept her company when she—very occasionally— worked with them.

But then she thought about the way people's eyes lit up when Marney told them about Lancaster Sound or the Amazon rivers or how seahorses had babies. She thought about Marney's face when she spoke to the tiniest of children and she knew exactly why Marney did what she did.

She didn't want to do anything else.

Ardella only hoped that her face—like Marney's and like Greg's—would begin to reflect the joy and passion they felt in their lives. She thought she was well on her way to getting there.

She could see it in the mirror—the difference between her old face and her new one. It wasn't that her skin was clearer or her eyes were brighter or her smile bigger, though it was all of that.

Ardella stood in front of the mirror in the changing room, the fluorescent lights glaring, and she examined the face in the mirror. It was still *her* face but it was at the same time a new face.

She'd acquired some fine lines around her eyes, because mostly every day she forgot her sunglasses and spent half the day squinting against the sun.

She'd changed color to reflect her surroundings, just like the chameleons in the rain forest room. Her skin was darker, slightly tanned. Warm.

And her eyes? Yes, they were brighter, but they were also more focused, more intense. Because Ardella now knew she'd made the right decision that day on the beach. The scrimping and saving over the next four years weren't going to matter nor were the eighty-hour weeks. The Ardella she saw in the mirror was a woman on a mission, a woman with a goal.

And it was a goal she was passionate about. No more endurance, no more just making it. Every single day would be an adventure, every single day a joy.

And all of that—not to mention the fact that maybe, just maybe, for the first time in her life she might be falling in love—was reflected in her face.

Ardella thought back over the summer. She'd made friends, she worked in the place she'd always dreamed of being, and she'd met Greg Angus. She definitely hadn't expected that. Meeting the co-director was one thing. Knowing he wanted to spend time with her was another. Knowing she might be falling in love with him? That was frightening and wonderful and painful all at once.

# CHAPTER FOURTEEN

*Humbug dascyllus (Dascyllus aruanus):*
*Loves reefs, eats plankton, benthic*
*invertebrates and algae. Very aggressive.*

Her last day before the end of summer and school and it was party time at the aquarium. The underground beluga viewing room was filled with people, everyone Ardella had met over the past summer, people she hadn't yet met because they were on a different schedule from her, people she'd only ever heard of—like the legendary founder of the aquarium.

And he even spoke to her; well, okay, he spoke to everyone. But Ardella was in her glory, here in the world she'd always wanted.

The food was amazing—seafood harvested from the cool waters of the Pacific—her ocean—and cooked by chefs from all over the world. Spring salmon cooked by Thai chefs, halibut cooked by Italian chefs and oysters prepared by African chefs.

There were photographs of the aquarium from its very inception, black-and-white ones, colored ones, photographs of the transformation of the place over the

past fifty years. There was a huge poster of the stamp that celebrated the anniversary—with a portrait of one of the belugas.

A string quartet played light and airy—though she thought it should be watery—music in the background and waitstaff hired for the occasion wandered through the crowd with trays of champagne and nibbles.

Ardella had never been to a party like this in her life.

Marney stood next to her, a glass of champagne in her hand while they pretended to listen to the speeches—the founder, the mayor, the premier of the province, a senator who once was the mayor and the city's coroner, the head of the Maritime Museum, a man who still spent much of his time searching for buried treasure—celebrating the aquarium's fiftieth anniversary.

"Did you ever think you'd be here?" she asked Ardella quietly. "I mean, you've been dreaming about this for almost thirty years—God, almost as long as this place has been around—and here you are. A part of it."

Ardella smiled and whispered back, "I knew I'd be here. Knowing kept me sane all those years, kept me putting one foot in front of the other. It kept me studying so I'd be ready."

She paused for a minute, thinking back on those years. "And," she continued, "the dream of this place made me able to love my mother and not resent her. Are you kidding? Being here is like being in Oz. Or Shangri-La.

"The only thing I didn't expect is that I'd make such great friends."

She turned away so Marney couldn't see the tears in her eyes but Marney wouldn't allow it. She carefully

put her glass down on the table beside them and put her arms around Ardella, the sniffles clear in her voice when she said, "I'm so glad you're here, so glad I met you."

"Hey, that's my line."

After this summer, Ardella knew that voice as well as she knew her own. Greg Angus, here at the end as he was at the beginning.

Okay, okay, it wasn't really the end, but it felt a bit that way. She'd be back in a couple of weeks, but only for one day a week. Maybe next summer she'd have the same long days of hard work—but it wasn't going to be the same without Nick and Terry and Joe.

And she wouldn't have the joy of discovering Marney, of discovering Greg, of discovering she was still a woman, a living, breathing, caring, sometimes frightened woman.

She hadn't allowed herself the luxury of those things—especially fear—for so long she almost didn't recognize it when it happened. The anxiety she'd felt on her first day, that was obvious, she'd spent twenty years experiencing it.

Ardella had felt anxious every single day, for her mother, mostly. But also about whether she'd be able to cope, whether she was capable of giving her mother the support and care she needed.

Every night she'd go to bed and worry about the next day. About the appointments, about the massages, about whether they should go for a walk and, if so, just how far her mother could manage. She worried about the menu for the next day. Would her mother be able to eat eggs? Or would a milk shake be better?

So, yes, Ardella was familiar with anxiety in all of its forms. But fear? She'd put that away for the duration. She couldn't afford it.

Now here she was, not just content, which was how she'd seen herself for all of her grown-up life, but joyful. And that was something she'd not expected.

She turned to Greg and to Marney, grabbed their hands and squeezed them.

"Thank you, both of you. I've had the best summer of my life."

She kissed Marney on the cheek, then turned to Greg. Should she or shouldn't she? Well, why the hell not?

She kissed him on the cheek.

He stopped her when she started to turn away, looking down at her with those ocean eyes, and then he smiled. And that smile contained all the secrets of the ocean, all the secrets of life, she thought.

Was she ready for them?

# CHAPTER FIFTEEN

*Sunflower star (Pycnopodia helianthoides):*
*Twenty-four arms distinguish this*
*magnificent star from others.*
*Voracious predator, when on the prowl*
*swings along on its 15,000 tube feet,*
*moving faster than any other sea star at*
*forty inches a minute.*

Greg watched Ardella as she moved through the crowd, saying goodbye to the temporary volunteers, the ones who were only with them for this one summer, saying "see you next year" to the volunteers who planned to return next summer.

He watched as she smiled at everyone, from the donors to the janitors to the women who worked in the restaurants and gift shop.

There was something different about her tonight, something he couldn't quite put his finger on. He knew what *he* was feeling—it was nostalgia, mostly.

He expected this summer to be boring but the board had said, he needed to know how they worked in the confined space of this building and not just out on the high seas.

They'd actually used the words *high seas* and Greg had laughed, planning to put in his one summer in the city and then go back out on the ship, but they'd been right. He'd learned a lot and enjoyed every minute of it.

Not all of it was attributable to Ardella, either, though she'd been a big part of reconciling him to being grounded.

Being here when Bobby was sick was another part of it. When he'd sat in the hospital for that week, waiting to see if the doctors could figure out what was wrong with his brother, he'd realized that he needed to be in one place, he needed to have a home.

If he'd been where he'd planned to be this summer— on a research vessel in Antarctica—Bobby could have died and Greg would have never seen him again. And seeing him lying on the hospital bed, so sick and frail, Greg had realized just how much he needed his brother. At least as much as Bobby needed him.

Greg and Bobby needed a home. They'd been without one for too long.

Oh, Bobby wouldn't be around much, vagabond that he was, but he needed some place to come to when he wasn't traveling. And Greg wanted that for him. And for himself. And especially, he whispered the wish, for Ardella.

Being grounded this summer had been good for him in all sorts of ways.

He'd seen the joy in children's faces as they watched the belugas and the sea otters. He'd seen what his work really meant to people and he was sure when they asked

him if he wanted to stay in the city, at the aquarium instead of out on the *high seas,* he would.

He'd already been looking at houses and fighting off the desire to—before he'd officially been appointed to it—put his name on the door of the empty office next to Denise.

That didn't mean he wouldn't take the occasional trip to the Arctic or the Amazon, because he would—the waters of the world were, after all, his home. But he was pretty sure his life was going to be lived mostly right here in this city, in this building. At least, he smiled to himself, for the next four years.

ARDELLA CIRCLED THE ROOM, making sure she said goodbye to everyone she'd met over the summer. She felt beautiful and happy and without a care in the world. It was her dress, she thought, the dress Marney helped her pick out.

She wore red, brilliant fire-engine red, and it felt like a million dollars on her, though Marney—the world's best shopper—took her to a consignment store to buy it. She had insisted that Ardella dress up for the party and insisted on shopping with her.

"I don't trust you," she said. "You'll say you're going to do it and then you'll show up in a black skirt and some silk blouse you've owned for fifteen years."

Ardella laughed, because that was exactly what she'd planned to do. She didn't have spare money for clothes. But Marney had found her this dress, literally forced her to try it on, and then haggled until even Ardella couldn't resist the price.

Marney was right.

Here she was and she felt his eyes following her and she knew exactly who it was, which man hadn't stopped watching her since she walked in the door. And it wasn't just the red dress, though maybe that was a small part of it.

Greg had seen her in shorts so filthy they were no longer white. He'd seen her cry. He'd seen her at the end of an excruciatingly long week, her hair hanging limp on her head, her eyes circled with black. He'd seen her after spending the morning fighting with a class of teenagers who were interested in anything but what she told them.

He'd seen her at her worst and he'd never once looked at her without love in his eyes.

Finally, Ardella gave in. She stopped racing around the room, stopped avoiding him.

She was careful to stop in an out-of-the-way corner and she waited while he made his way to her across the room.

Now she watched him, in his black tuxedo and brilliantly white shirt, watched while he stopped and spoke to the founder, watched the giant grin bloom on his face and was willing to bet the founder had offered him a permanent position on-site. She watched as he spoke to the volunteer coordinator and the president of the aquarium's largest corporate donor.

He was tall enough that for almost all of the conversations, he bent over to be heard through the raucous crowd, and he was beautiful enough that most of the women watched as he passed.

Ardella smiled as he burst out of the crowd and into the silent space she picked for this encounter.

"Hey," she said, holding out a glass of champagne.

"Hey," he replied, taking the glass she offered and placing it on the ledge behind him.

*No more games,* she thought. And she smiled up into his ocean eyes and waited.

She knew exactly what would happen. That was why she picked this isolated spot, why she'd been smiling the whole time she stood here, watching him make his way through the crowd to her.

The kiss, though, the kiss was far more than she expected.

And it was the perfect end to a perfect summer.

"It's not the end," Greg whispered, as if he read her mind. "It's the beginning."

Ardella nodded and leaned into him, knowing he was right, knowing that this summer had been the beginning of a new life for her. And it would be a much different life than the one she'd spent all those years imagining.

She'd have the work she'd always wanted, the aquarium, the creatures, the light and water and the smell of the world she craved.

She'd have friends—she smiled at the thought of Marney, of Joe and Kathleen, of Nick and Terry and all the other people she'd met over the summer, all the people she'd meet at school and over the years at the aquarium.

And she'd have a lover.

There was no doubt in his eyes as he looked at her,

no question in his body as he held her, no hesitation at all as he kissed her.

She turned in Greg's arms and looked through the glass at the belugas preening for the adoring crowds. She leaned back, her head against his shoulder, and sighed.

"It's perfect," she said.

Ardella felt the rumble of his "yes" against her back and placed her hands over his. "This is my place," she said.

"It's always been your place," Greg replied, kissing the top of her head. "We've been waiting for you."

* * * * *

no reason to suppose we'd need . . . no weapons at
all to be used.

She buried her face in his hand looked freer to
phone at the telephone, munching on the plate, showing
she leaned back. Her lips a cigarette lay somehow and
she had

"Stop, please," she said.

Abdiel felt the temple of his grief against her face
and placed her hand over his. "This is the place," he said.
"If you've been too much to." Gray rattled through
the top of her head. "Don't be too wound for you."

# Kokomo

Jennifer Greene

To all the boys we loved before…

# CHAPTER ONE

Talk about hellishly hot. The idiotic client had the demented idea to have a lunch meeting al fresco. Outside! Connecticut summers were traditionally warm, but it had been over a hundred degrees all week. Not just hot. Mean hot. Blistering, sick hot. Relentless hot.

Jane Whitcomb yanked open the door. The lobby of Bentham, James, Lambrect and Whitcomb was predictably cool, the décor soothing and tasteful, but nothing seemed to appease her cranky mood. She'd cinched the contract with the client—a downright brilliant deal, if she said so herself, and in spite of the sweaty, killer heat—but that didn't seem to lift her spirits, either.

As she clipped down the hall toward her office, young interns ducked from her sight. Those few bodies near the water cooler zoomed back to their offices with heads down. One hapless temp opened the door to the women's restroom, saw Jane, and headed right back into the restroom.

This wasn't the first time she'd noticed the phenomenon, but initially she hadn't connected the behavior with herself. Lately, though, it was hard to

avoid realizing that her coworkers' reaction to her had been steadily deteriorating. Jane's feelings were starting to feel bruised. Granted, for the past couple months she'd been in an incessant hurry and stressed to beat the band and tired from the inside out. But people were treating her as if she were…well, as if she were a bitch.

How could the once-most-popular girl in high school, the one they all nicknamed Peachy, the one everyone clamored to be with because she was fun and full of energy and ideas and laughter, possibly have turned into…well, into a bitch?

Whatever. A half mile of pink slips had accumulated by her phone over lunch. The files for the Baker, Spikas, Webster and Bailey contracts were heaped on her blotter. Her appointment calendar claimed she had a conflict—two conflicts—for later that afternoon, and the partners had called an impromptu emergency meeting over an imminent crisis with a client at four that day.

Absently she yanked open the desk drawer and scooped up some antacid tablets from her stock, then grabbed the phone. John—one of the partners—showed up in the doorway with his tie askew, looking frazzled, but she motioned him away. By then she was speed dialing through the problem list.

Halfway through the sixth call…it was the oddest thing…she developed a tic. Her right eye just kept trying to blink, nothing painful or frightening, but unsolvably annoying—and besides that, the last call required information from the Johnson brief.

The Johnson brief should have been on her desk. She

shifted through papers and files, then burrowed faster than a woodchuck digging for prey. Pencils flew. Paper clips dropped. Slips of paper and notes floated to the thick, plush blue carpet.

No Johnson brief showed up.

Eyes narrowed, Jane rounded the desk and stormed outside her office, only to see her assistant's desk—temporarily manned by a temp, yet another damn thing going wrong lately—was deserted. Surely this soon after lunch the darn woman couldn't be taking a break already? She zoomed down the hall and slapped open the door to the restroom.

"Marcia? You in here?"

A small voice from one of the locked stalls answered. "Yes, Ms. Whitcomb."

"Where'd you put the Johnson brief?"

"Ma'am...I'm in the bathroom. If you'd just wait for a minute or two—"

Hmmph. She hiked back to the office, and started another frantic search, thinking how the sam hill long could it take the woman to pee?

A strain of an old song filled her mind. She couldn't place it, couldn't remember all the words, but once she got the tune in her head, she couldn't shake it. "Aruba... Jamaica...Key Largo...Montego..."

The phone rang. She grabbed it. Finished that call and handled a second. Still, she rifled through every drawer, then the credenza and desktop for the Johnson brief. "Come on, pretty mama...."

DAMN it. She had to have the brief. Now. Yesterday. Partners were expected to bill seventy hours a week.

She'd been billing eighty to eighty-five. Awing them. Awing herself. Only she hadn't had a break since she could remember, and just possibly she had more balls in the air than hands to juggle them. "Kokomo…"

The tic in her eye wouldn't let UP. She jammed the heel of her hand against it, reached for the top shelf over the credenza, knowing perfectly well the brief couldn't possibly be up there—but it couldn't just walk away, either, and it had to be somewhere.

She couldn't reach the top shelf. Being five foot two was the bane of her life. Even three-inch heels didn't add enough height to look imposing, and right now, she was determined to search every inch of the office for the brief—no matter what it took.

She kicked off her heels, hiked up her skirt and climbed on top of her desk…which was when she noticed the temp standing in the doorway. Marcia was one of those women who somehow always managed to look vulnerable. She had mouse-brown hair, puppy-dog eyes and had the build of a cookie addict—plump and soft. At the moment she stood motionless, with an expression that looked as if she could start shaking any second.

"I was just…" Jane started to say, but then caught herself. Maybe it was the horror and fear in the temp's eyes, but she suddenly saw herself as the young woman seemed to be seeing her. Standing on top of her desk. The office in shambles. Paper and files everywhere. A cup overturned. Four lights blinking simultaneously on the phone. Her private fax was vomiting page after page in a bulimic fit, and the couch where clients were

supposed to be able to sit was completely covered in paper and fallout debris.

Jane found herself gulping. This was just never how she'd expected to behave as a lawyer.

This was never how she'd expected her work or her private life to turn out, either.

And suddenly something snapped inside her.

Slowly she climbed down from the desk. Even more slowly, she sank into her office chair. "Marcia," she said.

"Yes, Ms. Whitcomb."

"I need a break."

"Yes. You do. The whole office thinks you do."

"I haven't taken a vacation in three years." Now that that infamous "something" had snapped, it was like a hem on a skirt. Once the thread got loose, the whole thing unraveled. She knuckled her eyes for a moment, a little scared—as ridiculous as it sounded—that she just might cave in and cry. Then, of course, she pulled it back together. "I would appreciate it if you would get me plane tickets. For…"

The where-of-it was the major question, since she had absolutely no destination in mind. But then that song came back into her head, as if fate were just waiting to help her out that afternoon. "Kokomo. Round trip tickets to Kokomo. I want eight straight days. Set up the first and last nights in a hotel near the airport. I'll take care of the rest myself when I get there."

"Kokomo," Marcia said carefully. "Are you sure?"

"I am *dead* sure. In fact, I don't think I've been this

sure of anything since…" Who knew since when? Since she'd first heard that song a zillion summers ago. Since *that* long.

"But, Ms. Whitcomb—"

"Now. I want it done now. Just make the reservations on the soonest possible flight. Let me know the time. I don't want to hear another word about it."

"But Ms. Whitcomb—"

"Not another word. I mean it. I'm going to shut down my client projects, get things shifted and delegated so I can leave. But if there's a prayer in the universe of being on a plane to Kokomo by tomorrow, I want to be on it."

"Ms. Whitcomb, are you absolutely certain that—"

"Marcia." There now. Once she used that certain tone of voice, the temp shut up, nodded quickly and scurried out of sight.

Unfortunately, Jane realized she'd been a bitch again. It didn't make her feel good. Maybe there wasn't a justifiable excuse for behaving like a perimenopausal Wicked Witch of the West, but there actually was a reason.

She was miserable.

Who knew?

People not only avoided her; they'd been acting downright afraid of her. You'd think she might have picked up a few clues that people didn't want to be anywhere around her if they could help it. But that was precisely the kicker.

She hadn't noticed at all. She'd been running so fast, for so long, that she not only hadn't stopped to smell

the roses. She hadn't stopped long enough to realize she'd turned into a miserably unhappy sharp thorn.

WHEN JANE BOARDED the plane, her eyes were only open to half slits and she wasn't speaking—to anyone. Five in the morning wasn't her best hour. Because it had taken most of the night to prepare for being gone, she'd barely caught a couple hours of sleep. She hadn't even opened a suitcase until past two in the morning, but at least at that point, realized that packing didn't matter. She tossed some cosmetics and swimwear and shorts in a single bag and called it quits, knowing she could shop when she got there.

Now she stumbled down the narrow aisle, found her seat, hurled her purse down and strapped in. She didn't know how long the flight was. Didn't care. She'd only glanced at her e-ticket to know the flight time, and had ignored the rest of the arrangements Marcia had made just as happily. None of the details mattered now. The flight to Kokomo was surely long enough to catch several hours of sleep, and with a hotel pre-set up for the first night, she could catch even more. After that she had to do some thinking and planning, but not before.

The faces she passed vaguely registered. It wasn't a huge jet. The back of the plane was already filled, most of the passengers already tucked down and snoozing. But she passed a skinny businessman, a nerdy kid with a blond afro, a handsome guy in a military uniform, two teenage girls babbling to each other…when she finally located her seat, she thanked the travel gods for the empty seat next to her, but also noticed two white-

haired women in the seats across, both heavy set, who looked to be sound asleep.

She couldn't wait to do the same. She fixed a pillow behind her neck just so, sighed, and closed her eyes.

They popped back open. *Wide* open.

No one as exhausted as she was—days exhausted, weeks exhausted, MONTHS exhausted—could possibly have trouble sleeping.

Or so she told herself. Yet when she tried squeezing her eyes closed again, the lids jerked up faster than a jack-in-the-box.

As the jet engines revved for takeoff, in fact, she found her gaze fixed on the passenger three rows ahead.

She'd already noticed him. It was the good-looking guy in the military uniform, the one in the aisle of the emergency seat…she could see his long legs stretched out, see a wedge of his dark hair in profile, and even from here, she caught the shine of brass on the arm of his uniform. Still, those physical details weren't what snared her attention. There'd been something when she'd passed him….a flash in his dark eyes, something in his angular profile, the chin…that now struck her with a slap of recognition, as if she knew him.

She couldn't place a single person she knew in uniform—much less one who'd earned all that brass. She had to have imagined it…or maybe her pulse kicked her awake for a more obvious reason. He was one helluva good-looking guy.

It wasn't as if it mattered. In a thousand years she wouldn't give a stranger any serious thought…but that

didn't mean she was blind. He was definitely riveting enough to put some zest in a girl's heartbeat.

In her case, though, Jane wasn't dead sure if zest was a precise definition for the physical symptoms she was suffering. She forgot the guy and slammed her eyes closed again, all too aware that her heart was pounding. So was her pulse. And her temple.

It seemed as if that pounding had become a consuming way of life, like being miserable and mean and bitchy.

The only new symptom was fear. Something seemed to be very, very wrong with her. The last time she remembered putting herself through any serious self-analysis, she'd been a teenager—a bright, happy, driven teenager who'd known exactly what she wanted in life, gone after it, fought for it, and won it.

So how could she possibly be so unhappy when she had every darn thing she'd ever wanted?

Trying to relax, she forced her mind to concentrate on the Count The Blessing thing. Heaven knew, that took a while, because she really had a ton of them. When push came down to shove, she couldn't think of a single thing to complain about.

Her divorce was three years old—old enough for all the sharp edges to have faded. Cray had never cheated on her, never been abusive. He'd just been a parasite, the kind of guy who picked an ambitious wife so he could loll around and live off her earnings. Maybe she could have tolerated that longer if he'd just loved her— but whatever. The point was that she was happily single, and still downright thrilled to be free from Cray.

The kids were all doing fabulous—Bry married and spending a year in Alaska with his bride, Lar career-launched in Seattle and her baby was still home—Angel—but spending the summer on an exchange program in Europe before starting her senior year in college.

Her house was paid for. Her new white Lexus a love. Her closets filled with Elie Tahari and St. John's. And shoes. God knew, she had a weakness for shoes. All of it was paid for, though, and she'd earned every dime—had a lucrative, successful career. Lots of respect. She'd never wanted to be mediocre—she'd wanted to be an outstanding contract lawyer or nothing—and she'd met that goal, too.

She nestled her behind in the seat, determined to get more comfortable. The more blessings she counted, the more obvious it became. She was happy. She *had* to be happy.

So why in the Sam Hill was there salty moisture jammed up under her closed eyes?

When she got to that damned Caribbean island, Jane told herself, she was going to kick herself but good. And that old summer song suddenly strolled into her mind again. Soothing her. Easing away all that stress. "That's where I want to go…down to Kokomo…"

It was a minute later…no more. She positively hadn't slept a wink. Not a single one.

Yet she was suddenly startled to hear a young girl's voice rise in a scream of fear.

Instead of bright morning light pouring in the port windows, it was darker than pitch outside, and the

plane seemed to be pitching, as well. Another female voice cried out.

The pilot's voice came on the loudspeaker, his tone calm but terse.

"I know the turbulence is unpleasant, but please stay calm. As soon as we're on the ground, as fast as we can exit you all from the plane, we'll be aiming straight for a protected area. I understand that you'll be concerned about your luggage and your plans, but there will be no flights out of the Kokomo area until these storms have passed. We can't outrun these storms, folks, so just stay calm, and we'll be on the ground as fast as we can get you there…."

Jane heard him, but her attention was abruptly ransomed by the view outside her window. From a thick clot of smoky-black clouds, a funnel suddenly shot downward. Then a second funnel. When the jet turned to approach the runaway, a passenger on the other side of the aisle shrieked, "Tornadoes! We're all going to die! Can you see the tornadoes?"

But then another voice intervened. A man's voice, saying, "It's going to be all right. We'll be on the ground in less than a minute now. We're all going to be fine."

That voice…it was crazy, but Jane knew that voice.

Danger electrified the air in the cabin. It was hard to make sense of anything in the next few minutes—the crazy darkness. What time it was. Where they were. The storms had shown up from a crystal-clear sky as if from nowhere. The jet bounced on the tarmac, the brakes screeching no louder than everyone's heartbeats. Jane could taste fear at the back of her throat. Not the kind

of fear she associated with stress and pressure, but the other kind. The *real* kind.

Yet that man's voice kept echoing in her mind, butter-coating her nerves, soothing her. She just... believed that voice. Believed what he said about being fine. Some instinct kept reassuring her that she knew the voice, knew the man speaking, knew she could trust him.

The elderly man across the aisle suddenly looked right at her. "Where are we, do you know?" Jane asked.

"Kokomo," he responded. "And it seems like we're going to make it there by the skin of our teeth."

But when Jane looked out, past the black clouds and the tumultuous wind and deluge of a rain...she saw no sign of a tropical paradise. The view revealed a flat landscape, backdropped by the buildings of a middle-sized ordinary American town, with farm country visible in the far distance.

Naturally if they needed to make an emergency landing, it didn't matter where they were. But she was confused by the other passenger's response.

"This can't be Kokomo," she said.

The man raised one shaggy white eyebrow. "I promise you, it is. I was born in Kokomo, Indiana. I should know."

Kokomo, *Indiana?* Jane stared at the man in complete bewilderment—but a second later, the jet slammed to a stop and the passengers hustled toward the doors in a fury of frantic pandemonium.

# CHAPTER TWO

Jane couldn't possibly consider panicking, simply because everyone else was. The doors to the plane hadn't been opened yet, but people were too freaked to stay in their seats. The pilot and co-pilot swiftly emerged from the cockpit and tried to urge calm and quiet. And the man—the one in the uniform, the delicious one that Jane kept thinking she knew—emerged as another natural take-charge person.

The flight attendant would undoubtedly normally be of more help, but the girl looked young, as untried and scared as the passengers. "It's just unbelievable. There were a few rainstorms in the forecast, but nothing like this system, no threat of tornadoes or wind like this. The whole thing seemed to show up out of nowhere...."

"This way, people. Straight down the stairs and toward the open door. There's an attendant there...."

The older man in front of Jane stumbled. She grabbed his arm. The two teenagers up front were still shrieking and crying.

The uniformed man—*her* man—kept offering quiet, sensible advice. "Take your purse or bag, make sure you've got whatever medications or critical items you

were carrying with you. Nothing else. We can worry about everything else later. At the bottom of the stairs, walk with someone else. Prepare for the wind. That's it, that's it…"

When Jane reached him, it wasn't a thunderbolt from the tornado that hit her, but a different kind of thunderbolt entirely.

She *did* know him.

"You need help?" he asked her when she paused at the door.

"No, no, I'm fine!" It was no time to act like a blundering fool. If he recognized her, he didn't let on. But memories suddenly rushed at her with the force of a battering ram.

Henry White. That's who he was. Hank. Her Hank— once upon a time. Once upon a long, long ago time.

At the doorway to the plane the wind snarled around her, grabbing at her shirt, her hair, rain pummeling her with wild, sharp pellets. She was completely soaked in seconds, and gasped for air, yet there seemed nothing to breathe but that choking thick wind. Crazy things hurled through the air—chair legs and towels, pieces of metal and shreds of paper, branches when there wasn't a tree in sight. The howl of the storm made hearing any conversation impossible. Something stabbed her arm, stung. It was all she could do to hold the handrail and get down the stairs.

Someone gasped behind her—two women, both her mother's age—and because they were struggling just to stay on their feet, she reached for both of them.

The three ran toward the open door of the airport

terminal. Just negotiating those thirty yards seemed more challenging and exhausting than running miles.

"Come on, come on, come on!" A uniformed airport staff person brusquely grabbed at them, pulled them in, shoved them toward the right. "There. Keep going. Past the windows, past the revolving door. Then sit on the ground against the concrete wall. Hurry, everyone! Hurry, hurry!"

She heard it. The sounds outside changed. Suddenly it was more than storm, more than rain, but wind spiraling into a weapon. She did what everyone else did. Hurtled toward safety, packing close to everyone else, huddling down against the cold cement wall. She wrapped her arms around her knees and ducked her head.

People were crying. Men, women, made no difference. The whole corridor and terminal and anterooms were dim-dark—clearly they'd lost power. Yet even inside, protected by cement walls, Jane could hear the roar of wind, the menace of it.

She saw a dark shadow hustle into the area where they were, heard someone say, "My God, it hit the plane," and then none of them said or did anything. Just sat there, huddled and chilled and afraid. Waiting.

Vaguely she recognized that her left arm had a pretty good scrape, because blood had soaked through her salmon silk shirt.

And she was starting to feel chilled to the bone, whether from fear or being rain-soaked—or both. She always wore her hair short and neat, because there was no other way to control the thick curls, but now her hair

was all tangled and wet, too. Her pants, a silk twill, clung stickily to her thighs and butt.

Still, she was no more miserable than anyone else, and right then it kept hitting her: they were alive. Being alive hadn't struck her as amazing three hours ago, but it sure as hell did now. From moment to moment, her mind kept trying to wrap around being in Kokomo, *Indiana*—how in the universe could she have ended up here? Yet she remembered Marcia repeatedly asking her, are you sure, are you *sure*?…so she could all too easily piece together how this had happened.

Marcia hadn't believed she really meant Kokomo, Indiana, but Jane—being the bitch she'd turned into lately—hadn't really given the temp a chance to clarify her question. Or what she wanted.

And now none of that mattered anyway.

A tornado seemed to be an amazing equalizer.

So much of an equalizer that the only clear thought that kept surfacing in her head was Hank. Hank White.

It just struck her as crazily ironic. If she *had* to land in the middle of a tornado, she just wished it could be with a man she hadn't jilted in high school. A boy she'd once hurt as blithely as squashing a mosquito. A boy she'd treated very, very badly.

A boy who'd done nothing but love her, once upon a time.

She was still thinking about that, thinking about the summer of her senior year, the summer when she'd still believed in endless possibilities and "once upon a times," when the heartthrob of her old daydreams suddenly showed up in front of her.

He hunkered down, as if seeking to speak quietly without the rest of the passengers overhearing. But he clearly didn't recognize her. He just said, "My name's Henry White. Hank. You up for doing a little work? We could use a little organization and help."

"Sure," she said immediately, and pushed to her feet.

She wasn't the only one he'd picked. Another four passengers were quietly isolated from the pack—all men—and shown into a narrow back office. Their pilot, a pilot from another plane and several frazzled airport personnel were already there. Hank, though, was the one who spoke up.

"We're not facing an easy day ahead, as I'm sure you all already guessed. Tornadoes ripped through this whole area. We have no power here, beyond an emergency generator, and it's possible local hospitals or emergency services could need that more than we do. There are live wires all through the city of Kokomo and surrounding roads. Downed lines and trees and buildings are blocking the roads and tarmacs…"

He looked right at her, but no differently than he made eye contact with everyone else in the room. Jane kept thinking, surely she hadn't changed that much; he'd recognize her any second…yet he didn't seem to.

She, on the other hand, could hardly keep her eyes off him. He'd been an adorable boy. Shy and quiet, but still, he had that strong bone structure, the height, the sharp intelligence in his eyes that all set him apart. The dark eyes were downright dreamy—then and now. The shock of dark hair was extra striking next to his Irish-clear skin.

"At least there has only been our flight and one other that were stranded here. They were in the same boat that we were. No opportunity to divert to another airfield in time. The storms came up too fast, too unexpectedly. The point, though, is that we're all stranded here. We're not sure for how long, but our best guess is two or three days."

The others expressed sounds of dismay. Jane might have felt the same dismay…but she still couldn't take her eyes off Hank.

"We're safe," he said. "That's the good news. And frankly, it's damned good news. Those were hellacious storms. But the bad news is…things are going to get messy here."

"So what do we do to help?" Jane asked immediately.

Again, his gaze honed on her, still not with recognition—other than that he'd seemed to naturally isolate her, with some instinct that she'd keep a level head in a crisis.

"We need water. Food. Sanitation—the bathrooms are going to get rank damn fast if we can't flush. And we don't have shower facilities or spare water for washing. We'll also need sleeping arrangements. Someone to liaise with the passengers to make sure no one needs special medicine or care. The plane was damaged. But we'll be able to get luggage out, get people's things for a few days…nobody's going to be happy, but we should be able to cope well enough if we just organize and come together…."

Two male passengers wearing suits were given the

assignment of unloading luggage, blankets and pillows from the plane now that the wind had died down. The group talked about setting up staging areas, so belongings didn't get spread out all through the airport, and ways to address issues of security and privacy.

The airport staff and co-pilot got into a major discussion about sanitation. One of the passengers was an engineer, and already started rolling up his sleeves.

Jane opened her mouth several times to volunteer, but in the first round of acknowledged problems, everybody else seemed to sweep in ahead of her with some level of knowledge or expertise she didn't have. She had to admit, creating a soup kitchen or temporary latrines wasn't in any job description she'd ever had.

Still, everybody seemed to have a chore and major responsibility except for her. And as each person or pair hustled out to address their projects, suddenly there seemed no way left in the shadowy room but her and Hank.

"You didn't give me a job."

He leaned against a desk. "Actually, I left you the most critical one. Your name?"

"Jane," she said. "Jane Whitcomb." Instinctively she braced, because the instant she said her name, she thought it would click for him.

He'd remember her dumping him, what a heartless creep she'd been. And maybe she deserved his looking at her as if she were a worm in his past…but it was so odd. Because she wasn't remembering her rotten behavior half as much as she was suddenly recalling other parts of that long, hot summer. Like…his laying her

up against the high school brick wall and kissing her senseless.

Like…his lying next to her at the beach, both of them beaded with water under a hot sun, her pretending to nap but really fascinated by the rock-hard erection he kept trying to hide, her feeling sky-high powerful as a woman.

Like…the summer cotillion dance. The one where she'd worn a white strapless gown, long and silky. The one where the orchestra had started out playing traditional waltzes, but past ten, when most of the country club parents had started fading from sight and gone home, the musicians had loosened up and played some classic rock and roll. She didn't remember the songs, except for one. The Beach Boys one. The Kokomo one.

She'd been so happy that night, so high being with Hank…yet it wasn't Hank she'd gone home with.

It wasn't Hank she'd slept with.

It was another boy. Not a boy she loved. A boy she thought at the time—believed at the time—was her future.

"Are you with me so far, Jane?"

Swiftly she mentally slapped herself. "I'm sorry. I missed some of what you said. It's been such a stressful morning—"

"That's all right. But you really are the only one I think could do this well. We need to help people stay calm, not panic. We need someone to find out if there is anyone with special diet or health needs that should be addressed. We've got doers, but we don't have an assigned 'people person.' I think the flight attendant might normally do that job, but if you met her—"

"I understand."

"No one would listen to her. So it would really help if you could…" Suddenly he hesitated, and shook his head with a boyish laugh. "You're going to think this is crazy, but I keep getting the weirdest feeling that I've met you before."

She opened her mouth to respond, yet only a gulp emerged. Of course she was going to admit who she was, that they'd known each other before. Only…it suddenly wasn't that easy.

She didn't want him to hate her. Didn't want him to remember what she'd done.

Maybe more so, because in these past few days, she was coming to realize—with a whole lot of pain—that she was still that girl. Only aged. Not like wine, where age made it better. But more like champagne, where the grapes that once looked and tasted stupendous started to sour with time.

Not that she was sour, exactly. But…

She was.

Sour. On the inside.

But Hank was standing there—in the middle of a crisis, for Pete's sake—stuck waiting for an answer.

"You know me," she admitted. "We knew each other—"

But the pilot—Captain Bunker—abruptly popped his head in. "Hank, if you could come out here for a minute—"

"Sure, right away." And he was gone—but not before flashing her a swift, curious smile. "We'll catch up later."

She didn't see him again for ages. When everyone had gotten off the plane, gotten to safety, they'd all been quiet—fear-quiet—through the storms. But now the tornadoes were over, or everyone believed they were, and the terminal had turned into complete chaos. People wanted to go outside. Wanted food. Wanted to phone families and businesses. Wanted their luggage, their cars, their connections. Wanted to know what was going to happen next. When. How. Where. Why.

There were plenty of uniforms running around— whether they were airport staff or pilots or, like Hank, just a natural leader because of his military rank—so Jane found it bewildering how many hands plucked at her sleeve, chased after to ask her questions. But she suddenly got it, why Hank had pulled her from the crowd.

It was the female thing. The older women and kids especially wanted to ask a female, wanted female-type reassurance. And especially the women wanted answers to pressing personal problems.

"My sister…" The two white-haired ladies from the first row of first class looked like mirror-twins. "…has diabetes. And she had insulin in her purse. But now we don't know where her purse is. We think she left it on the plane, but now nobody will let us go back to the plane to look…."

"Okay," Jane said. "I'll get it. What's the purse look like? And do you need food right now?"

Then there was an old man on spindly legs, Walter, who pulled on her wrist. "Miss. My sister died. I'm here for the funeral. I need to go home."

"I understand. But I gather it's really dangerous out there, sir. Live electric wires in the roads. Big chunks of debris strewn on the road and runways. So for a while, the safest place we can be is right here. And whoever's in your family…they know. If they live locally, they just went through the same storms…and if they live close, they've heard about the tornadoes on the news. So they'll be worried, for sure, but we'll get you out of here just as soon as we can."

As she reached the door, it was the teenaged girls who ran her down. Neither were looking so perky now; they both had mascara running down their cheeks. "We need a bathroom."

"They're going to set up some kind of sanitation facilities as fast as they can. I'm guessing you can use the women's room to pee. But I don't know if or when we'll have some generator power, so for right now I'm guessing we just don't have water to flush or wash our hands."

"But I have to wash my face—"

"The only water we're going to use for a stretch here, is for drinking or food. I'm hoping that won't be for long—" She could see the girls were about to argue further, and decided she'd better come up with a diversion pronto. "I could really use your help, if you two wouldn't mind.

"Like," Jane said, "first just see if you can scout out the whole terminal facility for me. Check out the upstairs, see if there are any big rooms up there. If we're stuck for a couple of nights we might want to set up some privacy areas for men and women. Or just find out what the layout is like, okay?"

"Can we go behind the desks, even places like that?"
Both girls showed an immediate trigger of interest.

"You mean the private offices? Well…I think as long
as you're on a reconnaissance mission like this, it'll be
okay. If someone questions you, just tell them that Jane
asked you to do this job."

"Hey, that's cool."

Then there was an older man, Ronald, who hobbled
over with a walker to gravely state that he'd been in two
wars and three international conflicts, and what could
he do to help?

He looked so frail that she couldn't imagine anything
physical he could do, but she saw how clear and sharp
his eyes were. How proud.

And slowly she said, "It would really, really help if
you'd set up where you could see the front doors.
We've been all asked to stay inside for a while, to
make sure where everyone is, that all the passengers
are accounted for. And I guess, to make sure no one
goes out until the storm's damage has been determined. But I don't think there's any way everyone's
going to obey that. The smokers will be sneaking out,
for sure. But people are also curious, want to see
what's going on, want the fresh air. So…if you could
just station yourself by the doors? Take note if
someone leaves the building and let one of guys in
uniform know? Or me. I'll check back with you in a
little while."

He gave her a thumbs up. "I'm your man."

And that was when the thought clicked in her head.
People were understandably frustrated and upset—but

they would tend to panic less if everyone had something to *do*.

God knows she had a gift for being bossy. Might as well put it to use.

Hours later she was light-headed from lack of food; her Italian silk slacks were ruined, her feet were killing her and the scrape on her arm was angrily stinging. As she stole out a back door for a few seconds' break, though, she felt oddly exhilarated.

She hadn't thought of the office in hours. Hadn't been this long without a computer or phone since she could remember. And all the passengers, no matter how upset, seemed to assume she was a capable, warm-hearted woman—instead of the Bitch Times Three she'd turned into lately.

It was a long way from the Caribbean vacation she had in mind or desperately needed.

But she had the odd sensation of climbing in someone else's skin for a while. She had no idea whose—but it definitely wasn't her own. She got to be someone else today, and no one ever had to know otherwise.

She pushed open the farthest back door, the one that usually led passengers out to private flights. She expected no one would have any reason to be there, and she could catch a moment's privacy. Instead, the view stunned her into immediate silence.

The air was still hot, still humid, still choked with that electric smell warning of storms. The sky had all the blue leached from it, the color swirling with gray and yellow clouds, a moody wind still chasing debris in all directions.

On one runway, an orange truck sat on top of a white SUV. A hundred yards farther, a tree just lay on the blacktop...a huge, old tree with giant gnarly roots... even though there wasn't a forest or woods in sight. Part of a roof blocked a hangar. Garbage and paper and plastic and every other kind of trash looked as if a fairy-tale ogre had spilled massive messes from his garbage truck.

*Now* she got it. Why everyone had been urged to stay inside, why no one was likely to be traveling anywhere for hours, if not days. If the whole town was in as bad a shape as the airport, heaven knew how long it would take it clear it all.

Their plane didn't look exactly bad—assuming the hole it had put in the building wasn't too catastrophic. She could see the belly, where luggage was stored, almost emptied now and brought into the building. And then she noticed the fire.

At first she couldn't make sense of it, but then she had to smile. It looked as if five home gas barbecues had been nestled together to create a giant cook space. Judging from the pots and food, it appeared as if indi-vidual families—or restaurants—had emptied out their freezers, and rather than lose food because of the power outage, had simply contributed to a massive cooking effort. Heaven knew what the result would be. Or how long they would be eating whatever had gone into those big, fat pots. But they definitely weren't going to starve. The two plump ladies who'd sat in the first aisle looked as if they were in their glory, huge spoons in their hands, their pink cheeks double-flushed from their cooking.

"Peachy."

She whirled around, for the first time realizing that Hank had been outside, too, leaned against the building in the shade. He'd lost his military jacket, but not the bearing. Everything about him was hopelessly male. He'd so clearly grown into a guy comfortable in his own skin. A guy who'd become a leader, who didn't have to shout anything about his gender or his job or the success he'd made of his life. It was all there, in his clear dark eyes, his posture, the way he took in the world.

The way he looked at her.

And abruptly, she heard the "Peachy."

"You remembered," she said.

"I think I knew you the minute I laid eyes on you. But with the tornadoes—all this chaos—any connection just went to the back of my mind." He cocked his head, studying her. "Your hair's shorter. But otherwise you look the same."

"That's it. You're my hero forever." She told herself to smile, then realized she already was. "I wasn't sure if I wanted you to remember me. I'm pretty unhappy at the way I treated you years ago."

His eyebrows lifted. "All I remember is a great senior summer. And isn't this crazy? To meet up after all these years in a Kokomo, Indiana airport? Of all the places in the universe?"

"Beyond crazy—how do you happen to be here?"

"Grissom Air Force Base is a hop and jump from here. I have an old friend getting a promotion, flew in on the q.t. to be there for him. Or that was the plan. How about you?"

She started to answer, but his previous comment was still glued in her mind. All those summers ago, she'd hurt him badly, she knew. Yet now it so obviously didn't matter to him. He'd clearly made so much of his life that any memories of her were only a minor blip on his radar screen.

And that was a big thank heavens, she told herself. If the past didn't bother him, there was no reason to feel awkward. Or to carry around any more guilt. But…

It startled her.

That she was the one, that long-ago summer, who'd known exactly what she wanted from life. She'd pinned down a career, personal goals and needs, labeled the whole kind of future she wanted in every way.

Hank only had one goal that summer. To be with her.

Yet he was the one who looked happy now.

And she was the one hoping they'd be stranded with tornado weather just a little while longer so she didn't have to go back to her "wonderful" life.

# CHAPTER THREE

"But Jane. I don't understand why Joella gets a bed and I don't."

"There are only three cots in the whole building, Delores. The rest of us are lucky just to have carpet and blankets."

"But Joella only has arthritis. I'm a cancer survivor. And I have diabetes. I'm suffering a whole lot more than she is. On top of which, I think she took my hiddenite."

"Hiddenite?"

"Yes. You know about chakras, don't you? Well, I paid a lot for that mineral. And I was lying on the cot—just borrowing the cot for a while this afternoon, mind you, and it was after they delivered the luggage…"

"Uh-huh…"

"So I'd gotten out my hiddenite. Now there's only one way to use it right, I don't care what anybody says. You have to lie on your back and put the hiddenite stone right in the middle of your chest. It creates a feeling of harmony. But like I told my cousin Louise, I said, Louise, it's also very good for helping with heart palpitations. Only, next thing, I open my eyes and it's gone. I know Joella took it. I know. Because she always did

want whatever I had… She's jealous of me. That's what. Always has been—"

The intrepid Delores had followed her from one end of the building to the other. Tarps had been used to create makeshift curtains, allowing for some basic privacy between the genders. Jane had been running all day—as had everyone, she knew—hustling to make sleeping arrangements before they lost all natural light. It was nine now. Late enough. The accommodations weren't fancy, but between airline blankets and pillows, and the clothes people had packed in their suitcases, everyone had something to use as a pillow and a way to keep warm.

"Jane!"

One of the teenagers, the one with the pearl in her eyebrow, who was on the third change of clothes since getting her suitcase, accosted her before Delores had finished.

"Rina told me we couldn't use toilet paper."

Ah. All day long, said Rina had been spreading rumors, helping a certain group stay riled up ALL the time. "This is the thing, honey. We can't have normal sanitation when we're so limited on fresh water. So if we throw toilet paper in the toilets, it'll clog the system when we do get power back."

"But I have to use toilet paper."

Jane nodded. "And that's fine. But throw the toilet paper in the black plastic container in the restroom."

"You mean, in front of everybody?"

"Honey. We're all in the same boat. No one likes it."

"But it's so unclean and gross and embarrassing—"

"Uh-huh. For everyone. But at least we've got dry hand cleaner for everyone. I know it's a wild thought, but maybe you could skip using makeup just for these couple of days."

The sixteen-year-old looked at her as if she'd suggested walking naked down the street.

"Jane, you haven't answered *my* problem about the cot." Delores plucked at her sleeve again.

The blond man who'd sat at the back of the plane hailed her from across the room. "I've been trying to track you down, Jane." That morning, Dwight had had the look of a businessman, but he'd long lost the tie, added a day's stubble to his chin, and had mighty tired eyes.

"I know," she said gently. "You're terribly worried about your wife. I don't blame you." There were no functioning landlines, no way to plug in cell phones or laptop computers. The staff had gotten a generator going, but emergency needs had already taxed it to the limit—all of which Dwight knew. "I talked to the captain and to the airport staff. They're certain either police or National Guard will get in here by early tomorrow. The thing is, the whole city was hit so hard that we're just not a priority."

"I understand that. It's just….my Sara's pregnant—"

"And you're worried like hell." Jane squeezed his shoulder, swiftly, warmly, then let him go. "I would be, too. But I'm sure your wife's heard on the state and national news by now that we're okay. So there's every chance she knows where you are, and that you just can't temporarily reach her. And when we get some help in

here tomorrow, we'll have a way to get messages out. You're at the top of that list. I promise you won't be forgotten."

Delores was still trailing after her. "Jane," she said. "What about my cot?"

Well, she couldn't very well put off the lady any longer. She motioned her into the alcove that held the now-nonfunctional game and pop machines. An ideal place for a private conversation. "Delores," she said gently, "I think it's terrible, just terrible, that your friend Joella would take one of the few cots when you're suffering so much. But I think, ideally, what you could do is create a bed for yourself with clothes— bunching up soft spots and support exactly where you want it. A cot is just…hard. If you use clothes and pillows and soft jackets and all, you're going to have a much, much softer bed than your friend. Not that I'd tell her that."

"Oh, I won't," Delores assured her. She hesitated, but then remembered, "But what about the hiddenite she stole from me?"

"Now that's a very serious thing," she said gravely, thankful she'd had a couple neighbors who'd relentlessly enthused about certain new-age ideas. Possibly Delores had mangled the philosophical concepts to suit herself, but at least Jane understood the gist of the older woman's complaint. "But I don't think we'd want anyone else to hear about that hiddenite, would we? Because probably everybody'd want to steal it then."

"Oh! I didn't think of that! You're so right!"

"And if I know my chakras…and I do," Jane assured her.

"You do?"

"Oh, yes. So I know that the power of the stone will wear out unless it's cleansed and, um, discharged once a week in a bowl of sea salt."

Delores's jaw dropped. "You *do* know!"

"Doesn't everyone?" Jane added in a whisper, "The point is, that anyone who stole it would only get value from the mineral for a really short time. After that, there's no reason she shouldn't give it back to you. And once you discharge it, then it'll work for you again. Right?"

"Jane, Jane, Jane…you're one outstanding woman. Not like some of the riffraff on that plane."

"Thank you, Delores. I really appreciate…" From the corner of her eye, she saw Hank barely two yards away, hands on hips, rolling his eyes at her. "…your vote of support. I need to help Colonel White with something now, okay?"

"Certainly, dear, certainly…."

When the plump little lady wandered off, she faced Hank—who seemed to be crooking his finger at her. Apparently he'd overheard the conversation and seemed to think she'd suddenly turned into a lunatic.

"Look, you gave me the job of handling complaints! I'm trying to keep some of the trickier passengers off your back! I'm doing the best I can!"

Still, he motioned her closer.

"Okay, so I can't say I believe in magical minerals and mysticism and all, but I had to tell her something.

Most of the passengers are terrific. They're all stepping
up to be helpful. There are just a few who seem to be
on the pain-in-the-keester high maintenance list. I—"

Her voice failed her when he grabbed her hand. It
wasn't as if she minded if he touched her. It was just…a
surprise. The sudden warmth and zing of connection.
The way he slid his fingers between hers, the way teenagers held hands or at least the way *they'd* held hands
back when. At the time, holding hands had seemed
corny—even if she liked it—and now, well, he seemed
to be herding her past the ticket counter toward a private
door.

He glanced around, as if to insure no one was
looking, and then quickly opened the door and ushered
her inside.

"I think," he said, "that you've more than earned
combat pay. But since that isn't an option in these circumstances, the crew thought you'd earned a drink."

She blinked when she regarded the reprobates in the
back office. Only dim twilight filtered through the long
oblong window overlooking the tarmac. With drinking
water at a premium, clearly the group was trying not to
waste it. In fact, from the concentrated alcoholic fumes
in the small space, everyone had to be drinking straight
from either mini-airline bottles or their own private stash.

No one was exactly partying. It was just all the spiffy
uniforms of the staff that morning had suffered major
wrinkles, along with the bodies wearing them. The
group was sprawled on the floor under the window,
looking exhausted…but good-humored.

"We're all alive," the co-pilot from the second

stranded plane—George, she'd come to know—piped up by way of an excuse. "We thought we needed to celebrate that. On top of which, everybody put in a lion's effort today, and we'll all have to turn around and do the same tomorrow. So the consensus was that we should take five to click glasses together. Or paper cups, as it were. Jane—you've done more than your share."

"So has everyone," she said.

"What's your poison?" Hank asked.

"What's available?"

"Almost everything. As long as you don't want water with it or necessarily want more than an ounce at a time."

She laughed. "Scotch, then."

"Scotch? The girl has to have some Irish blood in her somewhere," Hank told the group approvingly.

Someone had lit a utility candle, plunked it in a glass on the desk. It flickered a pale light, not enough to il-luminate the handful of faces or the room...but it reminded Jane of campfires from when she was a girl, the shine of eyes and glow of cheeks in the darkness, the sense of belonging. When Hank handed her the Dixie cup of Scotch, she raised it to salute the group and then took a healthy sip.

It was bad Scotch. Ultra bad. So bad it burned holes in the back of her throat, yet for the first time in— weeks? months?—she felt herself relaxing. She eased down to the floor, cross-legged, inhaling the scents of the candle and heat and alcohol. The scents were hardly an aromatic perfume, but somehow, she associated the mix instinctively with safety.

It was like the co-pilot said. No matter how incon-

venient or uncomfortable or frustrated they may be…
they were alive. And coping pretty darn well together,
at least so far.

Jane realized Hank had plunked down next to her.
The others were talking, desultory fashion, about what
they were missing. The pilot had been en route to a
month's vacation. Two more days of flying and he'd
have been in Alaska, his favorite getaway spot. He
loved it all, the bears and salmon and eagles and
kayaking waters with whales.

Another man spoke up—a staff person from the
airport, although Jane didn't know his name. His four-
year-old was having a birthday tomorrow. A daughter.
He called her Bubble Face. He'd promised to be there,
and his wife… "Man, if my wife has to survive eleven
four-year-olds on her own, she'll never let me hear the
end of it. And Bubble Face, she's been talking about it
for weeks. What she's gonna wear. Whether she can
have purple frosting on her cake. Whether she's going
to get this certain doll. How she gets to put this sparkly
stuff on her fingers for the party. On and on."

Jane eased her back against an old-fashioned metal
desk. The metal was unyielding, but still felt cool, and
just having that physical support against her spine
relaxed her nerves another notch. She took another sip,
felt Hank glance at her.

She didn't look at him, though, but at the person in
the corner who was taking his turn talking. The co-pilot
from their plane, who she'd talked to a dozen times that
day. He looked a little too *GQ* to be military, but he was
a good-looking guy, and talked and walked like he

knew it. Still, he'd chipped in with humor and elbow grease just like everyone else all day.

And now he piped up, "You all sound like you had great stuff to go home to. But frankly, I don't mind being here. I just broke up with a woman I'd been seeing for almost two years. Really didn't want to go home. Still don't. I'm relieved as hell we're all okay— flying into that storm was no fun—and the forecasters should be horsewhipped, if you ask me. But there's nobody I'd rather fly with than Chuck. And so far I don't mind seeing this all as an adventure."

After that, it was Hank's turn at the conversational bat. A déjà vu sensation hit Jane when she saw how he suddenly ducked his head—it was a gesture he'd had, that long ago summer, when he was forced to talk about himself. He'd been an ace in the debate team, could speak in front of a group in high school. That never seemed his worry. He'd just never liked to draw attention to himself personally.

Still, he was game to answer how he'd come to be here and what the tornado had interrupted for him. "I was headed to Griffin Air Force base, to share in a promotion and celebration for an old friend. I grew up in Connecticut, but my home base has been Colorado Springs for years now. The Air Force Academy is there. Pikes Peak country. I've got two kids, grown, or the same as. Lost my wife a couple years ago to ovarian cancer, which was a bitch and a half. Sucked the life and heart out of our kids, same as it did me. But it's like the tornado. Sometimes you can't outrun it, so you just try to knuckle down and get on the other side…"

Hank scraped a hand through his hair, then leaned back against the cement wall. "Anyway…technically I doubt I'm missing anything. I have to believe everyone at Griffin's doing the same thing we're doing here. Chipping in. Doing whatever they can to help everybody past the mess of this storm. I'll eventually get to my friend, but right now, it's no hardship or problem for me to be here. Just as soon be part of doing what needs to be done, getting everybody fed and sheltered and eventually put on their way again…"

*Married,* she thought. Not that that was a surprise. Everyone she knew—at their age—had been married at least once by now. Sometimes twice.

Still, she absorbed the picture of his life those few words had framed for her. He'd obviously deeply loved his wife. Loved his kids. Created a life that really mattered to him.

That long ago summer…that Beach Boy summer… he'd not only trailed after her like a lovesick puppy. He'd seemed sure of nothing he wanted from his life. He'd had no career goals, no life plans, hadn't been sure of a single thing. Except that he wanted her.

She'd wanted him, too. But that had been about hormones and desire, and her parents had drilled into her how much fun that was—but how irrelevant to real life. Even before high school, she'd had a mapped-out life plan, with the ambition and determination and discipline to follow through. And because Hank hadn't been on her schedule, she'd jettisoned her feelings for him like yesterday's newspaper—not without guilt or regret. But because that's what she thought she had to do.

And now...lately, it wasn't as if she'd changed her mind about what was right or wrong. It was just...

She wanted to be Peachy again.

She wanted, just once, to taste again what it had been like, to be young and high and so sure of everything. To be wanted more than anything else in life. At least in someone's life.

"Jane?" The pilot's voice interrupted her mental mulling. "Your turn. Where were you trying to go when we got hit with these tornadoes?"

Good question, she thought. And gulped down the last of the amber fire in her Dixie cup, only wishing the Scotch could enable her to know that answer.

"Well...I'm a lawyer. A contract lawyer. I made partner last year in the firm I've been with for the last nine years. I'm divorced. Three kids, one in Seattle, one in Alaska, and my daughter's still in college, but Angel's in Europe for the summer right now in a school program. My home base is in Connecticut, Branbury...."

Even in the dark, she could feel the others looking at her, waiting.

And abruptly she realized that she was willingly offering up the facts. The surface information that gave the impression of a successful, happy life. The surface information she always willingly offered to anyone who asked.

But the others had shared something more personal. More honest. More...vulnerable.

For the first time in a long time, she wanted to do the same. This back room was dark and quiet and hot.

None of these people were ever likely to meet up with each other again. There was nothing to risk by offering something personal about herself out there.

But somehow...the words wouldn't come.

She tried to say something, but her throat dried up and she found herself swallowing, then swallowing again.

Finally she said, "Honestly, I haven't minded being here, helping out. So many people have it a lot worse."

She smiled, but it felt like a raw, fake smile. And when no one immediately responded or said anything, she lurched to her feet as if someone lit a fire beneath her fanny. "I loved the drink. Thanks for including me. But I just remembered that I promised to help one of the older passengers get settled...."

She barreled out of there so fast, she almost knocked over a waste basket. It took two fumbles for her to get the door open, but then she was outside, and the long, wide lobby of the terminal was darker than mud now that the sun was down.

A few yards away, two men were chatting, their silhouettes starkly clear against one window, the shadows of a husband and wife paired in another. The whole lobby had quieted down, with most trying to sleep. People had either grouped with newfound friends or whoever they'd been traveling with. Couples hadn't been separated, only the single passengers curtained off by gender. Jane suspected it wouldn't have mattered; the long, exhausting day had made almost everyone konk out early.

Not her. Her heart was beating louder than a noisy drum.

She wasn't used to acting like a fool. Not used to feeling like one. But the most unfamiliar sensation of all was tasting the flavor of loneliness, in her throat, in her heart. She seemed to be the only one wandering around solo.

Being alone was her own doing, her own fault, her own choice. She knew that. But the feeling of intense loneliness still burned, like the bullet of a sniper she'd never seen coming.

# CHAPTER FOUR

When Hank pushed open the door, it was barely 4:00 a.m. The sun hadn't cracked the horizon yet, but the sky had softened to a dark pearl-gray. Clouds were still restless, as if they couldn't forget the tumultuous storms from the day before, but a few stars poked through the cover.

It was light enough to see—at least to make out vague shapes—but more important, it was fresh outside. Cool enough to breathe.

Airports were his bailiwick. Instinctively, his gaze took in the damage to ramps, service vehicles, gates, chevrons—all the things that were going to need work before the airport was fully functional again.

Only two planes were in sight. All the other aircraft had been moved safely undercover before the tornadoes hit. Fuel and cargo trucks also appeared to have been locked up tight before the storms. The control tower, he already knew because he'd spent hours there yesterday, was also in good shape.

The smell of soup wafted from their hodgepodge of an outside kitchen—the same steak soup they'd had for dinner and were probably going to have, in some va-

riation, for the next couple meals as well. All freezers in the vicinity had lost power, and since steak was the most expensive thing being lost, it was the first food volunteered. Keeping the pots on the barbecue kept the food safe. Various passengers had volunteered to supervise the fire in shifts. The night volunteer was nodding off with a spoon in his hand.

The only other body outside was a small figure leaning against the outside wall.

Hank recognized her immediately, and hesitated— for a whole two seconds—before hiking over to her.

"Peachy." He spoke her name softly so he wouldn't startle her. She wasn't sleeping. Her tousled blond head was leaned back against the building, but her knees were cocked up, her posture clearly indicating someone who was tired but tense.

Her head whipped around the moment she heard his voice.

"Couldn't sleep inside?" he asked.

"I only wish," she said wryly. "But there's something about sleeping with a couple hundred strangers...."

He had to grin. "A little too personal for all of us, I'd guess." He edged down next to her, using the cool building for back support the way she did, cocking up his legs, same as her. Quietly he said, "Something seemed to upset you earlier."

She ducked that. "The whole group's great. So many people are pitching in to help."

"You, too."

"Yeah...but it's way easier for me to pitch in, than try to sit still with nothing to do." She added, "You

seemed to get elected boss of this mess, whether you wanted the job or not."

"Actually, there's a formal hierarchy set up for crisis situations in public places like airports, but this…well, there just hasn't been a reason to nail down roles quite like that. Maybe they're giving me a figurative chair at the head of the table, but it's more politeness than anything else, probably because the two pilots have the rank of captain, where I'm a colonel."

She glanced at him, obviously not taken in by his self-deprecating tone. "So a colonel is way higher than a captain," she murmured.

Again he had to grin. She obviously didn't have a clue about military rankings. No reason she should have. And he'd had enough talking about the "business" of their situation. "Right now I'd about kill for a good cup of coffee."

She closed her eyes, obviously swept away by the same fantasy. "Hazelnut. No sugar, no cream. Just a fresh-brewed hazelnut…"

"Hell, don't do that. I can almost taste it."

It was her turn to chuckle, and Hank realized it was the first time he'd seen a spontaneous smile from her…and suddenly, there it was. Even in the predawn dimness, even in the disheveled shape they both were, even with all the years passed between them…he remembered that smile.

He remembered *her,* the way he hadn't before.

Their gazes connected, held. Suddenly the morning air was electric, the mist whispering around the dew-drenched grounds surrounding them in privacy. She

was the only thing in life that seemed clear at that moment. Those amazing blue eyes. The petal soft skin, the thin little nose, the elegant cheekbones and high-arched brows. The tinyness of her. She was so short, so little, yet such a dynamo. A concentrated package of potent, pure female sexual energy.

He remembered that part of her as if it were yesterday. She'd always been so bursting with life. She'd always been driven to do things, to make a difference. She was passionate about every cause she took on, and had the backbone and determination to back up her dreams.

"Where *were* you going when we ran into that tornado weather yesterday?" he murmured.

"Right here."

"You mean *really* here? Kokomo, Indiana?" he asked disbelievingly.

She let out a humorous sigh. "Any way I say this, it's going to sound silly. Because it is. But yesterday morning, when I got on the plane...I was trying to follow an old summer dream."

"And that dream was...?"

"I wasn't headed to Kokomo, Indiana. I was trying to head for one of the Cayman Islands, the one that used to be named Kokomo. The one that was in the old Beach Boys song. Only a temp working in the office made the arrangements, and she apparently confused what I'd asked for and I was so darned busy I never looked or checked. She set up the tickets for the wrong Kokomo. It was just a totally silly goof."

He didn't know what to say. It *did* sound silly and impossible, but then, that was what mistakes usually

were. Unlikely twists in the road. Stop signs no one noticed. "Okay…I remember the song. But…what does the song have to do with the old summer dream you were following? You mean…you always wanted to vacation on a Caribbean island?"

"No." The first peak of pink frosted the horizon. The light was suddenly perfect, but he could see her more clearly. See those startling blue eyes, the blush of color on her cheeks. "I meant…I got this idea…I mean…"

He sensed she wasn't used to stumbling over her words, that possibly he'd stumbled into touchy territory for her. But she was tired, and it was dawn, and they knew each other way back when. Maybe the circumstances encouraged her to keep talking, even if she found it hard.

"I had this idea," she repeated, "that I just once wanted to feel the way I had when I was seventeen. That summer of our senior year."

He turned his head, listening.

"I was a self-centered brat back then," she said wryly.

"Hey. No, you weren't."

"Yeah, I was. But the good part, the part I wanted to feel again, was just the flavor of being happy that way again. I was so sure of what was right and wrong, so sure of where I was going, so sure that I could have everything that was important if I just worked for it…I *know,* this all sounds ridiculous. It was ridiculous back then, too. Cripes, I can't explain this."

She was right. Nothing she said made much sense to him. But if the words didn't add up, her tone of her

voice, her posture, her eyes did. She was unhappy. Terribly unhappy.

"You mentioned that you were a lawyer. A contract lawyer. If I remember right, that was exactly what you wanted, your law degree…."

"Oh, yeah. And that's just it. I bulldozed through life going after exactly what I wanted. And damn it, Hank, I *got* it. I was so positive that certain goals and achievements would make me happy. Instead, I feel as if I took a wrong turn. Back when I was young. Maybe even back in that summer of our senior year…." She hesitated, turned to face him. A whispery breeze suddenly silked strands of hair across her chin. She lifted a hand to push them away, her gaze still on his, intent, electric. Out of the blue, she said, "You really don't remember me, do you?"

"Of course I do. We've both been talking about that high school summer, knowing each other—"

She shook her head, swiftly, fiercely. "Yeah. You remember me in some vague way. But not really. Darn it, Hank. I hurt you. I was a bitch times three. Selfish. Thoughtless. And since fate handed us this unexpected chance to see each other again…I just want to say I'm sorry."

Hank's first instinct was to say an easy, "Hey, it's okay, forget it," but it obviously wasn't okay for her, wasn't something she'd forgotten. He racked his memory bank for that long-ago senior summer.

He'd had an embarrassingly painful crush on her— but then, so had every guy in the senior class.

Jane was the class goddess.

He was just a guy.

She'd been passionately involved in everything—class politics, world causes, grades, music. She'd led the prom committee and the cheerleading squad and all that obvious stuff the girls tended to like, but she'd also been the kind to pitch in after a football game to help clean up—and to spur everybody else to help. She was zesty and fun, full of spirit and laughter. Everybody liked her, but the guys…well, the guys groveled.

She was a little tiny for the average goddess sex symbol, but her small size just made the guys feel more protective. She was blond and adorable and ultra-feminine right down to her fingertips. Her family had big money, but she never acted like it.

He'd taken her to the summer country club cotillion, but not because he'd ever expected it to happen. For him, it had been like a winning lottery ticket falling out of the sky. He'd never had any intention of attending the white-tux dance thing…until Peachy turned into his date.

It was complicated, the way social politics in an upscale suburb always were. Peachy didn't need a date so much as an escort. His father and her father were both on the planning board. They arranged it—not like medieval fathers forcing their kids into a marriage, but just manipulating their kids into being allied for this event. Why, Hank couldn't remember. If he knew at the time, he hadn't cared. He only cared about getting his arms around his goddess.

She'd paired up with him a few times before that, but no different than she'd done things with a lot of guys.

She wasn't serious about anyone. If some event came up, she often impulsively included whatever guy was in her vicinity. God knew, he'd always made a point of being in her vicinity.

Hank remembered that dance. She'd come with him…but left with someone else.

He hadn't been exactly thrilled at that turn of events—but it hadn't hurt the way a bullet through his heart would have. At the time, it made sense to him. She'd gone off with a guy who was more in her league. Big money. Headed for an Ivy League college the way she was. When she'd taken off, there'd been no stunning blow, more like something he'd been waiting for—like knowing a final exam was coming, or facing a tetanus shot.

She was never going to end up with him, so he'd never allowed himself to fantasize in impossible directions like that. Hell, he was just glad to have the chance to do the escort thing, to get his arms around her for the dances, to have her looking up at him with those sassy blue eyes and perky grin.

"This is about that dance?" he asked slowly. "Your leaving with that other guy?"

She looked at him again. "That's part of what I'm sorry for, yes."

Now he felt even more confused. "There's more?"

"Yes. In fact, there's something I've been a whole lot more sorry for." And she reached for him.

If a lightning bolt hit him, Hank couldn't have been more stunned.

He was years distant from that green boy with his

tongue hanging out from yearning…he'd been married, loved from the heart and soul, and of course he recognized the click of chemistry. But a kiss from her—he just never expected it.

They were on a tarmac in Kokomo, Indiana, for Pete's sake. The sun was coming up fast and bright now. Debris from the tornado dominated the view. Mosquitoes were rising, along with already choking heat, and the asphalt felt gruff against their butts. There was just nothing, anywhere in sight or sound, conducive to romantic feelings.

Neither was her kiss, for that matter. She just seemed to twist around on her knees—a totally awkward position for her—clutch her hands on his shoulders for balance and then, eyes closed, plunk her mouth on his.

It was a crooked kiss.

A silly kiss.

A downright embarrassing kiss.

Even so, he caught a whiff of something he remembered. A scent, a taste. The shape of her mouth, the tilt of her head. Something that stirred memories he hadn't even known were stored like treasure in the memory banks of his brain.

For a second or two, anyway. Because that was as long as the kiss lasted.

She reared back, still twisted on her knees, her eyes popping wide and looking straight into his.

"Damn it," she said.

"Yeah, that's what I was thinking."

"I'm sorry. Really sorry." She sank back on her heels

then, but she was still facing him with a very odd, very determined, very thoughtful look.

He was looking at her, too, but not like before. He'd never felt fear flying an F-16, but her, now…he had the sudden, wary instinct that the bright, civilized, intelligent woman he'd once known as Peachy had a closet lioness in her. A lioness who could pounce without warning. "There's no reason to be *that* sorry," he said a little wryly. "I mean, I'm not sure what that was about, but…"

"I'll tell you," she said softly, bluntly. "I'd been thinking that there was a moment when my life took a major wrong turn, even if I didn't realize it at the time. And it was that summer you took me to that dance. The summer I took off on you. I remember the feeling when you kissed me, but the chemistry hadn't seemed that important then. I didn't value it. Didn't need it. Didn't think it mattered."

Whoa, he wanted to say, yet somehow couldn't. Between no sleep, no breakfast, that ram of a kiss, and now her sharing fiercely private revelations…he just couldn't seem to process it all, not coherently. "Peachy," he said gently, wanting to stop her before she said anything else. Who knew if she might really regret sharing such serious stuff with a man who'd long become a stranger to her?

"That chemistry did matter then, Hank. But not now." She shook her head with a self-deprecating chuckle. "Well, maybe I'm *not* sorry I kissed you. At least now I know for sure it's completely gone. There's nothing there."

Nothing there?

Hank told himself the only reason he felt ripped raw was because she'd stabbed his ego. Okay, he admitted it, he'd wanted her to feel a mighty attraction to him. What guy wouldn't want the goddess of his teenage fantasies to feel uncontrollable desire for him? And that reason for his ripped-raw feeling was true. At least ten percent true. But the other ninety percent of his psyche was suffering for an entirely different reason.

Of course the darned woman hadn't felt anything. She'd jammed her mouth on his and lifted it two seconds later.

It wasn't just that her kiss had been pale.

A two-second smooch didn't risk a damn thing.

There was no good sex without risk.

And if she was that hot to dive into old memories, then so could he. Because the only gold to win in life happened when you risked it all.

So he grabbed *her* this time. But softly. Wrapped his arms around her shoulders this time. But slowly.

And he lowered his mouth on hers this time, but definitely not in a flat, aggressive smack. He took her mouth, one sip at a time, deepened the kiss, one taste at a time. You couldn't get down to the level of yearning, unless you opened your heart to it. He'd learned that…well, God knew when. He just knew it. The way anybody who'd had good sex knew it.

Didn't take long.

Not with her.

Her right hand had been in startled midair when *this* kiss started. Now it was clinging around his waist, kneading the skin through his shirt. Her spine had been

stiff when he'd shifted her across his lap. Now it bowed, eased against his supportive arm. Her eyes had been stark open when he'd first hooked her close. Now those soft eyelids were closed, her pale lashes creating shadows on her cheeks, a flush of desire stroking her throat and cheeks with hectic color.

Oh, yeah. And she was kissing him back.

*This* was a kiss that involved tongues and teeth. A kiss that reached greedily for more feeling, more risk. A kiss that found both...then dove back for more.

Hank had the vague, mortifying awareness that he was turning back into an out-of-control teenage boy. He didn't get ruffled. In his life, in his career, control and character and strength were critical survival skills. In a crisis, he was the one who never lost it.

But he was sure as hell losing it now.

Again, suddenly, she jolted free, lifted her head and looked him straight in the eyes. Shock showed in her expression this time. Shock...and desire.

She started to say something, yet no sound came out of her mouth. Quicker than panic then, she pushed off his lap, stood, looked at the sun zooming up the sky, the light on the tarmac that hadn't been there minutes before, and shook her head as if she were trying to make sense from an incomprehensible world.

Again she tried to say something, but words refused to emerge from her mouth that time, too. Apparently giving up, she spun around, stumbled toward the door of the terminal, grappled twice with the pull bar before she could successfully open it, and then finally shot inside.

Hank stood and raked a hand through his hair. Nothing that just happened made sense. Nothing she'd done. Nothing he'd done.

He'd never been threatened by Peachy as a kid. Awed, yeah. Overwhelmed, oh, yeah. Wildly in-crush with, totally. But not intimidated by.

He couldn't think of much in life that intimidated him. God and war, naturally, but not people. People were mysteries he was interested in, comfortable with.

But the emotional place that woman had just taken him was an unknown, evocative ground, untested, off his map.

He was too damn old for those kinds of shenanigans, he told himself. But there it was. His heart was thudding like a muffled engine.

The man fifty yards across the tarmac—the volunteer manning the massive soup pots—had woken up and was standing up now. He waved, and if Hank wasn't mistaken, winked.

Pretty obvious he'd seen that kiss.

Pretty obvious he'd thought Hank had something hot going on.

Hell. The tornado was beginning to look like a lot easier crisis than Jane.

## CHAPTER FIVE

$J$ane tottered back into the terminal lobby and was immediately assaulted by the heat and rush of smells. It was the second day of no air-conditioning, no showers, and intrepid heat and humidity. The repercussions were starting to add up.

The smells weren't unpleasant—yet. But it'd be a good thing if they could air the place out today…better yet if they could all start leaving before much more time passed. And the chaos took her mind off Hank, at least for a time.

The night before, she'd set up a spot to sleep near the door. Now she dug in her bag, found fresh clothes and some toiletries and started trying to do a shape-up. She had makeup wipes to freshen her face. Deodorant. Under a light blanket, she peeled off clothes, pulled on yellow shorts and a wild yellow print top—one of the few outfits she'd tossed in for the island.

She ran a brush through her hair, pushed bare feet into flip-flops, and searched through her bag in the dim light until she finally located the finger-size teeth cleaners she always carried on planes.

By then, three people had yanked on the blanket to talk to her.

Because she was still rattled over Hank, the errant thought slipped into her mind that it would be impossible to have a love affair here. Even a one-night stand. Even a quickie. There wasn't an ounce of privacy to be had for love or money.

Not that she was thinking about quickies.

"What, Delores?" As she zipped up her bag, she found the new-age lady with the flowing gray hair, wringing her hands again.

"Someone took my celestite this time. I tried to find you before. But once everybody started getting up and moving around this morning, it was all crowded and confusing. And that's when I think somebody got into my suitcase and stole the celestite."

"Darn," Jane murmured.

"This isn't like the hiddenite. I *have* to have the celestite. It came from my grandmother, you see. It only works if it's given by a relative, so it's not like the thief could get any benefit from it. And it doesn't work unless the person's connected to both Capricorn and Gemini."

"Which of course you are," Jane said.

"Of course—"

"Have you been outside for breakfast yet?"

"I couldn't eat. I've been too upset."

"Okay. I want to hear all about the theft, but first let's go by your things, get any medication you're taking, then head outside for a little nourishment."

"I—"

"I know. You couldn't possibly eat. But you can tell me more while we're walking, okay?"

That idea calmed the older woman almost immedi-

ately. "Celestite works on the throat chakra, but that's not the point. The point is that it helps one get one's equilibrium back. It helps calm a person. It's been *very* hard to be calm since the tornadoes—"

"Yes, it sure is. That celestite—it's kind of a blue-white stone, isn't it?"

"Actually, it's a mineral, dear. Not just a stone. And this one has the darker blue shade, so it's much more powerful."

"And the points always have to point toward the sky or it doesn't work," Jane said, earning a huge sigh of relief from her ethereal sidekick.

"I knew you'd understand. So many people treat me like a batty old woman."

"No," Jane said disbelievingly, gave the older woman a hug, and moved on to the next problem.

People were increasingly anxious to contact loved ones, to get answers about when the airport would be running again, about how, when, and where they were getting out of here. There was plenty of food, because the loss of electricity meant everything in any freezer had to be used up or risk being spoiled, so there was still no end of stuff to fill the big pots outside. But they were going to run out of dishes or paper ways of serving things before much longer, and clean silverware was worth gold.

"You know…" A man named Ralph was helping her move a chair, using it to prop open a door to let more fresh air into the lobby. "I can't say I'm glad this happened. But…it's all kind of interesting. I never thought about any of these problems before."

"Neither had I," Jane admitted.

"Anything else we need to move?"

"No, but...you know where we've got all those people camped on the floor by the west entrance? I don't suppose you could coax them to relocate a little so there'd be a clear path to the door? Last night, people complained they couldn't move without stepping on someone else. If we could help them organize a little better..."

"Done," Ralph said, and took off.

A man broke his glasses. A rubber band provided a makeshift fix, but it took a while to locate a rubber band. Someone else needed first aid cream for a blister. The captain was organizing groups to move debris off the tarmac, so Jane put out the word. Another small group was walking outside, hoping to assess the vicinity around the airport, to see if there might be transportation or power within a walkable distance— or, for that matter, if there were others who needed help.

Jane kept thinking that she wasn't doing enough. She didn't know anything about sanitation or electricity or communications or any of the serious things going on. Yet by the time she ambled outside to grab some lunch around two, the bright hot sun illuminated two scrapes on her hands and a healthy bruise blooming on her knee.

"What on earth did you do to yourself?"

Hank's voice shivered on her nerves like a brush of silk. She whirled around. It was the first time she'd seen him since early that morning. She'd told herself

that she'd forgotten that exotic embrace between them—or imagined its power—but seeing him invoked fresh nerves all over again.

"I haven't a clue," she answered him, glancing down at the scrapes and bruises. "I haven't done a darn thing—"

"That's not what I've been hearing. The crew says you're the one keeping the passengers from imploding."

"Honestly, that's not true. Almost everyone's pulling their weight and then some."

"That's what I see, too. A few complainers, but that'd be true in every situation. And people are worried and frustrated. Who wouldn't be?"

He was holding a bowl, so was she. Almost everyone else had eaten lunch by that time. There were no surprises in the menu, beyond a few more peas and corn in the steak soup.

"I have to admit, I'd sure like a few more choices," she murmured.

Hank swiped two bottles of warm soda. "We're fast getting out of the mainstream drinks, too. Clearly mango guava juice was a little over-ordered by concession lady."

"I think most people are still thinking of it as picnicking, though. Making do."

"Me, too. But as soon as this is over, I want a drink with ice. And nothing that looks like hot soup."

"You're not kidding. Especially the ice!" He was making it easy to be with him, as if that wild moment that morning had never happened. That was okay by her. Nothing wrong with denial when a girl was des-

perate. She sank down in the shade of the building next to him. Since that morning, she was amazed how much had been done. "The whole tarmac looks cleared. I can't believe it!"

Hank nodded. "I don't know how soon we'll get repairs done from yesterday, but planes should start being able to land again shortly. And a truck made it from the Air Force base this morning—"

She was listening, but when he lifted a spoon to his mouth, she saw the streak of blood on the back of his arm. "Hank, what did you do?!"

He glanced down. "I think my elbow had an argument with a pair of pliers. And the pliers won."

"That needs some serious first aid, if not stitches."

"Says the lady with her own set of cuts and scrapes. And the blister on your hand has to smart."

With some bemusement, she noticed the bubble on her right palm. It looked particularly startling against...well, against such a pampered hand. She'd always had a major female streak about manicures, nice hand creams, pretty nails. Or she had until two days ago. Oddly enough, she felt a weird pride in the blister. "You know, it didn't hurt until you brought it up."

"That's it, blame me for your working like a dog," Hank teased.

She grinned—but then devoured the completely boring and unappetizing soup. For someone who loved sushi and a raw shrimp salad for lunch, preferably served with sterling and a snowy white linen napkin, she seemed to be falling on the soup like a pig—and a

greedy, hungry pig at that. "You're getting some first aid cream and a bandage for that arm, mister, just as soon as we finish lunch."

"And you're getting first aid and bandages for some blisters, missy, so don't try arguing with me."

"I suppose we could have an argument about who's bossier."

"I suppose you'd win," he said wryly.

"Of course I'd win. I'm the woman."

She yanked his chain for another few minutes, effortlessly, easily...before it suddenly hit her that she'd turned back into a teenager. Just like that, she was flirting with Hank again. Teasing a boy. Shooting him smiles and insults.

On top of an embrace that was still frying her brain when she thought about it.

Which, of course, she wasn't.

"Wait a minute. You said an Air Force truck made it here this morning?" By then they'd dumped their dishes and she was steering him toward the terminal office that stashed the first aid supplies.

"Yeah. We've been trying to pass the word. There probably isn't going to be electricity for a few more days yet. The whole town and surrounding area was hit by tornados, so there's no end of repairs that need to be done. But emergency services are now up and moving."

Two of the passengers were nurses, who'd been manning the first aid supplies since yesterday. But no one was there when Jane poked her head in, and it wasn't like it took a brain surgeon to clean his open cut and use some antiseptic.

*"Hey."*

"I'm sorry. There's no choice. Without plain old soap and water and sanitary conditions not exactly on a par with the Ritz afraid you really need an extra shot of alcohol there. In fact, I think you need a tetanus shot—"

"No."

She chuckled. "There isn't one. Relax. But how'd you get to be a colonel and still be such a sissy?"

"It's easy."

"Come on. Suck it up. The worst is over. Now it's just some antibiotic and a good tight bandage. I really think you should have a few stitches, but hopefully if the tape is snug enough, the cut will seal okay." Fixing the cut was no big deal, yet she still felt intensely conscious of his skin, the warmth of him, the closeness. She kept waiting for a sense of responsibility and guilt to hit. It didn't. Instead, she just kept wading in that tickle of desire whisking through her. How long had it been since she'd felt that basic old hormonal rush? It was fierce. Fun.

Silly.

But welcomed.

Suddenly his eyes were meeting hers again. "You were real brave when you were holding the alcohol, cookie. But now it's my turn. Let's see that blister."

"Hey," she yelped.

"Now how did you get to be a cutthroat, high-falutin' heartless lawyer if you were still such a sissy?"

"It was easy."

"Come on," he said. "Suck it up. It sounds like we're both going to be here for a maximum of another twenty-four hours."

"Pardon?" The sudden change in conversation shot her head up. He'd been holding her hand. Treating her blister with some kind of balm. That's all she'd been thinking about, all she'd been feeling, but now...she had to listen.

"We're definitely on a priority list to get us all out of here. Air Force base will make that easier. The National Guard's priority yesterday was taking on the sick and vulnerable, but we're not far down on the list after that. Kokomo doesn't need more visitors to feed and house. They'll get us shuttled out of here by late tomorrow, onto flights leaving from Indianapolis. You can pass the word along. I'm guessing it'll perk everyone up."

"Yeah, it will," she said. But it was weird, how low her heart suddenly sank.

It was going to be over. Soon. No more sleeping with a bunch of noisy, snoring, coughing strangers. No more bad smells. No more steak soup. No more dark, no more inconveniences, no more incessant heat. Life would get back to normal, with fresh showers and clean hair and real food. Computers. Cars. The whole ball of wax.

"Everyone'll be thrilled," she said hollowly. And tried to grapple with why she felt suddenly as if someone had socked her in the teeth. It was just...she'd been busier than a one-armed bandit. She was busy in her regular life, of course. Beyond belief busy. But here, she'd been feeling...useful. Feeling good. Feeling, well, young again.

"Peachy?" She felt Hank's knuckles gently touch her chin, coax her face up to his. "Hey." His tone lowered to baritone-butter. "What's wrong? Are those tears?"

She looked up at him. And then couldn't. A thug of emotion seemed to slug her in the heart. It hurt. The way her heart hadn't hurt in a very long time. She should be wanting to go back to her wonderful life. But the truth was…she didn't. Something was right here, that hadn't been right in her life in a very long time.

"Peachy?" he said again.

"I'm fine," she said. "Just had something in my eye." What else could she say? If she tried to really explain, he'd think she was crazy. Hell and a half, she knew she was reacting crazily. She didn't suddenly think Hank could or would or should be part of her life again. It was just…those kisses. And that for the first time in years, she'd felt young again. Young and bursting with hormones, bursting with hope and life. Feeling zingy and zesty on the inside. Feeling female. Inside and out.

"Okay, just say it. Whatever's wrong—"

But obviously she couldn't. And since she seemed stuck being in an immature, foolish way, she did what any mom knew worked. She took an immediate time out. Jerked to her feet and got out of Hank's sight.

Once away from the privacy of that back office, back in the wildly busy terminal again, her pulse almost immediately calmed down. People aimed for her faster than bullets—two had complaints, two had an argument they wanted her to settle. A man recovering from surgery had lost his walking cane. One of the passengers had seemed to disappear; no one knew where she was. And there was that announcement to spread through the group—that rescue was on the way and they'd be out of here as soon as sometime tomorrow.

She'd always loved it. Trouble. Confusion. The stuff normal people ran from. Probably she'd been drawn to lawyering because she loved sorting out messes, prioritizing the right from the more right, the wrong from the most wrong.

But right now, it wasn't about that. She just wanted to be too busy to think, and that was easier to accomplish than breathing. Every minute involved dealing with the unpredictable and unexpected and sometimes zany, working with all these strangers that she'd somehow bonded with.

Halfway through the afternoon, one of the airport staff tracked her down. She'd been outside, bringing a tray of drinks to the wheelchair group playing cards in the shade. "Got a message for you," the man named Brian told her.

She cocked her head.

"Your kids. Bry? Lar and Angel? They all knew the flight you were on, knew from the news that your flight had gotten stranded, didn't want to clog up emergency channels to find you…but they were worried. So they went through the National Guard to make sure you were okay. The message was that they loved you and to get in touch when you get out of here."

She smiled. "I've got great kids."

"Sounds like it."

She calmed down another notch. Hearing from the kids always did that. Even though they were all pretty independent now, launched in their own lives, the connection reminded her that wonderful love was just as real, even if they were physically distant from each other. It wasn't as if *everything* was wrong with her life.

It was just that *something* was.

And it had taken a tornado to make her notice.

Late afternoon, a big, noisy camouflage truck barreled down the runway—bringing everyone out of wherever they'd been hanging out and creating the atmosphere of a party. The guys had been delivering supplies to a local hospital and clinic. They had no news other than what the group already knew—that roads were being cleared, and they could expect buses to pick them up by late afternoon the next day to head for the Indianapolis airport. But they also brought supplies—boxes of ice and water, and enough plastic dishes and ware to get them through another day.

It wasn't as if they'd been stranded for years, but Jane found herself as boisterously happy as everyone else. The new bodies bought news. A reason to laugh. Stories to share. Affirmation that they'd all be home soon, that others were all right, that the tornadoes had destroyed tons of property but there'd been no deaths, no serious injuries.

Twice, Jane found herself searching the crowd for Hank.

The funny thing was…he was easy to find. He was everywhere, and since he was a half head taller than the average man, he was also easy to spot. And every time she located him, she found Hank looking straight at her. Finding *her*.

Unfortunately, there always seemed to be a dozen bodies between them. Or she'd be in the middle of a conversation or something else that had to be finished, and by the time she freed up to approach him, he was out of sight again.

Hank often seemed to be coming in and out of the air traffic control area, or hiking toward the plane maintenance area, or with the crew of people moving debris from the tarmac and roads.

Those were natural places for him to be, just like it was more natural for her to be in or around the terminal, because that was where the core group of passengers gathered—especially those who weren't as able and tended to have special needs.

By dusk that evening, though, the truck was long gone, dinner was long over, and Jane found herself outside. A group of passengers had congregated there and were just absently shooting some bull. Jane kept thinking what a motley and unlikely group they were—an old man with fierce eyebrows, one of the teenagers, a married couple who'd been headed to see their grandchildren, a nerdy kid from a prep school who'd been coming home for the weekend.

They all looked like fellow ruffians, with dirty hair and wrinkled clothes in general. They'd all snuck outside because of the heat, because they had nothing better to do. And normally they'd have nothing in common, but that was the thing.

They had the tornado in common.

They been stranded and survived and had each other in common.

Carl, the white-haired man, was a local farmer and looked the part. "Can't believe I'm stranded ten miles from home all this time. And when I get home, Leah's going to hose me down before she lets me in the house...." He shook his head, making them all laugh.

"I feel like I've been a year away from the Internet and e-mail." Rob, the studious young man, leaned his head back. "Last week, I couldn't have imagined it. But it hasn't been that bad."

"I don't think so, either," Margie, one of the volunteer cooks, piped up. "Something happens like this, it really shocks you into thinking, doesn't it? Nothing in life looks the same."

"We'll all be glad to get home after this," Carl said.

One by one, they wandered away. Rob wanted a walk. Heather wanted to find her friend. The others were hoping to settle down for the night, catch some sleep.

She wanted to do the same, yet she didn't go in after the others. She leaned back against the cool wall, closing her eyes, realizing yet again how everyone else couldn't wait to get home—except for her.

It wasn't that she didn't want to go home. She loved her home. Loved her kids. Once upon a time, she'd even loved her job, her whole life. Everything she worked for.

But she still didn't have a handle on what had gone wrong. Why and how she'd become a bitch. Why all the things she'd wanted so much, once upon a time, now seemed to give her no sense of satisfaction or reward.

"Peachy?"

Her head jerked up at the sound of Hank's voice.

# CHAPTER SIX

Seeing Jane, all alone, her head bent in a posture of such dejection…made something snap inside Hank.

She'd been on his mind all day. The way she'd suddenly taken off after he'd bandaged her hand. The hot sparkle of tears in her eyes, not because of the blister, but because of something else. Something that tore at his heart, just from looking at her face.

And that wasn't even counting the Armageddon of kisses from before that.

She lifted her eyes when she heard his voice. Dusk was falling fast now, the violet sky dusting everything with a soft jeweled glow. The same artist's palette colored her face. Her skin was so soft against the silhouette of the cement siding; her eyes, so full of shine and emotion.

"You're not sleepy yet?" he asked her.

"I only wish."

"Come on. Let's walk then."

"All right. Where to?"

He steered her toward the far hangar. Planes were his turf.

And almost everyone was settled down in the terminal or around the main buildings.

The minute they ambled inside, it was quieter. Cooler. A pair of guys were smoking, leaning against the outside wall, but when they saw him and Jane approaching, they waved and wandered off.

Deeper inside, it was darker than pitch, but an LED pocket flashlight illuminated the open door of a plane. The interior had been in the process of being cleaned when the storm came up, because the door was still open, a vacuum still in the aisle, trash scooped up and knotted tight. It was just empty. Port windows gleamed like black mirrors.

He clipped the LED light to the window. The light didn't reach the corners, but at least relieved the darkness. "Just sit anywhere," he suggested.

Instead of taking an airline seat, she eased down to the carpet near the open door and galley, near the glow of that pale light. He poked around, emerged with two mini bottles. "Scotch, I think. Pretty hard to see for sure. For darn sure, there's nothing to dilute it with."

She chuckled. "It'll do."

He decided to talk to her about his sons. Just because he'd wanted to tell her something more about his life. "They're both terrific kids. Bruce lost his way for a while, flunked out of college—but since then he's hit his stride, back to school, good job, the whole thing. Just got in with the wrong girl at the wrong time. Then the right girl at the right time. He's one of those men, where the woman in his life is always going to make the whole difference. He's never good when he's alone, needs the home thing. It's not how young men think. They're supposed to think of themselves as being happy

and carefree when they're bachelors. But he's my nester. Makes money hand over fist now, a baby on the way."

"You like your daughter-in-law?"

"Adore her. She was there for me, when my wife died. Just as much as my sons were."

By then he'd long hunkered down next to her. Both of them had kind of leaned back, half lying, looking either at each other or at the glimpse of stars from the open doorway. For a moment, though, a silence fell between them. Her eyes honed on his in the dark. And like she knew what he was thinking about—maybe what was hovering in her mind, too—started talking again.

"How about the other son?"

"Johnny." He gave a wry sigh. "Handsome as hell. Broken two hearts that I know of. Short of smacking him upside the head, not sure what I can do. He falls in love, then gallops down the road when it comes to commitment time."

"How old?"

"Twenty-four."

"Young yet, Hank."

"Yeah, I know. I wouldn't even want him settled yet, but I still worry about the pattern. He finished school, spent six months bumming in Europe on a shoestring, came home broke, thought he'd loaf around the house. And I let him…I *know* I should have gotten tough, but the truth was…I liked having him around."

"Is he still living with you?"

"Nope. Finally got a job. Boulder, Colorado. *Not* an

adult job, mind you, but at least there's a faint glimmer of responsibility showing up."

"And you're in Colorado Springs, so you can see him."

"Yup."

"What was she like, Hank? Your wife?"

He checked her mini bottle, but she was sipping it mighty slow, was a long way from a refill yet. So was he, but the subject made him pause and take a swallow. "She was...sturdy. Not in looks so much, as on the inside. Physically, she had kind of dark blond hair, always a sunburned nose. You'd never catch her inside if she had any excuse to be outdoors. She was raised an army brat, the kind of woman who..." He hesitated again, trying to frame his words. "She was the kind of woman who stood next to you. Not a lot of talk, but never running away when the going got tough."

"You loved her."

"With all my heart," he freely admitted.

"Anyone since?"

He said, "I want there to be. Some people don't understand that—how you could look for someone else if you lost a mate you really loved. But that's just the point. I know what a good marriage is. I know what good love can be. I'd want it for her. I want it again for myself."

"Of course you do."

"It's not that easy to find."

"No."

Her small laugh was as intimate as a kiss, making him think he'd better start another conversation, fast. "Your turn to spill. What was your ex like?"

"Hmm. Cray was good-looking. Smart. Came from a great family. He was…charming. An active dad, always happy to be with the kids, play with them."

"Sounds like a paragon. Only there has to be a catch or you'd still be married."

"Yup. He worked the first three years we were married. Then I got into a seriously good law firm, started bringing in real money. And he quit his job and started spending it. At first, that was totally okay with me. We both wanted a parent home when the kids were young. But then…it wasn't about parenting. He was always out playing, not there for the kids. Took up one expensive hobby after another. Spent days at the country club, just hanging around. He was an active, involved dad. Still is, in fact."

"But…"

"But he stopped pretending he was ever going to look for work. He liked his life, just as it was. Maybe that shouldn't have mattered to me." She looked up, an honest question in her eyes, one that had clearly haunted her. "I mean, what difference does it make if both have a formal job? Especially if one is more than capable of bringing in an adequate income for the household. It bugged me that I was being sexist, thinking the guy should pull some financial weight…"

"Maybe I'm reading something into this. But it doesn't sound as if the problem was about money."

She nodded, releasing an old sigh. "You said it. Money was the symptom. Not the illness itself. Cray…he liked playing for a lifestyle, had no interest in changing. And I stuck it out for a lot of years because

the kids were happy enough. It's not as if we were fighting and they were exposed to a lot of anger. But…at some point, it finally hit me, that he wanted my paycheck more than he wanted me. There hadn't been a real marriage in a long time."

"You didn't see it?"

"I hadn't wanted to see it." Again, she looked uncomfortable, as if she didn't often talk about her marriage, herself this way. Yet she didn't seem unwilling, only awkward at trying to get the words out. "I wanted to think that the man I was married to…loved me. Corny, huh? But that was the part that…shamed me. Diminished me. It's hard to explain, but when someone just stops loving you, not for a *reason,* but just because the feeling dies….I felt as if I were invisible. Not worth the emotion. Not important enough, interesting enough, to stir any emotion. I felt like a piece of furniture, a thing…."

Hank reached for her.

He didn't know how or why he'd started this conversation. Talking about exes and divorces and failed marriages sure as hell wasn't his thing. For that matter, he wasn't dead sure why he'd coaxed her into this walk, initiated the contact to begin with.

But he knew exactly why he reached for her. Knew exactly why he hooked an arm around her shoulder and leveled a long, hot kiss on her mouth.

Life beat everybody up. Nobody was exempt. Everybody lost the full-of-hell arrogance they had in their youth.

But he hated it, that Peachy had been beaten down. Yeah, she'd been thoughtless as a kid. But she also put

out five hundred percent of herself, all the time, to everyone, to everything. She left a lot of dust in her wake because she moved so fast. But nobody should have used her like that jerk had. Nobody should have taken advantage of that big heart, that exuberant energy, that hope and zest that had been so much a part of her.

That someone had cruelly taken her for granted killed him.

That someone made her feel like less of a woman killed him more.

That was his excuse for the first kiss. And the next five. And then, what the hell, he stopped pretending he needed excuses anyway.

"Hey," she murmured a little later. By then her yellow print top was gone. So was his shirt. One of her sandals. His shoes. "Are we really doing the swept-away thing? At our age?"

"I don't know what *you're* doing. But what I'm doing is living out an old summer fantasy. I used to daydream that you were crazy about me, couldn't get enough, were so hot to sleep with me that you couldn't stand it." He lifted his head from the delectable taste of her shoulder for a solid five seconds. "What can I say? I was a seventeen-year-old boy. Seventeen-year-old boys are always the star in their own fantasies. It's not my fault."

She chuckled…and then willfully arched her spine to invoke more full body contact between them. It was the kind of invitation he'd dreamed of when he was seventeen.

Come to think of it, he still dreamed about stuff like that.

But he'd also always dreamed about being a good lover for his woman, too. Then and now.

For damn sure, he wasn't leaving Peachy with any doubt about being wanted. About how special, how sexy, how unforgettable, how totally un-invisible she was.

The utilitarian airline carpet was a long way from a luxurious mattress. There were no pillows and the aisle was as narrow as a twin bed. Even with the open door, it was almost airless inside. Yet the physical discomforts of their surroundings only seemed to work for them, or so Hank thought. The miniature LED light hardly illuminated the deep darkness—not a night this dark, this hot.

But the heat that mattered was coming from her, not the temperature. And the intense darkness magnified his sensory awareness of her—her silky hair, drifting though his fingers. The satin smoothness of her skin, damp, sweet. The sound of her—not the sounds of an untried girl, but the sounds of a woman who wanted to be loved.

Peachy knew what she wanted, knew what she felt. Knew exactly how much trouble two adults could get into, if they really really worked at it.

And he was sure willing to work at it.

"Hank?" she murmured a while later. Two orgasms later, to be precise.

"Hmm?" Right then, he admitted conversation was the last thing on his mind…until she asked him her next question.

"Why did I ever, ever let you go?"

"Beats me. I was the best crush you ever had."

"Why didn't you tell me that at the time? Why didn't you chase me harder?"

"You're making this my fault?"

"That we never had sex before tonight? Damn straight. How could it be my fault? I had no way to know how good you were."

He had to grin. And tuck an errant strand around her ear, just so. "Hey, Peachy."

"What?"

"You were the fabulous lover, not me. In fact, you were beautiful, fabulous, and breathtaking. Better than any fantasy I ever had. And believe me, seventeen-year-old boys can have some Pulitzer prize level fantasies."

Initially she fell silent. "All right. I can't top that as a compliment. Or I *can*...but not until I catch my breath."

He didn't want her to catch her breath.

He wasn't dead sure he was up for a second round, hadn't tested the capacity of his virility in quite a while—and he kept hearing from guys his age that second and third rounds had gotten tricky. But maybe they were wrong.

Or maybe Peachy just inspired him to extraordinary heights. Or maybe depths.

"That was a sick, sick pun," she whispered later.

"I'm just saying. Who knew at my advanced age? So it must be your fault."

"What's *your* fault is that I'm probably going to walk bowlegged for quite a while. With rug burns on my fanny and whisker burns on my throat."

"And elsewhere."

She laughed, low and soft. "And elsewhere, you wicked man."

JANE WAS PRETTY SURE they dozed once or twice—at least she did—but every time she opened her eyes, they seemed to be talking. Not about anything heavy or meaningful.

He described his house in Colorado Springs.

She described her Connecticut place.

He told her about flying F-16s.

She told him about making partner and getting the kick-ass front office.

He talked about how lonely he'd been after his wife died, how dating sucked—but coming home to silence sucked even worse. He admitted how for a long time he just couldn't sleep in the king-sized bed without a body next to him. And he admitted, for a while, that he'd tried drinking himself to sleep, so he wouldn't have to face that lonely insomnia.

She told him how angry she'd been after the divorce. About how she hadn't wanted to be with anyone. How she hated being set up. How she hated sleeping in a king-sized bed alone. How she'd tried drinking herself to sleep with wine, but that hadn't worked, so she'd bought a queen-sized bed and gussied it up with fabulous 800 thread count sheets and down comforters and lace-edged pillows.

"Did that work?"

"Of course not. Nothing works," she said wryly. "Thank God time eventually makes it easier."

"For me, too. I don't mind being alone some of the time."

"Neither do I. I was lonelier in my marriage than I was after. There are parts of being single that I really like."

"There are parts I like, too. Like…eating what I

want. When I want. Not having to clean up anyone's messes but my own."

"No one to say 'I'm sorry' to."

She hesitated, not wanting to disagree with him, but she had to add, "I know it sounds goofy, but…to be honest, I miss having a body to say 'I'm sorry' to."

He hesitated then. "Hell. So do I."

When dawn was breaking, when she walked back to the terminal with him and separated just inside the door, Jane had the craziest, funniest realization. She was happy. Exhausted to beat the band, but still, exhilarated, smiling-on-the-inside happy, kicky-high. Soft happy. Honest happy.

Yet when she walked inside the women's room and clicked the latch on the stall door, she felt the sudden shock of huge, fat tears welling in her eyes. Welling, and then stinging out of control.

She sank against the door. That first round of tears turned into an inexplicable flood. She didn't even know why she was crying, but it was as if someone had flipped open a faucet and there was no shut-off valve.

Nothing seemed to stop it. She couldn't seem to catch her breath or her control.

For Pete's sake, she really *was* happy. She didn't regret a minute of the night with Hank—not a minute, not a second. She'd desperately wanted that chance again—the chance to feel the way she had that summer when she was seventeen, when all things were possible, and she owned her life and herself, and the future spread out in front of her with a limitless, wide-screen horizon.

Maybe that was what the tears were about. Rediscovering, through making love with Hank…

All she'd found.

And all she'd lost.

# CHAPTER SEVEN

"Jane! Jane! Are you in here?"

A trio of excited female voices made her gulp fast. Two seconds later, the women were pounding on the stall doors. "Are you in there? Jane, we need you. They said the buses are coming early! We're getting out of here! But Mary Bartholomew lost her glasses. And one of the men fell on a piece of glass. And—"

"I'm coming, I'm coming." Well, she wasn't coming *quite* that fast. Cripes, she hadn't even had time to pee, much less finish up her own personal meltdown. At least there was so little light in the restroom that no one could likely tell her eyes were red-rimmed or her hands were shaky.

And after that, there was no time to worry about herself anyway. The terminal lobby was in complete chaos. Actually, it had been in complete chaos for the last two days, but now it had turned into a regular Armageddon.

People had spread out their belongings over the whole lobby during the last couple days. Now they were trying to gather it all up. Immediately.

To add insult to injury, it had started raining—not a friendly little soaker but a heat-breaking torrential

downpour. The gloomy skies made the terminal darker and frayed tempers. The group who'd done such a great job of being good to each other and coming together suddenly seemed intent on having a group nervous breakdown.

"But Jane. How is Wilbur going to know where I am? What if no one picks me up?"

"But I don't understand, Jane. I don't think my flight leaves out of Indianapolis. I don't know anybody in Indianapolis."

"Jane! The captain told me that Henry and Bud are going to be on the first bus, and not me. I think I should be on the first bus. I have a bad knee—"

"Jane! Someone took my blue jacket!"

"Jane! I can't close my suitcase!"

"Jane! I can't find my suitcase!"

The co-pilot found her sometime before noon, shook his head when he found her knee-deep in the middle of some strange man's shorts and socks. "Is it like this for you at home?" he asked her wryly. "Every time I turn around, you're getting stuck with doing something you shouldn't have to do."

"Everybody's pitched in where they could, don't you think?"

"Not like you have. And that's why I stopped. Just to say…I'm sorry we met during a tornado, but hell, I really am glad to have known you."

Startled at the praise, she gave him a warm hug—but then went back to it. Through the whole chaotic morning, Hank still dominated her mind. Last night clung to her consciousness like dew on morning

grass—and so did trying to understand the inexplicable crying jag she'd had earlier. It all seemed mixed up with the whole crazy scene. Here she was, two days dirty, her hair unmentionable, no makeup, wearing clothes meant for some dad fool resort that she was probably never going to actually visit.

Yet above it all, beyond it all, she felt a sense of pride in herself that she hadn't felt in years. All the real accomplishments, all the stuff she'd achieved and worked so darn hard for and fought to win…yet here she was, separating two seniors from bickering over socks, and she felt proud of herself?

Maybe the tornado had brought on a heretofore unrecognized lunatic side of herself. Who knew?

Who had time to find out?

When the first bus left with a load of passengers, she looked around frantically for Hank. Everyone wasn't leaving at the same time, but she had to find him, had to speak to him before the chance was gone.

She'd already told the captain that she wasn't on the fast track many of the other passengers were. Of course, she was hot to get out of here, just like everyone else— but she had a week's vacation, and most certainly wasn't going near any Kokomo island at this point, so for her, it was just a matter of getting home to Connecticut. Others with more pressing responsibilities or problems could go first.

Only it didn't work out that way. For her or for Hank. Once the buses got there, they were herded like lemmings, no way to slow up the whole process.

Bare minutes before noon, Hank suddenly showed

up in front of her, a bag in his hand. "Peachy, you're harder to find than a raindrop in a storm."

This was so *not* how she wanted to say goodbye. She knew she looked like hell and a half, and there was just no way she could say anything meaningful, anything personal, with a zillion people milling around them— even assuming her tongue wasn't suddenly drier than the Sahara, which it most definitely was.

Still. She was an adult, not a seventeen-year-old girl any more. So she listened, while he explained there was a car waiting for him, and he was stuck on a fast exodus out of there. Then she straightened his collar, and took a good memory-installing look at that handsome face and roguish smile.

"If you think I'm going to forget this tornado, you're crazy," she said.

"If you think I'll ever forget *you* again, you're even crazier." He bent down, bussed her cheek—then hooked his jacket over his arm and leveled a serious kiss on her mouth. Not a long kiss, but one that was deep and hard and real.

She caught her breath. Or tried to. "If you'd kissed like that when we were seventeen, I'd never have let you go," she scolded.

"If you'd let me kiss you like that when we were seventeen, your dad would have gone after me with a shotgun."

"My dad was a pacifist."

Hank shook his head. "No dad is a pacifist where his gorgeous teenage daughter is concerned."

She knew people were looking at them. So did he. His

vehicle was waiting for him; the driver had already honked twice. They could hardly hold everybody up so they could keep on flirting like a pair of immature teenagers.

Yet he touched her hand once more, and looked at her once more—not like teenagers, not like flirting—but as if he really cared, as if she'd really touched him.

God knew, the last two days with him had really touched her.

And then he was gone. Striding away. Out the door…and out of her life.

WHEN JANE STEPPED OUT of the Lexus, the wind whipped open her suit jacket. It was the last day of summer. She could smell it in the wild, warm wind, in the brush of leaves in the air.

She raced up the steps to the lobby of Bentham, James, Lambrect and Whitcomb and escaped inside. Her three-inch heels clicked down the hall toward her office, sounding like a fast tap dance. A two-point-five million-dollar deal had gone down at lunch today, maybe not the moon, but still a big enough kerchunk to make her day when she nailed it. So maybe the three-inch heels and kick-ass Elie Tahari suit weren't factors, and possibly—the day after she was dead—she'd stop being quite so superstitious.

Interns scurried past her. A couple of the partners hung by the water cooler. She gave them a thumbs-up as she soared into her office—and then her ebullient mood suffered a tiny tank. Her office didn't look exactly like a pigsty, but it was getting there. The weeks since her return from Kokomo had been jam-packed with

business. Pyramids of files jockeyed for space on her desk. Pink and yellow slips decorated the surface by the phone.

Marcia—the temp who'd turned into a full-time girl Friday as of three weeks ago—showed up in the doorway, looking wary and ready to run if need be.

"How'd it go?" she asked carefully.

Jane bent down, rooted in her purse, and emerged with a bottle of Pinot Noir—San Ventre, 1997.

"Oh my God, oh my God," Marcia said. "For me?"

"And some extra loot in your check this week. We both put in a lot of hours on this nightmare. Appreciate all you did."

"You already gave me a raise—"

"Yeah, well, this is just some extra loot because you've had to put up with me. Who else would?" Jane grinned as she motioned toward all the notes. "Any calls that won't wait?"

"Two of your kids called. They were afraid they wouldn't catch you tomorrow for your birthday. They both said they'd try you later."

"They will. Or I'll call them, so it's on my dollar." She slipped off her suit jacket, then kicked off her heels and plunked onto her office chair. "My daughter's coming home from Europe on Friday. I'll be gone from the office as of noon."

"I'll bet you can't wait to see her."

"I can't. Best birthday present I could have." Without thinking, she started humming an old song. The title escaped her. It was just one of those really, really old ones with a catchy tune, the kind that you couldn't let

in your head because you could never get it out again. They'd been playing it on the radio on the route in from the restaurant. "Aruba…Jamaica…um, Marcia, this call from Griff Johnson. Was he ticked off again?"

Marcia's face changed expression. Her posture went from smiling and relaxed to smiling and just a wee bit wary again. "Truthfully, I've never spoken to the man when he wasn't ticked off. He wanted some further information on some tax ramifications—"

Jane nodded. "It's all right. That's what I thought. Every time he calls, he seems to think someone here should just instantly have an answer for him that second. Next time, put him straight to me. You don't have to put up with that verbal abuse from anyone, Marcia. Don't think it's expected. It'll never be expected. But we're almost done with this contract issue for him, and then that's the last we have to see of him."

"Thanks." Marcia suddenly shook her head with a little laugh. "Where's my boss?"

"Pardon?" More of those lyrics kept echoing in her head. Come on pretty mama…

"The bitch," Marcia said gently. "We're all wondering where she went. What you did with her. If she's ever coming back. Where you buried the body."

Jane laughed…but moments later, after Marcia left and she was digging through the archaeological mounds of work on her desk…it hit her. She was still humming.

Her inner bitch really was gone.

So was all that anger.

Nothing had been the same since the tornado...
since that god-awful campout and steak soup in
Kokomo.

Since Hank.

Friday afternoon, she drove to the airport to pick up
Angel. Her youngest daughter walked off the plane,
looking like a train wreck—blond hair all tumbled,
sleepy eyes, clothes all wrinkled. Jane took one look
and, laughing, wrapped her up in a bone-snuggling
hug. The others had left the nest, and this one was about
to. The summer in Europe had clearly matured her yet
another notch, but even this exhausted, her baby looked
precious and young as grass. "Happy to be home?"

"I had a *great* time. The whole summer was beyond
copacetic. But yeah, I can't wait to have my own bed,
my own pillow. I'm starving, Mom—"

"I expected you would be." It had to be fast food on
the way home—specifically French fries—because
Angel claimed she'd die if she couldn't have them immediately. She talked nonstop about what she'd seen,
what she'd done, how she could hardly wait to get back
to school, how she was sick of school, how her brothers
were, how she'd gotten food poisoning in Venice, how
she'd fallen in love in Vienna, how it had been dying
hot in Rome...

They were just walking in the door, dragging heaps
of luggage, when Jane's cell phone sang. She clicked
the on button, even as she started turning on lights
through the hall and living room.

It was only when she recognized Hank's voice that
she stopped buzzing around. Actually, everything

seemed to stop. Her feet, her hands, her brain. Her heart.

She was so stunned to hear that melt-quiet baritone that he spoke again. "Peachy? This is Peachy?"

"Yes." She shook her head and laughed. "Yes, of course it is. I just didn't expect to hear your voice. I didn't think you knew where I lived. I mean, we didn't give each other phone numbers or addresses...and I just didn't think that...I mean, you live so far. So I..."

Angel backed up from the kitchen to the hallway stairway to stare at her. You'd think she'd never heard her mother stutter before. Or maybe she'd never seen her mother sink down on the third stair step, a phone to her ear, and flush the color of rose petals.

When the call was over, Angel was still studying her as if a prehistoric archaeological artifact had suddenly been unearthed in her home. "What," she said, "has been going on while I was in Europe?"

"Nothing, honey. At least...I didn't think anything that momentous was."

"So who's the guy?"

"Who said it was a guy?"

"Mother." In two syllables, Angel expressed a symphonic range of dry humor. And then she looked hard at Jane again. "My God. You look younger. Did you have a face-lift?"

"No, of course not!"

Angel approached and squinted at her hard now. "And you look...oh my God. Happy. Not tired or stressed. This is getting scary. You either tell me who this guy is or I'm calling my brothers. Where does he

live? How serious is he? How serious are you? When am I going to meet him? What's he do for a living? Mom, you're not sleeping with him, are you?"

Jane stood up, hooked an arm around her daughter's neck in a mini-stranglehold, and dragged her nosy, prying youngest into the kitchen. She might just answer some of those questions. Later. When she was ready.

Just then, though, she just wanted to bask in that private, summer-warm feeling for just a few moments longer.

It wasn't Hank who'd changed her life. It was her. But he'd enabled her to remember what she'd lost, what she'd been missing.

Because of him, she'd taken a risk she'd been afraid to take for a very long time. To open up. To love.

To be loved.

He was flying this way in three weeks. Angel would be back in school by then. Jane would have the house to herself. She'd agreed to see him.

She wasn't going to put a fancy word on her hopes this soon. But now she knew—those old summer dreams hadn't died... but only opened up the possibilities.

# These billionaires are used to getting what they want...

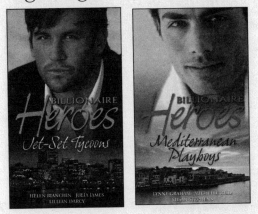

## ...and they want you in their bed!

**Billionaire Heroes:** *Jet-Set Billionaires*

*The Disobedient Bride* by Helen Bianchin
*His Wedding Ring of Revenge* by Julia James
*The Doctor's Fire Rescue* by Lilian Darcy

Available 1st August 2008

**Billionaire Heroes:** *Mediterranean Playboys*

*The Greek Tycoon's Convenient Mistress*
by Lynne Graham
*The Purchased Wife* by Michelle Reid
*The Spanish Billionaire's Mistress* by Susan Stephens

Available 5th September 2008

M&B

*100 Reasons to Celebrate*

**2008 is a very special year as we celebrate Mills and Boon's Centenary.**

Each month throughout the year there will be something new and exciting to mark the centenary, so watch for your favourite authors, captivating new stories, special limited edition collections…and more!